TO GET ME TO YOU

KAIT NOLAN

To Get Me To You

Written and published by Kait Nolan

Copyright 2014 Kait Nolan

Cover design by Lori Jackson

AUTHOR'S NOTE: The following is a work of fiction. All people, places, and events are purely products of the author's imagination. Any resemblance to actual people, places, or events is entirely coincidental.

To The Pie Society,

For your unflagging cheerleading, support, and stream of small town Southern gossip. You are an inspiration.

With love,

Kait

Dear Reader,

This book is set in the Deep South. As such, it contains a great deal of colorful, colloquial, and occasionally grammatically incorrect language. This is a deliberate choice on my part as an author to most accurately represent the region where I have lived my entire life. This book also contains swearing and pre-marital sex between the lead couple, as those things are part of the realistic lives of characters of this generation, and of many of my readers.

If any of these things are not your cup of

tea, please consider that you may not be the right audience for this book. There are scores of other books out there that are written with you in mind. In fact, I've got a list of some of my favorite authors who write on the sweeter side on my website at https://kaitnolan.com/on-the-sweeter-side/

If you choose to stick with me, I hope you enjoy!

Happy reading!

Kait

CHAPTER 1

THERE WAS NO ESCAPING now.

As the steady click of sensible heels on asphalt grew ever closer, Campbell Crawford shut his eyes and repressed a curse. Where the hell had she come from?

To give himself another few moments to arrange his face into something resembling polite civility, Cam ducked back into his truck.

"Mr. Crawford, I need a word." Agnes Crockett used the same stern tone she used to call his name when she'd taught trigonometry back in high school.

Resisting the urge to hunch his shoulders, Cam tucked a cardboard tube of landscaping blueprints under his arm and turned to face her. "Yes, Mrs. Crockett. What can I do for you?"

Mrs. Crockett peered up at him from beneath her umbrella, a bright floral affair completely at odds with her no-nonsense demeanor. "I have a matter that needs to be brought up at the next City Council meeting. It's about that stoplight at Market and Spring Street."

Not again. If he had a nickel for every time somebody griped about that stoplight, he could buy a round of drinks for everybody waiting inside the Mudcat Tavern.

"The city needs to fix the sensor. Cross traffic from Market Street gets stuck entirely too long, when nobody's even coming the other direction. Why, I sat there for a full *five minutes* today without a soul passing by on Spring Street, and I was late to Bitsy Elliott's daughter's baby shower. When is that sensor going to get fixed?"

Cam privately thought that, given the state of the city coffers, it would be more likely the stoplight would be entirely decommissioned and they'd go back to the four-way stop, but that wasn't something he was about to share with this particular constituent. "I certainly understand your concern, Mrs. Crockett. Now we talked about this the last time—"

"You said I had to fill out this form." She dug around in her purse and came up with a sheet of paper that she thrust at him. "I want that traffic light fixed."

Cam took the paper. She'd filled in the blanks by hand, her slanted scrawl covering most of the page. He bit back a sigh and refrained from mentioning that it was a web form she was supposed to submit online. "Ah, yes, ma'am. I'll see that it's put on the agenda for our next City Council meeting."

"See that you do. I've been put off for the *last time,* young man."

Aware that his shoulders had hunched up by

his ears, Cam forced them down. "Yes, ma'am. Now, if you'll excuse me, I've got to go meet a client." He tapped the blueprint tube and softened the diplomatic brushoff with a smile. "You have a good evenin', now."

He called the escape good when he made it to the door of the Mudcat without pursuit or an order to detention.

Somebody had Garth Brooks playing on the jukebox. The hot fiddle licks of "Callin' Baton Rouge" were punctuated by the crack of billiard balls from the far side of the bar. Christmas lights still twinkled around the perimeter, as they probably would until Valentine's Day or Easter. Cam felt some of the stress of the day leech out as he crossed to the high-top table in the corner, where his cousin, Miranda, was already taking a pull on a Sam Adams.

"You're late." She set down the bottle. "Had a real pisser of a day at the clinic, so I started without you. Two days after Christmas and there's already an outbreak of flu. And *not* the strain they were predicting when they formulated the flu shot this year. You have a client meeting?"

Cam laid the blueprint tube in another chair. "No, this was just cover. Got ambushed by Mrs. Crockett in the parking lot."

"The stoplight again?"

He cocked thumb and forefinger at her. "Got it in one. I'm late because I was working on mixing potting soil today, and I figured you'd appreciate me showering and changing first so as not to smell like manure."

Miranda leaned over and gave an exaggerated sniff as he shrugged out of his wet coat. "Much obliged then, cuz." She settled back in her chair. "Did you hear about Travis Hugget?"

"What about him?"

"Remember he's been dating that girl from college—Gwen something or other—long distance for more than a year, since she took that job in New York? Apparently, right before Christmas, he went up there to her fancy Wall Street office and proposed, right as the entire company was coming out of a staff meeting."

Poor bastard. He had plenty of reason to know that was a disaster waiting to happen.

"Not only did Gwen say yes, she quit her job right then and there, and they eloped."

Cam swiped Miranda's beer and tipped it back to wash the sour taste of envy from his mouth as he revised his opinion. *Lucky bastard.* "Good for them."

Aware of his cousin's *I shouldn't have said that* expression and sensing an imminent and entirely unnecessary apology, Cam wiped the scowl from his face. Christ, when was his family going to stop pussy footing around it?

Miranda's phone rang and she glanced at the screen. "It's Norah. I need to take this. Go get yourself a beer and bring me another since you polished mine off. And put in an order of cheese sticks while you're up there. I'm starving."

"Your wish." He saluted and headed for the bar, sending a silent thank you to Miranda's old college roommate for the distraction.

Adele Daly, the opinionated owner of the

Mudcat, worked the taps as she chatted with Abe Costello about Ole Miss's chance at making it to the Final Four.

"I'm tellin' you, if they can just take out Emory, they've got a shot," Abe insisted.

Adele slid a glass of IPA down the bar into a waiting hand. "My money's on State. They've been burning up the courts this season."

Easing between two stools, Cam propped himself on an elbow and nodded a hello to Abe. "Adele, would you be so kind as to get me a Killian's and put in an order for cheese sticks and another Sam Adams for Miranda?"

"You want a bottle or tap? Keg's fresh."

"Tap then. And better add some chili cheese fries to that order. Miranda doesn't strike me as being in a sharing mood tonight."

"You got it, sugar pie."

Cam lounged back against the bar and took note of the glass of scotch Abe was nursing. "Are we celebrating or commiserating?"

"Little bit of both. I got an offer on my land."

"That acreage over by Hope Springs?"

"Yep."

Cam straightened in surprise. Abe was a local man, born and raised in Wishful. That land parcel had been in his family for generations. "You're selling?"

"Thinkin' 'bout it. It's a damned good offer. Well above market value." He sipped the scotch and grimaced, more a testament to the situation than the drink.

"Who?"

"Nobody local."

Cam had figured that. Nobody local had that kind of money to throw around. In the wake of the plant closing, a lot of people didn't have any money at all. Heirloom Home Furnishings had been the primary employer in town. When they'd opted to move their operations to Mexico eight months ago, it had gutted the town's economy. That was just the latest blow in a long line of economic downturns over the last few decades. Their population was shrinking as more and more good people were forced to go elsewhere to support their families.

"But you can't sell. That land's part of your family history. Part of Wishful's history."

"History don't pay the bills, son."

It was an unfortunately familiar story. Loss of workforce and population also meant loss of business. Abe's farm supply company took a hit when Cam bought the nursery five years ago. Cam had a wider variety and better stock, and with local propagation, he was able to offer better prices than the other man. But nursery and garden stock wasn't Abe's bread and butter. If the farm supply was suffering, this was the first Cam had heard about it.

Adele set Cam's beer on the bar. "It's too bad the city can't make an offer on that parcel. Be nice to make a formal park out there by the springs. Like that plan you drew up. It'd be a great addition to the town."

Cam's mind started to spin. "Who's brokering the sale?"

"Sally Forester on my side. Other folks got an attorney from out of town."

"Hold off on making any final decisions, Abe. If anybody's gonna buy that property, the city ought to have first crack at it."

Abe grunted in acknowledgment, but it was a hollow victory. Buying more land was only one of many things the city couldn't afford to do. The truth was, the town he loved was dying, and Cam didn't know how much longer they could limp along as they were. What they needed was a miracle, and despite the holiday season, those were in pretty short supply.

"AND HOW IS my sister from another mister?" Miranda's voice rolled out of the car speakers, a welcome breath of the South that made Norah Burke ache with homesickness.

"Tired. It's a long drive back from New York."

"Why on earth didn't you fly?"

"Because nobody's invented a teleporter yet. Flying would take just as long, and I'd be one of a hundred other irritable sardines, who want to be home already. At least on the road it's quiet."

"You totally live in the wrong city for quiet. Are you home yet?"

"Got a couple more hours. But I'm about to break it up a bit and make a stop in your honor."

"Off I-90? Oh my God, are you in Morton? You're going to Have Your Cake, aren't you?"

Norah laughed at the mix of accusation and longing in her friend's tone. "Guilty."

The stretch of road immediately off the interstate had mushroomed in the past three years with the usual contingent of fast food restaurants, gas stations, and a couple of chain hotels. Pleased at the evidence of growth, Norah bypassed them all, following the signs for downtown and sending up a silent prayer that Have Your Cake would be open until six.

"Best road trip discovery *ever*. I love their caramel cake. The perfect marriage of salty and sweet, with four layers of lovely, moist cake... What made you decide to stop?"

"I was missing you." It was the truth, even if it didn't touch on all the whys. "How is everybody?"

As she navigated through town, Norah listened to her friend's account of this year's holiday hijinks. It was almost like listening to the summary of a Hallmark Channel movie, for all she could relate to Miranda's sprawling family, with aunts, uncles, and cousins galore. They were as close to normal as Norah ever got.

"—oh, and the boys had a poker tournament to decide who got the last slice of Grammy's chocolate pie."

Amusement and envy warred. Grammy's chocolate pie was a thing of legend. "Who won?"

"Reed, who was totally the dark horse in that race. Everybody assumed Mitch would win because he always does. He said to tell you hello, by the way."

"Tell him hi back and ask him when he's

coming to Chicago again for another architectural convention."

"I still can't believe you went on a date with my brother."

"It wasn't a date. It was a pity tour of the city, since you didn't warn him you wouldn't actually be able to leave the hospital to see him."

"That's why they call it residency. And anyway that's not the way *he* tells that story."

"Then Mitch is a liar liar pants on fire."

"Why don't you come down here and tell him that yourself? You keep promising to visit."

"I know, I know," Norah groaned. "It's been way too long. But work's been *crazy*. I had a hard enough time getting off to go to New York for the holiday. I can't possibly ask off again so soon. Maybe closer to summer."

"Summer? You *do* remember what Mississippi is like in the summer?"

"Honey, given the winter we've been having, I'd relish the chance to wear some short shorts and a tank top instead of a winter coat that makes me look like the Michelin Man."

"I'll remind you of that when you come and do your impression of the Wicked Witch of the West. How did Christmas go on your end? Was Rockefeller Center fabulous? I'm getting my vicarious white Christmas fix through you."

"It was gorgeous. The Plaza was amazing, and midnight mass at Saint Thomas was simply beautiful. Christmas in Manhattan is definitely a unique experience." And she'd have traded it all for one zany family dinner with the Campbells.

"Did your dad manage to refrain from harping on you about going back to law school?"

"Actually, he's dating somebody. Some high-powered exec who looks like Hollywood's idea of Wall Street. They went to Saint Bart's, so it was just me and Mom. *She* got called in to emergency surgery, so I spent my holiday bless-edly harp-free."

Miranda didn't buy her breezy, no-big-deal tone for a moment. "Wait, so you were *alone* for Christmas?"

Sensing the edge of a blistering rant, Norah felt compelled to head Miranda off. "Not all of it. Between surgeries, Mom and I had a blast shopping for Operation Santa Claus, and she got out of surgery in time for a late Christmas dinner."

"That's awful."

Norah bit back a sigh as she turned onto Main Street. Miranda's outrage on her behalf was well-intentioned, even if it solved exactly nothing. "Well, it was certainly better than if Dad had tried to include Lillian. We're a weirdly civilized modern family, but I don't think we're *that* civilized. Besides, it gave me some quiet time to catch up on this radical thing called reading for pleasure."

"You should've come here. You know you're always welcome."

Norah knew they'd fold her into the flock. It was part of the Campbells' charm. But there were a hundred reasons keeping her from following through on the invite Miranda made every year. "And I appreciate the offer. Now I'm going to let you go because I'm pretty sure I drove past Have Your Cake while I was running my mouth."

"Buy two pieces and have one in my name."

"And will those calories vicariously travel to *your* hips?" Norah circled the block for another pass.

"They will in spirit."

"Give your family my best."

"Love you."

"Love you back. Talk soon."

Norah didn't have to hunt for parking. But for a handful of cars, downtown Morton was deserted. She got out and climbed over the mounds of dirty snow to the sidewalk and took a good look around. No sign of Have Your Cake. Thinking she parked on the wrong block, she began to walk.

Maybe they're still on shortened holiday hours. Not what she'd have recommended to business owners in the wake of the holiday. They should've been taking advantage of post-

Christmas shoppers with gift certificates and Christmas money.

A shop window across the street had *Going Out of Business* painted across the glass. The sign above the awning indicated it had been a florist. Even with the poor economy and reduced discretionary income, a florist should have been able to make it through the Christmas season. In another window on her side, she saw a For Rent sign. A lone, headless mannequin stood inside, one arm lifted like it was waving good-bye. One empty retail space she could dismiss, but two? That didn't fit with her expectations.

Three years ago, she'd been brought in as the voice of the marketing team that convinced the town of Morton that Hugo's ValuCenter would be a partner to the community, a harbinger of new economic growth. She'd seen their multi-phase plan for sustainable community development, had been the one to sell city leaders on the concept. So why was everything closed?

The next couple of spaces were occupied by a law office and an accountant. But the space after that had a discreet For Sale sign and the name of a local real estate company. Cold fingers walked down her spine as Norah looked into every window on the entire three block stretch.

Based on the community development plan, downtown Morton should've been a bustling retail corridor, full of local vendors and craftspeople. Exactly what it had been, at the heart, when she and Miranda had discovered the place years ago, but bigger. And yet more than seventy percent of the retail space sat empty. It was such a far cry from the bustling, quirky town she remembered, she half wondered if she'd come to the wrong place.

"What the hell happened here?"

One business still had active clientele at this hour. Crossing the street, Norah stepped inside the Five O'Clock Shadow. The bar was dim and quiet. A few people looked up when she came in, then went back to their drinks. Their low murmurs of conversation barely competed with the classic rock playing over the speakers. She noted a handful of suits and some business casual attire, suggesting that this was probably a hang out for the office workers and city government employees who worked further down the street.

Loosening her scarf, Norah crossed to the bar, where a mustached man was drying glasses.

"What can I getcha?"

She slid onto a stool. "Directions, I hope. I'm from out of town, and it's been a few years since I came through here. I was hoping you could tell me where Have Your Cake moved to."

"Didn't move. Closed along with just about everything else down here."

She'd been afraid of that. "What happened?"

"Same as happened lots of other places. We got a Hugo's ValuCenter."

Norah swallowed, her throat suddenly dry. "I'd heard that they were in to being partners with the community."

The bartender snorted. "They're like any other politicians. Telling people exactly what they want to hear to get in, then going back on their word. Within six months of opening for business, they added an in-house florist, a bakery, a butcher, on top of all the other products they already carried. They undercut local prices, all in the name of *value.*" The word rolled off his tongue like something foul. "Local businesses couldn't compete. Those of us still standing are the ones who aren't in direct competition. Everybody else...*poof.*"

Numb, Norah thanked the bartender for his time and headed back to her car. Her stomach roiled.

Hugo's had done exactly what she'd promised the town they wouldn't do. She'd *seen* the proposal, *seen* the plans to integrate, not overtake the community. Was there a statute of limitations clause she'd missed? Had they performed some kind of bait and switch with the final contracts? Had her partner failed to do proper due diligence on the company? She had, in effect, lied to the townspeople. Used all her skill in persuasion to talk them into something that had decimated the character of the town.

How did this happen? Where did I screw up?

She didn't know. But as soon as she got to the office in the morning, she was going to find out.

CHAPTER 2

STANDING SHOULDER TO SHOULDER with her intern, Norah surveyed the mountains of folders spread across the conference table.

Cecily took a bracing breath. "This calls for ordering in. Do we want Chinese, Indian, or Greek?"

"None of the above. You are going home like the good little, not-excessively-overworked intern you're supposed to be."

"But I can help."

Aw, she's like your mini-me, Norah's conscience cooed. *The earnest, good-hearted worka-holic. Encourage that so y'all can have no life together.*

"It's not about can, it's about should. And you *should* have a life after work. Now go ahead and scoot or you're going to miss your TaeBo class."

"You did not just tell me to scoot. You've been talking to your Mississippi friend again."

Norah just arched a brow.

"Fine, fine. But I'll be here bright and early tomorrow. I've got some concepts kicking around in my head for the Rembrandt job."

"I look forward to hearing them. To. Mor. Row."

"Yes, boss."

As Cecily walked out, Norah's personal assistant walked in.

"Don't even start with me, Christoff."

"Not even back a day and you're covered up. We aren't *that* behind from the holiday."

As he moved toward her desk, Norah automatically closed the files she'd pulled herself earlier in the day. No reason to alert anyone else to her inquiries until she decided what to do about them.

"I'm just trying to get ahead a bit so I can take New Year's off."

He collapsed gracefully into one of the visitor's chairs and crossed his Ferragamo boots. "Honey, we both know you're going to bring your fabulous dress and get ready here, before you and Mr. Tall, Dark, and GQ show up fashionably late for whatever It Party is the place to be."

"Just because it's what we did last year…"

Christoff shut her up with a Look. He tapped the side of his nose. "I am wise to your ways, milady. You shouldn't be hitting the ground running this hard until after the first of the year."

Norah sighed. "I have my reasons. Now go ahead and get out of here. I mean it. Out of the office."

He crossed his arms. "I don't like abandoning you while you're drowning."

"I am not drowning. Go home and watch your DVR backlog of Project Runway. All this will still be here tomorrow."

"Only if you *promise* you're not going to work half the night. I'm calling up here in an hour to make sure you've left."

"Fair enough. I promise."

He made an *I'm watching you* gesture with his fingers. "I'll know if you just don't pick up."

He probably would. Norah had long since stopped wondering how Christoff knew the things he knew. She plastered on an indulgent smile and made shooing motions until he walked out of her office.

As soon as the door shut, Norah wilted, letting go of the *Everything's Okay* facade she'd been using all day. Everything was most definitely *not* okay. Rising, she crossed to the window of her office, staring out at the twinkling lights of the Chicago skyline. She'd worked her ass off for Helios Creative to earn that view, done good work. Exceptional work. She was tenacious and she was thorough. The harder the sell, the more determined she became, rallying to the challenge like a heavyweight going into a title fight. Her honeyed eloquence had produced the highest success rate of anyone in the firm, save her boss, and she'd rocketed through the ranks to Vice President of Sales, getting dubbed The Closer. Together, she and Pierce Vargas were an absolute marketing dream team. Everybody said so.

But what was the price? How many lives had she destroyed in her pursuit of success?

The door behind her opened, but she didn't turn.

"Finally took the lock off, huh? I was starting to wonder if you were avoiding me."

"I had a lot of work to do." She watched Pierce cross the room in the reflection, dispassionately noting the artfully mussed hair, the tailored suit trousers that still held a crease even at this late hour. He always looked like he'd stepped out of the pages of a magazine ad. So did she. It was part and parcel of the job. Perfect. Polished. Professional. As he slid his arms around her waist, they looked every bit the power couple.

Pierce dipped his head to press a kiss to her neck. "Welcome home, babe."

Norah stiffened and stepped away, wishing viciously for a tumbler of scotch she could drain before hurling the glass at his head.

Not a stupid man, Pierce stayed put, angling his head to study her. "Something wrong?"

"How long have we been partners?"

"In bed or out?" He flashed a glib smile. "Did I miss an anniversary or something?" When she didn't soften, he sobered. "We've been working together for a little over three years. Why?"

"I stopped in Morton on my trip back yesterday."

"Where?"

"Morton, Indiana. Hugo's ValuCenter hired us to convince the town to let them build there. Y'all brought me in to do the pitch on behalf of the clients."

"Okay. That was one of the first jobs we partnered on. So?"

"So the infrastructure of local businesses has been gutted. The downtown is all but dead because they completely violated their promise of non-competition in multiple areas. The promise *I* made the townspeople in good faith when I did the pitch."

Pierce's expression softened and he crossed to her. "Is that what's got you upset? Sure it sucks for them, but you didn't do anything wrong. It's business, and if the town didn't get a non-compete clause ironclad in the legal stuff, that's on them. It happens. It still has nothing to do with you. You did your job. We both did."

She spun away when he tried to pull her into his arms. "That's the problem."

"I don't follow."

Trembling with rage, Norah reached for the file on her desk, tossing it toward him. The contents spilled across the surface, onto the floor. Headlines jumped out in glaring black and white, damning Hugo's business practices, outing their impact on other small towns in other parts of the country. A stack of bad publicity that proved the company had never meant a word of the promises she'd made on their behalf. Publicity she hadn't seen when they brought her in at the last minute to do the pitch on behalf of Hugo's.

"You knew. You were the one who did due diligence on this job. You knew before I ever made the presentation, and you didn't tell me."

Pierce eased a hip back on the credenza and crossed his arms. "You're right. I didn't tell you."

"Why?"

"Because I knew you wouldn't do the job if you were aware of the company's…shall we say, checkered past."

"Of *course* I wouldn't have done it. It's an ethics violation, Pierce! We—or, at least, you—were aware that this company could seriously damage that community, and you said *nothing.*"

He shrugged. "It was a huge account, and the firm couldn't afford to lose it over your moral compass. So I gave you an edited version of the company's plans. It worked. The client was happy. And you were well on your way to this corner office. End of story."

"You *manipulated me*."

"Norah, you're really blowing this out of proportion—"

"Am I? Am I really? How often did you do this? How many times have you fed me a *revised* version of the truth and sent me in to *lie to people*?" She knew her voice was rising and struggled to find some control.

"Hey now, what is going on in here?" Philip Vargas, founder and CEO of Helios stepped through the door. "I can hear you from down the hall."

Norah turned to face her boss. "Philip, I am sorry to inform you that your son has committed a serious ethics violation. At least once, perhaps more, in the name of profit. And he dragged me in as an unwitting accomplice."

Philip gave an exaggerated sigh. "This is why we didn't tell you. You're our best closer. We couldn't have your over-developed conscience getting in the way."

She gaped at him. "*We*? You knew?"

"Of course, I knew. I know everything that goes on in my company. I know what assets I have and how best to use them."

Use. The word rang in her head. She was an asset. Never before had that word made her feel cheap.

Philip continued, "You happen to have an element of southern charm to go along with that keen mind. Clients eat it up. You do your job and you do it damned well. We just keep you informed about what you need to know to get the job done without you having hysterics over things like truth, justice, and the American way." The derision in his tone felt like acid.

With a dawning horror, Norah realized that neither Philip, nor Pierce, nor the company she'd devoted her life to for the last six years were who she thought they were. She was the only one in the room with an ounce of integrity. She squared her shoulders. "I won't be party to that kind of manipulation again."

Philip shrugged in a gesture so redolent of

Pierce only minutes before, Norah felt her head spin. "Fine. You're fired."

Norah's mouth dropped open.

"For every award you've won in this company's name, there are dozens of hungry young neophytes dying for your job. You're replaceable. And if you bother spreading this little story, you can be sure I'll blackball you. You won't ever work in this business again. Think about that while you're standing in line for unemployment."

She looked to Pierce, but he said nothing, looking disgusted by her behavior. A year and a half wasted on a man who couldn't be bothered to defend her. "We're through."

"Oh, I think that's been made abundantly clear."

Philip stepped out and called for the security guard. "Please escort Miss Burke from the building and take her keys once she's gathered her things. C'mon, son. I'll buy you a drink."

Norah was still staring at the door minutes after they walked out. Daryl, the security guard, stood awkwardly beside her desk as she piled her personal effects into a box. Riding on temper and righteous outrage as he escorted her to the elevator like some kind of criminal, Norah was grateful no one was left working late to bear witness to her humiliation.

Daryl didn't quite meet her eyes as the elevator doors opened at the parking garage. "I'm sorry about this ma'am, but it's company policy."

"Not your fault."

Fury carried her through traffic. Indignation had her deliberately taking the stairs up to her fourth floor apartment so she could burn off some of the excess energy. Not until she locked the door to her apartment and dumped the box on the kitchen table did anything else filter past that initial reaction of shock and outrage.

Shaking, Norah sank into a chair and buried her head in her hands.

"What have I done?"

CAM REALLY SHOULD'VE BEEN WORKING on year-end reports. It would save him time come tax season. Unfortunately, he much preferred mucking around in the dirt to the spreadsheets that tracked the income and expenses of his business. But since it was the dead of winter, that mostly meant mucking around in virtual dirt, except when he was in his greenhouses. Cam clicked his mouse and dragged to adjust the fence line on the park he wanted to build on Abe's land out at Hope Springs. He'd been fiddling with this design for the better part of four years, mostly for fun, but with a thread of pipe dream in the back of his mind. It had begun as a distraction for his mom while she was in chemo, and he'd made idiotic deals with God that if she made it through, he'd find a way to make it a reality.

Sandra had not only survived, she'd gotten re-elected mayor—a post she'd left for only a six-month hiatus during the worst of her treatments. Cam had taken that as a sign from the Universe that it was time to move forward with the park. His first year as a Councilman had quickly put an end to that idea. But he couldn't seem to let it go in the wake of Abe's announcement.

A murmur of voices preceded the unceremonious opening of his office door by his nursery manager, Violet. "See there, told you he wasn't really workin'."

Cam rose as his mother stepped inside.

"Hey baby. Sorry to interrupt."

He managed, just barely, to stop himself from asking if everything was okay. She was tired of the worry, tired of the solicitude, and just wanted life to get back to normal. "You're not interrupting a thing." He slid his arms carefully around her, thinking she still felt too fragile in his embrace.

"I'll just leave you two to it. Cam, I'm flipping the sign."

He let his mother go. "See you tomorrow, Vi."

Sandra peered, unabashed, at his monitor. "The park at the springs? What's got you looking at this again?"

"Did you know Abe's looking at selling his land out there?"

His mother eased into the chair on the other side of the desk. "No, I hadn't heard that."

Cam told her what he'd heard at the Mudcat the other night. "Any idea who the potential buyer might be?"

"Not a one. Do you think he's serious?"

"Seems like. I told him to hold off on making any final decisions."

Sandra looked at the screen then back at him. "You want the city to buy it."

"That's not news." Before she could say it, he said it himself. "I know the city can't afford it. But he can't sell that land, Mom. It can't change. It's too important to the history of the town. The springs are its heart."

Sandra gave him a look of affectionate forbearance. "The heart of this town is its people."

"And we're losing them left and right." How

many families had picked up and left in the last six months? "Everything's changing and I don't know how to stop it."

She rose and came around the desk to frame his face in her hands. "Oh my baby, you've never dealt well with change. That's probably my fault. I did everything I could to keep things the same for you after your dad left."

"You aren't to blame for anything that happened after that." God knew she'd done the best she could, and that was a damned sight better than plenty of people had with two parents.

"Be that as it may, the fact is that life is change. You either adapt and survive or you stagnate and die. I know you love Wishful exactly as it is, and you want to preserve it. That's admirable and is part of what endears you to many of your constituents. But if we're going to make it in today's world, we may have to do some things for our town that we won't necessarily like. We need jobs to keep the people. Without them, we have no town."

Something in her tone put him on edge. "Is

there something you're not telling me? Some new development?"

Sandra lifted her hands for peace. "I don't know anything yet. Vick's making noises about having some potentially interesting news by the next City Council meeting."

Cam scowled. City Planner Victor Burgess was as close as he had to a nemesis. Cam felt like he spent more than half his time and energy as a City Councilman trying to block whatever cock-eyed scheme Burgess came up with, in order to keep Wishful from turning into yet another soulless, cookie cutter suburbia. "God forbid the man actually spend some time thinking about what's truly *good* for this community."

"Now son, that's not fair. Vick does think he's doing what's best for Wishful. It just happens you two don't see eye to eye on what that actually is."

"And we never will."

"Campbell, our town is in trouble. Whatever it is he's got up his sleeve, I want you to give it a fair chance. Promise to at least hear him out."

Cam managed not to grind his teeth. "Yes, ma'am."

He understood that Wishful needed help. It needed jobs and an influx of serious cash into the economy. But he couldn't help hoping that there was some other way than courting the big industries that would come in and change the entire tone of the town.

"That's enough about that. No reason to borrow trouble before we absolutely have to. Are you about done here?"

"I ought to be working on year end reports but, as Violet pointed out, I'm not. You wanna go grab some dinner? We can be completely decadent and hit up Tosca. Ask for extra cheese on everything and tiramisu for dessert." Cam laid a hand over hers. "You deserve to splurge. You're still not back to fighting weight."

Sandra turned her palm up and squeezed his fingers. "It's been eighteen months, baby. I'm fine."

Eighteen months, two weeks, three days since the chemotherapy was pronounced a success. Cam wondered if he'd ever stop counting the days. Probably not, if only to give thanks for each additional one.

"Anyway, I can't. I'm going over to help Molly put together a welcome home party for Liam." She tugged her hand away and picked up her purse.

"Welcome home?"

"He's leaving the service and coming home to Wishful."

The eldest of four, Liam Montgomery and his two brothers had been in the Marines almost as long as Cam could remember. "Wow. I know she's thrilled. Anything I can do to help?" *Please say no.* All he really wanted at this point was to get on home. But if they needed anything, he'd suck it up and deal.

"Not right now, but I'll let you know. The party's at Speakeasy day after tomorrow."

Translation: *Your presence is expected.*

Cam held in a sigh. Yet another social engagement he couldn't dodge. At this rate he was earning some serious cave time. He rose to escort her out to her car. "I'll be sure to make some time to stop by and welcome him home."

Sandra rose to her toes to kiss his cheek. "Go home and enjoy your quiet, darlin'. I know you're always worn out by all the social of the holidays, and Miranda's going to expect you at her New Year's Eve party."

He groaned. "Why do I need to be there? The world is going to be there."

She patted his cheek. "Because you are *not* spending another year at home *alone* with your dog. You need to be out with other young people having a good time. And you will go because she's family and it will make her happy."

"Yes, ma'am."

Sometimes family obligations were a real bitch.

CHAPTER 3

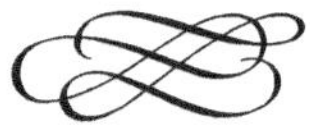

AT THE SOUND OF the crash, Norah jolted upright, hands clenching on the steering wheel as a scream clogged in her throat. But her car was still idling at the light, all in one piece. In park.

When had she done that?

Another tap came on the window. A tap. Not the crash in her dream. "Are you all right?"

Norah turned toward the muffled voice, her brain refusing to engage. A woman hunched outside the passenger side window, concern written across her face.

A car honked behind her, and Norah realized the light was finally green. Before she could shift back into drive, the big truck whipped around her to make the left on to Spring Street, proving that Chicago didn't have the market cornered on impatient drivers.

The woman still stood at the window. Norah rolled it down. "I'm…" What? Not fine. She'd just fallen asleep at the wheel at a stoplight. Thank God this was Wishful instead of somewhere with more traffic. "I must've dozed off."

The woman flashed a pair of dimples. "Well, it is a notoriously long light. Still, why don't you pull over up here and park? Come in and have some coffee." She gestured at the sign for Sweet Magnolias Bakery.

Getting off the road seemed like an excellent plan. "Yeah, okay."

Careful to actually watch for other vehicles, Norah made the turn and parked along the curb. The woman stood holding the door of the bakery open. She wore a red apron printed with a cartoon cat and the slogan *Sass. I haz it.* scrawled beneath.

"Thank you." Norah stepped inside. Scents of sweets and spice and chocolate wrapped around her like the welcoming arms of a favorite grandmother and her mouth immediately began to water.

"Have a seat." The woman gestured to the cluster of brightly painted, mismatched tables and chairs. "I saw you nod off in your car and thought I'd better check on you before you rolled into oncoming traffic."

"Thanks for that. The light was taking forever, and I must've slipped the car into park while I was waiting."

"Thank God for small mercies." She moved behind the stretch of glass cases to pour two cups of coffee. "The sensor's been broken since they put in the light. You were only out for a couple of minutes."

"Long enough to prove I need to get off the road." Norah accepted a steaming mug. "Thank you."

The proprietress slid into the chair across the table. "Long drive?"

"Set out from Chicago at five this morning after…not a lot of sleep." She'd decided it was time to get the hell out of town and finally make that visit to Miranda. Coming to Wishful was the only action she'd taken since her confrontation with Pierce and Philip that she *hadn't* questioned a thousand times over. Including the fact that when she left this morning, she'd mass blocked every area code in Chicago from her phone. For the next week, she was completely checking out.

"Oh you poor thing." The woman laid her hand over Norah's in a quick gesture of comfort. "Do you have much further to go?"

"Not too far." *Thank God.*

"Where are you headed?"

"Here."

The baker angled her head, clearly thinking. "Chicago…you're Miranda's friend, Norah."

Norah was too tired and too amused at how

things worked in small towns to be surprised. "Guilty."

"I'm Carolanne Wheeler. Nice to meet you."

Norah hummed an acknowledgment and sipped her drink. "You're a lifesaver with this coffee." She drank more and tried to get her sluggish brain in gear. "It's been a few years since I've been down to visit. Not since Miranda finished residency and came home to open her practice, but I don't remember you being here then."

"I wasn't. Only been open a couple of years."

"Are you from Wishful?"

Carolanne shook her head. "Atlanta originally. I had something of a personal crisis epiphany a few years ago and decided I needed a radical change. So I up and quit my job and moved here to open this place. With a stopover for pastry school."

Short of leaving the country, Norah couldn't imagine a more radical change. "And was that what you needed?"

"Best decision I ever made." She grinned.

"It's still a bit touch-and-go on the financial side, but that's the nature of opening a business anywhere. I love Wishful."

"I always have, too. I started coming here with Miranda when we were roommates back in college. It's a really special town."

"You know, Miranda was just in yesterday—she has a cupcake habit—and didn't say anything about you coming."

"She doesn't know. It was a spur of the moment trip. I needed some girl time, so I thought I'd surprise her. Speaking of which, I figure I could soften the imposition with sugar."

"I've got just the thing." Carolanne rose and circled around to pull a tray from the display case. "These are a devil's food cake with a peanut butter ganache and a peanut butter cup hidden in the center. I call them billionaires. Sweet and rich, with just a hint of salty. Perfectly sinful and exactly what a good man should be."

Norah decided she officially loved Carolanne. "I'll take one with a broody gaze and washboard abs."

Carolanne's laughter pealed and something in Norah loosened for the first time in days.

"Oh, you meant the cupcakes."

"Try one."

Norah bit in and groaned as pure decadence exploded in her mouth. "I'll take half a dozen."

As Carolanne rang up the sale, Norah finished her coffee and cupcake. "Thanks for the caffeine and chat. I think I'm awake enough to make it without passing out at the wheel again."

She handed over the box with a smile. "Welcome to Wishful, Norah. I hope you'll stay a while."

Fatigue still dragged at Norah as she stepped outside and back to her car. She drove past the large green that stretched the entire length of Main Street, scanning the shop windows from afar. The buildings themselves looked worn and aged. Comfortable with themselves. Much of the signage was faded, and definitely many of the awnings could use replacing. A few businesses had planters in front of their display windows. Empty this time of year. Everything would perk up, come spring. Local business owners would distract from the ancient brick and peeling paint with fresh plantings and clean, sparkling windows to display their wares. But for now, downtown looked frayed at the edges, as worn down and tired as Norah felt. But everything was still here. Not until the relief bled through her did she realize she'd expected Wishful to be as decimated as Morton.

The last few days had brought so much change. She needed something familiar. She needed Miranda, needed the rest of the crazy Campbell clan.

Norah didn't know what she'd tell them. She wasn't ready to admit she'd been fired. Burkes were raised not to make mistakes and ignorance didn't mitigate the enormity of the one she'd made.

Would it be better not to have found out? To go on with her high powered-life none the wiser?

No.

She recalled the look of derision on Philip's face, the disgust on Pierce's. No matter what happened from here on out, she was better off without them, better off knowing what kind of men they really were.

The receptionist was on the phone when Norah stepped into Miranda's clinic. The waiting room, like the parking lot outside, was almost empty. An older gentleman in a shearling coat sat reading a magazine. He looked up as she shut the door and gave her a wrinkled smile. Norah nodded and smiled back. He didn't appear to be sick, or agitated by the wait, so she assumed he was waiting on a patient in the back. Good. Maybe that meant Miranda was nearly through for the day.

A door beside the reception desk opened and a nurse in turquoise scrubs walked out. "I'm so sorry. We're just about to close, so this really isn't a good time for you to meet with Doctor—" The nurse cut herself off, eyes widening in surprise. "Norah! Oh my gosh, I thought you were a drug rep."

Norah grinned. "Hey Piper. Long time no see."

"Well I'll say. Damn, girl, how long's it been? Six years?"

"Seven." Norah shifted the cupcake box to give the other woman a one-armed hug. "Not since before you finished nursing school. You look fabulous."

Piper waved a hand. "I look like I've been dealing with a mad rush of flu patients. Don't worry. We've all been practically bathing in disinfectant. Miranda didn't tell me you were coming."

"She didn't know. I had an…unexpected opportunity to get away come up, and I took it."

"Well hallelujah for that. Miranda's going to be beside herself. Hang on a sec." Piper turned to the man in the corner and raised her voice to that register everyone used with the hard of hearing. "Mr. Tolleson, your wife is just about finished. We had to take some blood, so you be sure and take her to get something to eat straight after this. I hear it's meatloaf day at Dinner Belles. I know how Winnie likes her meatloaf."

Mr. Tolleson gave her a thumbs up.

Piper turned back to Norah and dropped her voice. "She has to come in for regular blood work. We help her make sure she gets a dinner date out of it."

Norah grinned. "I expect you could use some sustenance after such a long day." She lifted the cupcake box and opened the top.

"You are a saint. No, a goddess. Statues shall be erected in your honor." Piper grabbed a cupcake and wasted no time in taking a bite. Her head lolled back and she moaned theatrically.

The receptionist, a fortyish woman with a spray of freckles and vivid green eyes behind horn-rimmed glasses, hung up the phone with a clatter. "I swear, if I have to talk to that woman *one more time* this week…" She let the threat trail off.

Norah offered the box. "Cupcake?"

The woman lifted her fingers in the sign of the cross. "Get thee away, Satan!"

Piper took another bite of cupcake. "Shelby's on the Atkins diet."

"And after the week we've had already, my will power is at an all-time low. But thanks for the offer, sweetie."

"You should totally have waited to start until after New Year's. Who starts a diet the day after Christmas?" The groan of pleasure as Piper finished off the cupcake punctuated the lunacy of such a thing.

"The woman who ate half a chocolate chess pie out of stress due to the presence of her in-laws, that's who." Shelby shuddered. "How my husband came from those two, I will *never know.*"

The door to the exam rooms opened and Miranda edged out, her arm around an older lady. "Now you be sure to run right on over to the pharmacy and pick this up. I called it in already, so Riley ought to have it ready by the time you get there. You start it tonight at bedtime. And let me know if you have any side effects."

As the woman shuffled toward her waiting husband, Miranda shoved a hand through her thick blonde hair and turned, clearly checking for more patients. "Please tell me that's the—" Her eyes widened. "Norah!"

"Surprise." Norah grinned.

Miranda's white coat flared like a cape as she leapt across the room and wrapped Norah in a fierce hug. Norah held tight, burying her face against her friend's shoulder and breathing in the familiar scents of alcohol, starch, and new plastic. Something hot and tight lodged in her throat, and she had to fight to keep the smile in place. "God, I've missed you."

"It's *so* good to see you!"

"Sorry for just dropping in like this." Norah pulled back. "I hope your guest room is available."

"For you? Always. What are you doing here? I thought you couldn't get away again until summer."

It was on the tip of her tongue to let it all spill out. The fate of Morton. The firing. All the ugliness that had made her pack up and run. But shame and embarrassment locked her throat.

Something must've shown on her face because Miranda frowned and took her by the shoulders again. "Norah? What's wrong? Is it your parents?"

Norah shook her head. "I got dumped." *By my life.*

The immediate outpouring of sympathy and suggestions about what her ex could do with his manhood had her throat clogging yet again, even as Piper shoved a cupcake into her hand.

"Give us a chance to change clothes, and we'll go out tonight and drink to the shriveling of his dick. Liam Montgomery's welcome home party's going on over at Speakeasy right now anyway."

Norah let out a bark of laughter. "Oh God, as much fun as that sounds, I'm absolutely wiped. I've been up since four and drove straight through."

"Then we'll stay in and have Chinese and Ben and Jerry's before you crash."

"And tomorrow night you can flirt with the best male specimens Wishful has to offer," Piper added.

"Beg pardon?"

"I'm throwing a big New Year's Eve bash. Everybody who's anybody in our age bracket will be there."

"It'll be good for you." Piper looped an arm through hers. "An excuse to dress up, look fabulous, and party with people who have way better taste and sense than your ex. Throw off all this sad stuff."

Norah held back a grimace. Much as she enjoyed people, that kind of socializing was the last thing she was in the mood for. It was so incompatible with licking one's wounds. But she was the one who'd popped in unannounced. She couldn't expect everyone to change their plans to suit her. She mustered a sassy smile. "Well, I did pack this amazing dress."

"...AND we'll be taking applications for the future mother of my grandbabies right over here."

Cam laughed along with everyone else as big bad Staff Sergeant Liam Montgomery blushed all the way to the tips of his ears. "Mom!"

Molly pulled Liam down for a noisy kiss. "Kidding! Mostly. Please, everybody, enjoy the party!"

She and Liam stepped down from the tiny stage that usually hosted local musicians and karaoke. A big *Welcome Home!* banner stretched above their heads. Tables had been set up along one exposed brick wall, and they were lined with an assortment of Speakeasy's signature pizzas. Cam noticed Liam skirted these, giving a wide berth to everyone of the female persuasion.

The scents of spicy tomatoes, pepperoni, and yeasty crust set Cam's stomach to rumbling, reminding him he hadn't actually gotten around to lunch today, while he was pushing through those year-end reports at the nursery. But social duties had to be satisfied before his appetite. He cornered Liam as the other man lifted a beer from a passing tray.

"Welcome home, Staff Sergeant." Cam offered a hand.

"Good to be back." Liam shot a glance back at his mother. "I think."

"You had to know settling back here was gonna open you wide up for that. You're the oldest."

"Jesus. Is your Mama giving you grief about settling down?"

His family went well out of their way to avoid the topic of him and marriage, a state of affairs Cam was generally completely okay with. "Nope. That honor goes to Mitch."

"Then I expect he'll be happy to commiserate, now that I'm back."

"Gotta admit, I'm surprised. I always figured you for a lifer."

Liam's expression darkened for a fleeting instant and was gone. "Well, I did too, but things change."

"I was really sorry about your dad." A little over a year before, Liam's father, John, had dropped dead of an aneurysm while under the hood of his beloved 1969 Mustang.

"With Wynne off to New Orleans and both Jack and Cruz still in for a while, when this contract was up it just made the most sense to step off the train. Somebody needs to be home to look after Mom."

Cam smiled into his beer. "Don't let her hear you say that." The pint-sized Molly Montgomery had kept three sons, a daughter, and a husband in line, all while working a full-time job and regularly volunteering on various committees around town. She was a force to be reckoned with. But Cam understood the sentiment. After his mother's cancer diagnosis, he'd dropped out of grad school and come home to take care of her.

When Liam didn't respond, Cam followed his gaze across the room to a buxom brunette currently embracing Liam's sister, Wynne.

"Who is *that?*"

"Who? Riley?"

"*That's* Riley Gower?" Liam's eyes all but bugged out of his skull as she turned where he could see her face.

Cam elbowed him lightly in the ribs. "Pick your jaw up off the floor, man, before your mama sees you. Yeah, that's Riley Gower. I don't guess you've had occasion to see her since she grew up."

"She's my baby sister's best friend. I haven't seen her since I enlisted. She was a freshman in high school, I guess."

Which explained the shock. Since then, Riley had gone from awkward and a little bit heavy to 1940s bombshell.

"She bought out the pharmacy when your mom decided to semi-retire earlier this year," said Cam, though he was pretty sure, given the look on the other man's face, that wasn't the information he was looking for. "She's single."

Liam shook himself and turned his focus back to Cam. "What?"

"Riley. She's not seeing anybody."

"Wouldn't matter if she was. I was just…surprised, is all."

Yeah, you keep telling yourself that, buddy. But Cam gave the man a break and changed the subject. "So, what's the plan now that you're back?"

"I'm not sure what to do with myself just yet. It'll take time to get used to being without my unit, without orders, but, I have to say, I'm looking forward to being my own man."

"I'll certainly keep my ears open. If I hear of anybody looking to hire, I'll let you know."

"Appreciate it."

"Oh, you helping anybody find a job. That's rich, Crawford."

Cam turned toward the voice dripping with sarcasm and barely repressed venom.

Roy McKennon stepped up, a long-neck bottle hanging loose between two fingers. "The Councilman here has made it a *priority* to block any and all incoming industry to town. So don't be thinkin' he's got your best interests at heart."

Sometimes Cam really hated civil service. "Now Roy, that's not entirely accurate. There were reasons for—"

"Reasons?" Roy pivoted to face him. The slur in his voice made it evident he'd had more than a couple of beers. "What *reasons* do you have for stopping Ford from building that manufacturing plant here? What *reasons* do you have for denying hard-working people the possibility of a *job?*" Roy's voice was rising, and Cam was aware of others starting to look their way.

Cam knew he needed to diffuse the situation. "That's not what I was doing."

"I got three kids and a wife to support, boy. Since the plant closed, we've got no insurance. Had to go on goddamned assistance like a bunch of reprobates. April made me let her sign up for WIC and Medicaid just so the kids are covered. My youngest has chronic asthma." Roy punctuated each point with a jab to Cam's sternum.

Though his own temper stirred, Cam kept his voice level. "It's a tough place to be in, but there's no shame in asking for help when you need it."

That was absolutely the wrong thing to say. Roy's face reddened. "You've got no right! No goddamned right to do *anything* to stop job opportunities from coming to this town." He lunged for Cam, the bottle crashing to the floor as he swung one meaty fist.

Liam snagged Roy's arm, twisting it behind his back until the other man howled. "You need to settle on down now, Mr. McKennon. This isn't the place."

Speakeasy fell silent, all eyes turned on them.

Roy subsided in Liam's grip, his burst of liquid courage evidently spent. April McKennon, a worn-looking woman in her early forties, crossed the room, her face set in lines of abject mortification.

"We're going home." Her tone brooked no argument. "I'm very sorry for this. Liam, we welcome you back to Wishful and thank you for your service to our country."

"Yes ma'am." He released her husband. "Thank you."

"Get to the car, Roy."

Roy looked as if he might argue, but his wife just pointed with the well-honed authority of a mother of three, and he headed for the door.

April turned back toward Cam. "I'm sorry. Roy's a proud man, and this…financial down-turn has been really hard on him. He needs somebody to blame, and he's settled on you."

"I understand." Cam thought of the conversation with his mother about how they might have to do things they didn't necessarily like in order to save Wishful. "I swear to you, Mrs. McKennon, I'm trying my hardest to do what's best for this town."

"I'm sure you think you are." Without another word, she turned and followed her husband to the door, her head held high, her shoulders stiff.

Cam ached for her, knowing that the embarrassment over the scene her husband caused upset her as much as his unemployment.

Conversation gradually rose again in the wake of their departure. Cam rubbed a hand on the back of his neck as he turned back to Liam. "Well. Sorry 'bout that. I'm not exactly the most popular around here these days."

"Did you really block a Ford plant?"

Tucker McGee stepped up and handed Cam a beer. "Reckon you could use this. Cam was *not*, in fact, a one man army against Ford. He simply brought up all the relevant environmental impacts such a plant would have on the area, and the bulk of the City Council backed him up and decided it wasn't the right answer. Plus, I heard they got more favorable terms from some other state offering tax incentives and such that we couldn't."

"Not that the general public seems to be

aware of that. I was the most vocal opponent, so I'm the scapegoat for why we didn't get it. Times are really tough for a lot of folks." Aware that more people had queued up to talk to Liam, Cam gave in to his own keen desire to escape. "Anyway, I meant what I said. If I can do anything to help you find something, I will."

"Thanks again."

Tucker followed Cam over to the buffet. "It's not your fault, you know."

"I know that." But it was hard not to feel some responsibility as April's parting words echoed through his head. *I'm sure you think you are.* Was he wrong? His duty was to the townspeople, to his constituents, not just to further his own agenda of preserving the town exactly as he wanted it. He was starting to lose hope that there was any way to satisfy them and assuage his conscience.

CLAD in yoga pants and an ancient Ole Miss sweatshirt that was a dozen washings away from losing its collar, Norah sat curled on one end of Miranda's sofa, a pint of General Tso's chicken in her hands as the credits began to roll on *Serendipity.* They'd talked most of the way through the movie, catching up on things that hadn't come up in their twice weekly phone conversations. More relaxed than she'd been in ages, Norah let her head fall back to the cushions. "Chinese food and chick flicks. You do know how to take care of me."

"I am a medical professional." Miranda polished off the last of her sweet and sour chicken.

"I miss this. I miss *you.* Chicago hasn't been the same since you moved home."

"Feeling a bit like the last southerner standing?"

"Like a zoo exhibit at times." Norah grimaced.

"I know you love your job, and you've invested a lot in Helios, but there's nothing that says you can't move back below the Mason

Dixon line, you know. Especially since you're not tied to Pierce anymore."

Even less reason than you know. Now was the time to tell her the full truth, come clean about being fired. But she just...couldn't. Not yet. Because Miranda, God love her, was a steamroller, and she'd push as much as Norah's parents, albeit out of love rather than her own agenda. Norah just couldn't deal with that yet. Not until she'd reconciled it in her own mind, figured out what she was going to do next. The admission of failure would be easier to face with a plan. Right?

Not that she had any prior experience with failure. Burkes didn't fail. Period.

"Did that asshat break your heart, honey?"

Norah considered the question rather than offering the flip response that sprang to her lips. Had Pierce broken her heart? In the few days since she'd confronted him, she'd felt no grief over the loss of their relationship, only for the damage to her career.

"Less my heart and more my pride."

"Sometimes that hurts worse. And I'm going to make a confession here. I'm glad y'all broke up. He always felt like a very pretty accessory to that whole high-powered lifestyle rather than real relationship material."

Norah's mouth dropped open.

"I'm sorry, I know you must've seen something in him or you wouldn't have dated him in the first place but…you're worth so much more than that."

The laugh bubbled up, expanding in her chest until it burst out in a hoot. "Oh my God, Pierce would just *die.* A pretty accessory." Norah bent over in helpless giggles. "God, he really was." He was, she was shamed to realize, merely an extension of her career. And wasn't that a sad testament to the state of her life? The thought sobered her up. "But seriously, I'll take this as the sign it is."

"Of what?"

"That I'm not made for the kind of deep, long-term relationships that lead to marriage and family."

"That's horse shit."

The invective made Norah want to hug her all over again. God it was good to be back in the South.

"Is it? I'm ambitious and talented. The child of two equally ambitious, talented people who tried to make it work and failed spectacularly. Burkes excel professionally and absolutely tank in relationships."

"That doesn't mean you'll fail. Just means you haven't found the right guy."

"I can't imagine the right guy. The guy who can deal with my ambition and not expect me to put it away to do the whole wife and baby thing. I'd go crazy inside a year."

"I'm sorry, did it turn back to 1954 and I missed it? Live in the now, girl. Anyway, I think you're selling yourself short."

Norah jerked a shoulder. "And what about you? You've been doing the perpetually single dance since med school. If you made it past the third date, that was a long-term relationship."

"I'm careful," Miranda corrected. "Especially since I came home. Wishful is a pretty damned tiny dating pool, and it's not getting any bigger. Not usually anyway. I fully expect Liam to have half a dozen proposals before summer."

There was something in her friend's too off-hand manner. "That annoys you."

"What?"

"That all these women are going to be interested in this Liam guy. Who is he?"

Miranda waved a dismissive hand. "The Campbells and the Montgomerys have always been kind of intertwined. There are four of them and five of us in similar age ranges. Liam's the oldest. A good friend of Mitch's. He went straight into the Marines from high school. He just finished his third term and decided to move home to be closer to his mom. She's widowed."

"You like the hot ex-soldier," Norah proclaimed, happy to shift the conversation away from the dismal state of *her* love life.

"How do you know he's hot?"

"Goes without saying. He risked his life for our country."

"He was hot before that."

"I knew it! You like him!"

"I *did* like him. I had a ludicrous crush on him in high school, of the variety you can only have for your older brother's best friend. Of course, he never actually saw me as anything other than Randa Panda because my rat bastard of a brother told him I still had the bear I carried around as a toddler."

Norah winced in sympathy. "Have you seen him since high school?"

"Once at a Christmas party a few years back, when he was home on furlough. Where I was still Randa Panda. I freaking *hate* that nickname."

"So I gather you didn't have plans to show up at his welcome home party tonight in some knockout dress to make him realize you grew up?"

"Of course not." Miranda dimpled. "I invited him to *my* party tomorrow night, where I'll be wearing some knockout dress to make him realize I grew up. Not that I expect it to work, but it seems worth the effort to set the record straight."

"Even though you totally still have Pammy the Panda?"

"In the name of our decade of friendship, you will take that to your grave."

Norah nodded soberly. "Naturally."

"On that note, I have something for you." Miranda unfolded her long legs from the sofa and wandered into the kitchen. She returned a few minutes later with two slices of pie and a tiara.

"You got me a breakup pie?"

"Of course I did. You know the rule. 'When they don't stay, it's queen for a day.' So technically your queenship lasts through the party tomorrow." Miranda set the pie down and tucked the tiara in Norah's hair.

"Don't need to be queen. Just need my best gal pal."

"I'm always here. How long can you stay?"

There it was. Another opportunity to spill her guts. Norah tried to gather her courage as she dug into the French silk pie, but when she opened her mouth, a lie slipped out. "It's up in the air. I took a leave of absence. I need some time to figure things out." The last part, at least, was true.

You are an unmitigated coward.

"Good. You work too hard. Stay as long as you like. You know you've always got a place with me."

And that was why she'd come. Because wherever life took her, Miranda was always home.

Norah worked up a smile. "It's good to be back."

CAM WAS LATE TO the party and well aware he was gonna hear about it. He'd considered not coming at all, but he wouldn't put it past his cousins to come haul him bodily out of his house, and he preferred to show up under his own steam. Hush leapt down from the truck and Cam shut the door, trudging up the car-lined street toward Miranda's place. His dog ran ahead, darting from bush to tree to car tire to sniff. He was probably gonna hear about having brought her, too, but she'd been stuck in the house all day while he helped his mom prepare for *her* party, and Cam figured it was a good escape mechanism. Win-win.

He didn't bother knocking, just opened the front door and stepped inside. Music pumped through the lower floor, underscored by the din of conversation. People spilled into the rooms on either side of the entryway, surrounding the buffet in the dining room, trailing into the kitchen. Libation. That's what he needed before facing the firing squad.

"This is taking fashionably late to a new extreme, don't you think?" Tyler Edison looked amused from her post just inside the dining room.

"Yeah, well, my date took forever to get ready. All that primping."

"If I'd known fur was an option, I'd have brought her a playmate. Speaking of, you might want to nab her before she bowls over the impromptu guest of honor."

Cam spun just as Hush bolted into the den,

making a beeline for a brunette in a little black dress. He leapt forward, but before he could get out a command, the woman was turning and crouching in her high, high heels, arms open to receive a hundred pounds of enthusiastic canine. They collided with joyful sounds on both sides. Hush trembled with excitement, tail wagging ninety to nothing, imperiling the knees of everyone around them as the woman rubbed her down. "Aren't you just the sweetest thing? Who's a good girl? Who's a cute puppy?" She threw back her head in a laugh as his dog began bathing her face in kisses, her dark hair cascading in waves down her shoulders, her mouth curved in a smile that sucker punched Cam straight in the gut. His brain stuttered to a halt.

Wow.

"I don't think anybody would call her a puppy." Miranda turned a disapproving glare in his direction. "Cam, why in God's name did you bring your dog?"

"She's not two yet. Still a puppy." He crossed

to them and grabbed Hush by the collar. "And still learning her manners, I'm afraid. Sit, Hush."

After a moment of indecision, Hush plopped her butt to the floor, tail still thumping a steady tattoo.

The woman looked up at him, peat-dark eyes ripe with amusement. "Aren't you confusing her with multiple commands?"

She looked vaguely familiar, though Cam knew he'd never met her. No way would he have forgotten that smile. "No. Her name is Hush. It started out Sadie, but she talked so often the first few months and got told to hush, that's what she started coming to, so it stuck." He offered his hand and pulled her to her feet, sorry when her slim fingers released his.

"Oh Norah, your dress!"

That explained the familiarity. He'd seen pictures of Miranda's old college roommate. Cam looked down, noted the white dog hair clinging to the fabric and winced. "Sorry. I've got a lint roller in my truck. I can go get it, if you like."

"Oh smooth, Crawford," Piper crooned with a laugh. "Great first impression."

Norah waved a dismissive hand. "It's just fur. A perfectly reasonable price to pay for puppy kisses from this sweet baby." She scratched Hush under the chin, sent her back leg kicking. "You're just a big teddy bear, aren't you, girl?"

Delighted, Hush began to speak in her half howl, half singing voice as she slumped in a happy, boneless heap against Norah's legs.

Norah braced herself for the extra weight and laughed again. "I stand corrected. A Wookie in a dog suit."

"Half Alaskan malamute, half Great Pyrenees."

"And all fur." Miranda scowled. "Cam, she's shedding on *everything*."

"She's not hurting a thing. Are you, baby?" As if to illustrate the point, Norah slipped out of her shoes and dropped back to the floor, neatly tucking her legs so Hush could sprawl across her lap.

Miranda threw up her hands. "Fine. You two dog people have fun. I'm going to see if I need to put out more sausage balls."

"I'll come with." Piper followed her toward the dining room.

"Cam, if she gets into my buffet, it's your head."

"Yes, ma'am." He saluted his cousin and watched her stalk toward the refreshments, where Liam was chatting with Tucker. Time to test his good fortune. "Is this floor taken?"

"Have a seat."

He took up a position at the other end of his dog. "She's pissed at me."

"She'll get over it. We'll have to clean up the house again after the party anyway."

"I suspect I may have just drafted myself for that job."

"Well, you got points with *me* for bringing your dog to a people party."

"Despite the mess to your dress?"

"Dresses can be cleaned. I don't get to spend nearly enough time with dogs." When Hush shifted in her lap, pawing her hand closer to the broad expanse of chest, Norah obliged, wringing a contented sigh from his pooch.

"Don't have one yourself?"

"I live in an apartment and work long hours. It wouldn't be fair to have a dog under those circumstances. I could have a cat but…why?"

"True enough. Did you have dogs growing up?"

"The only place we lived that would've been good for a dog was Hattiesburg, and we left there when I was eleven and my folks divorced. After that it was a string of big cities. Houston, Cincinnati, Philadelphia. A year in Boston before I left for school. My mom is a gifted pediatric surgeon, who's always worked insane hours. My dad is a civil rights attorney who does the same, so a dog wasn't really an option in either household."

"That's just tragic."

"Little bit. But hard to argue when they're both out there fighting for the greater good."

There was something in her tone that made

him wonder what else they'd done or, more likely, hadn't done that she brushed off as being okay because they were doing good elsewhere.

"You never got one yourself?"

"I thought about it in college, but I knew I'd likely wind up back in the city for grad school. I promised myself if I ended up somewhere suitable after, then I'd get one. But I wound up staying in Chicago and—surprise, surprise—working as much as either of my parents." She shrugged and focused hard on sussing out the rest of Hush's favorite spots. "Sometimes I'll stop by the dog park down from my apartment and just sit a while and watch them play. It's relaxing." A faint wash of color stained her cheeks as she glanced up at him, before turning back to the dog.

Christ, she was breaking his heart. Cam couldn't imagine life without a dog. "Well, considering my dog appears to be completely besotted with you, seems like this trip should be a good opportunity for you to get your fill."

"You don't mind loaning her out?"

"She might come with her owner, when he can get free."

Norah angled her head to study him, the lift of her brows indicating she'd caught his subtle flirtation. "How is it we've never met before this? In all the years I've known Miranda, all the times I've come home with her, I've met your entire family, including your mom. But never you."

Cam leaned back against the wall, trailing his hand over Hush's flank as he considered the question. "Well, when y'all were in school at Ole Miss, I was over at Auburn. It's a much longer drive, so I didn't come home as often." A fact he now had cause to regret.

"You never visited Miranda in Chicago, while she was doing residency."

"Hate the city." He didn't bother repressing the automatic shudder. "And you haven't been back down here since she moved home. I'd have heard about it if you had. I've heard a great deal about you over the years. According to family reputation, you're damn near perfect."

Something flickered across her face at that, but her features smoothed quickly out into a self-deprecating smile. "Certifiable, type A overachiever, absolutely. But not perfect."

"Lies!"

They both looked up as Mitch ambled over.

"Don't listen to her, Cam. She's just being modest." He shifted his attention to Norah. "You've been hiding."

"Not hiding. You've been circulating. I'm pretty sure I saw you making eyes at the woman who runs the hardware store."

"Tyler? Nah. We're just friends. Besides, you know I only have eyes for urbane brunettes." Mitch held out both hands. "Come here and give me a hug."

Norah dislodged the dog and let Mitch draw her to her feet, where he promptly bent her back into a dip. "Hello gorgeous. I hear that a breakup pie was purchased last night and that you are, at long last, on the market again. Finally coming back to Mississippi to date me properly?"

Cam felt an immediate and irrational desire to call dibs.

When Mitch made to kiss her, Norah stopped his mouth with a finger. "Just because you're free with your kisses did not make it a date."

"It was totally a date." Mitch flashed an unrepentant grin.

"Liar, liar, pants on fire, Mitch Campbell."

Mitch laid a hand over his heart. "Darlin', you can light my pants on fire any time."

She slapped him hard on the ass. "That's as far as you're getting with me."

"More's the pity. Who was the idiot? That shark in Armani I met that time?"

A woman like her had been with a man like that?

"Pierce. Yes, that would be the idiot in question."

"Never did like him."

"You only met him once."

"He was too slick. And he had this look like he was calculating how he could use everything you said to his advantage."

"Well that's an astute observation. He did—does—exactly that. I never thought anything about it because that's something we both do for a living."

"With you it's personal, though. You're good because you can read people, figure out what they want, what they need, what they'll respond to. Because you legitimately give a damn about them getting the best outcome. Pierce seemed a lot more self-serving."

Because he was watching her, Cam saw the flash of surprise and relief before Norah leaned over and wrapped her arms around Mitch in a tight hug. "Thank you. I really needed to hear that."

Mitch ran a hand over her hair. "Hey, I've got your back. Do I need to make a trip up to kick his ass?"

She favored him with an indulgent smile. "As gratifying as that might be, having you brought up on assault charges in my honor isn't quite the resolution I had in mind."

"I guess that'd be kinda weird since y'all work together."

Cam caught the faint tightening around her mouth before she flashed another smile. If he hadn't seen the real thing when she'd fawned on Hush, he wouldn't have known the difference.

Something tender there.

"Lesson learned."

Mitch made a show of cracking his knuckles. "The offer to kick his ass still stands."

"You're sweet. Now go use your powers to woo some other unsuspecting female. I am wise to your ways."

"You wound me, madam."

"Pretty sure that ego of yours will survive." But Norah grinned as she said it.

Mitch grabbed her hand, lifted it to his lips. "Glad you made it down, finally."

She shook her head as he walked away. "Shameless."

Cam got to his feet. "He likes you."

"He likes everyone." Amusement still colored her tone. "I enjoy his company, enjoy flirting with him because he's exceptionally good at it, but it's never been a date."

Not for Mitch's lack of trying, Cam knew. His cousin was an incorrigible flirt who loved and appreciated women of all varieties. "Well now you're even more intriguing. Few women say no to Mitch."

Norah smiled. "Then he needs some practice. Besides, I don't have the energy to keep up with him."

"Really? According to family stories, you're the poster child for extrovert."

"I like people, and I'm good with them, which comes in handy in my line of work. But I spend so much time 'on' for my job, I need to be able to turn it off and decompress the rest of the time. Mitch never turns off. The one time he visited for longer than two days, I wanted to sleep for a week."

Cam took a closer look, noting the subtle strain and the tension in her posture now that she wasn't distracted by petting Hush. "You needed to recharge when you came here."

She looked up at him, lifting a brow.

"One introvert recognizes the signs of another. You weren't expecting a big party."

"No, but I dropped in completely unannounced, and it's hard to consider a night of good company a hardship." Her hand dropped back to Hush, scratching absently behind her ears.

The feeling of unexpected kinship surprised him. "I'll drink to that."

"That might be a little difficult, as neither of us presently has a drink."

"An oversight easily rectified. What can I get you?"

"I'd love a cider. Thanks." At the sight of something across the room, she loosed a quiet sigh and braced herself.

Tucker was headed their way. "Listen, why don't you take Hush out back, get some air and a few minutes of quiet. I'll run interference and meet you out there."

Gratitude flashed in her eyes. "That's the best offer I've had all night."

"Go make your escape." *Time for an interception.*

NORAH STEPPED into the relative quiet of the night, Hush close on her heels. There were too many people in the house, too many familiar faces she'd met over the years, and they all had expectations about who she was, how she should behave. The last thing she wanted to do was talk about her exploits and successes, or entertain them with tales of the fast-paced, jet-setter life they imagined she led. She felt like a fraud. Keeping up the mask, subtly steering the conversation away from herself was taking all her energy. At least midnight wasn't that far off.

Surely the party wouldn't last too much past that.

Hush peeled away to make a sniffing exploration of the fence perimeter. Norah walked out into the yard and looked up at the stars. Millions of tiny pinpricks winking against a sea of velvety black. She thought she could pick out the Big Dipper and maybe Orion's Belt. *I should've paid more attention when I took all those out-of-towners to the planetarium.*

Cam stepped up beside her. "Bet you don't get skies like these in Chicago."

Norah accepted the bottle he held out. "No, definitely not. I'm surprised nobody's spilled out. It's a gorgeous night."

"It's below freezing."

"Pssh. There's six inches of fresh snow on the ground and sub-zero wind chills in Chicago right now. This is balmy."

"Balmy or not, you're going to freeze in that dress."

As if to illustrate his point, a frigid wind stirred the trees, painting gooseflesh along her exposed skin. The warmth of Cam's coat settled around her shoulders, draping almost all the way to her hemline. It smelled of him, of green, growing things that reminded her of the long, lazy summer days of childhood. Appealing. Like the man himself and his ridiculously charming dog.

"Thanks, but won't you get cold now?" She looked over in time to see the flash of his smile and wished her eyes had adjusted enough to catch the wink of dimples she'd seen inside. She had a serious weakness for dimples.

"First, I have sleeves. Second, manly men don't get cold." He took a long pull on his beer. "But I can go back in if you'd rather be alone."

She studied his shadowed face. "You'd really be okay with that, wouldn't you? With rescuing me and being sent back inside."

"You needed a chance to breathe. I don't expect some kind of reward for recognizing that."

How incredibly refreshing. "That kind of intuition is rare and highly under-appreciated.

You're the only person in there who recognized that I was about ready to crawl out of my skin."

"I get the need for quiet. I don't much like people horning in on mine, but that's the nature of the holidays, especially in my family."

"Well you have my thanks. And my company if you want it."

"In that case, c'mon." Cam grabbed her free hand and led her around the side of the house. A porch swing dangled from the limb of a massive oak tree. "We'll be more out of the wind here."

He sat, tugging her down beside him. One arm draped along the back of the swing. The move was such a classic, Norah's lips twitched into a smile. But he didn't shift to curve his arm around her shoulders or pull her closer. Instead, he leaned his head back and looked back up at the night sky. In the summer, when the tree leafed out, this would be a quiet, shady spot. For now, there was still a good view of the stars through the bare branches. The music inside was a low murmur through the glass.

Norah took the opportunity to study him from the corner of her eye. He was leaner than Mitch, though just as tall, with the blond hair characteristic of most of the Campbell clan. His was a good face, she decided. Not classically handsome like Pierce, but caught somewhere between boyish and rugged. It was a *real* face, and just now it was relaxed in lines of utter contentment.

"I envy you." She didn't realize she'd said it aloud until he looked over at her.

"Why?"

Your family. Your comfort in your life. Your direction. But she could say none of those things. "Your ability to relax. I'm terrible at it."

"You're still on city speed. I expect it takes practice. Lean on back."

She tried to force herself to relax, but was too aware of the weight of his arm on the swing behind her and the heat of his leg pressed companionably against hers on the tiny seat. If she really relaxed, she'd be snuggling into him.

"There's nothing you have to do, nothing

demanding your attention. No reason why you can't stop a while."

Norah couldn't stop the bitter laugh. "You have no idea how true that is."

"Sounds like there's a story there."

"Not a good one."

"That why you can't relax?"

"Yeah."

Cam toed the swing into motion and momentum did what she couldn't, tipping her back into the crook of his arm. She was so damned tired, and it felt so nice to lean against him, she let herself have the illusory comfort of contact. Simple and undemanding. God, when was the last time anyone just let her *be?*

"I'm a good listener." The quiet statement got to her.

"I haven't even told Miranda why I'm really here." She didn't mean to say it. But the dark and the closeness seemed to invite confidences as much as he did.

"Not just a visit, then."

"I'm running away." Oh, it galled her to admit it.

Cam stopped their rocking, tension snapping into his body. When he spoke, his voice was carefully controlled. "Did the ex hurt you?"

"No. No, not the way you mean. I'm not coming from an abusive relationship or something. Despite its longevity, I'm not entirely sure it even merits the term relationship."

He relaxed again and Norah felt the stroke of his hand down the length of her hair, the touch of hands that knew how to handle delicate things. Not that she'd ever thought of herself as delicate. She remembered that he ran a nursery and spent his days with plants. That explained the scents on his coat.

Cam said nothing as her brain continued to spin, just kept stroking her hair. Why should that small thing be so soothing? She found the words spilling out in a whisper. "I got fired."

He didn't flinch, didn't pause, just shifted his hand beneath her hair to rub at the tension in her nape. "Why?"

"I found out my firm had engaged in ethics violations. Had involved me in ethics violations by withholding certain information."

"Your firm or your ex?"

Oh, he was astute. "Both. I confronted them about it and said I wouldn't be party to any more of that sort of practice. Evidently, I over-estimated my importance to the firm."

"Is there some professional organization you can report them to? Some group that can sanction them or yank their license or whatever?"

"We don't have any kind of body like that. The American Marketing Association and the Public Relations Society of America have codes of ethics, but membership isn't mandatory. There's not really anybody who can do a damned thing. There's no ethics police."

"Well that sucks. Either way it sounds like you're better off out of there. They weren't your caliber of people."

"Knowing I have the moral high ground is cold comfort when it comes to trying to get another job without references. I've been with this firm since graduate school."

"References or not, I'm sure your work speaks for itself. Not to mention your academic credentials. Twice valedictorian, top of your class at Northwestern. Taylor medalist at Ole Miss."

Norah sat up to look at him. "How do you know all that?"

"Miranda talks a lot. She's really proud of you. Come back here." Cam pulled her back where she'd been tucked up against him. "Is that why you haven't told her? Are you worried she'll think of you differently?"

"No. I know she loves me no matter what, which is why I came. But I know her. She'll try to steamroll me to make a big change, and right now I just...I guess I'm still trying to wrap my head around it."

"I'm hearing a lot more upset about the job than the guy."

He was fishing and Norah knew it. She found she didn't actually mind. "The job mattered. Pierce didn't. Or rather, he was an extension of the job. Work has always defined my life, defined me. I don't know who I am without it."

"You're more than your job, Norah. From my point of view, you're a woman who takes her commitments and responsibilities very seriously. Clearly your parents did a great job instilling in you a hard work ethic, but they missed out on some of the essentials."

Norah bristled and started to sit up, but he held her in place.

"Don't get your dander up. I'm not insulting your folks. But they clearly didn't teach you that the other side of hard work is play. That sometimes you just need to be still. That it's okay to just *be.* They didn't teach you the value of sitting on a swing in the dark or dancing under the stars. All that's important too."

She tried to imagine her parents doing any of those things and couldn't see it. Her father was always working on some brief and, when she wasn't at the hospital, her mother was always keeping up-to-date with the medical literature, even over Saturday morning coffee. And Norah had followed right along in their footsteps within the confines of her own field. She understood work. Work had always been a constant. It made sense in a world that otherwise often didn't seem to follow any rules.

"Did I piss you off?"

"No, I was just trying to remember the last time I truly just chilled. Went to a movie without trying to analyze the advertising campaign or to a party without automatically building mental dossiers on all the attendees. And I…can't."

"Seems like maybe you need a remedial course in just plain living."

Christ, that was sad. "Are you volunteering as teacher?"

"Why not? I'm here, you're here, and they're playing one of my favorites." Cam brought the swing to a stop and rose, setting both their drinks at the base of the tree. He held out a hand. "Dance with me."

Norah laid her hand in his, letting the coat fall to the swing as she stood and stepped into him. She didn't notice the cold, not when the warmth of his hand curved at her waist and he began circling her to the quiet rhythm. She angled her head, straining to identify the music because it seemed safer to focus on that than on how it felt to be pressed almost against him. "Moon River. Old school."

"Other kids got *Goodnight Moon.* I got this."

The idea of it delighted her. "Please tell me you had one of those Fisher Price record players in your room."

"For a little while, but it didn't survive my cousins very long. No, I had this little tape deck thing. Mom filled up both sides of a tape with the song, and every night she'd put me to bed and press play. I'd fall asleep serenaded by Sinatra."

"That sounds lovely." Smiling, she tipped her head back to look at the sky again. "This is lovely."

"So are you."

Her eyes had adjusted enough to see his face in the faint cast of light from the house, and what she saw there made her pulse leap. *Foolish*, she thought. Theirs was a temporary intimacy, a product of shared secrets and darkness. But for all that it was fleeting, it was so incredibly tempting to give into the desire to touch and be touched. To feel, for a little while, as if she wasn't alone.

One corner of Cam's mouth lifted, drawing her gaze. God, he had beautiful lips. As the instrumental solo began, he slid one hand around her back, shifting from a dance to an embrace. Her hand flexed on his shoulder, with nerves or to get a better grip on him, she didn't know. But he didn't kiss her, instead nudging her head to his shoulder and resting a cheek on her hair. After a brief flare of disappointment, she relaxed against him and lost herself to the music and the solid, steady feel of him against her. By the time the song ended, Norah found herself soothed, as much by the man as the dance.

Reluctant to step away, she lifted her head.

"I feel better. Thanks for listening. And for the dance."

"Anytime." Cam brushed the hair back from her face with another of those feather-soft touches.

Inside, somebody shouted. The music cut off and the countdown began.

Cam didn't drop his hand. With each second that ticked by, Norah's heart kicked harder.

"…six…five…"

He stroked his thumb along the curve of her cheek, and she couldn't stop herself from leaning into the touch.

"…three…two…one!"

"Happy New Year," she whispered.

He bent his head so she felt the warmth of his breath. "Happy New Year."

They held, trembling, at that delicious edge of temptation as noisemakers and whoops sounded from inside. She didn't know who moved first, only that his hand tangled in her hair and the mouth pressed to hers was no gossamer brush of lips. Heat sparked between them, rushing along her skin, heady and welcome.

God, yes.

She rose up, twining her arms around his neck to draw him closer and held on for the ride. He changed the angle, drew them both deeper into the kiss. The taste of him punched into her and lit up nerve endings she hadn't known existed. It was so wholly unexpected and *glorious* to be lost in a tangle of sensations and needs.

"Hush! Get out of my flower bed!"

Norah broke off, reflexively turning her head toward Miranda's shout. Cam made a growl of protest.

"Um…" It was all she could manage with her brain cells obliterated. She was deliciously dizzy, still gripping his shoulders for balance.

He pressed his brow to hers, his breath gratifyingly unsteady. "How long are you staying?"

"Longer now, I think."

"Good." Reluctance in every gesture, he

eased back and released her. "I've gotta go rescue my dog."

Still swaying, Norah watched him walk back around the side of the house to accept Miranda's wrath. She lifted a hand to her still tingling lips and let out a trembling exhale.

Oh boy.

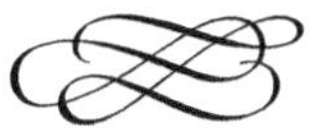

"YOU'RE WOOL GATHERING."

NORAH looked up at the accusation, noting the mix of amusement and concern in her companion's eyes. He flashed an easy smile in response to her sheepish expression, and it was a lovely smile. But it wasn't the one she wanted to see.

"Sorry, Mitch. I'm afraid I'm not the best company."

"He's not worth it."

"Who?" She hoped she didn't look guilty.

"The shark. He didn't deserve you."

"I wasn't thinking about Pierce." She'd been thinking of Cam and wondering why he hadn't been at the New Year's Day bowl game marathon at his aunt and uncle's house.

"Have you got some other reason for frowning, sugar?" He leaned back in the booth, arms spread out along the back in a relaxed posture that invited confidences. Norah had reason to know it was, quite often, his default position, part of what made him so appealing. She also knew she could move around to his side of the booth and burrow in for one of his bear hugs, and he'd listen and make outraged noises in all the right places because he cared. She'd always loved that about him. But when she broke her silence, it needed to be with Miranda first.

"You mean other than the fact that I will soon have to return to the land of crappy tea?" She sipped at the perfectly mixed, syrupy beverage in her glass.

"Ah, work then. You know you're not supposed to think about work when you're on vacation."

"And when have you ever known me not to think about work?"

"You're the poster child for workaholic."

"It ain't good for a body to do nothin' but work." Mama Pearl, the heart, soul, and very opinionated mouth of Dinner Belles, leaned over to refill the half-empty glass of sweet tea.

"I've been hearing that a lot lately." Norah thought again of Cam. *You're more than your job,* he'd said. *Then what the hell am I?*

"Maybe it's the good Lord sendin' you a message to slow down, child. Time you be payin' attention. It shouldn't take you three years to come back down to visit family." The broad, dark face was set in lines of censure.

Norah loved that Wishful was a place where they understood that family was more than blood. "Yes ma'am, you're absolutely right. Thank you for the pie, by the way. It was fabulous."

"Maybe you'll pick better next time."

"I could hardly pick worse."

"Need to skip out on all them Yankee boys and come find yourself a good Southern man."

Mitch stretched his arms wide across the back of the booth. "I keep telling her I'm available. She keeps breaking my heart."

He was handsome, funny, loyal. They had history. But he just didn't make her heart race. Unlike his quieter cousin. "I'm pretty sure your heart is made of silly putty and easily mended. You fall in love as often as some men change socks."

"What can I say? Women are fascinating creatures and there are so many flavors to try."

Mama Pearl wagged one stubby finger in his face. "One of these days, Mitch Campbell, you gonna find yourself one that ruins you for all others, and we all gonna enjoy the show."

Norah laughed as Mama Pearl ambled away to another table. "Oh, I would love to be around to see the woman who manages *that*."

"You could be. What's *really* holding you in Chicago?"

Less than you can imagine. But that was on

the list of things she really didn't want to think about just now. "And what would a high-powered marketing executive do down here?"

"I'm sure you could charm everybody into something. I never met anybody who could say no to you."

"Oh they exist. They're just really rare. But seriously, I could work up full marketing campaigns for every business in town in a year—not that most of them would even see the need for my kind of skills—then what? I have an urban skill set."

"There are urban centers below the Mason-Dixon line. You'd at least be close enough to visit more easily and more often. And we could steal you for Christmas. Miranda told me what happened this year."

Norah shrugged. "It's the Burke way. We are our own brand of dysfunction."

"Which is why we made you an honorary Campbell years ago."

"Don't think I don't appreciate that. Your family means more to me than you can possibly know. But what would my mother do? Dad's finally moving on. She's married to her work. I'm not leaving her alone for the holidays."

"You know perfectly well we'd welcome her with open arms. It'd be good for her."

Norah tried to imagine her very serious mother in the middle of the usual chaos that defined the Campbells and couldn't. She and Miranda could carry on a conversation over mutual medical geekage, but what would she say to everyone else? She had no life outside work. Then again, when Norah was in Chicago, neither did she.

Because that, too, trod too close to subjects she wasn't ready to think about, Norah switched topics. "You ever think about leaving?"

"Not really."

"That surprises me. You love the city. The energy, the people."

"I do. But I like home, too. I've got a good thing going here. Not a lot of inducement to leave. But for the right job—or the right woman —I might."

"You'd change your whole life for a woman?"

"Sure. You can always find another job. Love is a much rarer phenomenon. You find it, you best hang on to it."

She hummed a non-committal note.

"Sorry, sugar. That's probably still a bit sensitive, yet."

"Not sensitive at all. I wasn't in love with Pierce. Not if the mark of love is being willing to change everything for him. If that's what love is, I've never been in love before. I can't fathom being willing to change my entire career for a guy."

"There's a first time for everything."

For other people, maybe. But that wasn't the kind of stock she came from. Burkes existed for career alone. That's just the way it was.

CAM MANAGED to time things so that he was climbing out of his truck about the time Norah stepped out of Dinner Belles with Mitch. Hush leapt out of the truck and made a beeline for her, all wags and Wookie greetings. When she started to jump, Norah held up a hand and gave a command. His enthusiastic pooch actually sat, tail sweeping the sidewalk as she waited for pets and praise. Wonders never ceased.

Cam's own heart began to gallop as Norah looked up from his dog and shot a wide smile in his direction. Jesus, he hadn't been this nervous-excited since he'd asked Laura Hollingsworth to junior prom.

Get a grip. Advice that might've been good to take before he'd executed acts of Bond-worthy subterfuge with his family in order to find out Norah's schedule so he could casually run into her in town. He hadn't been able to wait nine hours before wanting to see her again, but he'd managed to hold off on just showing up at Miranda's the day after the party. They'd want girlfriend time, and his cousin was not, on any level, a morning person. Besides, he didn't need to come off as some over-eager schoolboy. Or worse, a pushy, obsessed lunatic. But surely two days was within the realm of reasonable.

"Is this a conspiracy?" She divided the smile between him and Mitch. "The rest of the Campbell clan working to make sure I'm not bored on my vacation while Miranda's at work?"

"Hey, you know I hate to eat alone."

"I had to come into town for some errands." A half lie. Cam had made up errands so he had to come into town.

"Then perhaps you'd let me steal your dog for a few hours." Hush, leaning against Norah's legs and looking up in adoration, was clearly on board with that plan.

"That could probably be arranged."

"I gotta get back to work. You have time to drop Norah off at Miranda's on your way back to the nursery?"

"Sure."

"Then unless you object, I'll leave you in my cousin's capable hands."

Yes, please. Cam shoved those hands in his pockets and rocked back on his heels, working to keep his face neutral.

"I can think of worse company."

Mitch gave Norah a squeeze. "I'll see you later, then."

They stayed silent, both watching as he walked away. When he was out of earshot, Norah tipped her head toward him. "Are you particularly busy at work or can I steal you along with Hush?"

"Are you tryin' to talk me into playin' hooky, Miss Burke?"

"I absolutely am. Somebody told me recently I needed to play more." Though her face was sober, her eyes shone with amusement. "Seemed like good advice."

"Far be it for me to refuse a lady." He gestured toward the town green. "Shall we walk?"

They fell into step, Hush prancing a few paces ahead. Cam itched to take her hand, just for the chance to touch her. But this was downtown Wishful. That'd be as good as taking out a billboard declaring his intentions. He didn't even know what they were yet. He only knew that she was the first woman to truly spark his interest in years and that kiss had been…epic. Today was about finding out if they were on the same page with that interest and, if he was lucky, getting his mouth on her again.

She started to pull ahead of him, legs moving with a brisk efficiency.

"You in a hurry?"

She jerked almost to a stop, then into motion again with her eyes on his feet. "You can take the girl out of the city. But seriously, your legs are a foot longer than mine. You don't walk, you mosey."

"Moseying is good when you want to enjoy somebody's company."

The noise she made might've been a laugh. "I'm out of practice with that, too, I guess."

Cam couldn't help himself. He rubbed a

hand down her back. "That wasn't meant as a criticism."

She shifted ever so slightly into his touch. "I suppose I stay wound pretty tight."

"Don't apologize. You've got reason to be." As they walked, he noted the fine lines of strain still around her eyes and guessed she still hadn't come clean to Miranda about her job. But he said nothing, placing a hand at the small of her back to steer her toward the fountain. "That's what hooky is for, anyway. Finding your way to unwind."

"Would you believe I have never played hooky in my life?"

He glanced at her, this type-A, perfectionist overachiever, with a strong moral compass and staunch belief in The Rules, and smiled. "Somehow that doesn't surprise me about you. But rumor has it you're a quick study for anything you set your mind to."

"I do have that reputation. So what are the rules of playing hooky?"

"Rule 1: Never feel guilty for playing hooky."

"Well, I'm not the one legitimately playing hooky today."

"And I feel not a qualm about it, so we're good on that front. It's one of the best parts of being your own boss. Rule 2: Choose your company wisely. You want a partner in crime, not someone who will bail on you if things get dicey."

She laughed. "And what constitutes dicey for grown ups who don't have the threat of detention or parents?"

"Woman, there is no statute of limitations on parental disapproval when you live in the same town. Especially not a small town where everybody knows everybody else. Do you have any idea how *hard* it was getting away with *anything* when we were teenagers?"

"Somehow, I imagine you and Mitch still managed just fine."

"Well, necessity *is* the mother of invention. It was more often me and Tucker McGee and our friend Brody—he's not here anymore—sometimes Miranda, though she was more goody two shoes. Mitch was three years ahead of us in school."

"I can't wrap my brain around what that's like. Growing up in one place, having friends for that long. I bounced around so much after my parents' divorce that I didn't make connections with people. Not really. Not until Miranda. And if she didn't hang on as tightly as she does, I don't know if I'd have kept up with her as well as I have. You're really lucky to have that." There was no mistaking the expression of longing on her face.

Cam didn't know what to say. He'd never given a thought to having that foundation to fall back on. It simply was. Friends. Family. Community. You fought with them and fought for them because that's what you did for what you loved. It hurt him to think she'd never known that, and he wondered what she fought for in their stead, wondered, too, why he was aching for a woman he barely knew.

"We don't mind sharing."

That made her smile. "I know. Which is why I've shamelessly adopted your entire family."

"Does that make us cousins in a complicated, Southern sort of way? Because this is Mississippi and we definitely don't need any more fodder for jokes around here."

"You mean, like, the fact that there's still a law on the books that says three women in a room together, barefoot, makes an orgy?"

"What?"

"That was a favorite of ours to laugh about at our sorority house in college."

"So you're saying all the fantasies we guys have about sorority houses are true? Pillow fights and sexy pajamas and all?"

Norah waggled her eyebrows at him. "Wouldn't you like to know?"

Cam sank down on the edge of the fountain that dated back to just after the Civil War. He patted the ledge. "Sit."

He liked the neat way she tucked her legs, even in jeans. She always managed to look put together and elegant, which made him wonder what she'd looked like all mussed up.

"Have you made your wish yet?" He swiveled toward the water so their knees bumped. She didn't move away.

"My wish?"

"Sure." Cam dipped his fingers into the few inches of frigid rainwater in the basin. Coins glimmered below the surface. "The fountain itself might not have run for years, but people still make wishes. Don't tell me after all the years you've been coming here, you've never made a wish."

"Never have. I'm much more a *If you want something to happen you have to make it happen* kind of girl."

"There's a lot to be said for self sufficiency and drive. But sometimes you need a little help."

"Does it work?"

"Mmm, hard to say. When I was sixteen, I wished for a really hot car. Sure enough, I got a hot one all right. The AC never did work in that thing."

She laughed. "If that's not clear illustration that you should be careful what you wish for, I don't know what is."

"Other folks have had better luck. Uncle Pete came here before he proposed to Aunt Liz and wished she'd say yes. Obviously that worked out."

Her smile was just a little dreamy. "They're great together." She trailed her fingers through the water. "Has the city ever tried to fix it so it'll run again?"

"'Bout the time I was in middle school, they did a whole big thing trying to replace the copper pipes out to the springs. They figured it had collapsed somewhere in the last hundred and fifty years or so. But the lines were completely intact. They never did figure out what the problem is."

"Wait, the fountain is supposed to be fed from Hope Springs?"

"Yep."

"That's rather poetic, somehow. And sad. Like the fountain dried up as hope in Wishful did."

"You think Wishful doesn't have hope?"

She looked around what they could see of Main Street, and Cam wondered what she saw. "I think it's suffered a lot of economic downturns over time, like lots of small towns."

"You're not wrong. We've lost a lot of our industry and about a third of our population over the last thirty years."

"That weighs on you."

Cam arched a brow.

"You aren't the only one who's observant. This is your town. You want to save it."

"Yeah. Yeah, I do. It's why I ran for City Council. Well, partly. It started as a means to keep an eye on my mother when she went back to work. Gave me a reason to stop by during the day to check on her without looking like I was checking on her."

"Did she buy it?"

"Of course not. But turns out I actually like

the job. Most of the time. Sometimes it's really frustrating to be in a position to effect change but not actually be able to change a damn thing."

"Sounds like you have something to wish for yourself."

"So I do." Cam fished a couple of quarters out of his pocket and placed one in Norah's hand, letting his fingers linger over her palm. "I will if you will."

"Okay." Her fingers curled around his briefly before sliding away to wrap around the coin.

When she closed her eyes—probably considering her wording carefully after the warning of his first car—he almost threw caution to the wind and leaned in to kiss her.

Cam pondered his own wish as he watched her, thinking of fate and chemistry and what might've happened if they'd crossed paths back in college. He couldn't alter the past, but he had a lot more confidence in his ability to impact the future—at least on one point. So when she opened her eyes and said, "On three," it was the town he thought of.

I wish for a miracle to save Wishful.

"One. Two. Three."

They tossed their coins, watched them hit the water with a soft *plunk.*

The fountain belched.

Norah jolted and Cam stared as a spurt of water bubbled up from the mouth of the fountain and trickled down the stone. Nothing else. Just that one, short blast of water.

"Does it usually do that?"

"Never has for me before." *Strange. Damned strange.* "Must be air in the pipes." He rose. "C'mon. It's cold. Let's go get some coffee."

Could I drag Cam into the pantry without anyone noticing?

Norah glanced at the door to the kitchen, wondering what excuse she could concoct to get them both away from the game table. From the other side of the Monopoly board, Cam's mouth quirked, as if he knew exactly where her thoughts had veered. He probably did. The man had an uncanny ability to read her.

"Community Chest." Mitch picked up one of the cards. "Get out of jail free card. Sweet! I'll just hang on to this. Your turn, sister dear." He passed the dice to Miranda and game play continued around the table.

In all the years she'd been coming home with Miranda, Norah had always appreciated the big, messy Campbell family. After being shuttled from one single-parent household to the other for more than half her life, being surrounded by all of them was like being plunked down in the midst of *Cheaper By The Dozen,* in the best possible way. She'd never had cause to regret that there were quite so many of them. Until Cam.

By mutual agreement, they'd kept their involvement quiet. The secret was both exhausting and exhilarating. On the surface, Cam was easy with her around his family, adopting a more muted form of the flirtation and teasing she got from Mitch and Reed. But there was nothing muted about the look in his eyes when they met hers and nothing simple about the spark she felt from the brush of his fingers as he handed over the dice. Flustered, Norah struggled not to jerk her hand back.

Secret Relationship 101: Pretend all is normal.

Norah rolled the dice, took her turn.

In the past week, Cam had introduced her to quite a few other life lessons she'd bypassed as a teenager, training her on how to sneak around all his myriad relatives in order to meet him. She hadn't quite resorted to climbing out her bedroom window and shimmying down the sycamore tree, but a time or two, it had been a near thing. The friend finder app they'd both installed on their phones helped arrange some "accidental" meetings, but it seemed every time they turned around, one or more of the Campbells was popping up to keep her from being bored during her stay. At this point, she'd relish the chance to be bored.

Play circled back around to Mitch. He rolled the dice and tapped his race car all the way to Park Place.

Glad of the distraction, Norah held out her hand. "Welcome to the Grand Royale Hotel at Park Place. I hope you'll enjoy your stay. That'll be $1500, please."

Mitch eyed the cash in his hand, before flashing a glib smile. "Maybe we can come to some kind of mutually satisfying arrangement?"

"This isn't that sort of establishment, sir."

He waggled his eyebrows. "Your foot is saying otherwise."

Norah arched her own brow. "I'm sitting on my feet."

"Then who's trying to play footsie?" Mitch leaned back to check the tangle of legs beneath the table.

Norah caught the momentary flash of alarm across Cam's face and nearly erupted into giggles. To cover for them both, she put on a mock stern face. "Your stalling tactics aren't going to work. Pay up, bucko."

Grumbling, Mitch made the necessary arrangements with the bank—aka Uncle Pete—and handed over the cash. "Heartless real estate mogul."

"Aw, it's not personal, sweetie, it's business."

Miranda rolled the dice. "I did warn you, she's brutal at Monopoly."

"Oh, who are you kidding? I'm ruthless at all games. I make no denials or apologies."

"And we love you anyway." Miranda moved her thimble. "Speaking of business, how much longer can you stay away from yours?"

Norah managed not to look at Cam—barely. He was still the only one she'd told about being fired. And despite the fact that they'd spent every night on the phone, talking till the wee hours about everything under the sun, they'd carefully steered clear of discussing when she was leaving. *If we ignore it, the white elephant doesn't actually exist.*

Except now Miranda had put it right out

there. Because if Norah was really here on a true vacation from her former job, she'd absolutely have to be getting back. *Damn it.*

"I feel like I just got here."

"Well, it is the first vacation longer than a holiday weekend you've taken since I moved back home."

"Seems a shame to head on back to the city when you only just now slowed down," Cam remarked.

Norah glanced at him but saw no censure. He was leaving this news for her, as she'd asked.

"Do you have the extra leave time to take?" Aunt Liz asked.

"I've got more leave time than I know what to do with." It wasn't a complete lie. She'd had almost two months built up when she got axed. Four, if she counted major medical.

Aunt Liz clapped her hands together. "Then stay a while longer. We haven't gotten to see you nearly enough this visit."

The actual decision was easy. Chicago felt worlds away, and she was in no shape to be making major life decisions at the moment. As Cam had said, she'd only just slowed down. Plus, she wanted—needed—time to explore this unexpected spark with him.

"There are any number of hungry young neophytes dying to step into my shoes. I expect they'll find a way to do without me." Because her face felt suddenly brittle, Norah flashed her best sales smile and changed the subject. "If I asked super sweetly, could I talk anybody else into a fire and hot chocolate?"

"Yes!" Mitch shot a fist into the air. "A hot chocolate break will give me a chance to plot my comeback."

Miranda patted him on the arm. "You hang on to that delusion, big brother. I'll help with the beverages."

"I could use a chance to stretch my legs." Norah unfolded from her chair. "I'll get the firewood."

Cam pushed back from the table. "I'll help you. Uncle Pete, make sure Mitch doesn't mess with the bank."

Norah slipped out the door before Mitch finished protesting. The woodpile was at the far side of the yard, flanking the garden shed, well away from the cedar shingles of the house. She'd already made it halfway across the lawn by the time Cam caught up.

"Hold it. Put this on."

Turning, she saw he'd stopped to grab her coat. "It's not that cold to me. Thicker blood, remember?"

"Humor me." He held it so she could slip her arms inside.

Relenting, she did as he asked, then immediately crossed her arms because she did feel cold. But she knew it had nothing to do with the temperature.

"What's wrong?"

She looked over her shoulder at him. "How did you know?"

"I know your real smile. That wasn't it." Cam squeezed her shoulders. "You okay?"

"I keep thinking I am, and then something brings it all back up again.

"It's gonna keep happening until you tell them."

Norah hunched her shoulders. "I know. Doesn't make it any easier."

"I don't think this kind of thing is ever easy. It's a Band-aid yank sort of situation."

They circled around the wood pile to the back side of the shed.

"I guess…there's a part of me that feels like if I keep it to myself, if I don't actually say it out loud, then it can still go away. That they'll figure out they've shot themselves in the foot and call begging me to come back."

"Do you want them to ask you back?"

"God, yes." Catching sight of his carefully blank expression, she laid both hands on his arms. "Only so I can tell them to stick it where the sun don't shine. I couldn't go back to that. Not knowing what I know now."

Cam relaxed and pulled her close. "You'll figure the rest out, Wonder Woman. I have faith."

Norah burrowed in, wrapping her arms

around him beneath his open coat. "I'm glad one of us does."

He stroked a hand down her hair. "I get that you don't want to spread this around and why you're not keen on announcing it to the whole family, but I really think you'll feel better if you at least talk to Miranda."

"I feel better when I'm with you." She tipped her head back to look at him. "You're solid. Steady."

His lips twisted in an expression that couldn't be termed a smile. "Yep, that's me. Solid, steady, boring Cam. Everybody says so."

"Then everybody's wrong. You're not boring. Not at all. You're just...subtle," she decided. "I guess next to Mitch or Reed or Tucker, people probably tend to overlook that." She slid her hands up to brace on his shoulders, rising to her toes until she was close enough to feel the warmth of his breath. "Solid and steady really works for me."

Now he did smile. "Happy to oblige." Dipping his head, he brushed his lips over hers, testing. They both listened.

"We have maybe two minutes before somebody starts wondering where we are," he murmured.

"Then we'd better make the most of them."

Cam's eyes darkened, his lips curving into a hungry smile that had Norah's toes curling. He backed her against the shed and boxed her in with his arms. She loved it, loved that instant leap of her heart, the catch of her breath as he took her mouth. Wanting to feel the heat of him, she slid her fingers into the open collar of his shirt to rest against his skin. His pulse thundered, and she loved that, too. How could such a quiet, steady man be so…potent?

His head snapped up, and Norah made some soft, incoherent sound of protest before she heard what he'd heard. Footsteps across the dead grass.

Releasing her, he eased open the door to the shed and stepped inside. "Pull out your phone. Flashlight."

She didn't stop to ask him why, just did as he asked, raising the poor light above her head to partially illuminate the gloom within. Cam was shifting through the contents of the shed when Miranda came around and blocked the light.

"What on earth are you doing?"

"Looking for the wood sling," Cam replied, not a trace of breathlessness in his voice.

"It was by the back door." Miranda held it up.

"My mistake." Cam stepped out of the shed, apparently back under control. "Norah, you wanna grab some kindling off that end?"

Norah followed him out and started gathering the smaller bits, as asked, hoping her flush would be attributed to the cold.

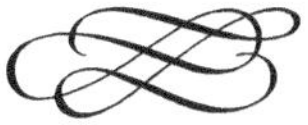

CHAPTER 6

TUCKER MCGEE WAS A hard-core flirt. The man practically oozed charm, so the fact that he was currently oozing said charm all over Norah had Cam grinding his teeth and repressing the urge to plant a fist in his friend's face. He wasn't concerned Tucker was actually getting somewhere with her, but that was *his* woman, and he hadn't even gotten a chance to greet her before Tucker had swooped in to escort her from the car to the refreshment tables. Not that Cam could give her the greeting he wanted with Miranda trailing right behind, looking irritable.

"—and here, the *pièce de résistance*, s'mores fixin's. And over here we have the roasting rods." Tucker pulled a slim handled rod from a cluster in a tube and handed it to her, hilt first.

Norah inspected it. The metal was bent back on itself and wrapped to make a sturdy handle. "Swanky. I thought you were supposed to use coat hangers."

"That's for amateurs. We take the art of bonfire to the next level. Do you need a refresher on the proper roasting technique?"

"I'm not that citified."

Tucker held up both hands in a gesture of peace. "Just checking. I didn't know."

"There's something else you don't know about me."

"And what's that?"

She sank into a fencing stance. "I am not left handed." Tossing the rod to her right hand, she lunged forward.

Hooting with laughter, Tucker stumbled

back, grabbing another rod on the fly and bringing it up to parry. Having spent half his life on the stage in one community theater production or another, Tucker was given to theatrics. He let them fly with flashy swordsmanship and more quotes from *The Princess Bride* as the pair of them circled around the refreshment tables.

Cam watched as Norah steadily drove him back, her movements tight and controlled compared to Tucker's dramatics. "She actually knows how to fence, doesn't she."

"Yep. Three years of fencing club in college."

Cam chuckled, waiting for Norah to hand Tucker his ass.

"Be careful, cousin."

Cam pretended not to hear the warning in Miranda's voice. "Mmm?"

She looked up at him. "Look, I'm not blind. I see how you are around Norah. You aren't obvious, like Mitch, but you watch her when she walks into a room. You're into her."

He should've known Miranda would

notice *something*. She knew him better than almost anyone. "Well, yeah. Last time I checked, I do have a pulse."

"It's not a good idea."

Right, because he'd proved he couldn't make good choices in the relationship department on his own and needed to submit the candidates for review. Cam chained down the surge of temper and kept his voice even. "Are you warning me off for her sake or for mine?"

"Both. I don't think she's in a good place right now. I know something's going on with her that she hasn't told me, and I'm worried about her. But quite apart from that, you know exactly why I think she's a bad idea for you."

Cam scowled. "It's not the same."

"Don't get pissy. I just don't want to see either of you get hurt." She shot a glance back at Norah, who handily disarmed Tucker. "You've both been hurt enough."

"Thanks for the warning, but I'm a big boy. I can take care of myself."

"Surrender, McGee! You're bested!" Norah shouted in triumph.

Tucker dropped to his knees, the tip of her impromptu sword at his throat. "I yield, milady. Do with me what you will. Only tell me you'll come back and do the fight choreography for our summer production of *The Pirates of Penzance*."

She mimed cutting an *N* in the air, then bowed to enthusiastic applause. "Acquire me marshmallows, and I might consider it."

"As you wish." Tucker scrambled up as Norah turned to join Cam and Miranda by the fire, her cheeks flushed from cold and exertion.

"You seem quite cheerful," Cam observed.

"Winning agrees with me."

"Your marshmallows, milady." Tucker presented them with a flourish.

"Thanks." She threaded one on the rod and held it into the fire.

Tucker made a sound of protest. "I thought you remembered how to do this."

Ignoring him, Norah lifted the marshmallow free of the blaze, watching it burn for a minute before she blew out the flame and tipped the rod toward Miranda. "Perfectly charred, exactly as you like it. A peace offering because I know you didn't want to come out tonight."

Miranda plucked off the marshmallow, tossing it from hand to hand to cool before chomping in. "Your tribute is appreciated. Make me another, and I might even forget I've already stopped feeling my ass." She rotated so her backside faced the bonfire.

"It's not that cold." Norah stuck the second marshmallow into the flames.

"You haven't been below the Mason-Dixon long enough to lose your tolerance yet. One summer down here and you'll be back to freezing at forty degrees, like the rest of us."

Faint strains of music limited Norah's retort to, "Wimp," as she dug out her phone. One look at the display had her smile fading. "Excuse me." She passed the roasting rod to Miranda and strode toward the line of cars parked at the edge of the pasture.

Cam gave her five minutes' lead time before he headed in the same direction on the pretense of grabbing a blanket from the truck for his cousin. He found Norah leaning against the wheel-well of his truck, hidden from view by a Suburban. Her hands were empty.

"Who was that?"

She grimaced. "My dad."

"Did you tell him?"

"No. Because I'm a coward. He just wanted to check in since he's finally back from Saint Bart's."

Cam leaned beside her. "Have you told anybody else?"

"Just you." She flashed a humorless smile. "Somehow, you've become my official secret keeper. I don't know if that's because you're circumspect or because you're one of the secrets."

"The sneaking around we've done the last two weeks isn't what's putting those shadows under your eyes." He skimmed a thumb down her cheek. "Honey, you're not built for keeping secrets. Hanging on to this is eating you up inside."

"I can't come clean about it until I've figured everything out."

"Have you actually been working on that?"

She dropped her gaze. "I've been trying to figure you out."

He tipped her face back up. "I'm a simple guy."

She frowned. "You want people to think you are. You've got this easy, good ole boy, Zen gardener thing going on. But really you're hanging out behind the scenes taking care of everybody around you, all quiet-like, so most of them don't even realize it. Me included. Did you think I wouldn't notice? Nobody takes care of me, Cam."

He braced himself, scrambling to think of some response that would make her see that it had nothing to do with him thinking she wasn't capable of taking care of herself.

She laid a hand over his heart. "Most people

assume I don't need anything or anyone. I've got years of experience proving exactly that. It means a lot to me that you see that I'm not invincible, that you'd do what you can to lighten the load in such a way that it's supportive rather than overbearing. But until I figure out some direction, I'm kind of stuck in the stewing portion of the process."

Because her fingers felt like ice, he took them between his hands and began to rub. "Has it occurred to you that coming clean might help you figure it out? That holding on to this secret is keeping you from moving forward? You're so focused on the dread, you can't look beyond it to what's next."

"I don't *know* what's next." Frustration sharpened her tone.

"Maybe you don't. And that's okay. But I'm gonna make some observations. You're happy here. You're among friends and family. I haven't seen you look anything but stressed out and unhappy whenever Chicago comes up. That ought to tell you something."

"I haven't been happy in Chicago for a long time."

Cam could tell the admission was grudging. "Well, there you go. Seems like a pretty big sign from the Universe. If your life isn't making you happy, you change it. Period."

Norah stared at him as if he'd just started speaking ancient Greek. "I can't just change everything without a lot of careful thought."

"That's fine, if that's what you need to do. You take your time, consider all the angles. Just be sure to factor this into the equation." He pressed her back against the truck and lowered his mouth to hers.

She rose to meet him, hungry, heated, her hands sliding up his chest and into his hair. God, he loved how responsive she was, loved knowing that beneath that calm, collected exterior, she was a fever.

Still waters...

With considerable effort, Cam eased back, waiting a moment for his breath to even out.

"You matter, Norah. I didn't expect it, wasn't looking for it. But there it is."

"This was supposed to be a vacation for me. Downtime and a chance to think. You were supposed to be a distraction. I didn't expect…more."

Neither had he. And thank God for defied expectations. "Life would be pretty boring if we always got what we expected."

"Cam! I'm freezing my butt off. Did you get lost?" Miranda's shout came from somewhere down the line of vehicles.

They untangled themselves in a hurry, and Cam pulled open the door to grab the blanket from the backseat. "Go do your analysis, Wonder Woman. I'll still be here when you're through."

"Get in here and give me a hug." Lisbet Campbell opened the front door to Grammy Campbell's house and pulled Norah in for a good, hard squeeze. "It's so good to see you."

"You just saw me last week." Norah hung on, nonetheless, basking in the feeling of momness in her embrace.

"Yes, but we don't know how much longer you get to stay, so every time I see you is like a fresh visit," Aunt Liz said.

Since Norah had no answer to that question, she searched for a new topic. "Grammy painted."

"Oh my goodness, yes." The woman herself came bustling in from the kitchen, a vintage half apron tied around her slim hips. "Hello, sugar."

Grammy was the only member of the Campbell clan shorter than Norah's 5'4". Norah could only presume that Grammy's statuesque children were rocking some of her late husband's genes. He'd passed before Norah had a chance to meet him. Grammy's hug was like being embraced by a stick of summer-scented dynamite. How she managed to smell like honeysuckle in the dead of winter, Norah had no idea.

"She has us rearranging something every other weekend." But Uncle Pete softened the gripe with a smile. Tall and broad, like Mitch, Uncle Pete's blond hair had silvered completely since Miranda had first brought Norah home. "Come on over here, honey."

Norah moved from one to the other, giving in to the urge to press her cheek to the aged flannel of his shirt. He smelled faintly of sawdust and motor oil.

She eased back. "You've been out on your motorcycle."

Aunt Liz grinned. "We had a date for lunch. Rode up to Little Mountain for a picnic."

"Wanna go for another ride?"

Grammy intervened. "Not until after dinner. It won't be long. I just need to make the gravy."

Norah sniffed, drooled a little. "Is that country fried steak?"

"And mashed potatoes, homemade biscuits,

and the last of the purple hull peas from the freezer."

All of her favorites. Norah mimed a kowtow. "I'm not worthy."

"Of course you are. It's not every day I get to cook for my other granddaughter. Come on back to the kitchen."

The kitchen was a wide, spacious room with windows that overlooked what Norah knew was a long slope of yard. Not that she could see any of it now in the winter dark. Cherry cabinets stretched all the way to the top of the ten-foot ceiling and dark granite countertops gleamed. Mitch hunched over one, gingerly lifting a cloth napkin in a basket.

"Mitch, get your hands out of that bread basket!"

He jerked his hand back as if she'd slapped it. "But Grammy…"

"You can wait fifteen minutes without starving to death." Grammy picked up a spoon and waved him away.

From the kitchen table Aunt Anita, Reed

and Ava's mom, waved hello. Several shoeboxes and photo albums were spread out across the surface.

"What're you working on?" Norah slipped off her coat and peeked.

"Torture," Reed said, a bouquet of silverware in his hand. "She's organizing family photo albums, meaning she's accruing blackmail material."

"I'm doing no such thing." Anita shooed him into the dining room to finish setting the table.

With a roll of his eyes, Miranda's dark-haired cousin disappeared into the other room. Norah slid into a chair and reached for the nearest album. "May I?"

"Knock yourself out, hon."

The first page was full of pictures from their childhood. A gap-toothed Miranda, maybe five or six, sat beside another grinning, tow-headed boy. "Is that Mitch? No, he'd have been much bigger than you at that age. Cam?"

Miranda came to lean over her shoulder.

"Yeah, back then, people often mistook us for twins. We're only three months apart."

"I can see why. He looks so much like his mom."

Miranda flipped the page and pointed to another shot, this one of Sandra and Cam, identical smiles beaming at the camera. "Check her out."

"She looks so *young*."

"Younger than us."

And already a mom of a six- or seven-year old. Norah couldn't fathom that. In the next photo, he wore a baseball uniform and mugged for the camera beside another man.

"Who's this?"

"Cam's dad. May he rot in hell."

Norah lifted a brow. "Is he dead?"

"Officially, no. As far as our family is concerned, he might as well be."

Studying the photo, Norah thought she could see something of Cam's build in his father, but nothing more. Everything else was pure Campbell. "What happened?"

Grammy picked up the thread. "He and Sandra were high school sweethearts. Got married straight after graduation. It wasn't an… easy marriage."

"It was a mistake," Uncle Pete said with an uncharacteristic scowl.

"It wasn't a mistake because it led to Cam," Grammy corrected.

"She should have dumped his ass right after Cam was born," Uncle Jimmy put in.

"Well now, that may be. But that's not how it happened. Waylan was the kind of guy who's never satisfied with what he's got. Always wanting something more, admiring the greener grass and all that. He took keeping up with the Joneses to a whole new level. When Cam was eleven, Waylan left in pursuit of his grand ambitions, abandoning them on the verge of bankruptcy. Just got up one morning, told Sandy he was leaving. No discussion, no argument. And he left. Without even telling Cam goodbye. The divorce papers arrived a few days later."

Norah straightened in outrage. "Who *does* that?"

"The weak. They were well rid of him." Anita tugged the album over and passed Norah a different one. "Better memories in here."

The next album started with Reed's high school graduation. He grinned, arms around both his parents in what appeared to be a high school gym. His cap was cocked rakishly atop a shaggy mop of hair and his chin sported a faint scruff of goatee. The camera flash glinted off the lenses of some truly awful black-framed glasses.

The man in question wandered back in from the dining room, clean-shaven and wearing a pair of horn-rims that accentuated his hazel eyes. The hair that had looked merely unkempt back then now edged toward attractively rumpled.

"I had no idea you were a hipster before it was cool," Norah teased.

Reed came to peer over her shoulder and groaned. "See, told you. Blackmail material." At her peals of laughter, he said, "Yeah, you keep on laughing. You're in all this somewhere."

"I am?" Norah immediately began to wonder which of her and Miranda's antics they'd managed to capture on film.

Reed flipped a few pages, bringing up a shot of Norah doubled over with hilarity, hair hanging in wet ropes down her shoulders as multiple water balloons exploded around her. "See, wet t-shirt contest."

"That's a *swimsuit* under that t-shirt."

"Didn't you end up nailing Mitch with the water hose?" Miranda slipped into the chair beside her.

Mitch bent to look over her shoulder. "You totally did."

"Hey, you boys unearthed contraband Su-perSoakers. It was only fair."

"We got our revenge." Mitch flipped to the next page with a picture of him dangling her upside down from the knees after he'd wrested the hose away.

Miranda chuckled. "You're *so* lucky that

wasn't me. I'd have pantsed you from that position."

"I had no desire to be that up close and personal with your brother's—" She could hardly say *junk* in front of Grammy. "—well. I was laughing too hard to retaliate by that point anyway."

They kept turning pages, filling in Norah's gaps in family knowledge with stories and jokes. Cam appeared again in the later album pages. He looked more like Mitch back then, easier and more carefree. That had to be before his mother's cancer.

"Ugh, somebody get a Sharpie," Miranda said. "I need to draw some devil horns."

"On who?"

"*Her.*" Miranda thumped a finger against the face of a red-head Norah didn't recognize.

Norah studied the picture. The girl was tall. A younger Cam, maybe twenty or so, stood with his arm around her shoulders, easily able to look into her laughing face. She was gorgeous, with perfect creamy skin and blue eyes that seemed to wink at the camera. And he was in love with her.

The punch of jealousy was quick and vicious, despite the fact that this was obviously years ago.

"Who is she?"

"Melody." Miranda sneered the name. "Cam's college girlfriend."

"I'm getting a very powerful sense of gut-hating here. Why?"

Aunt Anita picked up the thread. "Oh, he dated that piece of work all through college. She was bright, beautiful, and always had an eye on bigger, better things."

"In a grass is always greener, cheated on him kind of way?"

"Not that we know of," Aunt Liz said. "But ruthlessly ambitious. Top of her class. She couldn't wait to get out of the South."

"She was a nice enough girl," Uncle Pete added. "Polite whenever she came to visit."

Aunt Liz snorted. "Polite. Sure. She had all you men practically drooling."

"Gross." Miranda grimaced.

"He was planning to propose," Reed said. "But the weekend he came home to buy the ring was when the news broke about Aunt Sandy's cancer. It was bad. Really, really bad. Cam quit school and came home to take care of her."

"And this Melody had a problem with that?" Norah couldn't fathom the kind of person who would.

"No, not as such," Miranda said. "The issue came when it was time for her to go to grad school. Melody got into law school at Ole Miss and George Mason. But she'd applied before the cancer, and Aunt Sandy was in bad shape, to the point the doctors didn't think she was going to make it. You remember how bad it was. Cam was devastated. Any decent human being would've stayed close to support him."

The outcome was painfully obvious. "She picked George Mason."

"It was the better, more prestigious program. She believed if she turned them down, she'd never get another shot at it, and her career was too important to put on hold."

"So she dumped him?"

"Not then," Anita said. "They did the long distance thing for a while. Couple years, if I remember. He didn't see much of her. She didn't come down here much, and he wasn't willing to go far from Sandy. At least not until she'd stabilized. Even then, we had to practically kick him out of the house to make him go up to Virginia to surprise her."

"He drove up and came back in just over twenty-four hours," Aunt Liz said. "Never did tell us what happened, just that they'd decided to go their separate ways, that they wanted different things. Cam's not the sort to bad-mouth anybody."

Grammy harumphed. "You ask me, they could've figured that out without all that driving. *I* think she'd moved right on without him and didn't have the decency to say so on account of she couldn't figure out how to break it to him given what was going on with Sandy. Figure our boy walked in on something."

"I wouldn't put it past her." Miranda flung a hand toward the album. "I mean, seriously. What kind of woman puts her own ambitions ahead of what's supposed to be the most important relationship in her life?"

A woman who wants more out of life than being a wife and mother, trapped in a small town that doesn't support her career choices. But she kept the comment to herself. She didn't condone the way Melody had handled the situation, but she understood the choice the girl had faced in a way that no one else here could. She understood because she'd watched her mother live with the wrong one for far too long and then dealt with the fallout when Margaret finally made the tough call that her career and the lives she could save were more important than family.

"At least she figured it out before he married her. Before there was a child to be impacted by the inevitable divorce."

Miranda leaned in to give Norah a hug. "You shouldn't have had to pay for your parents' selfishness."

"It's better than if they'd stayed together. All those years before the divorce was like watching my mother slowly die. Better that they be true to who they really are, what they really want."

Which leaves me, where exactly? Norah wondered. *Who am I and what do I want?*

A month ago she could've answered that question without hesitation. But now? Here she was without the job she'd worked her ass off to earn, unexpectedly involved with a man who'd so rapidly worked his way under her skin, she couldn't imagine going back to a life without him in it. But neither could she imagine what life *with* him in it would look like. And she was lying to her best friend and the rest of his family about their involvement because, quite clearly, they wouldn't approve.

When exactly had she become someone

who knowingly hid the truth? *So much for that moral compass.*

Reed jolted her back to the conversation. "Either way, she did a number on him. As far as we know, he hasn't had more than a couple of dates with anybody since his mom went into remission."

Yeah, about that...

"So Mitch is dating enough for them both?" she asked, hoping to shift the conversation.

"Hey! I resemble that remark."

Aunt Liz put in her two cents. "Cam needs to find a nice local girl. That boy was made for marriage, family, and babies. He needs somebody that can actually appreciate the deep sunk roots he has here instead of being all bound up in career."

In other words, someone who isn't me, Norah thought. And that was the clincher of all of it. She recognized and respected Cam's roots, found his connection to family and the community unaccountably appealing. But she wasn't local—*couldn't* be local and keep the career she'd poured herself into. And even if, by some miracle, she could sort *that* mess out, she wasn't made for a traditional role of wife and mother any more than her mother had been.

Grammy pivoted with a casserole dish in her hands. "Everybody take a bowl into the dining room. Dinner is served!"

Norah stood and took the bread basket on autopilot, but she found she'd lost her appetite.

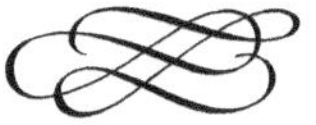

VICK BURGESS WAS SMILING when Cam walked into the City Council meeting Monday evening. His teeth flashed white in his too-tan-for-winter face, making Cam think of politicians and used car salesmen. Anything that made Vick smile was likely to be bad. He was speaking to another man dressed in a too-expensive suit that screamed city slicker. What was an outsider doing in their City Council meeting?

Across the room, Sandra caught Cam's eye. She fixed him with a *Be nice* Look that just solidified the dread curling through his gut. But Cam held his tongue and took his place at the conference table next to Edgar Falk.

Vick clasped his hands. "Since everybody's here, perhaps we can get started? Avery, are you ready?"

Avery Cahill, Sandra's personal assistant and the official City Recorder, took her position at his mother's right hand, fingers poised over a tidy little laptop. "I am."

"Okay then, let's get this show on the road." Sandra rapped her gavel. "As Mayor, I now call this closed meeting of the City Council to order."

Ed lifted a hand, spotted with age, and waited for acknowledgment. "Motion to approve the minutes from the December 12th meeting."

Cam seconded.

"All in favor of approving the minutes from our previous meeting?" Everyone present lifted a hand. "Minutes approved."

Grace Handeford spoke next. "Motion to

approve the docket of claims for tonight's meeting."

"What's on it?" asked Hank van Buren. "I didn't get a copy of the memo."

"It's probably in your spam folder. I keep telling you to check it," Grace chided. "Just the charge for replacing the street lights with more cost-efficient halogen bulbs."

"Is that a sweeping change or something to be implemented as the bulbs go out?" Connie Lockwood's French manicured nails tapped against her pen as she scribbled notes.

Grace slipped her reading glasses on and peered at the memo. "This is for the supply of bulbs. It doesn't address when the change would be made."

They debated the merits of both options before finally approving the claim.

"Are there any amendments to the agenda?" Sandra asked.

Cam thought about Mrs. Crockett and the stoplight, but he was too worried about the newcomer to bring it up. When no changes were raised, she turned her attention to Vick. "Very well. I shall turn the floor over to City Planner Victor Burgess."

Vick beamed. Cam thought about how much he wanted to plant a fist in the other man's face.

"Thank you, madam Mayor. I'd like to take this opportunity to introduce Bill Sutto." The suit lifted a hand and offered an ingratiating smile. "Bill is a representative from GrandGoods."

Connie sat up straighter. "The bulk buyer's club?"

Vick's car salesman grinned widened. "The very same."

"I love that place. I go every time I head down to Jackson to visit my sister."

"Well, you may not have to drive that far in the future. They're looking to expand their market share in Mississippi, and Wishful is a potential site."

Hello red flag number one. Cam crossed his arms. "What sense does that make? We don't have the population base to support a store of that size. They only build in cities or big interstate hubs. We're neither."

Sutto answered that charge. "You raise a good point. And it's true that up to this point, we have focused on sites that meet those criteria. But Wishful is centralized. So much of Mississippi's population is considered rural by population standards. Right now, we have a GrandGoods down on the coast in Biloxi, one in Jackson, and one in Southaven. That leaves the north central portion of the state unserved. Wishful occupies a central location that could draw citizens from Oxford, the Golden Triangle area, and all the rural counties between. That's a few hundred thousand people right there, within an hour and a half radius, with no shopping alternative that would provide the same benefits."

"Why would you choose to build here rather

than in, say, Tupelo?" Grace asked. "That would hit almost all the same areas."

"That's a great question, Grace." Sutto beamed as if she were a prize pupil. "Tupelo already has a Sam's Club. GrandGoods is more interested in expanding into an area with no existing competition. We want to pilot test a store on a slightly smaller scale in a rural location. And we want Wishful."

"Just imagine what that kind of business would draw to town," Grace said.

A sense of deep unease unfurled inside Cam at the thought. GrandGoods would bring customers, sure, but it would also bring urban bloat. More chains, more franchises, more depersonalization.

Vick picked up the thread again. "Not only work for the labor hired to build the store and the jobs created for the people to work in it. But it would pull in people from all over to shop here. That would provide a really nice chunk of additional revenue that we could use."

At what cost? Cam exchanged a Look with his mother. Very little was as cut and dry as they were making it out to be. "I have serious reservations about how a business like that would impact the community. Yeah, it'd mean short term jobs for those involved with construction, provided GrandGoods did actually hire local labor. And probably longer term jobs for those needed to run the store. But what impact will it have on competing local businesses? What percentage of the people who come in from surrounding areas will actually stop in at other businesses here? And what about the increased burden on the infrastructure? All that extra traffic that isn't part of our tax base and isn't going to be paying for upkeep of roads."

All solicitousness, Sutto nodded. "Those are completely valid concerns. First off, let me assure you that GrandGoods fully intends to recruit local labor for construction of the store, should our proposal be accepted. As to the impact on competing local businesses, we don't foresee that being an issue. GrandGoods is a particular type of store and shouldn't infringe on the smaller, niche businesses already established. We have no intention of damaging the character of your town but, rather, believe that we can enhance it."

Cam doubted that.

"I've got a presentation of our full proposal prepared that will, I hope, answer more of your questions. If you'd direct your attention up here, please."

Somebody dimmed the lights for Sutto's PowerPoint presentation. Cam sat through it, listening to the spin and the promises and the buzzwords with half an ear as he observed the reactions of the other Councilmen. By the end, they were all nodding, smiling, some of them actually *excited*. Not a damned one of them seemed concerned that a formal proposal presented to the city was only subject to the rules already contained in the zoning code. As far as Cam knew, that meant just a weak site plan review stood between Wishful and this store should the proposal be accepted.

Sandra steepled her fingers. "You make compelling arguments."

Beneath the table, Cam's hands fisted. Sutto had neatly skirted the issue of strain on infrastructure and overplayed the limited benefit Wishful would receive from sales tax. Had anyone noticed but him?

"Certainly, I think he's made enough valid points that we should enter into more formal discussion of the proposal," Ed agreed.

"Of course, we want to allow you ample time to make an informed, educated decision, as well as an opportunity to discuss any issues you may have with our proposal."

Vick began gathering up his papers. "I'll get all of you a copy of the full proposal tomorrow morning."

Cam swallowed down his rage. "I can promise you, we'll have plenty of questions."

A date was set for the next City Council meeting, which Bill Sutto would return for. That gave Cam fourteen days to figure out how the hell he was going to derail this.

"There's one thing you haven't mentioned yet. Where exactly do you propose building this store?"

"Oh we're already in negotiations for a parcel of land on the outskirts of town."

Cam tensed, already knowing the answer before Vick clarified, "Abe Costello's land out near Hope Springs. It's fitting, don't you think, that the business that can bring hope back to this town be situated right there."

It was a minor miracle Cam managed to stay in his seat. "I'd hope that you would consider other sites with less historical significance."

Vick waved that away as if it meant nothing. "The site isn't the most important. We'll find a place for it. The point is that even you can't stop all progress, Crawford. We have ambitions for our town."

Ambition was exactly what Cam was afraid of. In his experience, ambition destroyed everything it touched, and he wasn't about to stand by and allow it to change the heart of his town.

"Over my dead body." The all but shouted pronouncement was punctuated by Cam slamming the front door.

The entire Campbell clan went silent, waiting to find out what was going on. He stalked into the room, hands balled to fists, face set. Norah could see the worry beneath the simmering temper and struggled not to cross over to try and soothe.

"Campbell Alexander Crawford, you go right back out that door and prove you know how to enter it in a civilized manner," Grammy snapped.

A muscle ticked in his jaw, but Cam did an about face and followed his grandmother's order.

Aunt Liz rose. "What on earth?"

"I take it the City Council meeting didn't go well?" Miranda asked dryly.

"That depends on who you ask." Sandra sank into a chair.

The front door opened and shut again, softer this time. Cam prowled back into the living room. "I apologize, Grammy."

His grandmother sniffed. "Do you want cobbler before or after you tell us what you're tantruming about?"

"Respectfully, I don't want any cobbler."

"Oh, man," Mitch said, "it must be bad."

"I'm evidently the only one to think so," Cam growled.

"Maybe you should start at the beginning," Reed suggested.

"At tonight's City Council meeting, we received a formal proposal from GrandGoods."

Norah's hand fisted on the arm of the sofa. "The megastore?"

He nodded. "They want to use Wishful as a pilot site for a new, smaller store designed to expand their market share into more rural locales. I have a number of problems with it, not the least of which is that they've already made an offer on the property where they want to build—the acreage owned by Abe Costello that wraps around two sides of Hope Springs. They want to put a goddamned parking lot almost to the edge of the springs."

Norah expected Grammy to call him out on his language, but she said nothing.

"We can block that," his mother said. "If not the direct purchase of the property, then the zoning restrictions on what and how they could build on it."

"We need to do a hell of a lot more than that to update the zoning code. Have you even *looked* at the minimal site review process out there? I have. And we don't have time to change that before the Council meets again in two weeks to talk about this. You saw everybody in that room. I was the only one thinking in terms other than 'Ooo, shopping.'"

"Campbell." Sandra's tone was a warning.

"I don't want our history paved over by some soulless corporate giant."

"We don't know that it would be that bad. Their presentation—"

Cam interrupted. "The guy gave an impressive presentation. Slick. Too slick."

"What exactly was their pitch?" Uncle Pete asked.

"They don't want to damage the identity of the town," Sandra began.

"Of course, they'll lead with that." Norah's chest went tight. Unable to keep still, she shoved to her feet, tucking her hands beneath her arms. "They want to get your guard down. I bet they said that they're on the side of the people. That their philosophy is to embrace the identity of the community and that the store and the town will be equal partners. They'll offer choice and convenience to the masses. Jobs and an influx of capital to the local economy. They probably rounded things out with a nice speech about how there's value in the future and that progress lives on. How'm I doing?"

Cam stared at her with disbelief. "What? Were you hiding under the table in the Council chambers? How do you know all that?"

Norah closed her eyes and felt the blood drain out of her cheeks. "Because it's what *I* said. On behalf of one of their biggest competitors, in another small town, just like this one." She began to pace the room, her steps short and jerky. There wasn't enough space for what she was feeling amid all these people. "I told them all of that and more. I convinced them everything would be great. That Hugo's would be an asset and partner to the community. And within three years, seventy percent of the businesses downtown had been wiped out and the town was so swollen from urban sprawl, it was barely recognizable." She looked at Miranda. "Have Your Cake was gone."

"Morton."

"I didn't know." Not that saying so made it any better. "Not until my drive back from New York. I tried to stop in and downtown was a ghost town. So I asked one of the locals what happened. Hugo's came in and violated pretty much every selling point I'd used to get them into the community. As soon as I saw what happened, I went straight to the office and dug into the old files. And it was all there. Helios was working as an extension of Hugo's marketing and sales team, as a third party. My partner did the due diligence—that was his job as Market Research Director—and he didn't bother to share the facts and the bad publicity the company had gotten elsewhere because he didn't want my inconvenient moral compass to get in the way of closing the deal. I wasn't on the development team. They just brought me in at the end to do the pitch to Morton for Hugo's because closing the deal is my specialty, and I have a gift for bringing creative campaigns to life. I was just the face, the voice, the charm. What did I need with the truth? Apparently that's been standard operating procedure the last few years—or so he said when I confronted him about it. And our boss knew and encouraged it, because I was just an asset to be used, and they figured that was the best way to handle me. I have absolutely no idea how many other lives I've managed to ruin in the name of profit. I didn't get a chance to find out before they fired me."

"Oh honey." Miranda was off the sofa in an instant, pulling Norah into a hard hug. "That's why you've been able to stay so long?"

Norah ducked her head. "Yeah."

"Why didn't you *tell* me?"

She felt her lips twist into a sardonic smile. "Because Burkes don't fail and we sure as hell don't get fired." She hissed out a breath and stepped away, waving an impatient hand. "But that isn't my point. The only reason I'm bringing any of this up is that GrandGoods is going to have someone like me on their side. They're going to make it sound like a dream come true and have an answer to downplay or eliminate all of your concerns. They're going to offer jobs and discounts and services, and the public is going to eat it up because the economy is in the toilet, and they want someone big to come in and save them."

"I saw some of that just in the other Council

members. I've got two weeks to change their minds."

Norah fixed her gaze on him. "If you want to play David to their Goliath, you're going to need a helluva lot more than a rock. It doesn't matter how well you think you know people here. GrandGoods is going to make this come down to economic survival, and by the time they're through, people will believe that they're some kind of savior. At least until they get here and the blindfold comes off. By then it'll be too late. You *can't* let that happen here, Cam."

"I don't intend to."

"Excuse me for interjecting," Uncle Jimmy said, "but exactly how do you intend to stop it? In two weeks, no less. The public's going to want this, once word gets out. Like Norah said, that's just the economic climate we're in."

"It's going to take a miracle," Anita said.

Something lightened in Cam's face, a dawning realization. "No, it's going to take somebody to counteract whatever silver-tongued devil they send. I can't think of anybody better than the woman who once sold solar panels to an oil man." He shifted his gaze back to Norah. "You said I need something bigger than a rock. You're the next best thing to having an inside man. You've proved you know how they think, how they'll approach this. And I know you know how to counter all that. So stay. Stay and make this fight less David versus Goliath and more Sparta versus the Persian army. You're pissed off, and you have every right to be for how your firm used you. So take all that anger and use it. Redirect it to a new target and fight for us. We'll hire you freelance."

She thought back to the day they'd gone to the fountain, to the wish she'd made.

I wish for my time here to show me the right path, what my purpose really is.

Was it really so simple? So perfectly aligned with circumstance?

The whole idea of it smacked far too much of fate, which wasn't a concept Norah was comfortable with. She believed in making her own fate, her own destiny. And yet, how could she say no to a chance to put her skills to use and stop the ruination of the town she loved, to atone, in part, for the damage she'd inadvertently done elsewhere.

Then there was Cam. If she agreed to do this, she had to end things. Anything else would be leading him on. She *couldn't* stay forever, and remaining involved for however long this campaign might take would just make that ultimate parting worse for both of them in the end. Knowing what she knew now about his history… They'd slid too far, too fast already, getting so emotionally tangled, she hadn't been able to think beyond the now to the practicalities of the future.

Resolute, Norah squared her shoulders. "I'll fight for you, but I'll do it pro bono."

Cam frowned. "That hardly seems fair to you. You're doing a job; you should get paid for it."

She shook her head. "I've got a lot of work to do to balance out the bad karma for what I did in Morton."

"That wasn't your fault."

"Of course it's my fault. They only reason they were there at all was because I convinced those people it was a good idea. You can pretty it up all you want, but I *lied* to them. *I* did that."

"You were manipulated."

"That's no excuse. I should have double checked his work, should've followed up, done my own digging...*something.*" Cam opened his mouth to say something else, but Norah held up a hand. "We can argue about my culpability until we're blue in the face, but I won't budge on this. I was exceptionally well paid for what I did, and I worked too damned much to spend much of it. I don't need the money right now. I need the fight. Let me do this my way."

"Okay. Your way, then." Cam offered his hand.

Norah took it, curling her fingers around his in a firm shake. "Cry 'havoc' and let slip the dogs of war. Clear your schedule, Leonidas. We've got a lot of work to do."

He smiled, the tension visibly draining out of him. "Let's give 'em hell."

Grammy stepped toward the kitchen. "Save your hell raisin' for after cobbler. No war was ever won on an empty stomach."

"If there's one thing I've learned," Cam said, "it's to always respect my elders."

CHAPTER 8

"YOU LIVE…IN A barn." Norah made the statement slowly, as if that might make it a dream.

"Above one, actually." Cam climbed out of the truck and reached for the bags in the backseat.

"Um…why?"

"It happens the house that was here burned to the ground a few years back. The owners didn't have the means or desire to rebuild. So I bought it and all the land that went with it. The barn loft was easy enough to convert into an apartment. Mitch and a few other friends helped me do it the summer I bought the place. I keep meaning to start on a house, but it...just hasn't been a priority. Come on in and let's see how far I've offended your city girl sensibilities."

Norah climbed out of his truck and stalked around the front. "Just because I've lived in cities more than half my life doesn't change the fact that I'm Mississippi born and bred."

He chuckled at the irritated twitch to her hips and led her up the stairs to the converted loft. Hush met them at the door, wagging in ecstasy at her visitor. While she and Norah greeted each other as if it'd been years rather than a few hours since they'd played together, Cam brushed past them and deposited the bags on the coffee table.

"Can I get you anything? There's a pitcher of tea in the fridge. Or beer if you want."

Norah extricated herself from the dog and finally stepped inside, her heels clicking across the hardwood floors he'd sanded and stained himself. "Coffee, if you've got it."

"Comin' right up."

Hush bounced across the room and laid claim to her end of the sofa. As he set up the coffee to brew, Cam watched Norah taking in his space and wondered what she saw. Would she notice the reclaimed wood they'd fashioned into window seats and cabinetry along the length of both long walls? Or the solid butcher block counters polished to a gleam? Would she appreciate the small touches of the antique and the rustic? Or would she only see the lack of sleek and modern?

Norah turned a slow circle. "It's...wonderful. Cozy."

Something in him eased at that. She really wasn't the city girl he teased her of being. Not completely. "It's unique anyway. I like my privacy."

By the time French roast dripped through the filter, Norah had commandeered the coffee table. Her assortment of new notepads was laid out by size, and she was in the process of orga-nizing the pens by color.

"You had multiple colored highlighters and sticky notes when you studied in college, didn't you?"

"Of course I did. There were flashcards, too. I made everybody play Trivial Pursuit to study."

Amused and happy to have her in his space, alone, he flopped down beside her on the sofa and tugged her into his lap. He cut off her squeal of surprise with a kiss.

"Mmm, I've been waiting for that for days." Nibbling his way down her throat, he said, "Been waiting to get you here all to myself for longer."

"Stop." Norah's voice was a trifle breathless as she slapped a hand to his chest and shoved back. "We need to talk."

"Talk." The universal warning signal for re-lationships everywhere. Where was she going with this?

"I—oh for heaven's sake, I can't do this in your lap." She extricated herself and took a breath. "Look, what we're trying to do here is huge. It's going to take a lot of work, and I need to be at the top of my game. I can't do that if you're scrambling my brains every other minute with your mouth."

Cam fought the grin for all of two seconds.

"Don't look so pleased with yourself, Campbell." Her narrow-eyed glare was entirely ruined by the twitch of her own lips

"Hard not to be when you're exactly where I want you. Almost." He managed not to glance at the door to the bedroom as he curled his hand around hers and stroked a thumb over her wrist. Her pulse jumped and that pleased him as well.

"This—you and me—it's complicated."

"Doesn't have to be." He didn't want it to be. He wanted things to be simple.

"It's complicated." Those expressive eyes were full of so much doubt and uncertainty. "I don't know what the hell I'm doing with my life."

"So? You don't have to have a plan for everything all the time."

"I do. Do you know the last time I didn't know exactly where my life was going and how I was going to get there? Fifth grade, when my parents divorced and had to sort out custody, which was really trying to work out whose career trying to save the world was inconvenienced the least by having to deal with me. I don't just bounce along without a plan. Ever. Because I have to *know* I have somewhere to land."

Cam bled for her. He knew what it was to be abandoned by a parent because of career. But at least he'd had his mom. He'd always been able to count on her. On the rest of his family. He wanted to tug Norah back into his arms, but he didn't think she'd let him. Not just now.

"Miranda and her family—*your* family and this town have been that for me. So I intend to win this war. I won't watch what happened to Morton happen here. I can't."

She carried so much guilt. He wanted to

ease that burden for her but didn't know what he could say that she would believe. So he just brushed the hair back from her face and said in all seriousness, "We won't."

Norah shifted back, as if his touch pained her.

Cam felt the first hints of true unease slither through him. "What's wrong?"

"It can't work, Cam."

His heart began to thud. "What can't?"

Her eyes, those lovely, dark eyes, were full of apology. "Us."

The hand he still held was trembling, and she looked on the verge of tears. But he couldn't shove down the temper and disbelief, "I think the last two weeks are pretty damned good evidence to the contrary."

"This isn't about compatibility or attraction. But there's no future here. There never was. I was always leaving, at some point. I have a life, a career to salvage. You just made me forget that for a while. Staying to run this campaign is a delay of the inevitable. We're not fling kind of people, and I think it's wiser to stop things before they go any further."

"I pretty much blew wisdom all to hell the moment I decided to kiss you."

"We got in over our heads. I'm just trying to do the right thing here. I don't want to hurt you, but my life isn't here. Not beyond the temporary."

More than half the reason he'd asked her to stay was to give her a legitimate reason not to go back, to continue to explore what was growing between them. And she was all set to walk away.

Same song, different verse.

"If you truly think the life you left behind is worth more than what you've found here, then you've just failed Life Lessons 101. Miserably."

She flinched and pulled her hand free. "We've established that's the one area Burkes regularly fail at. Please don't be angry. We have to be able to work together on this campaign."

Of course. The campaign. No matter what was going on between them, he needed her to help save his town. She'd agreed to stay, however long it took. So he'd use that and find a way to convince her that there were more important things in life than career and prove that she had a place here, if only she was willing to take it.

So Cam stopped arguing. "Fine."

Norah blinked at him. "Fine?"

"That's not unreasonable logic." Cam went to pour coffee because he needed to put some physical distance between them. "I don't like it, don't agree with it. But there are bigger things at stake here than us. We don't have a lot of time to put this together. Just two weeks until the next City Council meeting. What's next?"

Her shift into work mode was almost like seeing a set change for a play. She squared her shoulders, shutting her emotions away, and reached for one of the legal pads. Cam wished he could do the same as easily.

"Who has final say on this decision? Is this going to be a vote of the City Council or will it go out for a public ballot?"

"As the law currently stands, it's a City Council vote."

"So our goal is to persuade the decision makers to say no." She scribbled that at the top. "There are two avenues to do that, and we'll follow through on them both. On your side, you'll be fighting this from within the system of city government. You know, or can find out, all the steps in the whole process of going from proposal to approval where there's an opportunity to stop them in their tracks."

"There aren't nearly enough of those steps for my taste."

"Nevertheless, we're working with what we've got. You'll be focusing on how the store would harm the community and the economy —and first thing tomorrow you should request an economic impact study from an independent contractor. Morton didn't do that and should have."

Cam stole one of the smaller pads and began to make his own list. "What about you?"

"My efforts will be geared toward showing

how many members of the community support a 'no' vote."

"Considering how many people we hypothesize will want a 'yes,' how do you plan to do that?"

"By educating the public—and myself—on the hidden costs of big box stores and creating a campaign to get the word out about that. But to do that I need data. About forty percent of persuasion is knowing your audience. I want to do a focus group with the local Chamber of Commerce."

And a challenge straight out of the gate. "That's gonna be a bit tough. The Chamber of Commerce is more or less defunct."

"How defunct?"

"Well, I can't really remember the last time they met. They never formally disbanded, but they haven't actually *done* anything in a good five, maybe seven years. Not since I bought the nursery, and I'm technically a member."

"Well then, now's the time to revive it. Local businesses are going to be the biggest potential allies in this fight, as they're the ones who have the most to lose."

He couldn't fault her logic. "I'll make some calls, put something together."

"Good. Let me know when and where. If we can get a venue with a marker or chalkboard, that would be really helpful, but in a pinch I can pick up a flip chart and easel." She began listing things out in a smaller notebook.

"Should be able to set something up at the community center. I'm pretty sure they've got markerboards floating around there some-where. I'll go by and book the space tomorrow."

"Good. Do you think they'd be willing to show up out of concern and civic duty or should we offer incentives?"

He offered her a steaming mug. "Incentives?"

"Feeding people is always a popular way to get butts in chairs."

"I expect we can get people to show up ei-ther way."

"Then we'll save that for when we have a

head count to see if it's within the budget. What *is* the budget?"

"Budget?" When he'd concocted this plan, he hadn't thought that far ahead.

"My skills aren't the only expense of a marketing campaign."

Maybe it's a good thing she decided to do this pro bono. "I'd have to do some figuring."

"This isn't a big city, so the big ticket items like TV spots are unnecessary and wouldn't be hitting our target audience anyway. We'll focus on guerrilla marketing and low budget, grassroots tactics." She made more notes, this time on one of the larger pads.

"Guerrilla marketing? Do I need to pick up some greasepaint and a ghillie suit?"

"Guerrilla marketing focuses on tactics outside the traditional realm—thinking outside the box instead of focusing on mass marketing through traditional media. Ideally we'd have a much longer period of time to build something, but since we don't, it's vital that we define our target audience, figure out who the best local influencers are—that's where I hope to loop in the local business owners—and get them to help spread the word. This is a small town. Everybody knows everybody else, and gossip is the currency of the day. Our goal is to get that working to our advantage to get a Shop Local campaign off the ground."

He blinked at her, trying to process everything she'd said. "Wow. That's…I don't know. A bit more elaborate than I was expecting."

"That's not even a full basic prospectus. What exactly did you think you were asking me to do?"

He'd been trying to give her a reason to stay that she could justify without getting into the murky issue of their relationship. The relationship she'd just broken off. "I didn't look much beyond the fact that you were an ally. After the City Council meeting tonight, those were in pretty short supply."

Cam saw her reach toward him, as if to lay her hand over his, then stop. "Well, I am that. I love Wishful. I always have. If I can do something to preserve it, I absolutely will. But we have to have a plan for that. I'll do some research, see if there happens to be some kind of smoking gun of bad press on GrandGoods, but chances are there won't be. We need to be prepared to give the town an alternative."

"An alternative?"

"Part of why GrandGoods is going to be so appealing is because it's something different from the status quo. If they have no other options, people will make the shitty choice just because it's there."

"That's what I'm afraid of. Burgess—the City Planner—has always had this tendency to over-emphasize industrial recruiting. I understand that. It's the loss of industry that got us into this financial state to start with, but in all of his efforts to woo companies into coming here, he pays almost no attention to improving the quality of life in the community. Prosperous small town economies are built on the foundation of strong communities. We've lost so much in the last decade, and part of that is community spirit. But we only have two weeks. I have no idea what we could do in that span to remind people of that, let alone give them a true economic alternative. We have virtually no resources, little support. And as much as I believe you are Wonder Woman, I don't know if even you can pull this off."

"Have a little faith, Cam, and people might surprise you."

"I'll do my best." But he was afraid faith, like allies, was in very short supply.

THE STREETS of downtown Wishful were all but empty, shrouded in winter quiet. In another hour or so, the get to school and work hustle would begin, and businesses would open for another day. For now, it was just Cam and the silence of the green, exactly as he liked it. Even in the winter, it felt like a postcard of his own little slice of paradise. He'd fight tooth and nail to keep it that way.

Wanting to stretch his legs, he parked across the green and walked the couple of blocks to his destination. With the nursery being somewhat out from town, he made it a point to drive in and patronize other local businesses at least once most days. He considered it good for the local economy and part of his job as a City Councilman to be visible and social—connected to his constituents. As he was bound for City Hall, he set his sights on The Daily Grind and a caffeinated form of olive branch to hopefully smooth his way.

As soon as he stepped through the door, Cassie Callister called out, "Just the man I wanted to see! Do a girl a favor and give me the scoop on this proposed store before Mama Pearl hears."

Being one of the two major gossip hubs of town, Cassie and the staff of The Grind were in a constant competition with Mama Pearl at Dinner Belles to be the first to know anything worth knowing. Given the general consensus that Mama Pearl was somehow psychic—Violet swore to it on a stack of Bibles—Cam was pretty sure she was in a perpetual lead.

"Do I even want to know who got the gossip train moving on this?"

Cassie grinned. "You know I never reveal my sources."

"Hook me up with a straight Americano, a white chocolate mocha, and whatever Avery's go to is this month, and I'll consider it."

"I'm on it. All to go?"

"Yep."

While she bustled behind the counter, Cam scoped out the handful of other patrons. A few familiar faces, but nobody that sent up red flags that he should keep his mouth shut, so as Cassie handed over his coffee, he said, "We've had a formal proposal by GrandGoods for store development."

Cassie made a face. "Homogenized, big bulk, over processed, sweat shop supporting robots."

"Then you'll want to be at the Chamber of Commerce meeting later this week to get in on the ground floor of things."

"Ooo, are we staging a protest? A picket line? A sit in?"

He chuckled, thinking Cassie was born in the wrong decade. "I think the expert helping out has some other ideas."

"Well count me in. When and where, my friend?"

"Not sure just yet. Soon. I've still gotta book the community center, but I'll let you know as soon as I do."

"I'll be there with bells on."

As it was early yet, Cam made his way down Main Street without the usual stop and greet that would've tripled his time. The guard's station at the front desk of City Hall was empty. Old Jerry Noble wouldn't be on duty until the hall officially opened at eight. Cam bypassed the metal detector and headed up the stairs to his mother's office on the second floor.

Avery looked up as he came in. "She's been here since seven."

"Thought she might be." He held out the double shot espresso.

"Bless you." She dropped her voice as she took the proffered coffee. "She's in a mood."

"Afraid I'm not gonna be helping that."

"I figured as much."

"Ah well, forewarned is forearmed."

"For what it's worth, we're both on your side."

"Thanks for that." He rapped on the door, lifting a brow at the curt invitation before he stepped inside.

His mother looked up from the desk. "Don't you start on me, Campbell. I'm already having a lousy morning."

Cam revised his strategy. "Who's starting something? I'm just here bearing legal stimulants and checking in before I head out to the nursery for the day." He passed her the caffeine and sugar bomb he knew she loved but would never order for herself. "What's wrong?"

"Chief Curry just submitted his resignation, pending the hire of a replacement."

"He what?" Robert Curry had been Chief of

Police in Wishful since…forever. Which, now that Cam thought about it, might be the why.

"He wants to retire, damn him. Like we need more change right now. I told him we'd take it under advisement, but we have to do a nation-wide search and that takes time."

"He doesn't think anyone in the department is up to the task?"

"There's one person who will probably apply, but a nationwide search is the only way to do things fairly and be certain we have the best candidate. Either way, it has to wait until this GrandGoods thing is settled. Now go ahead and spit out whatever it is you came here to say about it."

Cam kept his face impassive.

"Don't take that innocent face with me, young man. It didn't work when you were five and it won't work now. I'm sure you and Norah came up with something to make my life diffi-cult during your powwow last night."

No, the difficulty Norah presented the night before had nothing to do with his mother.

"We are not out to make your life difficult, Mom."

"You're going to put me in a position to play referee between you and Vick Burgess, even though I technically agree with you, because I have to be the mayor, not your mother, if I want the decision to be accepted by the public. That makes my life difficult."

Too restless to sit, Cam stood and began moving around her office. "If Norah's plan works, the public is going to be on our side and this isn't going to come down to a brawl—metaphoric or otherwise—between me and Vick."

Sandra gave a wary look. "And what exactly is her plan?"

"Garner public support for a 'no' vote by educating them on the true impact of big box stores."

"And you think people will listen to her as an outsider?"

He picked up the photo of the old Hoka Theater in Oxford and put it back again. "She's less outsider than this representative from GrandGoods. A lot of people know her through Miranda, since she's been coming here so many years. You've met her. What do you think?"

"I look at her and I see her father."

Whatever he'd expected her to say, that wasn't it. "You know her dad?"

"By reputation. Her father was a fraternity brother of your dad's."

Cam jolted at that. Having lived his entire life in Mississippi, he knew the whole state was one big small town, and there were seldom more than a couple of degrees of separation between people. But a connection between Norah's dad and his own? That was...unexpected.

"What was he like?"

"Joseph Burke was a shooting star. I've known very few people as brilliant, driven, or unyieldingly competitive. He was the guy everybody knew on campus, partly because he was student body president, and partly because that's just who he was. He spoke and people listened. He's a gifted orator. Once he left Ole Miss, he went on to Harvard Law."

Exactly the kind of man his father would envy.

"Norah's very like him in a lot of ways."

Cam couldn't argue with that description, and yet he saw so much more in her than that. And judging by the tilt of his mother's head, as if she hadn't quite finished her thought, she saw something else too.

"I sense a 'but' in there."

"But, I don't think he'd do what she's doing."

"Which part? Working pro bono?"

"Working on this at all. Everything Joseph did was to get the hell out of Mississippi. He was never satisfied being a big fish in a small pond. He wanted to be a big fish in an ocean. The kind of man who wanted to save the world —and get credit for it."

Perhaps Norah's dad had more in common with Cam's after all.

"From what she's said about him, he's been

exceptionally successful at that. But Norah's not like that."

"No, I don't think she is. I don't think she'd have stayed friends with Miranda, kept coming back here all these years if she was."

"She has no financial stake in the decision, so less reason to be biased. I think that's in our favor."

"She seemed pretty biased to me."

"No more than I am. She got a really raw deal. And nothing anybody can say will convince her that she didn't personally have a hand in destroying that other town."

"Shouldering all that responsibility." Sandra shook her head. "Reminds me of someone else I know." She lifted a meaningful brow at him.

Cam shrugged. "Apple. Tree." He pointed a finger at his chest, then at her.

"True enough. Now what is it you really want this morning?" Her manner relaxed, and Cam knew the brief diversionary conversation had been the right move.

"I think we should commission an independent economic impact study. Bring in an expert who doesn't have a horse in this race to look at the local economy and actually project what GrandGoods will do to it, good or bad. It will help us all make a more informed decision."

"That seems completely logical. Why bring this directly to me?"

"Because I figure it stands a better chance of happening if it comes from you. You can strong arm Vick where I can't if he kicks up a fuss."

"I hate how much of this job is making other people play nice."

"You had plenty of practice corralling me and the cousins over the years."

She fixed him with a gimlet eye. "I could ground all of you."

Cam grinned.

"I'll set up a meeting." She dialed Vick's extension, obviously surprised when he answered after the second ring. Cam checked his watch. Not yet eight. Vick was getting a bright and early start after his apparent success at last night's Council meeting. Sandra asked him to come up for a quick chat.

"Should I vamoose?"

"No need for that."

Vick was all smiles when he strode in a few minutes later. He opened his mouth, ostensibly to spew some effusive pleasantries, but Sandra cut him off, back to the curt irritation she'd displayed when Cam had arrived.

"I'll be brief. Before things go any further on the GrandGoods proposal, I want an economic impact study conducted. Paid for by the city, conducted by an independent agent with no ties to GrandGoods. This project is significantly different from any of the proposals we've entertained before, and I want to make absolutely certain we proceed with as much information as possible."

"I think that's a very sensible suggestion, Sandra. I'd be happy to get right on that this morning and compile a list of possible contractors."

His ready agreement threw Cam. Where

was the antagonism? The arguments against slowing the process?

"That would be great. I've got a full plate sorting through other things today."

With another of those used car salesman grins, Vick walked right back out.

"There. That was relatively painless, for once."

Painless and Vick didn't go together. "I don't trust him. He never agrees to anything that easily."

"I take it as a sign he's trying to play nice. I suggest you do the same. Now skedaddle on to work yourself. I've got work to do."

CHAPTER 9

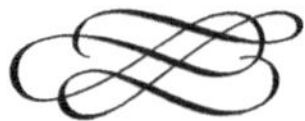

"—THE COUNCIL HAS AGREED to a delay of the vote until receipt of the economic impact study, so we've got a bit of a reprieve until the report comes back." Cam's announcement to the twenty or so members of the Chamber of Commerce scattered on the bleachers of the community center was met with grim focus.

Norah could work with that. What she wasn't sure she could continue to do was work with Cam. He hadn't pushed, hadn't guilted, hadn't even alluded to their brief relationship.

But compartmentalizing what she felt for him was taking more than half the energy she needed to be devoting to the campaign. She could usually lose herself in the work, but seeing him day in, day out was slowly driving her mad.

Realizing he was done introducing her, Norah took his place up front, already refining her pitch, shifting from training to instinct. "Usually how this works is I'd go with all the glitz and glam, lay out my credentials and awards to establish myself as the resident expert before launching into my pitch. But this isn't a boardroom and y'all don't care about that. Most of you don't know me. Those who do probably know little more than my connection to the Campbell family. So here's what you need to know in a nutshell: I may not be from here, but I love this town, and I don't want to see it desecrated by GrandGoods or any other corporate giant seeking to come in and carve out a place without consideration of the community at large. I have the skill set, the time, the passion, and the commitment to see that that doesn't happen."

She paused a few beats, noting body language as some, like Tyler and the sweet-faced brunette who ran the pharmacy, leaned forward, engaged. Mama Pearl folded both arms across her ample bosom, her strangely ageless face set in lines of skepticism. Norah had faced tougher crowds.

"But I can't fight this war alone. And make no mistake—this *is* a war. GrandGoods and all they represent are a threat to the culture and way of life here. Your City Planner would have you believe otherwise."

She turned and rotated the markerboard Cam had dragged in for her before the meeting so they could see the list she'd made. "Mr. Burgess would have you believe that Grand-Goods will create jobs. Obviously, with Wishful's economy being in its current state, that would be a great thing. If it were true. In fact, studies by independent economists prove that big box stores eliminate more retail jobs than they create. And the jobs they *do* create tend to be part time, low wages, with no benefits." She drew a line through the first myth and moved on to the second. "He says GrandGoods will boost local tax revenue. That's a big catch-22. Whatever tax benefits GrandGoods may provide will be negated by the cost of providing public services like roads, additional miles of utilities, more of a drain on fire and police time. Not to mention that cities that approve big box development often experience a decline in property and sales tax revenue from existing local businesses. That would be all of you." She crossed another line off.

"He'll tell you that GrandGoods will grow the economy, when, in fact, chains like them actually shrink the volume of activity in the local economy. As local business owners, you hire more local workers, purchase more goods and services from other local businesses, and contribute more to local charities than a big box counterpart would." Another strike out. "GrandGoods is supposed to bring competition and choice for the consumer. But what competition will remain when they edge you out of business? A town this size cannot reasonably absorb a store of that scale without considerable revenue losses to existing businesses. And there's absolutely no guarantee of quality or customer service." She axed that one from the list and drew a circle around the remaining myth she intended to bust.

"Perhaps most important, they're going to tell you that GrandGoods and other big box stores like it are the only option for saving your flagging economy. Mr. Burgess is focused on big industry, big box stores, big solutions to an understandably big and intimidating problem. And a lot of people think like he does. But the fact is, there *are* other solutions. Solutions that will protect and enhance your businesses and create a climate that will appeal to entrepreneurs seeking viable locations for small business investment."

A hand shot up from the back row. Sandy

hair with purple streaks. The owner of The Daily Grind.

"Yes Cassie?"

"That all sounds great, but it also sounds like a really long-term kind of project. Even with a few weeks' reprieve from a decision about GrandGoods, how can we possibly make enough of a difference to stop it?"

"You're right." Norah nodded. "You're absolutely right. It *is* a long-term kind of project. And I tell you that because I want to give y'all a hint of the bigger picture. But our goal—I think we're all agreed on this—is to stop GrandGoods. In order to do that, we need to sway the decision makers to *say* no. That means the rest of the City Council."

"And how are we gonna do that?" Mama Pearl demanded.

Norah let her smile spread wide. "You're going to do what you do best. Share your wisdom with anybody and everybody who comes in your door."

There was a ripple of laughter at that. One

corner of Mama Pearl's generous mouth quirked up. Her approximation of a grudging smile.

"All of you are here because you're business owners. As such, you have contact on a daily basis with the citizens of Wishful. I'd wager most of you know the majority of your clientele by face, if not full names with family histories attached. You're influencers in this community. What I need you to do is spread the word. Get people talking about this situation and be frank about your problems with the proposal. Most of all, it will be your job to utilize whatever gossip trees you have in place to make sure that everybody knows that we're forming a citizens coalition, and we want them to join."

Pharmacy girl lifted a timid hand.

Norah pointed to give her the floor. "I'm sorry, what was your name?"

"Riley Gower. What exactly will we be doing with a citizens coalition?"

"I'm glad you asked. Apart from pulling to-gether as many like-minded people as we can, the coalition will have two primary goals. The first will be to continue to spread the word and educate the public about this issue. Our country is notoriously inactive when it comes to taking action on a political front. Most people don't take the time to educate themselves about the issues and prefer their news delivered in a soundbyte. We need to work to change that here. The second goal of the coalition will be to establish an effective Shop Local campaign. We want you to retain the customer base you have and remind everyone else why local is better, in an effort to get them to spend more of their dollars here rather than taking business elsewhere to places like Lawley or Jackson or online."

Her audience peppered her with questions for the next half hour. Norah answered them, expanding and elaborating as she could, making note of anything she didn't know so she could research further before the coalition meeting. When they wound down, Norah spread her hands. "Well, troops. I hope I've given you a good information base to work from on this and sufficient reason to act. Can I count on y'all to be my front line recruiters?"

"Aye aye, General!" Cassie Callister called.

Not everyone was quite as enthusiastic, but the prevailing consensus was a yes.

Cam stepped forward. "We've got information packets on the table by the door if you'd like to do more research yourself before talking to others."

For the duration of her talk, he'd hung back, generally out of her sight. She'd been relieved at that, knowing that her gaze would've strayed too often to him. But it also meant she hadn't been able to watch *his* reactions to her presentation. It was foolish to be nervous about that. She'd accomplished what she set out to do tonight. But it still felt important that he be happy with her work. He was, after all, sort of her client.

Everybody filed out except Tyler, who stood talking with Cam.

"Nicely done, Wonder Woman. I'm not surprised, but I'm suitably impressed."

"It's a start," Norah acknowledged.

"Well, I for one am looking forward to seeing your plan of attack. And to seeing how well you can herd cats, because that's totally what that coalition meeting will be." Tyler seemed faintly amused at the thought.

They wouldn't be the first cats she'd herded. "One challenge at a time."

"What's next?" Tyler asked.

"Individual recruitment of other business owners for the coalition." Norah turned to Cam. "Do you have that list for me? We can split them down the middle to get done faster."

"I do, but I think it's best if we go together. A lot of people still don't know you. They all know me, so I can get you in the door, smooth the way."

"Can you afford to take that much time away from the nursery? It'll probably take a few days to hit up everybody."

"Violet runs a tight ship and this is a priority."

Three full days working side-by-side. Oh goodie. "Okay then. We should start tomorrow."

Cam's stomach gave an audible gurgle. "You wanna go debrief over food? Figure out the schedule"

Norah felt almost weak with relief. "Can't. Tyler and I are meeting Miranda and Piper for dinner at Speakeasy."

"Beer, pizza, and gossip. Pretty sure there will be discussion about who Liam Montgomery is stepping out with."

"He's only been back a few weeks. How do you know he's stepping out with anybody?" Cam asked.

"I don't, but it's hella fun to torture Miranda." Tyler grinned.

"Does she actually still have a thing for him?"

"She says she doesn't. I'm pretty sure she'd just

like the chance to be seen as something other than Randa Panda. If that dress she wore New Year's Eve didn't do the trick, I'm not sure anything will."

"I can't believe she didn't murder Mitch for that one," Tyler said.

"Miranda is a big believer in the idea that revenge is a dish best served cold." Cam looked back to Norah. "Anyway, you want to do breakfast in the morning? We can go over the recruitment plan for the rest of the week before you take Hush for your play date."

"Works for me. You make coffee. I'll bring food."

"If you want something other than Frosted Flakes, that's probably best."

"Frosted Flakes? What are you, ten?"

"Hey, they're grrrrreat! Besides, what's the point of being a grown up if you can't eat all the stuff your mom wouldn't let you have when you were a kid?"

"I can think of a few other better reasons to be a grown up," Norah said.

Cam shot her a look so full of heat, she almost took a step back.

Jesus, that's so not what I meant. But, of course, now the thought was in her head. She needed to get out of here before she broke into a sweat. "We should probably get going, Tyler. We're going to be late."

"Y'all go ahead. I'll lock up here. I'll see you in the morning, Wonder Woman. Say seven-thirty? Violet's got a thing, so I need to be at the nursery to open by nine. Then we can hit the streets around noon."

"Sure. Tomorrow."

The cold night air was a relief. Tyler had left her truck at the hardware store, so she hitched a ride with Norah to the pizzeria.

Tyler tugged her seatbelt into place. "So, how long has that been going on?"

Norah tightened her hands on the wheel, hoping she misunderstood. "How long has what been going on?"

"You and Cam."

Norah kept her eyes on the road. "There is

no me and Cam."

"If there's not, then there should be. The pair of you are throwing off enough sexual tension to power the county for a month."

God, she felt it. Focusing on not reacting, Norah kept her voice even. "That would be very complicated considering my life isn't actually here beyond the temporary."

"Maybe, but it'd sure be a helluva lot of fun."

"I didn't come down here looking for fun." She hadn't come down here looking for a relationship of any kind.

"Maybe not, but it's worth grabbing while you can. You never know when you'll lose it." Her tone didn't change, but there was some subtle thread of pain underlying Tyler's words that distracted Norah from her own problems.

"I'm thinking there's a story behind that wisdom."

"One for another time. Tonight is for girls only."

As she followed Tyler into the pizzeria, Norah wondered if she was right. Was it worth grabbing onto while she could, even knowing the whole thing had an expiration date? Was the pleasure worth the ultimate pain?

If she'd had only herself to consider, maybe she could believe that. But she couldn't, *wouldn't* knowingly put Cam in a position that would build false hope for a future they couldn't have. He'd been through enough.

"AND THAT'S another one ticked off." Norah made a triumphant and dramatic check on the legal pad in her lap.

Cam turned his eyes away from that lap and the slim black skirt that'd had "Barracuda" running through his head since she'd slid into his truck that morning. Why had he thought this was a good idea?

"You knew exactly how that would go before we even walked in there, didn't you?" He cranked the engine. "Down to the fact that Abe wasn't going to listen to a word I said."

"Yep."

"And you let me walk in there and try to talk to him anyway." Figuring old school Abe wouldn't respond well to Norah's city slicker suit and fancy shoes, Cam had thought it best to take the lead.

"I did."

"Was that to prove a point?"

Norah smiled, and it was almost a real one. "A little. But it also set up a little good cop/bad cop. You went in there expecting him to see you as an enemy, and he did. I was a sweet little gal in need of rescuing by a big, strong, experienced man. I was no threat."

"No threat, my ass. That was a friggin' work of art how you herded him around to volunteering like it was all his idea. You got him to do exactly what you wanted."

"Yes. Yes, I did." Her lips curved in an expression of smug satisfaction that shot his internal temperature up a good ten degrees.

Cam shifted in his seat. "Objectively, I knew you were good, but I don't think I really grasped what that meant. I honestly did *not* expect you to pull that off."

"Abe Costello is hardly the first good ol' boy I've ever had to deal with. The South doesn't have the market cornered on old school male chauvinists. I made it out of there without getting my ass pinched, so I call that a win on multiple fronts."

And that just made him think about palming her ass. *Business. Stick to business.* "Who's next?"

She consulted the ever-present list. "Brister Construction."

"That'll be Burt Brister. Another of those good ol' boys."

Norah crossed her legs in that slim black skirt, drawing his eye. "Then I'll charm him just as easily."

Cam found that the mantle of optimism didn't rest so comfortably on his own shoulders. In his experience, nothing worth having came easy, so he kept waiting for the other shoe to drop. But despite their personal differences, he did trust Norah, and she *had* just successfully talked Abe Costello into coming to the coalition meeting to hear her out, so for her sake, he was trying to rein in his natural skepticism.

The huge doors of the garage that housed all the heavy equipment were closed and only one aging work truck with the Brister insignia was parked in the gravel lot when they pulled up.

"Think they're out on a job?" Norah asked.

"Not likely this time of year. Personal vehicles would be parked around back."

Not even a receptionist sat at the front desk when they stepped inside.

"Maybe we should come back later."

Cam moved further inside. "Somebody's here if the door's unlocked. Hello?"

The clatter of plastic wheels sounded from the back and someone stepped out of an office. Burt Brister had always reminded Cam of General Custer, with the long, sandy mustache framing his mouth, a mouth that was very definitely unsmiling as he stepped forward. "Can I help you?"

"Campbell Crawford, sir. I believe you know my mother, the mayor."

Burt angled his head in acknowledgment and took Cam's offered hand.

"And this is Norah Burke. We were hoping you had a few minutes to talk to us."

"Got more free minutes than I'd like just now. Come on back." He shifted some files out of the two chairs in front of his battered metal desk and gestured for them to sit. His own chair creaked as he sat and looked the two of them over. "Y'all lookin' to build a house?"

Norah, who'd opened her mouth to start whatever spiel she'd been planning, looked startled. "Sorry?"

Cam thought about what they must look like, a young couple ready to take the next step in life and wanting new digs to go with it. Since that was exactly the direction he'd been headed in when she broke things off, the question put a strain on his already volatile mood. "Ah, no sir. We're here on another matter entirely. Are you aware that the city has been approached with a proposal by GrandGoods?"

"I heard rumblings about something. Didn't know the particulars."

Norah picked up the thread. "Provided they pass the approval process, they intend to build a 150,000 square foot store in Wishful."

Burt straightened a little in his chair, his eyes sharpening. "Go on."

She laid it out for him, explaining the proposal and the problems such a project would present for the town. "As a local business owner, I'm sure you can appreciate the importance of preserving the character of Wishful and preventing the uncontrolled urban sprawl that would inevitably follow should GrandGoods be allowed to go ahead with their project. That's why we'd like to invite you to come to the citizens' coalition meeting next week, to be a part of the community's voice in letting the local policy-makers know that this isn't the direction Wishful should go."

"No."

Cam caught the momentary stunned expression on Norah's face before she recovered enough to reply. "I can understand how that might be your instinctive response, but surely it would be better to reserve your final decision until after you've attended the meeting, heard what others have to say."

"Young lady, I'm not going to join your coalition. I will, in fact, be first in line to submit a bid for the GrandGoods contract. I support the growth of commercial real estate such a store would bring to town."

"Aren't you the least bit concerned about the negative impact—"

Burt broke in. "Let me tell you about negative impact. I built this business from the ground up. Over the last twenty-five years, I've expanded my operations, my crew. And with the tanking economy, do you know how many good people I've had to let go? Twelve. Not because they did shoddy work or anything wrong but simply because we don't have the level of work we need to pay them. I've had to cut back the hours on dozens more."

Cam felt his gut clench, thinking again of Roy McKennon's desperation and wounded pride over the loss of his ability to provide for his family. Here was more of the same.

"I want to hire those men back. I want to protect the jobs of the ones I still have. I have to look out for my employees, for their families. They depend on me for their livelihood, so from my perspective, supporting GrandGoods is the *only* decision."

It made sense. Here was that rock and a hard place his mother had warned him about. More people who'd be lost if they couldn't find work. More of the soul of his town destroyed by a bad economy.

"Do you have any idea the kind of security a job like that would give them? You'll forgive me if I think that's a helluva lot more important than some kind of misplaced nostalgia for how this town used to be."

When Norah looked as if she might try some other tack, Cam sat forward. "We absolutely appreciate your position, Burt. Thanks for hearing us out. We'll let you get back to your day."

Cam recognized the mutinous expression in Norah's eyes as he said their goodbyes and herded her toward the door, but she kept her mouth shut until they were shut inside his truck again.

"What the hell was that?"

"A tactical retreat. You weren't going to change his mind."

"You don't know that. You didn't even let me try to counter his position."

"No. Because we shouldn't try to counter his position, Norah. Absolutely nothing we can say or do is going to provide the kind of work opportunities he needs to be able to offer his employees. He's right. From his standpoint, GrandGoods and everything that comes with it is exactly what his business needs."

Norah exhaled long and slow. "Okay, fair point. He's not the right target audience for this message. We aren't going to convince every-body, and that's okay."

"Is it? Is it really okay to the twenty percent of our population who are unemployed? What we're doing isn't helping them. Do we even have the right to be pushing to stop this?"

She laid a hand on his arm. "No decision is going to make everyone happy."

He looked down at her fingers, slim and delicate. "Yeah, you specialize in those, don't you."

When she pulled her hand away, he bit back a curse. He knew this wasn't easy on her either, could see the strain she was under. But, of course, she didn't actually respond to his jab. The matter was already settled in her mind.

"You have to look at the bigger picture, at the long-term impacts, to determine what's best for the majority."

Were they still talking about the town?

"Seems like looking out for the majority still means the minority gets shit on."

"Campbell, you can't save everybody. Not all at once. Just because what we're trying to do isn't the right thing for some people doesn't mean that we're wrong or that we should stop. The alternative means that the minority gets bigger. You're maybe too close to this. That minority is personal for you, people you know, people you care about. And I know it hurts you that you can't fix it for them because that's how you're built. It's one of the things I admire about you. But I think, in this case, it's making this whole situation harder on you than it might otherwise be."

He could see her point, but that did nothing to assuage the guilt that had dogged him since his encounter with April and Roy McKennon.

"Maybe I should do the rest on my own."

He wanted to let her. To just walk away from the torture of having her right there and yet completely out of reach. But she'd been right about one thing. This was about more than them. If she was going to go, then he had to at least save the town she was leaving behind.

"No. I said I'd help with this part. And you're right, we can't please everybody. It's just…hard coming up against completely reasonable opposition."

"I know." She shoved the legal pad into her briefcase. "Let's take a break and get some lunch before we pick back up with the rest of the list. I bet Mama Pearl has a pie that's a cure-all for personal guilt crises."

Because he knew an olive branch when he heard one, Cam forced a smile. "That's the best idea you've had all day."

NORAH EYED THE VIBRATING phone like a pit viper as it danced across Miranda's coffee table. Her father. For the sixth time in the last hour. No voicemails.

He knew.

Stop being a coward, she ordered herself. *Get it over with.*

The phone felt heavy in her sweaty hand. "Dad."

"What the hell is this about you being *fired?*"

She winced and pulled the phone away from her ear as he continued.

"What the hell is going on, Norah? Where have you been?"

Her head began to throb. "If you'll stop yelling for five minutes, I'll tell you." Norah slid off the sofa to pace and rub at her temples. She gave her father a bare bones account of the events that led to her termination. With every step, every word, her shoulders tightened.

"No, sir, I'm not legally liable for anything. Neither I nor Helios broke any official laws."

"Do you have copies of all the legal paperwork between Hugo's and the city?"

Because, of course, her word on the stand wasn't good enough. She was supposed to produce evidence. "Why would I? We didn't have that kind of role in the project. We didn't make any decisions, sign any documents short of the standard contracts we sign with all clients, outlining our scope of work." She wrapped one arm tight around her middle and did an about face, heading toward the dining room. "Mine was a moral objection to the actions of the firm, not an actual legal issue."

"Do you know what this could do to your career?"

I should hang up. But years of conditioned behavior had her staying on the line, continuing to defend her decisions in the hope that one day she'd argue well enough that he'd see her side—maybe even offer approval. But today wasn't going to be that day. She made another circuit, living room to dining room and back before stopping to drop her head back against the nearest wall as she listened to what he imagined was counsel but came across more like orders.

God, she wanted Cam. Wanted his support, his level head, his touch. But that wasn't an option. So she steeled her spine as she'd done for the last twenty years. "With all due respect, Dad, I'll handle it. I know this was never the career you or Mom would've picked for me, but that's not the point. It's what I chose."

"It was a poor decision."

And you never get tired of reminding me of that. "Yes, you both made it quite clear that you didn't agree with that decision. That doesn't make what I do have less value."

"I'm really disappointed in you, Norah. You have so much potential and you continue to waste it, wasting all the advantages your mother and I worked to give you. I really expected better of you."

She blanched, staying silent as she absorbed that blow. When she answered, her voice was small and oh so tired. "You're entitled to your opinion, Dad, just like I'm entitled to mine. Whatever I do next will still be what I choose. I'm not going to suddenly turn around and go back to law or medical school because it's what *you* want. Now, you've been informed. Go ahead and call Mom and share your mutual disappointment in me. I've got work to do."

Without giving him a chance to respond, Norah hung up. Then she turned her phone completely off and crossed to lay it on the coffee table with meticulous care, before she could give in to the impulse to hurl it against the wall.

Damn him. Damn him and all his expectations and guilt trips and goddamned cross examinations. It's my life.

And it was a mess. She'd stubbornly put off dealing with it in the name of saving Wishful. But if she was to have any kind of career to go back to when the campaign was done, she had to get off her ass and start taking steps to straighten things out.

Even the idea of it left her feeling hollow and exhausted. But that was pretty par for the course these days.

The sound of the doorbell had her groaning. Company was the last thing she wanted. But it might be about the campaign. So many balls were up in the air, she really couldn't afford to leave her phone off for long.

Schooling her features into an expression of polite welcome, Norah opened the door.

Piper bounced inside. "This is a kidnapping!"

Norah stared at the very short skirt and

pink straw cowboy hat her friend was sporting. "I'm sorry, what?"

"We failed to adhere to our sacred duty upon your arrival and must now rectify that oversight."

"Which sacred duty is that?"

"The part where we go out dancing and drink to the shriveling of your ex's dick." This was stated in a tone of *duh.*

"She's bloodthirsty, our Piper," Tyler said from the doorway.

It was a sentiment Norah could get behind, even if the object of her ire was a little different. "While I appreciate the thought, I've got a lot of work to do."

The coalition meeting had gone well. She'd successfully sold them on a Shop Local campaign and laid the foundation for a grassroots movement. But even with the help of the new coalition chairwoman, Molly Montgomery—who evidently had a membership or officer position in every civic group in town—it meant her workload had quadrupled.

"All work and no play makes Norah a dull girl," Piper sang.

"All work and no play makes Norah a successful girl." She returned to her position on the sofa.

"There is more to life than work."

An ache bloomed in Norah's chest as she thought of Cam and his life lessons. There'd been no more of them since she broke things off. Not a surprise. And not that there'd been time. They'd both been working their asses off to get this campaign off the ground.

"You might as well give in," Tyler added. "She doesn't take no for an answer."

Norah looked down at her yoga pants and sweatshirt. "I'm hardly dressed for going out. And Miranda will be home from her ER rotation in an hour."

"She's meeting us there when she gets off." Piper stepped over the piles of folders and tugged Norah up. "Come on."

Norah had no intention of going. She had census data to dig through and city tax records to analyze. Not to mention the website mock-up she wanted to finish before the next coalition meeting. But forty-five minutes later, she was being hustled through the door of the Mudcat Tavern, fully made up and wearing borrowed cowboy boots, as Piper had declared her knee-high English riding boots "too citified for this kind of dancing" and insisted that they did not meet Bitch Boot status. Norah was pretty sure some kind of magic had been involved.

The pretty, older bartender flashed a welcoming smile. "What'll it be ladies?"

Piper slapped the bar. "Adele, we're here for the Three Furies. Norah here has been wronged by an idiot man."

More than one.

"Is there any other kind?" Adele asked.

Norah exercised more caution than Piper. "And what exactly does the Three Furies entail?"

"It's a tradition of long standing, dating back to just after college when He Who Is Not Worth

Naming walked out of my life," Tyler explained. "First shot is tequila because you're drinking to forget a worm. Second shot is whiskey, in honor of the fire in your belly. Third shot is Jaeger, which will kick all asses. And after each, you get a shot at Bob the Bastard."

"Bob the Bastard?"

Adele lifted a sad burlap…thing from behind the counter. It had a crude face embroidered on and four rough limbs flung out akimbo. A fifth…protuberance was painted in red between the legs.

"Is that…a voodoo doll?"

"Sort of. We mount him on the dartboard and take shots at his nuts. It's terribly cathartic. I think this is actually Bob the Sixth. The Three Furies is a popular ritual." Tyler patted Bob on the head.

"It's one that has stood us in good stead, and as you are now officially a part of the Sisterhood, it is your duty to participate," Piper said.

Norah wondered what sisterhood that was, exactly. "Oh, well I don't do shots. I'm more a sedate glass of wine or the occasional glass of Scotch kind of girl. And, really, I'm over it. Not even on the rebound." Why should she waste time thinking about Pierce when she was already half crazy for a better man she wouldn't let herself have?

Piper gave her a baleful glance. "Are you seriously not going to cooperate?"

The idea of throwing darts at Pierce's junk in effigy *was* pretty appealing. All this mess had started with him. "Well, if it's *that* important to you."

"Damn straight."

Adele set out a salted shot glass and poured the tequila while Tyler affixed Bob to one of the dart boards on the wall. A cheer went up around the bar.

"Okay Norah, you have to name him," Tyler called.

"Pierce Vargas."

"Here hangs the bastard Pierce Vargas, Asshole of the First Degree," Tyler intoned. "Administering his sentence is Norah Burke, the

Supremely Wronged Party. Norah, you may begin when ready."

When in Rome. Norah took the shot, wincing at the burn as she bit the lime. God, tequila was nasty. Piper offered up the first dart and she took her position behind the line. After clearing the pucker from her face, Norah zeroed in on the doll less than eight feet away.

"Feel free to list his crimes."

"For being a lying douchenozzle."

Bringing Pierce's smug, supercilious face to mind, she let the dart fly. It embedded in one of the arms. The crowd cheered.

"Not bad." Piper nodded in approval. "Extra points for using 'douchenozzle' correctly in a sentence. That counts as first blood. Bet you can do better, though. Adele, bring on the Jack!"

"Shouldn't I eat something first?" Norah tried to remember if she'd had lunch.

"We'll order after you're done. Don't want to lose your momentum."

If only my Chicago colleagues could see me now. She accepted the second glass. All those pretentious, self-absorbed professionals would consider this behavior completely unseemly. The idea made her grin as she took the second shot. The whiskey went down easier, smoothing some of the edges she hadn't realized she'd been carrying around. Maybe they were on to something with this whole thing.

The dart Piper handed her felt warm in her palm.

"For not appreciating that I was the best thing to ever happen to you."

You were supposed to exhale when throwing, right? Or maybe that was just archery. She couldn't remember, but it seemed like a good idea, so when Norah stepped up to the line, she took a series of deep breaths as she aimed. On a last gust, she released with a snap. It hit a mere half inch below the desired target, to the collective groans of the audience.

"That's okay, honey. You've still got one more to go," Piper said.

Norah returned to the bar for the Jaeger.

"Hail, hail, the gang's all here!" Turning, she

saw Tucker crossing the bar, Cam, Mitch, and Liam Montgomery right behind.

Cam. Of *course,* he was here. Because it wasn't enough that she should see him every day in a work capacity, and almost as often through all her Campbell family interactions. She really needed the Universe to mock her further by throwing him in her path some more with a *Nana nana boo boo, look what you gave up* for good measure.

God, he looked good. He also looked just a little bit pissed off. She wondered if Tucker and company had dragged him out of his cave like she'd been dragged out of hers.

"Who's the poor bastard being skewered?" Tucker inquired.

By way of answer, Norah lifted the shot of Jaeger in a toast before tossing it back with a prayer that it would strengthen her resolve. Her cheeks felt flushed as she slapped the glass down on the bar and returned to position for her final shot.

"For my career, you unscrupulous, exploitive son of a bitch." Norah flung the dart, wishing it was something more substantial, like a knife, as it zoomed forward and buried itself in the doll's painted scrotum.

The crowd—the females anyway—burst into cheers and applause. Norah took an exaggerated bow and regretted it as the room took a bit of a dip along with it. Food. Food was an immediate priority. And water. Like, a gallon of it. She managed to straighten without lurching.

Mitch swaggered over. "Is this an All-Men-Suck hen party, or can we join you?"

"Better check Norah for sharp, pointy objects," Cam said. "Clearly she's dangerous with them."

Norah assumed a superior air. "He deserved it."

Piper was grinning like a loon, her arm already looped through Liam's, so evidently this was to be a mixed party. *Hooray, a new challenge to resist Cam, this time with diminished capacity.* Norah knew after the lengths they'd gone to getting her here, neither woman was going to just let her go on home, so she didn't voice the protest.

They commandeered a booth in the corner and put in orders for appetizers. Even as the others broke into a babble of joking conversation, Norah could feel Cam's eyes on her.

"Are you okay?" He had to lean in close to be heard over the music, and Norah shivered at the feel of his breath on her ear.

"Not even close." She tossed back a glass of water as if it were another shot.

"What happened?"

"Talked to my dad."

Cam winced. "As bad as you expected?"

"Worse." She wished he'd rub her nape, banish some of the tension. But he didn't touch her. Because they didn't do that anymore. She wasn't his to take care of.

"I'm sorry."

Norah jerked her shoulders. "Over now." Flashing a smile that was probably more of a snarl, she asked, "And how was your day?"

"Could've been better. The economic impact

report will be in tomorrow. The Council is convening tomorrow afternoon to go over it and vote."

The shots turned to acid in her stomach. "So soon? I thought we weren't expecting it for another month?"

"So did I. Apparently when they said they'd fast-track it, they really meant it."

Had she done enough? She'd expected to have another month to shift public opinion, get the other Council members on their side. There had barely been time to get the Shop Local campaign off the ground, let alone finish with all the public education components of her plan. At this point, all their hopes were pinned on the results of that study.

"I'm sure it'll be fine." She knew the power of optimism. "All our research suggests that the economic impact would be overwhelmingly negative. Any firm worth its salt is going to find the same."

"I hope you're right. Either way, tomorrow is D-Day."

It was a sobering thought. Another sign from the Universe that her time here was winding up. Her mind automatically shifted to the action plan for the coalition, wondering how she should alter the timeline to see that the Shop Local campaign was truly sustainable on its own. Because an end to the anti-GrandGoods campaign meant an end to her time in Wishful. And an end to her time with Cam. She told herself it would be easier away from him, back in the real world, where everyone had expectations and the standard operating procedure was looking out for number one.

And when had she become a woman who looked for easy?

"You two look entirely too serious. I know just the way to turn that frown upside down." Tucker grabbed her hand. "Come on, sugar."

"No, no, no, nono. I don't—oh Jesus." Abruptly, she found herself spun in some complicated sequence as an Alan Jackson song rocked out from the juke box.

Tyler waved after them. "Don't worry. Tucker makes everybody look good!"

Despite his lousy mood, Cam couldn't help but be amused as Tucker dragged a very panicked Norah out on the dance floor. Piper wasn't far behind, Liam in tow.

Mitch turned and offered a hand to Tyler, "May I have this dance, fair lady? We could put them to shame or die trying."

"Not even for you, dear heart."

He mimed brushing away tears. "In that case, beer. Pitcher?"

"Get a couple," Cam said. "Pretty sure Liam's gonna need a lot to recover from Piper's enthusiasm."

"Soldier boy's got game," Tyler observed as Mitch headed for the bar.

"Not yo' mama's Texas two step, right there. That's, like, the Magic Mike version."

She slanted him a Look.

"What? I saw the previews."

Cam's gaze was drawn inexorably back to Norah, who looked beyond uncomfortable on the dance floor. Tucker might as well have been trying to swing dance with a fence post for all the natural grace and rhythm she displayed. It was so absolutely counter to the way she usually conducted herself, he almost wanted to laugh.

"You know, I wouldn't have believed it if I hadn't seen it for myself. There really *is* something Norah's not good at. Do you suppose it's the alcohol?"

"No, bless her heart. She hasn't got an ounce of rhythm and isn't following his lead at all," Tyler said. "Of course, he's tryin' to showboat and going way above a basic skill level."

Cam thought back to New Year's. She hadn't had any trouble following *his* lead.

"Okay, so I have no idea what excuse y'all are using to keep yourselves from following through on the sparks you throw off every time you get within ten feet of each other, but I'm pretty sure we've taken out her half of them with those shots. So what are you going to do about it, Crawford?"

Cam cut a glance toward Tyler. "Do about it?"

"Why *else* do you think I got Tucker to drag you out tonight? Don't even try to tell me you don't have a thing for her. I've known you too many years for that to fly. You've never looked at any woman like that."

Uncomfortable, Cam wondered if any of his family had made the same observation.

"She looks at you the same way when she thinks nobody's looking. Whatever her objections are, they have nothing to do with lack of interest. Don't tell me you're going to waste this opportunity to work on her when her shields are down."

"You are a sneaky bitch."

"You love me," she said, smug.

"Yes, yes, I do." He'd wanted an opportunity to prove to Norah that there were more important things in life than career. Judging by the nut shot she'd taken at Bob the Bastard, she absolutely wasn't in a frame of mind to let go of that perspective. "I don't know how much good it'll do, though."

"Never know until you try. You could start by going to rescue her. I don't think I've ever seen a woman look terrified of dancing with Tucker before. That's a really impressive use of multiple left feet."

Seeing his very nosy cousin returning with pitchers and glasses, Cam saluted Tyler and made his escape. The choice at the jukebox was easy. He made his selection and wove his way through the crowd just in time to keep Norah from crashing into another couple, as Tucker's attempted spin completely got away from him.

"This is an intervention. You're turning this poor woman into a weapon. Go get a beer."

"I tried…to tell you…I can't dance. Seriously."

Tucker held up his hands in surrender. She started to follow him back to the table, but Cam caught her neatly around the waist and spun her into his arms as the music he'd chosen began to play. "My turn."

She angled her head, listening to the music. "The Dance? Really?"

"Seemed appropriate."

"Is this meant to be romantic or a guilt trip?"

"Neither. It's nostalgic. Some things really are simple. Come here." As he had New Year's Eve, Cam nudged her head toward his shoulder.

She didn't fight him. Her body curved toward his as if just as starved for contact as he was. How had it only been a month since he'd held her? It felt like years. As they circled the floor, the tension he'd noted when he'd walked in bled away, leaving her warm and pliant in his arms. He didn't think of the town, didn't think of the campaign, or the fact that after tomorrow she could be leaving. He thought only of how right she felt pressed against him and that he'd do almost anything to keep her there.

When Norah lifted her head, her face was flushed, her eyes over-bright. Cam didn't want to move, didn't want to let her go, but the music swung into something upbeat. Around them, patrons formed into lines and launched into a grapevine.

"Let's step outside for some air." There were things he wanted—needed—to give voice to, and the middle of a crowded dance floor wasn't the place.

She nodded once and let him guide her with a hand at the small of her back toward the back door. By grace of the frigid temperatures, the porch designated for outdoor dining and smoking was empty. Norah went straight to the railing and leaned against it, lifting her face to the sky. Cam resisted the urge to move in behind her, boxing her in, and instead leaned beside her, his arm brushing hers.

"I miss simple." She sighed and tipped her head against his arm. "I miss you."

He hadn't expected the admission and credited lowered inhibitions due to the Three Furies. "You don't have to. I've been right here the whole time. And for all your talk, you haven't gone anywhere, not yet."

"But I will. Not tomorrow. Probably not next week. I don't *know* when I'm leaving. But I have to start taking control of my life again. If that conversation with my father did anything, it lit a fire under me to finally start facing the long job search. I can't keep putting it off."

Nothing had changed. After all these weeks, all her involvement in the community, she still didn't think she belonged here. He was losing her, back to the life she'd come here to escape. Because he was perilously close to begging, Cam kept his mouth shut, fisting both hands around the railing until the wrought iron began to creak.

She mistook the reason for his silence. "I promise you, I won't go until Wishful is safe. And I don't make promises I can't keep."

He believed her. And cursed himself for wishing more danger on his town, just so she'd stay.

If he said nothing now, if he let her walk away, he'd regret it for the rest of his life.

Cam turned her to face him. "Isn't it worth

grabbing whatever happiness we can, while we can?" He could feel the pull between them, always the pull.

She leaned toward him, yearning written clearly on her face. But mixed with it was equal parts sadness and resignation. "It isn't about happiness."

"Why the hell not?"

"Because there are bigger things at stake."

"I get that you've got this mission, this purpose. I support that. Hell, I asked you to take it on. But that doesn't mean you can't take something for yourself. Even Wonder Woman had Steve Trevor."

"You're no Steve Trevor."

Before Cam could process the insult of that, she was reaching up, cupping his jaw. "Steve Trevor didn't recognize what was right in front of him. You actually *see* me."

What he saw was a brilliant, beautiful woman with an inexplicably fast hold on his heart and a mule-headed resistance to taking it.

He turned his face into her touch, needing the connection.

Her thumb traced the arch of his cheek. "Do you know how rare that is?"

Cam covered her hand with his. "Do you know how rare *this* is? Don't you think it's worth hanging on to?"

"Campbell." She swayed toward him. "I..."

He might've said any number of things to try to persuade her, or he might've just given in and kissed her, as he'd wanted to do pretty much since the moment he'd stopped. But Fate, cruel bitch that she was, had other plans in the form of his meddling cousin, who came barreling out the door like an overgrown golden retriever.

Mitch drew up short, his mouth dropping open as he took in their embrace in a glance. "I...uh...just came to say the food's ready. And Miranda's here."

"Great. I'm starved." Norah tapped Cam's cheek gently. "Thanks for the dance, Leonidas." She stepped away from him with the grace that completely eluded her on the dance floor and made her way to the door with the careful deliberation of the inebriated.

"You got it okay there, sugar?"

She gave Mitch a thumbs up and the door swung shut behind her.

Cam started to follow, to make sure she got through the dancing throng safely—thumbs up be damned—, but Mitch slapped a palm against his chest. "Hold it. What was that?"

"That was none of your business." He tried to push past, but for all his general good humor, Mitch was bigger, broader, and when he didn't want to be moved, he couldn't be without considerably more force than Cam was prepared to use.

"You've got a thing for Norah."

"Congratulations, you have eyes in your head."

"Eyes enough to see that was not a casual flirtation."

"You got a problem with that, cuz?" Cam knew Mitch found Norah attractive, but he'd assumed the flirtation was the same knee-jerk reaction his cousin had to most women. He wasn't worried about competition—Norah had made it perfectly clear where she stood—but Mitch didn't know that.

"No." And there was nothing of Mitch's usual playfulness in his tone. "Are you okay?"

"Am I—what?"

"Norah's a sweetheart, but a shoot down is a shoot down, and I know you haven't really been interested in anybody in a long time."

He thought she wasn't interested. Cam almost laughed. Lack of interest he could deal with. If this whole thing was legitimately one-sided, he'd just accept and move on. No harm, no foul. But she was balking out of…what? Some principled bullshit that if it couldn't last, it wasn't worth pursuing at all? Did she think they could just turn it off like a switch?

Well, if she had, it wasn't working. For either of them.

"Cam?"

"Yeah, I'm fine."

And there it was. That Look. That careful, piteous look his entire family had been using since Melody walked away years before. Because they all thought she'd broken something in him and had adopted a standard operating procedure of treating him with kid gloves when it came to women and relationships. It drove Cam batshit crazy.

As Mitch stared him down, a sick suspicion trickled through Cam's gut. Had his family infected Norah with that absurdity? It was exactly why Miranda thought they were a bad idea. Had she warned Norah away after he'd blown off her caution at the bonfire? Was that at the root of Norah's reluctance to be with him? Because she thought he was broken, too?

"I said, I'm fine, Mitch. I don't need some touchy feely intervention here."

This time, when Cam stepped forward, Mitch gave way and let him inside.

Norah hadn't made it back to the table. She was, instead, in a line with Piper, Liam, Tucker, and Tyler executing the electric slide with more enthusiasm than skill. At least she didn't seem in danger of injuring anybody dancing solo.

From the sidelines, Miranda was staring. "How much has she had to drink?"

"The Three Furies. Piper's idea, apparently." He studied his cousin, wondering if she'd stabbed him in the back in the name of protection.

"What?"

Not the time. "C'mon, there's food." He gestured toward their booth, then turned and signaled Tucker out on the floor.

Cam and Miranda slid in on opposite sides of the long table, squeezing to make room for everyone else as they came out of the dancing throng in a pack. As she went to make the single step into the booth, Norah missed and toppled. Cam lunged over, barely catching her before her head cracked against the table. She thumped into his chest, hands clutching at his shoulders.

"Whoa there. I've gotcha."

She looked up from her perch, and her eyes

were huge. "Sorry. It's the boots," she said, very seriously. "Piper wouldn't let me wear mine."

"Pretty sure it's not just the boots. I think you're officially cut off." He righted her so she could crawl into the booth beside him.

"No." Norah jabbed a finger into his chest for emphasis. The gesture seemed to distract her a bit, as she flattened her hand over his heart and frowned. "I cut myself off. That's totally the problem. Being cut off sucks."

"Yes, yes it does."

She lifted her eyes to his again, resolute and clearly very, very drunk. "I *told* you. Is the responsible thing to do."

"So you did." Whatever composure she'd managed to cobble together out on the patio was eradicated. Apparently the full force of the shots had hit her somewhere out on the dance floor.

"Tell you a secret." She leaned in, bracing herself on Cam's shoulder as she tried to tuck one foot beneath her on the seat. "I really hate being the responsible one all the time. But I'm really, really good at it. Can't let anybody else pay for my mistakes. No, sir." She hiccupped.

"I'm pretty sure you'll be paying for this one in the morning."

"Jesus, Piper, did you really have her do the Three Furies on an empty stomach?" Miranda demanded. "She *never* has more than one drink. *Ever.*"

"What? She's totally fine."

"No, really, I am." Norah, finally seated, balanced with one hand on Cam's thigh—Jesus—as she leaned in to grab a French fry. "Piper was right. I tooootally needed to take a break."

"I'm pretty sure you need to be mainlining some water," Miranda said. "Or you'll be flirting with the fourth Fury in the form of a massive hangover in the morning."

"Yes, Mom."

Norah applied herself to the task with the same single-minded focus she applied to everything. She dutifully ate and drank everything pushed on her, staying quiet as conversation flowed around her and the others got up, now and then, to dance some more. Cam assumed her silence had more to do with the topics of conversation—local gossip about people she didn't know—until he felt a weight heavy against his arm.

"And that would be the other reason she never has more than one," Miranda said. "She falls asleep. She almost never stops, so when something does finally knock her on her ass, she stays down."

Because no one takes care of her. When she'd cut things off, he'd stopped trying. He regretted it now, seeing the hollows in her cheeks. Had she been sleeping? Eating enough? "She's been working herself into the ground."

"It's what she does. You give her a war and she'll fight it, with or without an army. She has more heart and generosity than anyone I know, but it takes a toll on her." Miranda sighed. "I need to be getting home. I've got an early day tomorrow. It'll take an act of God to wake her up."

"Let her sleep. I'll help you get her home."

Cam reached around and lifted Norah into his arms. She snuggled into him, one arm curling around his neck, the other resting against his chest as she nuzzled into the juncture of his neck and shoulder. It was a childlike motion, trusting and vulnerable. Norah wasn't a woman who accepted or showed vulnerability, and Cam felt something in him stutter. He needed to take care of this woman. Needed to keep her safe, to make her smile. He just plain needed her. And whether she wanted to or not, she needed him, too.

Miranda slid out of the booth.

Resisting the urge to stroke Norah's hair back or press a kiss to her head, he slid out himself and hoisted Norah up. "Come on, Wonder Woman. Time for you to sleep it off."

CHAPTER 11

"WE OFFICIALLY SWEPT THE entire letters to the editor section for the last three days." Grammy checked a list. "That brings our total to…sixteen."

Norah fought to keep her voice level and professional. "Excellent. Are your letter writers prepared to expand the scope? We really want to get the word out regionally. Hit up the papers in Lawley, Oxford, Starkville, all the areas that would be impacted by this change."

"I'll get them started tonight."

She paused to guzzle the fresh glass of water

Aunt Liz had set out for her. Now if only she had an aspirin the size of Alabama. No one had said a word about the fact that she looked like death—she was good with makeup—but Aunt Liz's silent solicitude made her wonder if last night's antics had already spread around town, or at least through the family.

The front door opened. "Honey, I'm *hoooome!*"

Norah held in a groan—something she'd become a champ at since she left the house this morning with one of the worst hangovers of her life—as Mitch strolled, whistling, into the living room. He was one of the last people she wanted to see right now. Along with everyone else who'd been at the Mudcat for her encounter with the Three Furies last night. She was never going drinking with Piper, ever again.

"Well, hey there, sugar. I didn't expect you to be up at all today, let alone among the land of the living."

"I feel like death warmed over, but I'm not

going to shirk my duty because of one supremely bad decision." She didn't know for sure what she'd done to embarrass herself beyond that horrific dance with Tucker, but she had dim memories of admitting to Cam that she missed him and then crawling into his lap to sleep. She was really hoping that part was a dream. And then there was the matter of how the hell she'd gotten home. Miranda hadn't said and Norah hadn't asked.

She consulted her notepad. "Next order of business: The coalition's order of pamphlets and fliers at Poor Richard's is ready. It needs to be picked up and distributed."

Mitch flopped down on the sofa and stretched out his long, long legs. "I should be able to get to that between site visits."

"I've got the list of who needs to get what," Aunt Liz said. "If you can bring everything by this evening, I can work on getting that sorted."

"Great. The media campaign is going well. I'm scheduled for an interview at the radio station at the end of the week. That, in conjunction with the spot WCBI did with Molly last week about the coalition, is a really great start. We're getting the word out and, in a lot of cases, are the first side of this many people are hearing. Now we just have to keep it up so we stay at the forefront of people's minds. I'm still waiting to hear back from WTVA."

The front door opened again, and Norah felt her heart leap, knowing it was Cam. A strange mix of emotions swirled through her. Hope that their hard work had paid off, that Wishful was safe. Terror, too, that all this might be over, that her alleged reason for being here was finished, and she would have to make the hard decision about what came next without the benefit of external factors dictating her actions. That she'd have to walk away from him for real.

Cam's face was rigid when he walked into the room.

Norah was on her feet, across the room to him before she could stop herself. "What?"

"Read it." He thrust a wad of papers at her.

The economic impact report.

Frowning as he moved off to pace with frenetic irritation, she began to read. Her stomach sank as she hit the second page, but she kept reading, searching for the qualifying argument, the refutation that would've signified balanced investigation. It never came.

"This can't be right. This contradicts almost everything I've read in the literature.

"The Council voted. I was the lone dissenting voice. GrandGoods' proposal was approved, and they're moving forward with the hearing for a special use permit. No one but me is going to vote against it after this."

Norah's mind went immediately to damage control. "That's a public hearing?"

Cam's nod was tight. "Public hearing, but still ultimately a Council vote."

"Then we ramp up our efforts to educate the public, get them out to attend the hearing. You need to put in a formal request to the firm who did the evaluation to have them present for the hearing so they can answer questions. We're going to get a rebuttal by then. We need a second opinion. Someone *not* hired by Vick."

"How? It was a minor miracle this got pushed through in a month. Where the hell do you think you're going to get a second opinion in a week or two?"

"I don't know yet, but I'll find someone. Have a little—"

"Faith?" The word was bitter, brittle with lack of belief. "Because that's gotten us so far up to now."

Norah felt the sting of his frustrated dejection. She could see it in the set of his chin, the defeated look in his eyes. God, how could he give up so easily? Was the rest of the town so easily cowed, so devoid of hope? If they were, she was fighting a losing battle, and the enemy wasn't GrandGoods.

Norah put the thought out of her mind. She had one war to fight right now, one stubborn man to convince. She crossed the room toward him. "What would you have done if I hadn't been here when the GrandGoods proposal came in? If I hadn't been here to tell you expressly what it could mean?"

"I'd have fought it, regardless."

"How? Would you have mobilized the citizenry? Even thought to get an economic impact study? Would you have had the grounds to delay things this far?"

A muscle in his jaw jumped. "I don't know."

Norah nodded. "You're out of your depth. You knew that when you asked me to stay. Now I know this is frustrating. It's not what we'd hoped for. But this is just a battle, Cam. It's not the war."

"They're not going to listen. They don't *want* to listen. How can you possibly combat that?"

All the Campbells had similar streaks of mulish stubbornness. After years of living with Miranda, Norah was well-versed in the various shades of that expression, so she knew she wasn't making a dent. She shifted tactics. "What were you doing when you were fifteen?"

"What?"

"When you were fifteen. What were you doing? School? Sports? Dating? Getting your learner's permit to drive?"

"Yeah, all that, I guess. Why?"

"When I was fifteen, I was in Cincinnati with my mom. Public school. New kid...again. And I still managed to get elected class president. While in office, I used my position to orchestrate the clean up and rehab of half a dozen inner-city playgrounds and started an urban gardening initiative that's still in operation. Sixteen was Philadelphia. Dad that year. Catholic school. I was a youth activist for the ACLU. Seventeen, I was in Boston with Mom again. Private school. I interned with Amnesty International. Oh, followed by a summer internship at the Smithsonian while Dad was in D.C. arguing with Congress. So while you got to live your life and be a normal teenager who did normal teenager things, I was being shaped and trained to be an extension of my parents' successes. That is what my parents expected of me. Because that's what Burkes are supposed to do. We save the world. Except not me.

"No, I eschewed Harvard, avoided law school, ran from med school. I built a god-damned good career in a field that has absolutely nothing to do with the humanitarian background my parents gave me. A fact which my father, in particular, takes great pains to remind me is a waste of my potential and the advantages they worked to give me. When he's not busy cross-examining me about my decisions. That's what he said to me when I finally talked to him yesterday. That he was *disappointed* in me. That he expected *better* of me. After all but demanding the legal documents related to the sordid affair of Morton to prove I didn't actually know anything underhanded was taking place."

Miranda made an inarticulate sound of rage—the same emotion Norah could see echoed in Cam's face.

"Your father's an asshole." She appreciated the growl in his voice that said exactly what he'd like to do to her dad.

"He's an idealist with a very explicitly defined vision that doesn't take anyone else's wants into account. And he happens to know exactly which ribs to shove the knife between to try to manipulate me into doing what he wants. The fact is, he's right. After everything that happened in Morton, *I* expect better of me. I *was* given every advantage, every possible form of training to do great things, to take on any challenge and come out the victor. I may disagree with my parents on the nature of what those great things are, but through circumstance or fate or the alignment of the goddamn stars, I was brought here, right now, for this." *For you.* The certainty of the thought gave her pause, but she didn't voice it. "I have exactly the skillset and the indefatigable ego needed for the job. I may not be saving the world by my parents' standards, but by damn I'm going to save yours. So you have five more minutes to waste on this useless pity party before I expect you to get your ass back to work. Do I make myself clear?"

From somewhere behind her, Mitch said, "And though she be but wee, she is mighty."

Norah felt her lips twitch, but didn't look away from Cam.

"Are you always this fearless?"

Fearless. What a joke. But Norah supposed it probably did look like that from the outside. Because she acted rather than standing paralyzed in the face of challenge.

"Courage isn't the absence of fear, but rather the judgment that something else is more important. Wishful is more important." And so was Cam, though Norah didn't give voice to that thought either.

"What about your job search?"

"I made you a promise, and I intend to keep it. If that means further damage to my career, then at least I'll be able to sleep at night." She turned away because she couldn't bear the hopeless expression on his face. "Mitch, can you move those site visits this afternoon?"

"I can and will. What are your orders, my general?"

"You're coming with me." She pulled out her phone and dialed before the plan had fully solidified in her brain.

"Edison Hardware."

"Tyler, it's Norah. Have you got somebody who can man the store for a few hours?"

"I can call in Dad. What's up?"

"I need your design skills."

Norah could hear the other woman's interest pique. "For what?"

A miracle. "Tell you when I get there. Mitch and I will be in to pick you up in half an hour."

She called Molly next, arranged for the coalition chair to meet them downtown. Then and only then did she turn to Cam. He hadn't moved from where she'd interrupted his pacing. She couldn't read his shuttered expression, couldn't tell if she'd crossed a line or pissed him off.

"Five minutes are up. Are you coming?"

"There's something else I need to do first." Without another glance her way, he stalked from the room.

Speechless, she stared after him. He'd walked away. She didn't know what she'd wanted, exactly. For him to leap enthusiastically back into the cause. To say, "I trust you. I'm sorry I doubted. What next?" To say he believed in her and her ability to pull this off. To show *any* kind of willingness to keep fighting. Because, Lord knew, she could use some of that support right now.

But maybe he didn't believe.

And that meant she'd failed where it mattered most.

Aunt Liz wrapped an arm around Norah's shoulders. "He'll come around."

Norah wasn't at all sure that he would. But that was a disappointment that would have to wait until she'd finished her own fight.

HUSH'S BERSERKER mode let Cam know that Norah had finally come in search of him, despite the drizzling rain. He continued to sip at his beer, simply calling out, "It's open!" when she knocked.

The fruits of the afternoon's labor sat in a neat stack on the counter, highlighted and cross referenced with the same level of precision he expected from Norah herself. He wasn't leaving anything open to misinterpretation. Giving this to her at all was a calculated risk. But it was one he had to take or he wouldn't be able to live with himself. She had a right to know.

Though she lit up in response to the dog, Norah had lost her smile by the time she made it through the gauntlet of Hush's enthusiastic greeting and crossed the room. "You never made it downtown." Her tone was cool.

"Sorry. I had some Council business to take care of."

One delicate brow arched.

"The firm that did the impact study will be attending the hearing when it's scheduled." No reason for her to think he was bailing now.

"Good. Were they difficult to track down?"

Translation: *Where were you the rest of the afternoon?*

"No. I was also working on lining up a second evaluation. Avery's boyfriend, Dillon, is working on his MBA up at Ole Miss. He's checking to see if any of his professors could do it, or know of someone who can. There's also the possibility of getting one or more of them to the hearing to rebut based on the literature, even if we don't manage to get a full second evaluation. We should hear something in a day or two."

Her poker face melted into a smile of approval. "Excellent."

Cam hesitated. "There's something else. I was following up on some leads."

She sat at the counter. "On what?"

"I think it's better if you read that for yourself." He handed the sheaf of papers to her. "I highlighted the relevant passages."

Her long, graceful fingers flexed at the edges of the paper as she read the letterhead: *City of Morton, Indiana.* The blood drained out of her cheeks, only to creep back up from her neck in a flush of shame. Not the reaction he'd expected, and not at all his intention.

"Where did you get this?" Her words came out in a thin, almost whisper. She didn't look up, didn't turn past the cover letter.

"I made some calls. Skip to the highlighted stuff."

She didn't skip ahead. She read through every line, and Cam struggled not to rush her.

Neon yellow highlighter screamed from the page. Norah's flush faded as she read it. Her hands fumbled, flipping to the next page and the next, reading the evidence he'd gathered. It all painted a pretty damning picture. Of Philip Vargas.

Fumbling gave way to stillness as she read the final page. She drew a shuddering breath and laid the paperwork on the counter with the same careful deliberation she might use handling a bomb. A sure sign she was trying to control some strong emotion. Cam expected relief or shock, or maybe even anger. But when

Norah lifted her head, the mask of professionalism was shattered by…pain.

Thinking perhaps she'd misunderstood, Cam leapt to reassure. "It wasn't you. That proves it."

She just shook her head. "Only you. Only you would think to do this."

Something was horribly wrong. He'd made some egregious miscalculation. This wasn't how she was supposed to react.

"Norah—"

"You make this so goddamned *hard,*" she whispered, fisting both hands and pressing them to her eyes.

What?

Stunned, Cam could only watch as Norah shoved back from the counter, movements no longer controlled or precise. Her hands trembled as she grabbed up the paperwork. "What the hell am I supposed to do with this?" Her eyes glimmered with unshed tears, but there was also an underlying heat he didn't understand

"Do with it?"

"Other men give flowers or jewelry. And you hand me absolution. *No one* else would think to chase this down. No one else would even know how."

"What you said about your dad wanting evidence gave me the idea. It's all a matter of public record. I just had one of their city councilmen copy it all for me."

"Of course you did." She threw her hands toward the ceiling in a gesture of…what? Exasperation? "I am trying so, so hard to do the right thing here. I can resist your charm. I can resist your dimples. I can resist the chemistry between us, though I've lost sleep over it. But this—" She shook the papers now crushed in her hand. "—how am I supposed to defend against this?"

Cam's brain was starting to catch up to hers. Maybe. "I didn't do it because I expected something from you. You made your position clear. I did it because I can't stand to see you beating yourself up over something that I knew couldn't be your fault. You have a right to know the truth."

"I know. I know, and that makes it almost worse somehow. Because that's who you are. This honorable, thoughtful, amazing man. Still taking care of me, even though I pushed you away." She sounded furious about that as she whirled away to pace. "I thought it would be easier if I stayed away from you. As if that was going to stop everything in its tracks. But it hasn't. God, it hasn't." One hand rubbed absently at her chest, as if to ease an ache. "I see you every day and I try to pretend that you fit the same niche as Mitch or Reed. But you don't. And, damn it, my resolve is only so strong."

Relief and hope struggled for dominance in his chest. "Well, thank God for that. I've been waiting for you to come to your senses for a month. I don't understand why you thought we should fight this in the first place."

"I told you—"

"Yes, you *told* me. *You* decided that breaking

things off was the right thing. But the right thing for who, Norah?"

"You!"

"Why?"

"Because you deserve so much more than a relationship with an expiration date."

"Why are you so certain there's gonna be one?"

"Didn't you listen to *anything* I said to you a month ago?"

"I listened to a whole lot of bullshit about how you were always going to leave. But you didn't say whatever you were really thinking. Something flipped that switch for you. Was it Miranda? Did she warn you off? Say we were a bad idea?"

She shook her head. "She didn't have to. I know we're a bad idea."

"Why? Make your case, Norah. Make me understand why you won't give this a chance."

He watched her try to pull together the professionalism she so often wore like armor, hated that she felt a need for it.

"I'm a bad bet. I can't be what you need, what you really want."

"What is it you think that is?"

"You're meant for marriage and family. Children. A traditional life."

The image of a little girl with his eyes and her dark curls, crowned with a big pink bow, came fast and clear in his mind.

"That's not me, Cam."

Her words of denial did nothing to stop the picture that had taken root and begun to bloom. He could see it so easily, almost as easily as he could see a truth about her that she didn't even see herself. "I've never met anyone who wants marriage and family and roots more than you. You want all the things you didn't have growing up or you wouldn't find my crazy family so appealing." Unable to stop himself, he reached out, slid a hand around her nape and tilted her face up toward his. "You *fit here*. Can't you see that?"

"It's an illusion. I'm career and ambition. Things I can't pursue here, not really."

"You're more than that."

"Am I? Or is it that you can't believe I could be like Melody?"

Whatever argument he'd thought she'd pull out, it wasn't that. "Leaving aside the fact that I've never actually told you about my ex and that my family is apparently a bunch of incurable gossips, that's absolute bullshit."

"Really? Bright. Top of my class. Ruthlessly ambitious. Always with an eye on bigger, better things. That all applies to me as much as it did to her."

"On the surface, maybe it does. But it's all in the execution, in what those traits drove her to do. Melody would never have put her career on hold to save this town. You're *nothing* like her."

The stubborn jut to Norah's chin said she wasn't buying it. How could he convince her that this comparison was complete lunacy?

"If you'd been with me when I dropped out of grad school because my mother had cancer, would you have gone off to Northwestern anyway?"

"Of course not. I'd have deferred enrollment and been right there with you, while I had my mother pulling every contact she had to get your mom in to see the best cancer specialists in the country, instead of just stopping with a few phone calls."

Cam's brain ground to a halt as her words sank in. He thought back to those panicked weeks after the diagnosis, the talk of waiting lists and more exams, and all the roadblocks that stood between them and the aggressive treatment his mother needed. And then they'd seemed to disappear. "That's how she got into MD Anderson so fast, isn't it? You made that call."

Norah shrugged. "Sure. What's the point in being related to one of the top surgeons in the country if you can't actually use those connections when it matters? It was important to your family, and your family's important to me. It was the right thing to do."

His heart was thudding so fast and hard as the ramifications unfolded in his mind. That one small action on her part might've been the thing that kept his mother from dying. Cam framed her face with careful hands and lowered his forehead to hers. "Jesus. You did what you could to help, and you hadn't even met me yet. That's who you are. Melody walked away when I needed her most. You're *nothing* like her."

Norah lifted her hands, curled them around his forearms. "I'm enough like her to be bad for you."

"While I appreciate the sentiment, that isn't your call. It should be *my* choice. And I choose you."

A strange mix of pleasure and pain flickered across her face. Had anyone ever put her first? Not her parents. Certainly not her asshole ex.

"I'll always choose you. Because you're worth the risk."

She was wavering, his name a plea on her lips.

"What are you so afraid of, Norah?"

"You," she whispered. "You call me fearless, but I'm not. Not when it comes to this. I'm terrified of how you make me feel. Because you tempt me. You make me want things I've never wanted before, make me see how my mother got seduced into believing that marriage and family was what *she* wanted. I don't want to be like her, don't want to chase this beautiful thing and then wake up one day and realize I'm suffocating and have to get out. I have that potential in me, and I can't—*won't* risk hurting you like that. You've had enough important people walk away from you."

"The fact that you're even worried about this proves just how different from them you are. You're not like Melody. You're not like my father or your mother. You're not doomed to making any of the same mistakes or choices."

"But—"

"But nothing. Am I afraid there's a chance this won't pan out? Sure. That's a possibility in any relationship. But you said yourself, courage isn't the absence of fear. It's the judgment that something else is more important. This is more important. *You're* more important, and I choose to take the risk. Take it with me."

Cam watched the last of her resolve crumble. And at long last, she melted into him, sliding her hands up his shoulders and lifting her mouth toward his.

For the first time tears tasted sweet.

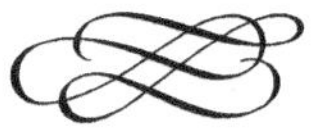

ORAH WAS RUNNING LATE. Her meeting in Oxford had taken longer than expected, but the end results were well worth it. Come Saturday, they just might pull off her lunatic scheme.

The downside was she had to head straight to Grammy's for family dinner, where Cam was supposed to have broken the news about their involvement. Terror at the family's possible reactions dimmed the effervescent thrill of finally giving in and letting herself want, letting herself have. If this relationship blew up in their faces, they'd keep Cam. He was blood. But where would that leave her? Cut off from the family she was closer to than her own?

Maybe it would be fine, as he expected. He was so blithely unconcerned about what they thought. But just in case, she'd been mentally rehearsing her defense. Not that the Campbells would ever put her on the witness stand like her father, but a lifetime of training was hard to break.

"Now or never," she muttered, stepping inside.

The babble of voices and laughter led her back to the living room. Norah didn't let herself linger in the hall trying to gauge the mood. She could already hear some heated debate going on about the last Mississippi State basketball game. Whatever they thought about her and Cam, it wasn't the current topic of conversation.

"Sorry I'm late."

"Welcome back. How was Oxford?" Miranda had to raise her voice to be heard over her uncle.

"I don't even want to talk about the traffic. They've completely changed how you go through part of campus. I wound up somewhere by the football stadium trying to get out. But I got Ajax for lunch, so win."

"Squash dressing and jalapeno cornbread make up for a multitude of sins."

Okay, so nobody was looking at her weird. That was positive.

Cam rose from where he'd been slouched in a chair beside the door. He cupped the back of her neck and brought her mouth to his. Her body gave one, quick jolt before she melted against him. Mindful of their audience, she didn't give in to the urge to dive deeper, but her hands were fisted in his shirt as he eased back. He was grinning, and Norah found herself grinning foolishly in response.

"Hi," he said.

"Hi back."

"How did your mystery meeting go?"

"Really well, I…" Norah trailed off, realizing the room had fallen dead silent. She could feel the weight of eyes, sense the shock along her skin, though she didn't look away from Cam. "You didn't tell them."

"I've always been a much bigger fan of showing than telling." He was still grinning, entirely unrepentant.

Though exasperation warred with nerves, she kept her voice light. "Here's a lesson from the professional: When your audience looks like you just dropped an atomic bomb, you need to work on your delivery."

He dragged his gaze from her to take in the reactions she hadn't gotten up the courage to face. The grin faded, chased away by confusion and the first sparks of anger. Norah felt his tension ratchet up to match hers.

As bad as she'd feared then.

With a bracing breath, Norah squared her shoulders and stepped back to face the music with all the gravity and enthusiasm of meeting a firing squad. When she would've stood alone,

Cam laced his fingers through hers and stepped up beside her. A unified front. She squeezed his hand, grateful for the support.

Grammy's eyebrows were lost somewhere under her fluffy silver bangs. Miranda remained completely unreadable. Everyone else's eyes were round as dinner plates. Only Aunt Liz looked positively ecstatic, her lips curved, her hands clasped as if she'd clapped them in delight. Sandra apparently wasn't here yet.

"Seriously?" Mitch gaped. "You and Cam?"

"Me and Cam." Despite the awkward situation, saying it still gave her a little thrill.

"Did not call that one," Reed said.

"Well they have been spending a lot of time together with the coalition," Aunt Liz pointed out.

"Yeah but—" Anita trailed off. "Are you sure this is wise?"

"Wise?" Cam's voice dropped to one step above a growl.

Before he popped off to tell his aunt exactly where she could shove her opinions on the wisdom of their relationship, Norah pivoted into him, laying a hand on his chest. "Don't. They love you. They've got a right to their concerns."

The temper in his eyes didn't cool. "I'm not just gonna stand here and—"

"Campbell, stop." She framed his face. "You've already slain my dragon. They're not insulting me. They're not attacking me. And I guarantee they don't have a single objection I didn't already throw at you. You won me over. Let me win them. I came prepared for this. You're not used to being cross-examined and forced to defend your decisions. I am."

"You don't have to defend anything." Miranda looked horrified at the very idea.

Norah shifted to face her. "You're right, I don't. I don't owe y'all an explanation or promises or justification. But I'll give them anyway because I love and respect this family and the place you've given me in it over the years. So please, just listen."

She paused to pull her thoughts together,

steadied when Cam slid an arm around her waist.

"I know I'm not what you want for him." Several of them started to speak, but Norah just held up a hand. "I'm not. You'd like to see him with some local girl with roots dug as deep as his. Somebody content with a traditional role of wife and mother, who doesn't have the kind of aspirations that would ever pull her—or him —away from here. And I don't blame you for that. Everybody who ever mattered put their ambitions before him. You want assurances that I'll never do that, and I can't give them.

"I *am* ambitious and competitive and very, very good at what I do. I was raised to be that way by two brilliant, broken people who wouldn't recognize a functional, healthy relationship if it knocked them over the head. The only thing they ever taught me about relationships is that they're secondary. That personal wants take a backseat to the greater good. And you know what? I'm done." It felt good to say it, to *mean* it. "I'm done being selfless. I'm done being rational and logical and thinking fifteen steps ahead of everybody else. I'm done living my life based on someone else's expectations.

"The fact is, Cam's the best man I know." Norah looked up, met his eyes, because the rest of this was as much for him as his family. "He matters. More than anyone ever has, or I wouldn't still be here. I don't have the first clue how this is going to work in the long term, but I'm sure as hell not going to apologize for not being willing to walk away from the chance to find out."

"Nor should you have to."

Norah closed her eyes and wished the sudden burst of mortification had enough gravitational force to suck her into the ground. Of course. Of *course* Sandra was standing right behind them. Why that was somehow worse than baring her soul to the rest of the Campbell clan, Norah didn't quite know, but as Sandra came into the room, circling past them, Norah's ears burned, and the pulse that had calmed by taking control of the situation began to thump erratically. She forced herself to stand straight and meet the other woman's gaze instead of tucking into Cam to hide. He stood close, pressed against her back. A solid support but not an unnecessary shield.

"Allow me to apologize for the rest of the family for making you feel uncomfortable and like you needed to defend yourself. It was wholly unnecessary. You aren't careless with people, Norah. I certainly don't think you'll be careless with Cam, particularly as you know exactly what it feels like to be second to someone else's ambitions."

Norah opened her mouth, closed it again. That wasn't an insight she'd expected from someone in this family, and she didn't know what to say, so she inclined her head in acknowledgment of the point.

"I think it's high time *both* of you were a little selfish, and I, for one, am glad you've stopped dancing around each other."

"Wait, you knew?" Cam sounded so affronted.

Sandra shot him an amused look. "Of course, I knew. I'm your mother."

"How?"

"The same way I knew you, Tucker, and Brody rolled Aggie Crockett's yard after she gave you a B on your midterm in trig. I just know."

Norah felt Cam's jolt of surprise and almost laughed, thinking of his complaint about how hard it was to get away with anything growing up.

Sandra turned to Norah and took her free hand. "It's a smart thing for a mother to learn to care for the woman her son chooses. It's a real gift to legitimately like and respect her. I've had occasion to know the difference. So, not that you need it, but consider this my blessing."

Absolutely flummoxed and moved by the show of support, Norah could only stammer. "I —thank you."

Releasing Norah, Sandra cheerfully turned to the rest of the family. "Mom, the pot roast smells amazing. Please tell me there are mashed potatoes."

"Only a boatload."

"Excellent. I'm starving."

DINNER WAS A STRANGELY NORMAL AFFAIR, which left Norah feeling completely off balance.

"So, who are you kids taking to the Valentine's dance?" Sandra asked.

Norah laughed, assuming she was teasing to keep the tone light.

Then Reed spoke up. "Lynnette Rainey."

"Isn't she one of the members of your book club?" Miranda passed the platter of roast beef.

"She is. Which means I won't get bored."

Mitch dumped a healthy lake of gravy on his mashed potatoes and pot roast. "Cuz, if you need a book club assignment to keep you from getting bored on a date, you clearly need to revisit the definition of date."

"It's a PG function, son," Uncle Pete said.

Baffled, Norah looked around the table. "Did I step into a Twilight Zone episode set back in high school?"

"Wishful has an annual Valentine's dance," Aunt Liz explained. "Here, have a roll."

Norah took one and passed the bread basket to Cam on her right. "Really?"

"Since we don't have a lot of the things people in big cities do for the occasion, we make our own fun," Sandra said. "Old school style. It's a nice change from the winter doldrums."

"I'm afraid most of my knowledge of school dances comes from John Hughes movies."

"You never went to a high school dance?" Cam looked appalled.

"I'm sorry, have we had *any* conversation that would lead you to believe that I did anything normal in high school?"

"Not even prom?"

"It may shock you to know that high school boys found me intimidating. Apparently the fact that I didn't feel the need to hide my brain was a turn off."

"Bless your heart. We need to rectify some of these holes in your life experience." Cam lifted her hand and adopted a hopeful expression. "So will you and your devastatingly attractive brain be my valentine?"

Charmed, she repressed a grin and pretended to consider. "And what exactly would that entail?"

"Drinking probably spiked punch—"

"Definitely spiked. Tucker's coming," Mitch said.

"—and dancing under crepe paper banners and construction paper hearts in the community center gym. It'll be completely cheesetastic, nostalgic, and—"

"Perfect." Norah kissed his cheek. "Though we'll all be up early on Saturday for work."

"Ah yes, your mysterious plan. And when are you going to let us in on the rest of it?"

"On Saturday. Everybody knows what they

need to know. The rest is a surprise." And she was still working out some of the details.

"So not even a clue as to what you were doing in Oxford today?"

"Not a one."

"Cam hates surprises," Sandra said. "I used to have to hide his Christmas presents at friends' houses because he'd get into the closet and peek under the wrapping paper. As if I wasn't going to be able to tell he'd untaped the end."

"I was eight!"

"I caught you doing that at thirteen."

"Well it was an important year. I had to know if I was getting the new Nintendo."

"And did you?" Norah asked.

"Eventually. After I caught him snooping, I decided he'd have to wait until his birthday for that one," Sandra said.

"I thought she'd returned it. And after I'd saved my allowance to buy two games so that I could play on Christmas Day."

"You never peeked again, did you?"

"No ma'am. I learned my lesson. Still hate surprises, though. Unless they're related to dessert." Cam looked hopefully at Grammy.

"There might be pecan pie and ice cream. But clean up, first."

"The boys have dish duty," Miranda declared. "I'm stealing Norah."

Nothing in her tone suggested she was angry, but Norah felt the anxiety creep back up her spine. Of everyone, Miranda's was the reaction she was most worried about. As they pushed back from the table, Cam skimmed a hand down her shoulder. No matter what, he'd be waiting for her on the other side. Bolstered, she followed Miranda out to the sun porch.

They sat on the glider swing, toeing it into motion in tandem. When the strain of silence became too much, Norah said, "I'm sorry I didn't tell you."

"I'm guessing you don't mean tonight. How long has this thing with you and Cam been going on?"

"That's a little complicated to answer."

"Before this GrandGoods campaign?"

Better to bring out the truth now than never. "Pretty much since the moment we met."

"New Year's?"

Norah nodded.

"Really? Why didn't you say anything?"

"Initially, because I was blind-sided. I certainly didn't come down here looking for a relationship. Everybody knew I was fresh off a break up with Pierce, and I didn't want anyone to think I was using Cam for some kind of rebound."

Miranda was quiet for a moment. "I wasn't so much worried about that, but I wouldn't have pegged you as being in a good place for a relationship. Which I told Cam flat out."

Norah's heart gave a sick lurch. "You warned him off me?"

"Not because I think you're bad for him or vice versa but just…I saw how he looked at you, and I could see a lot of potential for hurt on both sides."

Norah absorbed that as the glider continued

to rock. "Well, you aren't wrong. Things got really serious, really fast, and I didn't know what to do about it. I was still trying to work out what to do about my career, and, frankly, I didn't think the family would approve of the idea of me with Cam. So when he asked me to stay for this war against GrandGoods, I broke things off."

"You ended things because of me. Because of everything we said that night about Melody. You thought we'd compare you to her."

"On the surface, it isn't an inappropriate comparison."

"God, Norah, I'm sorry. I'd never in a million years think you'd do to him what she did. You're nothing like her."

"That's what Cam said. But even without that, I thought stopping things before they went any further was best for both of us. It's an impossible relationship. He's small town and I'm big city. I know perfectly well he's part of the fabric of this place. I'd never dream of asking him to leave it. And Wishful doesn't exactly have need of a high-powered marketing executive under normal circumstances. I'd never be cruel about it, but my leaving at some point seemed pretty inevitable, and I didn't want to hurt him."

"So what changed?"

"Nothing. And everything." Norah sighed and laughed a little. "Breaking things off didn't make me any less crazy about him. With all the time we've spent together, I didn't do anything but make us both miserable by holding us apart. And then yesterday…Do you know what he did?"

"Does this have something to do with that whole dragon slaying thing you mentioned?"

"He got in touch with the City Council of Morton and got copies of all the paperwork related to their consideration and approval of Hugo's, and he dug through all of it until he found proof that it wasn't me who convinced them to change the terms. It was my boss. He not only found hard-core exculpatory evidence—Miranda, he had the whole thing highlighted and sticky tabbed as thoroughly as I would."

Miranda's lips twitched. "It's a wise man who recognizes the key to your heart lies in color-coded organization."

"How can I not fall for a man like that?"

"I'd say you'd be pretty hard pressed. Are you in love with him?"

She'd vowed she'd be honest. "If I wasn't already, I'm pretty sure I took a swan dive off that cliff without a parachute last night. It's completely insane. Every single objection I raised is still valid, every problem still an issue. But I know if I don't go after this with everything I've got, I'll regret it for the rest of my life."

"Love isn't supposed to be sane and logical. You'll figure the rest of it out. Problems without solutions are your specialty, remember?"

"Yeah. I may need you to keep reminding me of that when I start to freak out."

"I can do that." She leaned forward and tugged Norah into a hard hug. "For the record,

I think you two will be great together. Melody wasn't right for him, not because she was ambitious but because she was a bitch."

Norah laughed. "Good to know."

"Now come on. If we want to score any pie, we'd better get back in there."

CHAPTER 13

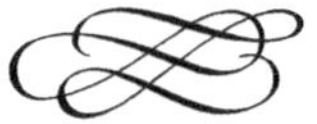

"**Y**OU BROUGHT ME A corsage." This was said in a tone of *awww*, accompanied by a look of stunned pleasure on Norah's face that completely eradicated the feeling of idiocy Cam had felt on buying it.

"Well, it's part of that whole dance experience. It seemed the thing to do. I wasn't sure what you'd be wearing, so I figured wrist made more sense than something you pinned on. You look amazing, by the way." He had a soft spot for that little black dress from New Year's, now sans Hush hair and paired with some short jacket that stopped at the base of her shoulders.

"Put it on." Beaming, she held out her wrist and waited while he fastened on the simple red rose corsage.

"It's a bit trite, but Trudy up in the floral section of McSweeney's Market doesn't have a whole lot to work with. We don't have a proper florist anymore."

"It's perfect." Her eyes, deep and dark and serious, searched his for a long moment before she rose to brush her lips over his, a feat much more easily managed in the heels she wore. "God, you're sweet. Thank you."

He was feeling something in response to that kiss but sweet wasn't it.

"Just let me go grab my coat." She sprinted up the stairs at a speed that should've been impossible in the ridiculous and very sexy shoes.

Miranda picked up her purse. "You know, I feel like part of me should be gagging at the cuteness here, but the pair of you are just too adorable."

"Is that approval, cuz?"

"That was exceptionally thoughtful."

Cam shrugged. "It's just a flower."

"Admittedly it doesn't top digging up evidence clearing her of blame for what happened in Morton, but still, thoughtful. It's normal. She hasn't had a lot of that in her life.

"Too many people look at her and see what she can do, not who she is. And she's spent a long damned time buying into it. I aim to change that, give her a little balance."

Miranda studied him with open curiosity. "You get her. Most people don't. They like her, are impressed by her, but they don't understand her."

They don't love her. He cast a glance back up the stairs. "I've been waiting for her all my life."

Miranda gave an uncharacteristically watery, "Oh, Cam" as she reached up to cup his face.

He gave her a squeeze. "Jesus, don't cry. You'll mess up your makeup."

"I'm allowed to get emotional over the fact

that my favorite cousin is in love with my best friend."

"Yeah well, pull yourself together. I'm not ready to tell her yet. She's wigged out enough about how fast this is moving."

"Fair enough. A word of advice, though, as somebody who's known her a lot longer than you. If she balks or tries to run, go after her. Hang on. No one else ever has."

Norah's footsteps from upstairs put a stop to any reply he might've made. She descended the stairs at a considerably more sedate pace, a coat draped over one arm and a bulging messenger bag slung over her shoulder. "Sorry. I had to throw some things together."

Cam eyed the bag with suspicion. "If that's more of your folders and legal pads, we're going to have to have a serious talk."

She stopped in front of him with a slow, sexy smile. "Talking wasn't what I had in mind."

His mouth went dry.

Miranda did an abrupt about face. "I'll take my own car."

"Don't wait up," Norah murmured. As the door shut behind his cousin, she said, "When I make up my mind about something, I'm all in." When he said nothing, the smiled dimmed a fraction. "Is this okay? It seemed more practical than getting up an hour earlier than the crack of dawn to come back over here for clothes before our work day tomorrow."

He gripped her hips, already imagining the feel of bare skin. "God bless your practical soul."

She blocked his mouth with two fingers. "Oh no. If you get that mouth on me, we won't make it to the dance."

"I fail to see the problem with this plan."

"You promised me crepe paper streamers and construction paper hearts. I expect you to deliver."

Cam sucked in a long breath and worked on chaining down his roaring libido. "So I did."

"Besides—" She scraped one nail lightly down the column of his throat to trace his collarbone. "—there's something to be said for anticipation."

"Yeah, it just might kill me." He opened the front door. "Get in the truck, woman, before I go all caveman and throw you over my shoulder."

"Promises promises."

With a considerable show of self restraint, Cam drove to the community center rather than back to his place. He had himself under control—mostly—and was calculating how long it would take to give her the classic high school dance experience before he moved her along to their private after party, when the sound of raised voices spilled out along with music from the open door.

"What on earth?" Norah asked.

Cam quickened his pace. The last thing they needed was some kind of fight breaking out.

"Now Jim, nobody wants any ugliness." Mamie Landen, who sported a lemon yellow hairdo tall enough to commune with God on its own, had both hands fisted on her generous hips.

Jim Vernon, one of Vick's cronies, stood before the ticket table, red-faced and sputtering, while his wife looked on with pinched lips. "It ain't right."

"What's the trouble here?" Cam asked.

"They've gone and doubled the cover in the name of a 'fund raiser.'" Jim actually used air quotes.

Cam looked to Mamie for explanation.

"The dance committee decided to use this as an opportunity for an additional fundraiser for the coalition. Half the proceeds go toward the cost of the party, the other half to the downtown revitalization project." She turned a glare on Jim. "It's a good cause."

It was also the first Cam was hearing of it. A quick glance at Norah said she'd been unaware of the plan as well. He slipped out his wallet and offered Mamie a smile. "Two please."

"That'll be forty dollars."

Cam slid out two twenties and passed them

over. "A small price to pay for a good cause and a night out with my best girl. There's nothin' like dancing cheek to cheek with your sweetheart, with the lights down low and good music playin', don't you think, Jim?"

Plainly Jim didn't agree, but his wife Irene turned that pinched expression on him, arms crossed.

"We oughta be able to choose whether or not to donate."

"That wouldn't make for a very effective fundraiser. Nobody's making you pay anything. You're welcome to turn right back around and leave. But if you expect to see your favorite fried chicken any time in the next decade, you'll quit being a cheapskate and bring your wife in to enjoy the party."

Evidently realizing the wisdom of this advice, Jim stopped arguing and pulled out his wallet.

"We appreciate your community spirit. Y'all have a good time." Crisis averted, Cam took Norah's hand and tugged her toward the gym.

"I wonder how many people have had that reaction?"

They stepped inside to find a packed dance floor and at least a hundred people crowded around the tables. "Not that many."

The promised crepe paper streamers and construction paper hearts dripped from the ceiling, but the dance committee had classed the place up a bit this year with the addition of little tea light candles and mason jars of flowers on each of the covered tables. Adele's second in command, Joe Fowler, manned a cash bar adjacent to the punch station. A DJ was set up at one end of the gym. On the dance floor, a trio of older women were shaking their collective groove thing, gyrating with their hands in the air as Sir Mix-a-lot's "Baby Got Back" rocked out over the PA. As he watched, one of them began to twerk.

"Oh God," Cam grimaced. "I could've gone my whole life and not seen that."

"She's got better rhythm than I do."

"Shut your mouth. That's my seventh grade

English teacher, Mrs. Jennings. She usually doesn't get that…enthusiastic until after several glasses of wine."

"You've had occasion to see that before?"

"She cuts loose at every non-Baptist wedding reception where there's alcohol." Spying a pack of old ladies headed their way, he wrapped an arm around Norah's waist and said, "Brace yourself. You were worried about the family. You didn't give a single thought to our debut to the rest of the town."

She laughed. "What?"

"It's the Casserole Patrol." He pasted a smile in place to greet them.

Without preamble, Miss Betty Monroe asked, "Did you try my Jello mold?"

"I'm afraid we haven't had the opportunity. We just got here." He began introductions, but Miss Maudie Bell Ramsey rolled right on over him.

"Well, of course, we know who Norah is. Glad to see you've got the good sense to snatch her up."

"Been wonderin' who was going to take you off the market after all this time," Delia Watson said. "S'pose it makes sense. If you were gonna pick a local, you'd have done it by now. Who are your people, honey?"

Before he could come up with a means of rescuing Norah from the question, she launched in, explaining that while her mother was a Royce from Charlotte, NC, her father hailed from Bay St. Louis. "His family went way back in the area, so I actually have very old Mississippi roots."

"Do you still have kin there?"

"My grandparents passed when I was little. I don't think there are any relatives still there now. At least not more than distant cousins I've never met."

"Burke." Miss Maudie Bell tapped her chin in thought. "That wouldn't happen to be Benjamin Burke, would it?"

"Anderson. Benjamin was his first cousin on his daddy's side, I think."

There followed a complicated discussion

about how Miss Maudie Bell's family was connected to Norah's.

Cam stroked a thumb over the pulse in her wrist and felt it jump, though she didn't falter in saying her grandmother had been a Fitzpatrick before her marriage.

"So I reckon that makes us third or fourth cousins, twice removed," Miss Maudie Bell concluded in triumph. "See there, bet you didn't know you had family here."

"No, I certainly didn't! Not beyond the Campbells, whom I'm not *actually* related to."

Miss Betty beamed at the pair of them. "Oh, I expect that won't stay the case too long."

Miss Delia nudged Miss Maudie Bell conspiratorially. "These two will make beautiful babies, don't you think?"

Norah froze, mouth half open, cheeks flushing pink.

Cam was searching for a polite way to redirect the conversation when his mother's personal assistant neatly inserted herself into the conversation, laying a hand on Cam's arm. "I'm sorry, ladies, I need to steal the Councilman and Norah. City business."

Cam could've kissed her. He offered a rueful smile to the Casserole Patrol. "Duty calls. Excuse us."

Avery led them through the crowd to where Dillon had a table staked out. She made quick introductions and sat, accepting the glass of punch he offered. "You looked like you needed rescuing."

"I'm pretty sure they just married us off and gave us 2.5 kids."

"Five more minutes and the kids would be named and their college funds started." Cam turned to Avery, "You're getting a raise. I don't know where we're finding the money, but I owe you."

"Feel free to bring that up at the next City Council meeting. But anyway, it wasn't a lie. We have news."

Cam and Norah slid into chairs. Beneath the tablecloth, Norah laid a hand on his thigh and started to drag it higher. Tensing, he pinned her hand in place with his own and struggled to focus.

"One of my professors looked over the economic impact study," Dillon said. "It's not wrong—if this was the 1980s. Their conclusions are founded in old theories, old data. She doesn't have time to get through a full study herself before the meeting, but she'll absolutely be here to help rebut and tear them apart in the court of public opinion."

"Excellent." Norah's eyes brightened with challenge.

Cam could already see the gears in her brain starting to turn, sorting out the best means of presenting the rebuttal. Before she could get immersed in more discussion, he shoved back from the table and tugged her up. "Nope. No more work tonight. No more thinking. I brought you here to dance, and by damn, we're going to dance."

"See y'all in the morning," she called as he dragged her toward the middle of the gym.

Of course it wasn't that easy. They made it

all of fifteen feet before she got stopped by Babette Wofford of Brides and Belles.

"We have a little problem about tomorrow."

Norah gave him a look of apology. "Five minutes."

"Five minutes."

As soon as she stepped away, Tully Kauffman snagged him wanting to talk about why the trash pick up schedule should be changed. He listened with half an ear, watching as Norah crossed the room, getting stopped another four times by various other people before she made it over to Molly Montgomery and a cluster of other coalition members. She listened intently, offered some response.

"—if you switched Cedar Hills to Tuesday-Friday and put Garrett Park on Monday-Thursday..."

Five minutes turned into fifteen, then edged into twenty before Norah managed to separate herself from the group. Cam had long since stopped paying attention to Tully's treatise about the trash schedule. When Norah finally stepped away and looked at him, Cam felt the punch of it from across the room. She angled her head just slightly toward the far end of the gym where one set of the expandable bleachers was deployed.

Cam grabbed Tucker as he passed. "Tuck, didn't you need to talk to Tully about that thing?"

He didn't wait for assent before breaking away to head toward the bleachers. Norah did the same, holding his gaze as she skirted the periphery. Another half dozen people tried to stop him for one reason or another, but rudeness be damned, he kept going, never losing eye contact as they inched ever closer to their destination.

"Crawford!" Quentin Irby stepped right into his path. "I've been wanting to set up an appointment with you to talk about a new landscaping project for my wife for our thirtieth anniversary."

Mitch appeared out of nowhere, swinging an arm around Quentin's shoulders. "Now if you really want to impress Janine, you'll let me have a go at putting that sunroom off the back of the house. You know she's been wanting one for years now."

"Oh yeah?"

Cam blessed his cousin as he shook loose and made it the last twenty feet to the dark corner where Norah waited.

She pulled him underneath the bleachers. Her hands fisted in his shirt, as she dragged his mouth to hers in a long devouring kiss that had every drop of blood draining from his head. "What's the quickest way out of here?"

"I thought you wanted to dance." He tugged her head gently back so he could taste the line of her throat.

"God." She shuddered. "Changed my mind. Too many damned people here. We'll never even make it to the dance floor without being unforgivably rude."

"Then allow me to introduce you to the time-honored tradition of sneaking out past the chaperones."

NORAH ALREADY HAD Cam's sport coat off and his shirt untucked by the time they stumbled their way inside his loft. He spun her, using her body to shut the door, then pressing her up against it, cursing when he couldn't dislodge the bolero jacket.

"Give me just a second," she gasped, breathless as he ran his hands up her hips, around to cup her ass.

The floor abruptly shifted beneath them. Norah hung on, shielded from the sudden earthquake by Cam's body.

"Down. *Down,* damn it!"

Not an earthquake. Hush.

Norah reeled a little as Cam let her go and reached for the dog, who'd jumped up against his back in greeting.

"Get the damned jacket off. I'll take care of her." He yanked open the door again and dragged a whining Hush down the stairs.

"C'mon girl, there's bacon downstairs. You want some bacon?"

Norah shucked the jacket and considered stripping off the rest to speed things along. Her pulse hummed in delicious anticipation. She'd wanted him since that first night, wanted to lose herself in the heat they made together. With the feelings she'd developed since—she was all but drunk with desire.

In less than two minutes, Cam bounded back through the door, shutting and locking it. Hush howled from the barn below, sounding for all the world as if she'd been put in prison.

"I feel bad for her. She sounds so pitiful."

"We'll make it up to her," Cam assured her as he crossed the room to the stereo. "I'll fix her chicken and peanut butter. But I don't have any intention of being interrupted before morning."

"Thank God for that. I've had enough interruptions for the night."

Something slow and jazzy spilled out from the speakers to block out the sound of the dog.

"There won't be any more, so let's slow things down a bit."

She shook her head, reaching for him again and making quick work of the buttons of his shirt. "Fast now to take the edge off. Slow later." Parting the fabric, she gripped one side in each fist and pulled him to her so she could nip lightly at the tendon in his throat.

"But I like the edge." Nudging one strap of her dress down her shoulder, he followed the trail with his mouth.

Her body tightened, her breath skipping in response. "The edge makes me crazy."

"I'm gonna make you crazier." Cam backed her across the loft, toward the bedroom, sliding down the other strap. "See, I've had considerable time to think about what I wanted to do when I got you here like this."

"Oh yeah?" She shoved the shirt from his shoulders. He was beautifully made, the lean lines of his muscles sculpted from hard physical labor rather than a gym. She wanted to map him with her hands, learn his contours with her mouth.

"One thing I've noticed about you is that you never stop thinking. The wheels in that sexy brain of yours are always turning. So I've got one goal." He dragged down the zipper of her dress, until the only thing holding it up was the press of his body to hers.

"Which is?"

"To make them stop."

"That's a pretty big goal. Nobody's ever managed it."

"I think you'll find I'm up to the task." Proof of that fact pressed into her belly.

"You're up to something."

His smile spread, slow and wicked as he eased away from her to finish shedding the shirt.

Norah crossed one arm over her breast to hold the dress in place and offered a smile of her own as she backed away into one of the silvered squares of moonlight spilling through the intermittent skylights. From the shadows, she could feel Cam watching as she let the dress peel away, sliding down her body, until she stepped gingerly out of it.

"Sweet Mary, mother of God," he breathed.

"I did a little shopping when I was in Oxford."

His fingers reverently traced the line of the garters that held up the sheer, thigh high stockings. "If I'd known you were wearing this, we'd never have made it to the dance."

"If I'd known everybody and their brother was going to treat tonight as another day at the office, I'd have said we could just skip it." And yet something about the interruptions had felt good. Because it meant she was a part of something. That people trusted her enough to come to her for help.

"It's part of being in the public eye. They'll be back at it tomorrow. But not tonight. The rest of tonight is for us."

He pulled her in, his broad palms skimming up the bare skin of her back as he took her mouth in a slow drugging kiss that blurred the details of the rest of the evening. He drew the straps of her bra down and away, baring her breasts. They felt full and heavy, cupped in his calloused palms. She pressed into his touch, sweeping her tongue into his mouth, inviting the same as she struggled to take control.

But he wouldn't be rushed.

He stroked, tasted, and explored until her breath hitched and her legs trembled. Dizzy, she realized he'd lured her, one sexy step at a time into the bedroom. A wide shaft of moonlight haloed the bed. She wanted him there, wanted to watch the slick play of muscle as he moved inside her and they lost themselves to oblivion.

But Cam apparently had other ideas. He knelt before her, bringing her hands to his shoulders for balance as he slipped off first one shoe, then the other, until she stood, swaying a little in her stockinged feet. With more of that infinite patience, he detached one garter and began to roll the stocking down, following the trail with his lips.

"Christ, Cam, glaciers are faster than this."

He ran a hand up her bared leg and slid a finger beneath the edge of her panties, stroking through the drenched heat. "But glaciers aren't this hot."

Norah's legs jerked, and she swore at him as he chuckled, returning to the other stocking. She was going to incinerate before he ever finished. Every inch of her skin felt tight and hot as he finally slipped off the panties and garter belt.

He nudged her legs further apart, gripping just below her ass. "I've dreamed of having you like this, at my mercy."

The heat of his breath against her sex caused another slow pull in her belly. "I'm not seeing a lot of mercy."

"I haven't even gotten started yet." He pressed his mouth between her thighs.

The orgasm whipped through her like lightning. Gasping for breath, muscles quaking, Cam's hold was the only thing keeping her upright. She rode the knife edge between pleasure and pain, her vision blurring as he sucked and licked and drove her ruthlessly, relentlessly up again.

At the cusp of that next, brutal peak, he stopped. Norah whimpered as he eased her back from the edge, rising from his crouch to lay her, at last, on the bed. A rustle of clothes, the rip of foil, and the mattress dipped beneath his weight as he came back to her, skin against glorious skin. Opening her arms, she got her wish, watching his face in the silvered light as he slid smoothly inside her. Home.

They held there, joined and trembling, and she stared into eyes gone dark with passion.

I love you.

It was too soon to say the words, but she lay one hand over his heart and threaded the other through the hair at his nape.

He began to move, a slow retreat and thrust that seated him deeper with every stroke. Her body arched, straining for more of that exquisite friction. She murmured his name, drawing him down to take his mouth.

Sensation built upon sensation as he picked up speed, at last losing that infinite patience as he drove them up that final crest toward release. His breath went ragged, his body tensing. Wrapping her legs tight around his waist, she held him deep as he lost himself, and moments later flew joyfully over the edge behind him.

He weighed a ton. Her face pressed into his throat, breathing in the healthy scent of sweat and sex and Cam, Norah decided she was entirely okay with that. Her body felt loose and used and relaxed for—possibly the first time in her life. With a little purr, she stretched beneath him, running one foot up the back of his thigh.

"Well, you are nothing if not a man of your word."

"Mmm?"

"Apparently mine wasn't the only brain you obliterated."

"You aren't supposed to be able to form coherent sentences yet."

She nuzzled his ear. "I'm an overachiever."

"I'm starting to learn that about you. Give me a year or so, I'll catch up."

"You know, for once, I'm not on city speed. I don't want to go anywhere or do anything but stay right here with you." *For maybe the rest of my life.*

The realization had her heart kicking back into high gear. She wanted a life with him, wanted a future with him. And tonight had given her a glimpse of what that might look like. It wasn't the kind of clear-cut plan she liked, more a glimmer of possibility. But she hugged that glimmer close to her heart as she held him close to her body. A secret wish.

It was terrifying and exhilarating. And when her practical side tried to point out the problems, Norah reminded herself that if it could happen anywhere, it could happen here. Wishful was, after all, a town where wishes came true.

CHAPTER 14

"... OH, AND WE FINALLY found a venue for that fund-raiser dinner," Molly said. "Tom Thatcher's going to host it at The Spring House. It is, unfortunately, a much smaller location, so we're limited to about half the head count, but we're working on ways to maximize that."

"Then I need to finish drafting the press release for the regional newspapers." Norah checked her watch for the fifteenth time before scanning the crowd assembled on the town green. Eighty-three locals had shown in response to the call. The bulk were members of the coalition or related to someone who was. Several had tool belts slung around their hips. All were dressed for a day of hard, messy labor. While they were waiting for her instructions, most circulated through the line of the coffee station generously provided by Cassie Callister. Some of them for the second time.

It wasn't enough people to execute her plan. Not by a long shot. Molly followed her gaze but said nothing about the turnout. This was Norah's show, and the coalition chair was standing back, letting her run it.

Had her Hail Mary failed? Had the promise she'd elicited earlier in the week meant nothing? The timing hadn't been awesome, what with today being the morning after Valentine's Day, but she'd thought surely *some* of them would show.

Cam joined them where they stood across from City Hall. "The natives are getting restless."

She checked her watch again. Nearly half an hour past time to start.

Cam reached up, began to knead at her shoulders, and she leaned into him, her mind taking a quick detour to how those hands had felt, slow and languid in the hour before dawn. The morning air wasn't frigid enough to cool the blush that heated her cheeks.

"I think this is all we're gonna get, Wonder Woman. We'd best prioritize the work that needs doing and see what we can manage with this group."

Tearing her brain back to the issue at hand she said, "Just wait a little bit longer." Even she heard the trace of stubborn desperation in her voice.

"Honey, if you wait any longer, you're gonna start losing your workforce." He nodded to where a contingent had broken off and headed toward Sweet Magnolias. "We need to go ahead and get started with what we've got."

Disappointment weighed heavy as she nodded. "Who's got the bullhorn?"

Norah retrieved it from Liam. Stepping onto the ledge of the fountain, she put on her best cheerleader face as she called out, "Good morning! First off, I want to thank all of y'all for giving up your Saturday to work. We've got tons to do and a somewhat smaller group than expected, so it's important that we prioritize our projects." Since she'd been so closed-mouthed about her full plan, no one knew exactly how short they truly were on man power except for her co-conspirators, Mitch and Tyler. "The goal of this work weekend is to give downtown Wishful a makeover. We want to clean up and spiff up the area with much-needed curb appeal. In the long-term, we have plans to address each individual business on Main Street, but for today, we're going to focus on the public spaces, those that will impact everybody."

She gaged the level of interest and enthusiasm, scanning faces as she spoke. "We're going to divide you into teams based on skill sets. Those with any sort of construction experience will be working with Mitch Campbell on things like external repairs and awning replacement. Another group will be pressure washing the sidewalks and building exteriors. Others will be on trash pick up. Others on painting, once the buildings dry from their washing. The gardeners among you will be working with Cam Crawford to get trees planted and new planter boxes installed and filled. On the front end, this is all about window dressing, making down-town appealing so people will want to stop in and stay a while. We want to get people *in the door*. And if, at the end of the day, we've still got time, we'll revisit some of those individual businesses and see what we're able to ac-complish."

"And how exactly are you going to prioritize those?" called a voice from the back. "Are you the person who will make the decision which businesses are important enough to move to the front of the line?"

Norah peered through the crowd, trying to find the speaker as several folks started nodding. She struggled to maintain a friendly face as she recognized Vick Burgess. Of course he'd show up trying to sow seeds of dissension when they were already low on workers.

"All the businesses will be addressed eventually. What gets dealt with today will depend upon how much time and man power is available once the main public spaces are complete."

"But how will that be decided?"

She bit down on her temper as she noted more than a few people murmuring in agreement. They didn't need his brand of bullshit today. She'd pulled these people together and they couldn't afford to lose a single one. "Given our current turnout, the likelihood that we will make it past the public spaces today is highly unlikely. Speculation on what's to be done next is a moot point until such a time as we know we have the opportunity to do additional work. Those business owners who are in the greatest hurry are free to come speak to me after work assignments have been passed out. We'll see what we can work out."

"Why don't you just admit you've bitten off more than you can chew with this project of yours? It's pretty cruel to get everybody's hopes up and then renege on your promises."

She was going to kill him. Surely nobody would blame her if he turned up floating in Hope Springs. Except it seemed a shame to taint the springs.

"Listen—" Before she could actually give voice to the insult all but choking to get out, someone laid on their car horn. Norah turned to see an aging Grand Cherokee turning onto Main Street. Behind it came a procession of other unfamiliar vehicles. As the Jeep pulled to the curb, a blonde head rose up out of the sun roof, and Norah began to smile.

"Sorry we're late!" the girl called. "Last night's formal ran a little later than expected and we had to make a stop to roust out the boys. We didn't figure you'd mind if we brought some friends."

"The more the merrier," Norah shouted, leaping down from her post and crossing to the newcomer. Cam followed, close on her heels.

"Where should we park?"

"Tucker!" Norah called.

He bounded over, taking in the line of idling cars. "Yes'm?"

"Will you direct our volunteers over to Church Street? I've already cleared it with First Baptist and First Methodist to use their parking lots."

The girl dropped back through the sun roof and opened the back passenger door, offering her seat to Tucker. "Hop on in."

The Jeep pulled away from the curb and led the caravan around the green and off again. Behind her, the townsfolk stared as vehicle after vehicle rolled past.

"Who are all these people?" Cam stared in no little bit of awe.

Norah grinned up at him. "The cavalry." She turned to introduce him to the bouncy blonde in a pink hoodie with Ole Miss stitched across the front and an anchor embroidered on one side. "Cam, I'd like you to meet Chelsea Patterson, junior marketing major at Ole Miss and current chair of public relations for Delta Gamma."

Cam shook her hand and offered a confused smile. "I still don't understand."

"I was the DG PR chair back when I was at Ole Miss. Part of that job has to do with organizing philanthropic activities. At their heart, sororities are service organizations and members are expected to put in a certain number of service hours each semester. I went up to Oxford on Tuesday to meet with my old chapter to offer up this service opportunity."

"We weren't about to turn down a request for help from one of our most distinguished alumnae," Chelsea said.

"So who exactly were these extras you recruited?"

"Oh, well Lacey—she's our chapter president," Chelsea added for Cam's benefit, "—is dating the president of Sigma Chi, so she talked him into offering up his chapter for slave labor today."

"Strong backs are more than welcome."

Chelsea flashed a satisfied smile. "Aaaaand I called up our sister chapter at MSU to set up a little friendly competition. They should be here, right about…now." She pointed to the opposite side of the green where a second string of vehicles led by a Toyota flying maroon and white window flags was coming to a stop at the opposite curb.

Norah swung an arm around the girl's shoulders and sent up a prayer of thanks. "Chelsea, you're a woman after my own heart."

It took another half hour for everybody to park. They far outstripped the space available on Church Street. By the time everybody had walked back to the green, cars were lining the entire downtown area, including all the cross streets, and the crowd had swelled to nearly twice the force she'd originally expected.

Norah took up her bullhorn again. "Before we get started today, I'd like to offer up a warm

Wishful welcome to the Delta Gammas from Ole Miss!" The girls cheered. "The Sigma Chis from Ole Miss!" The guys hooted and shouted. "And the Delta Gammas from Mississippi State!" The girls hollered and clapped. "I'd like to thank you all so much for coming. For those of you who don't know, my name is Norah Burke, and I'm your de facto general for the day. Now that the remainder of our army has arrived, here's our revised plan."

Norah took great pleasure in the sour expression on Vick's face as she laid out the full scope of her vision. She took even more in the infectious enthusiasm of her cavalry as it spread to the locals.

"Before you leave today, each of you should stop by and see Richard Patton to give your name and T-shirt size. Richard wave for everybody." The wiry, balding owner of the print shop lifted a hand. "You'll be getting a free commemorative shirt for your efforts! And now I'm going to turn you over to Molly Montgomery, who will divide you into groups."

Norah stepped down and handed off the bullhorn.

Cam fell into step with her as she circled around the crowd. "Not to be a buzz kill, but who's going to pay for all those shirts?"

"I intend to sweet talk all the local businesses who are getting makeovers today into donating toward the effort. Their logos will go on the shirt. That's two hundred and fifty walking advertisements out there, to go along with the free labor. That's what you call a good investment. We're going to pull this off in spades. Vick can just stick that in his pipe and smoke it."

IT GOT WORSE before it got better. Old awnings came down, old paint was knocked off with the dirt when many of the buildings were washed, and more than one downtown business was in total chaos, filled with bodies shifting displays, cleaning, rearranging stock. Cam hoped like hell none of their volunteers decided to employ the five-finger discount.

Norah caught him staring in horror at all the furniture being hauled out of Lickety Split and turned him firmly away. "It's all getting re-painted."

Similar forms of disorder appeared to be going on inside every business. "The chaos, it burns." He shuddered

"I know, I know. The disorganization offends your sensibilities. There is a plan for each and every one. I swear. Tyler, Mitch, and I worked it out before we ever started."

"If you say so." He didn't bother to hide the skepticism.

She gave him a smacking kiss. "Go play in the dirt and leave the organizing to us. And maybe use the opportunity to charm some of your compatriots on the Council." She nodded to where Grace Handeford and Hank van Buren were listening closely as Violet instructed them on the proper means of planting a multi-season hanging basket. "I had Molly put them on your team, just in case."

"Sneaky sneaky. I like that about you."

With a saucy wink, she left him, calling out for Dillon, who had a pair of chairs from the ice cream parlor tucked under either arm.

Cam crossed over to join his official crew for the day.

He had twenty people to manage, most of whom were regulars at the nursery. Four of them were on the Black List and not allowed to touch any plants they hadn't already paid for—per Violet's orders. Since the object of this project was downtown beautification, Cam wasn't going to argue with her. It wouldn't do for everything those folks planted to wither up and die in two days, as their track records suggested. He put them to work mounting the special brackets they'd ordered on the light posts running the length of Main Street. Violet had the hanging basket and planter folks well in hand, so the remaining few were designated tree planters. Which would've been fine if the damned tree spade on the Bobcat hadn't blown a valve. With that one, single problem, a couple hours of work turned into an impossible task.

"Son of a bitch." Cam slapped a hand against the Bobcat.

"Having a bit of bad luck there, Crawford?"

Cam turned and tensed as he caught sight of Roy McKennon. He looked rough, but sober in Carhartts and a flannel shirt. Had he been here from the start? Cam couldn't remember. He hadn't seen Roy since Liam's welcome home party, and he didn't imagine that the other man had changed his opinion on what Cam was trying to do regarding GrandGoods. Was he angry enough to try to sabotage the equipment?

"Little equipment malfunction, as it happens." Cam kept his tone neutral.

Roy looked from the Bobcat to the nursery truck, where more than a dozen trees waited to be planted. "You ain't gonna get that done with whatcha got."

That was the plain truth, and Cam couldn't argue it. He'd have to go track down Norah, see if she wanted them to try to put in what they could the old-fashioned way or hold off until he could get the tree spade repaired. "It's always somethin'."

"Reckon you could use some strong backs."

"Sorry?"

"I happen to know some." The older man turned and whistled.

Across the green, nearly a dozen men broke away from a cluster of pick-up trucks and headed their way.

Catching Cam's wary look, Roy said, "We came to work, same as everybody else. Be obliged if you'd let us help."

Too stunned to reply, Cam could only stare for a moment.

"I may not agree with you on all your politics, but it's a good thing y'all are doin' here. Been a long time since Wishful had something good."

"Hopefully this is the start of a new trend." Cam offered a hand. "I'd appreciate the help."

When Roy's friends joined them, Cam divided them into teams of three and assigned them spots to dig, giving instructions on width and depth of the holes they'd need for the root balls of the Bradford pears they were putting in. He wiped out Tyler's supply of shovels to cover the extra labor, but it was well worth it seeing the teamwork and camaraderie among men who hadn't had reason to smile in a good long while.

More than an hour passed before he made it back to Hank and Grace, who were discussing the congestion of vehicles from all the out of town volunteers.

"I'm pretty sure I saw Aggie Crockett circle the block four times without finding a space," Hank said.

It was exactly the opening he needed. "That's just a fraction of the kind of impact GrandGoods would have," Cam said. "The typical warehouse club of the size they propose has average of five *thousand* vehicle trips *per* weekday, depending on the size of the store. And weekends are bigger."

"That's…a lot," Grace admitted.

"That's more than double our entire population of drivers. We've got to think about expenses for the city, like road maintenance and police force that would be required to compensate for an increase of that magnitude."

"It would be a significant burden on our existing tax base." Hank looked reflective. "Certainly, supplemental funding from the state hasn't been forthcoming. I don't see that getting any better in the future. Not under the current administration anyway."

"So, if they built, we'd get the excess traffic from people who don't live here, don't contribute to the roads they're wearing out. And on top of that, all the land in the general vicinity of the store would decrease in property value because of traffic and noise and the kind of chain-oriented urban bloat that tends to go along *with* these big box stores. And that's not even touching on the impacts on the environment."

"You raise some good points, Cam. But what's the alternative?" Grace asked.

"If we focus on revitalizing downtown, really supporting local retail and creating a climate that will appeal to entrepreneurs looking for good locations to invest in small business, it's a benefit to the entire community. People don't have to drive as far to conduct their day to day business. That means fewer vehicle miles logged, lower accident rates, lower vehicle emissions. And it encourages more of a walking culture, which improves the health of the local populace *and* strengthens community ties because people are out and about and interacting instead of trapped behind the wheel."

"I certainly like the *idea* of that."

"The fact is, we don't *need* what Grand-Goods is offering. We don't need someone from outside to come in and save us. Not at that kind of expense. We can take care of our own if we're just willing to work together to find a solution that will truly benefit the community."

"That's not going to be a popular position," Hank said.

"It's not our job to be popular." Cam had resigned himself to that a long time ago. "It's our job to work in the best interests of Wishful. And that means looking at long-term impact. Look, I don't want to belabor the point. Just promise me you'll consider that when you cast your vote about GrandGoods and their proposal."

"Fair enough." Grace packed the soil around the roots of some ivy. Dusting her hands off, she straightened, looking at something back toward the green. "Is that Abe Costello?"

"That's sure as heck his championship smoker."

Cam turned to look. "What on earth?" As he watched, Abe backed the enormous trailer onto the green. "I'd best go see what this is about. Can you two finish up these planters and get them in place?"

"Go ahead, son. We can handle a bunch of pansies," Hank said.

The truck was parked and the driver out of the cab by the time Cam made it over.

"Uh, Abe. Whatcha doing with Black Beauty here?"

The old man merely grunted and lowered the trailer foot. "Got a bunch of volunteers. They gotta eat. Least we can do to feed 'em for their trouble. McSweeney's is donating fixins, the Rotary Club is donating burgers and hot dogs for lunch, the Kiwanis Club is demolishing the butcher section for supper, and the Methodist, Baptist, and Presbyterian women's groups are in some kind of competition to donate sides."

Cam blinked at him, his brain not quite catching up to what he'd heard. "You're planning to feed the volunteers?"

"That's what I said. Don't just stand there, boy. Help me get this wood out of the truck."

Cam leapt into action.

Smoke was curling toward the sky by the time he got back to the landscaping. As the afternoon progressed and the scents of grilling meat filled downtown, more tables and tents popped up on the green. Clay Turner hauled out the PA system from the community center and added a party feel to the proceedings, playing DJ while the work progressed at a furious pace.

It shouldn't have come together so fast. Not given the state downtown was in that morning. But by the time the news van pulled up late that afternoon, every business downtown had at least one fresh coat of paint, windows sparkled, displays had been updated, and the concrete planters had been set in intervals along Main Street, a pop of color that tied in with the new hanging baskets mounted on all the light poles. Teams were working on getting up new awnings as the reporter climbed out.

Norah appeared from somewhere, managing to look polished and put together in her jeans and camp shirt, despite the paint liberally streaking her legs. She shook hands with the reporter and launched into an animated explanation of what was going on, gesturing to various businesses along Main Street.

His mother stepped up to join him.

"Hey." Cam pulled her in for a one-armed hug. "I haven't seen you all day."

"I've been recovering the booths at Dinner Belles. They're a bit harder than the dining room chairs I did last year, but they came together."

"It seems everything's coming together. In more ways than one."

She looked around in satisfaction. "This is amazing. I haven't seen this kind of community spirit and unity in years. It's all because of you and Norah."

"We make a good team." Cam turned his gaze back to where she stood with the reporter. "But none of this would've happened without her. She single-handedly brought in a freaking army. Just by asking."

"Sometimes that's all it takes, for someone to have the courage to ask. She's not afraid to do that. She doesn't expect everyone to jump at the snap of her fingers, and she's not…entitled like her father, but she's not afraid to ask because she knows her mind and she knows her worth. I hope you know it, too."

"I've been counting my blessings since the day she walked into my life."

"Good." Leaning up to press her cheek to his, she said, "In case nobody else has said it, thanks for taking the hard stance on this GrandGoods thing, baby. It's what needed to be done."

"For the first time, I'm starting to believe that with Norah's help, it just might be enough."

CHAPTER 15

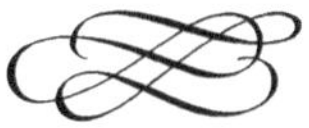

"VALENTINE'S DAY MAY BE over, but love is still in the air here in the tiny town of Wishful. Residents and volunteers gathered today to give downtown some much needed TLC. I'm here with Norah Burke, public relations chairwoman of the citizens coalition behind the project. Can you tell us a little about what's going on here?"

Norah leaned forward from the sofa, her hand clamped around Cam's as she and the rest of the Campbells watched the interview on the ten o'clock news. The station played the whole thing, unedited, as she succinctly explained the origins of the coalition, the threat to their small town way of life, and their hope of reminding the people of what's really important. She came off as charming, erudite, and welcoming, finishing up with an invite to everyone in the viewing area to come by and see what they'd been missing. The camera cut from her to a sequence of shots showing updates in progress or finished, before panning back to the green and the cookout, where the reporter remarked about the outpouring of support from the community for the volunteers. That observation was backed up by a half dozen one liners of gratitude from said volunteers, capped off by Chelsea Patterson, who said "From the moment we arrived, they made us feel like we were home."

"There you have it. The restoration of this little slice of Southern Americana, where visitors will find friendly faces and a touch of home. And, if they're lucky, a little romance in the process." This last was accompanied by a zoom in on Cam, who'd surprised Norah with a deep dip and an enthusiastic kiss to celebrate the success of the day. She hadn't realized they'd still been filming. "I'm Deanna Fossett, WTVA News. Back to you, Cathy."

Norah leapt off the couch executed a victory boogie around the den. "Yes. Yes! You cannot *buy* coverage like that."

"The camera loves you," Cam remarked.

She waved that off. "You're biased. But tying Wishful to the idea that it feels like home. Genius. People *love* that. God bless, Chelsea. I would absolutely hire that girl if I could."

"Why don't you?" Aunt Liz asked.

"Well, aside from the fact that she hasn't graduated yet and isn't actually looking for a job, I'm not being paid myself, so I would have nothing to pay *her*, even if she did want to come work for me."

"You don't right *now*, but you could. Did you ever consider opening your own firm?"

"That would require a lot of capital, a lot of risk for not very good odds of success. Under the best of circumstances the majority of small businesses fail within two years. These aren't the best of circumstances. A town of five thousand doesn't have a lot of need for what I do."

"I think the last couple of months have proven that to the contrary." Cam snagged her hand and tugged her into his lap.

Exhausted, she tumbled into it, snuggling in and sliding an arm around his shoulders so she could finger the fine hair at his nape. She could go to sleep right here…

Norah realized in the expectant pause that she was supposed to respond and worked to keep her brain online for just a little longer. "I've done good work for the coalition, but that's not a paying job, nor is it going to turn into one, unfortunately. The city can't afford to hire me, even if they *were* inclined to create a new position. I've seen your books. The budget's an absolute mess, and I don't know who's doing the accounting, but I think they're dyslexic because there are a lot of discrepancies in the numbers I saw."

"Wait, what?" Cam stopped stroking her back.

"In those city records I analyzed for the last decade, the numbers are all kinds of wonky. I'm sure it's not as bad as it seemed. I'm not an accountant, after all, and I didn't dig all that deep. But really, y'all should look into proper accounting software to keep up with stuff. All those paper ledgers leave so much room for error."

"I'll have a word with the comptroller," Sandra said. "That's something that I admit I let slide without enough oversight during my treatment."

"But back to the question at hand," Aunt Liz insisted.

Norah felt a prickle of annoyance. They meant well, all of them. But this wasn't a topic of conversation she really wanted to deal with right now. It was ruining her lovely high from the day's success. Wanting to stay and being *able* to stay were two entirely different things, and she lived in the real world. "I am a marketing executive. And Wishful *doesn't* have much need of that." God knew, she didn't have the energy to contemplate a total career change, even if she wanted one.

"How big a geographic area does metro Chicago cover?" Mitch asked.

"I don't have a clue. Why?"

Mitch googled it from his phone. "Nearly 5500 square kilometers. That's something like 3400 square miles."

"Okay." If there was a point, she was missing it.

"It's got a relative population density of about nine and a half million people," Reed added.

"And if I were half awake, I could probably give you an arm-long list of entertaining fac-toids about it. I still don't see where you're going with this."

"My point is that's a lot of physical territory, and it includes a lot of communities. And I know for a fact your firm did work outside the city."

"So?" Still baffled, Norah wondered what she was missing with her sleep-deprived brain.

Cam slid a hand beneath the fall of her hair to rub at the knots left by the hours of painting and hauling. "I think the point he's making is that just because Wishful is only five thousand people, there are a lot more towns in the area. It isn't the sort of population density of Chicago, but—well, to use the same argument GrandGoods is using to base a store here, you've got a few hundred thousand people in an hour and a half radius. A whole lot of them are business owners. If you opened your own firm here as a home base, there's nothing stopping you from reaching out to them."

"Or from reaching out further than that online," Miranda added. "You're good with web work. I'm sure there are all sorts of potential clients you wouldn't necessarily need to meet with in person. For stuff like that, it wouldn't matter where you were based. And there's no rule that says you can't travel to meet somebody if you needed to. You did that with Helios all the time."

Feeling hemmed in, Norah struggled to find patience and a rational argument that they'd accept. It wasn't that she didn't have the capital to start her own firm. But money wasn't the only consideration. She had the will-power and the know-how but absolutely no reputation to speak of outside world she'd walked away from. There was no way to do what she'd done before. There wouldn't be the epic corporate accounts, the fast-paced, high-powered *everything* without the glowing recommendation of Philip Vargas.

But had she missed *any* of that since she came to Wishful? Had she once given thought to her corner office or the intra-office politics that had been so much a part of the game that kind of career demanded? She certainly didn't miss Chicago itself. For all that most of her life had been spent in big cities, she appreciated the slower pace of small towns. And she appreciated the people, the personal, the messy community ties she'd found in Wishful. All the things her colleagues would've been scrambling to escape, she actually *liked*. She loved that people here knew her name and gave a damn about her personal life—even if that was mostly as a source of good-natured gossip—because they wouldn't ask if they didn't care, if they didn't feel that in some small way, she was one of theirs.

Norah had wanted that all her life.

But the question of whether she'd be happy in Wishful wasn't actually at issue. No, the question was whether she could be successful in Wishful. They'd made strides, begun to implement changes that would, over time, help keep the town afloat. But afloat was a long way from financially viable as a business location. It wasn't that she was looking to replicate her six-figure salary. The cost of living in Mississippi was the lowest in the country. But she had serious doubts about whether there was sufficient business, even in that hour and a half radius, to make a marketing firm, even one with a payroll of just her, sustainable. They needed to make the *town* sustainable first.

Don't you want a piece of that? Don't you want to save this place every bit as much as Cam? Who better to spearhead that movement than you?

So maybe it *wasn't* such a crazy idea. It would be hard work. Harder even than she'd put in on this anti-GrandGoods campaign. But if she could pull it off…

"I couldn't even begin to think about something that risky without conducting a market analysis, assessing what competition there is in the area, what the best means of reaching people here would be. Then there'd be the issue of the legalities of starting my own company—"

"That's easy enough," Uncle Pete said. "Got all the information on that right here." He tapped a manila envelope on the end table.

Before she could even ask why he had all that pulled together, Mitch jumped in. "You'd need office space. I've been giving some thought to that, actually." Pulling out his digital tablet, he opened some files and handed it over.

The image on the screen was dark, dusty, and loaded with boxes.

"What am I looking at?"

"Is that the old train depot?" Cam asked.

"Yep. It hasn't been used for anything but storage for…man, I don't know. Twenty years. But—" Mitch leaned over and swiped to the next image. "—it has potential."

The concept was fabulous. It retained the historic character of the exposed brick, the struts and beams. But he'd opened the walls, replaced some of the windows to let in the light. There were offices, three of them, divided by glass walls, so as not to block the light, and a small conference room, in addition to a comfortable waiting area for greeting clients. Another swipe revealed the interior of the largest office. Of all of them, Mitch was the only one who'd seen that corner office she'd left behind. He knew how she liked to work and had taken that into account, adding a massive corkboard wall on one side and a giant freestanding glass board on the other for brainstorming. The third wall opened up into a huge picture window overlooking the town green.

Her stomach tied itself in knots of slippery, professional lust. She shook her head. "No, I'm sorry, Mitch."

"Sorry?"

"I'm not going to change my mind and marry you just because you designed my dream office. It was a valiant effort, though."

Mitch laughed. "Hard to compete when I know it was never really a contest."

"We put together a list of potential clients." Anita handed over yet another manila envelope.

Frowning Norah took it, sliding out a thick stack of what turned out to be signed letters of intention.

"It's more or less everyone you've worked with since you got here," Grammy said. "Plus a few others."

Norah said nothing, eyes moving from one Campbell to the next.

Mitch had sobered. "We felt bad about how

we reacted, and we really wanted to show you that we're behind you a hundred percent."

Cam bristled. "So you decided to make the decision for her and back her into a corner?"

Of course, he would understand her hesitation. Her parents had been doing the same thing for years, trying to force her hand, albeit with far less consideration of her own wants and preferences. Cam himself had gone out of his way to avoid talking about the future, to keep her from feeling pressured.

"I'm sure that wasn't their intention."

Aunt Liz looked stricken. "No! We just wanted to be supportive. To try to make it an easier decision."

"Oh, no we absolutely colluded to railroad you," Miranda said. "Because we love you and that's what we do in this family. You love us, so you'll forgive us for essentially beating you over the head with this after you've put in a full day's work on three hours of sleep."

Norah felt her cheeks heat. She didn't dare look at Cam to see if he was blushing or otherwise looked incriminating. Miranda knew she'd slept at his place. Norah didn't know if the rest of the family did and wasn't quite ready to look them in the eye to find out. So she kept her eyes on her friend. "The fact that you pull no punches is one of the things I love most about you."

"You've been too busy busting your ass trying to outflank GrandGoods to give much consideration to a real job. I know you. It never occurred to you to create one for yourself."

"You're right. It didn't. I've deliberately kept myself too busy to think about it because, I guess I was afraid if I did, I wouldn't be able to think of a viable way I could stay." She looked down at the stack of letters and smiled. "So thank you for opening my eyes to the possibility."

Picking up Mitch's tablet, she opened up the concept sketches again. "Who owns this property?"

"The city," Sandra said. "As Mitch said, it's

not been used for anything but storage in ages. I don't think there'd be any fuss over selling."

Norah looked to Cam. "Can you get the keys?"

He angled his head, a faint curve to the corners of his mouth that was just enough to make his dimples wink. "That can be arranged."

THE OLD TRAIN DEPOT WAS, as advertised, a glorified storage unit. File cabinets and boxes of who knew what from decades of running a town were stacked cheek by jowl around an assortment of discarded office furniture all through the space. But what Norah saw as she looked through it a few days later was the vision Mitch had planted in her head.

"It was really smart of Mitch to do this."

"Do what?" Cam asked.

"Make me lust over what this space could be. It was smart of all of them to give me the pitch for what my own firm here could be like."

He scowled. "They shouldn't have pressured you."

"It means a lot to me that you don't. That you're giving me time to figure things out. I know it has to be hard on you to stay in the here and now without talking about the future. You're just as much a planner as I am."

"I don't have to talk about it to believe in it. I'm a patient guy. I know you'll get there in your own time."

This was where he put his faith, his hope, and it humbled her.

"Maybe a little less time, thanks to your very nosy family." She leaned back against a desk. "I want to stay, Cam."

It wasn't the declaration she wanted to make. Or, at least, not the only one. But it was enough to make his eyes light.

"I've been afraid to admit to myself how badly I want that because I couldn't see how I could make it work. They gave me an option I hadn't considered. I don't know if it's actually what I'll end up doing, but they showed me a way I could maybe legitimately have my cake and eat it too. That makes up for the pushy."

"The idea of opening your own firm really hadn't occurred to you?"

"It really hadn't. I mean, maybe down the road in another decade or so, when I had more experience, more awards, a more solid reputation to base a firm around. But those things don't matter so much here. And I've discovered through my work with the coalition that I really like running stuff."

"You're good at it. And I believe we've discussed the benefits of being your own boss."

Norah could think of a lot more inventive ways to play hooky now than what they'd managed so far. The sparkle in Cam's eye said he could, too. Because that glint was dangerous, she turned her mind to the details of the firm she hadn't yet decided to open. "I'd need to come up with a name. And a logo. And a business plan. That should actually come first." Her fingers began to clench, and she automatically started looking around for pen and paper.

Cam reached into the pocket of his cargo pants and produced a small notepad. At her start of surprise, he said, "I started carrying it weeks ago after watching you write all the way up to your elbow when you couldn't find paper." He dug back in the pocket and came up with a pen. "Here. Purple for brainstorming."

Her chest went tight, her throat thick.

"It is purple, right? I thought the blue was for action items."

"It is."

He looked vaguely uncertain. "What is this look?"

"This is me going completely gooey. Like homemade marshmallow fluff gooey."

"My family handed you half a business concept and a pen makes you gooey?"

"The fact that you know my color coding system, what it's for, and that you have—" She tugged open the pocket to check. "—all the major colors in your pocket just in case I need them makes me gooey."

"You have them organized in at least four

places at my apartment. It isn't hard to grab a handful and go."

Norah leaned in to brush her mouth over his. "It's observant and thoughtful. You're always doing stuff like this, all these little signs that show you're paying attention. That you see me. You just…undo me."

He stepped close, crowding her back against a desk until he'd caged her between it and his body. "I like seeing you undone. It's those business suits."

"What?" She couldn't breathe with him this close. Not when she could feel the heat of him and her hands itched to tug at his shirt until she found skin.

"You're always so neat and tidy. Put together. It makes me want to muss you up. Even more now that I know how gorgeous you are when you come apart from my hands. My mouth."

The gravel in his voice, the memories he evoked, had her going hot and wet.

"Cam."

"Hmm?"

"What are you doing?"

"We're done with business for the day. And I've got my mind on pleasure." Cam dipped his head to kiss a trail along the column of her throat. She dropped her pen.

God. "I can see that." He found a particularly sensitive spot behind her ear that made her shudder and fist a hand in his shirt. "Cam."

"Mmm?" He slipped his hands beneath the hem of her sweater, skimming along her spine in a stroke that made her arch like a cat.

"You're distracting me."

She felt his lips curve against her throat. "That's the idea."

Those *hands.* How was she supposed to think with them on her?

There were really good, rational reasons hanging out at the periphery of her mind about why this wasn't a good idea. She came close to grasping at them, then he slid his hands around her ribcage, up to cradle her breasts. His thumbs brushed the stiffened peaks through her bra and a bolt of heat shot straight to her center. Norah dragged his head down and took his mouth in a hungry, open-mouthed kiss. The taste of him punched into her and fried what remained of her synapses, leaving her desperate and wanting.

As he gripped her hips and lifted her onto the desk, she was already tugging his shirt free. Stepping between the V of her thighs, Cam dragged her forward until they were pressed, center to center, separated only by a few inconvenient layers.

The slap of the door had them both freezing.

"Well, this is awkward."

Tucker. Norah didn't have to see his face to know he was grinning.

Cam slid his hands free of her sweater and tugged it down. He eased back, just a bit for decency—as if it wasn't too late for that—but continued to block her with his body.

"Christ, McGee, could you possibly have worse timing?"

"I'm pretty sure five minutes later would've been worse."

"Oh God, I'm just going to die now." Norah buried her face in Cam's chest and willed them both to sink through the floor.

Cam swore.

"Come on man, you didn't put a sock on the door or anything."

"You're going to turn around and leave, right now, without another word, or you're going to end up with my fist in your face."

"No can do, buddy boy. I've been dispatched by Violet to drag you in by your hair if necessary. She's been trying to get you for an hour. She said there's some problem with the Keaney job for tomorrow."

"Damn it. Fine. I'll take care of it."

"Oh no, I'm supposed to make sure your ass actually gets to the nursery. I have been threatened with having my pie privileges revoked at Dinner Belles. You know she could talk her mama into it. I'm not willing to risk it. Happy to give you time to compose yourself, though.

I'll just be outside."

The door thumped shut behind them.

Cam dropped his forehead to hers. "That's not how I saw that going."

"I officially cannot show my face in town, ever again. I should sneak out under cover of darkness, while I still can."

"It was just Tucker. He'll give me shit about it, but it's nothing to worry about. And it's not like people don't know we're involved."

"Knowing we're involved and knowing we almost…on a desk, *in a public building* are totally different things."

"Only semi-public. It's not usually open."

"So not the point. This is not the place for a quickie."

He cupped her cheek, rubbed a thumb across her lips. "A quickie wasn't what I had in mind."

Norah closed her eyes, absorbing the touch. "Then it's a good thing we got interrupted."

"I can be done with this in forty-five minutes. An hour, tops."

And if she was lucky, she wouldn't spontaneously combust in the meantime. "Meet you at your place."

Norah waited until she was sure Cam and Tucker would be gone, until she was sure she could walk without the friction of her slacks making her blush. Then she locked the door to the depot and crossed the green toward her car, parked at the opposite end, near the fountain. The evening air was cool, and she was grateful for the dark. Nobody who saw her in the glow of the street lamps would notice anything amiss. Probably. The few souls she saw were headed for Dinner Belles or Speakeasy, or slipping into the Mudcat for a beer. All save one, who stood very still beside the fountain. Something in his posture was unbearably sad.

She almost didn't stop. In Chicago, she'd have gone straight for her car without giving the guy more than a passing glance. But this wasn't Chicago, so she slowed, stepping quietly up beside him. Dressed in jeans and a black pea coat, Norah pegged him to be in his late forties, a bit younger and a lot fitter than her father. And he looked…lost. Not like he needed directions somewhere local, but direction for his life.

"It's beautiful, isn't it?"

"Always was," the stranger agreed. "Though it still ran the last time I was here."

"Been away a while?"

"Almost thirty years."

"Long time. Was this home?"

He shook his head, not taking his eyes off the fountain. "I loved a girl from here once."

And clearly, he'd lost her somehow. Still caught up in the heady promise of a future with Cam, the thought made her ache for whatever put that look of heartbreak on this man's face.

"Is she what brought you back?" Norah asked gently.

"The memory of her." He finally shifted his attention to Norah, expression sharpening with recognition. "And you, actually. I was in Jackson on business and saw you on the news last night. Norah Burke, right?"

She suppressed her instinctive whoop at the

fact that they'd made it outside the regional news. "I'm afraid you have me at a disadvantage, sir."

"Gerald Peyton." He offered his hand.

She took it, appreciating the quick, businesslike shake before he released her.

"So indulge my curiosity," she said, knowing she'd already asked him a more personal question than this, "what about the interview made you come back to Wishful?"

Gerald lifted a brow.

"I'm in marketing, so I'm always working on refining my campaigns, seeing what works, what doesn't."

"And you're marketing the town?"

"Something like that," she said, and waited.

"The reminder of my personal connection was part of it. I was nostalgic. But it was the fountain. This place always reminds me that hope springs eternal."

The familiar phrase circled around in her head. "I expect everybody could use a little reminder of that from time to time," she said. "It's certainly why I came."

"Yeah? Where'd you blow in from?"

"The Windy City, as it happens. I came for family and got caught up in the cause."

"And a relationship, apparently," he noted with amusement. "Or was that dip staged?"

"Nope, not staged. Just a very unexpected side effect of a wish."

His look was more one of curiosity than contempt. "You believe in that stuff?"

"I didn't when I got here, but I think I'm changing my mind."

They both looked back at the fountain.

"Are you going to make one?" she asked.

"That didn't turn out so well for me last time."

"Cam told me you have to be really careful what you wish for. It can rebound badly."

"Cam? Mr. Dip?"

Norah smiled. "Campbell Crawford. He's one of the City Councilmen."

"Crawford?" Gerald went still.

"His mom Sandra is mayor. Did you know her?"

Something flickered across his face and was gone. "No. No, I didn't know her. Just recognized the name."

"It might've been somebody from Cam's dad's side that you knew. I'm afraid I don't know anything about the Crawford side. His dad left years ago, and I don't think there are any relatives still here from that branch." She laughed at herself. "Sorry. They're rubbing off on me. Can't seem to have a conversation without talking about who's related to who anymore."

"It's the way of the south. Listen, it was nice to meet you. Good luck with your campaign. It's not often in life you get a second chance at something, and this town really deserves one."

He turned to walk away.

"Mr. Peyton?" Gerald glanced over his shoulder. "I hope you find what you're looking for."

"So do I."

CAM DUG THE BLADE of his sharp shooter shovel into the earth and blessed the groundhog for having given the middle finger to winter. The rising, early spring temperatures had landscaping clients coming out of the woodwork, which meant he could finally get his hands dirty with something other than political bullshit. The weeping cherry trees that hadn't arrived in yesterday's shipment were easily traded out for Japanese magnolias, so, with the exception of Dewey May, who hadn't shown, he and his crew were going full-tilt on the demolition of Moriah Keaney's dated, overgrown front flowerbeds.

An hour and a half into the job, Cam was getting worried. Dewey hadn't called in. He was the soul of responsibility. He'd fallen on hard times, another victim of the plant closing. Cam plugged him into the crew as often as possible for part-time work, just to help him keep his family afloat. That hadn't been often during the slow winter.

Cam paused in his work to try the house phone again. No answer. He tried Dewey's cell, wondering if he'd misdialed the first time, but the recorded message told him the number was no longer in service. "Hey, anybody know if Dewey got a new cell number?"

Steve Vessey paused to mop his brow with a faded bandana. "I think he had to let his cell service go. They had to keep the land line because of the kids, you know?"

None of the rest of the crew knew where he was.

Prying up the overgrown boxwood hedge,

Cam decided that if he'd heard nothing in another hour, he'd take a break and get Violet to call over to check with Dewey's wife Pauline at the salon where she worked.

Even as Cam dragged the boxwood to the trailer to haul off, Dewey's ancient, mud brown Chevy rumbled up and parked behind the line of vehicles.

He leapt out and made a beeline for Cam. "I'm sorry. I'm so sorry I'm late." A moon-faced man with a body like a fireplug, Dewey picked up the other side of the hedge and helped Cam heave it into the trailer. "I'll understand if you had to replace me for this job."

"We're fine. Is everything all right with you, though? Nothing's amiss with the kids or Pauline?"

"Oh no. Didn't mean to worry you. I was up at the job fair. It took a lot longer than I expected."

"What job fair?"

"Up at the community center. That new

store GrandGoods is up there taking applications."

An event like that would've required special permission. It should've gone through cursory City Council review, and yet this was the first Cam was hearing of it.

Something must've shown in his expression because Dewey flushed. "I know you're against them coming, Cam. But Pauline really wanted me to put in an application."

"Certainly, she did. You have a duty to apply for anything you can to support your family. I understand that." But he sure as hell needed to find out what was going on.

Giving instructions to Dewey about what needed to be done before lunch, Cam rinsed off his hands and headed into town.

There was a line. It snaked out of the community center doors and wrapped down the sidewalk, all the way around the quarter mile walking track next door. A banner was tied up on the side of the building with the GrandGoods logo, proclaiming NOW HIRING. Cam parked down by Poor Richard's Print Shop and walked the three blocks back. He didn't miss the assorted grumbles from the masses as he strode past them all and went inside.

Tables were set up in the gymnasium. Bill Sutto was there, along with four other people wearing GrandGoods polo shirts, each talking to prospective employees. And, of course, in the thick of it all stood Vick Burgess.

"What's going on here? Who authorized this?"

"Why, the City Council did," Vick said with an avuncular smile. "You didn't get the memo?"

"I most certainly did not." Cam was willing to bet the bastard hadn't even sent him the email.

"It passed the others with a quick review. Nobody saw any reason not to get the ball rolling since GrandGoods was approved. The people need the boost of some good news."

"Nothing is definite yet. They still have to obtain the special use permit before they even complete the purchase of the land. What's it going to do to community morale to get hopes up for a job, only to have the company defeated?"

Vick looked around at all the people. "Are you really so naive you think it won't pass?"

Cam skimmed the crowd, noting as many familiar faces as strangers. This would pull in people all over the county and beyond. They'd get ten times the number of applicants they needed for a store the size they proposed. Under those circumstances, GrandGoods could afford to be choosy and pay low. The supply of potential workers was sufficient that no one would risk complaining because any job was better than none.

"When are you going to realize that you're out-gunned on this, Crawford? You and your coalition are on a little island all your own, where it apparently rains glitter and everybody shits rainbows. This is reality. This is the future. You'd better get used to it."

"I will fight you and this until my last breath."

"What do you think you can do in two days?"

Cam had no answer for that. Knowing there was nothing he could do to stop the job fair from proceeding, he turned to leave. "This isn't over."

"It was over before you started," Vick called after him.

Cam stalked out, noting with disgust and disappointment a few members of the coalition standing in line. Dave Lautner and Jordan Linley deliberately shifted away as Cam walked by, as if to pretend they didn't see him, but the flush of red creeping up their necks belied the innocent gesture.

Cam didn't stop. In his present mood, he sure as hell wasn't in the right frame of mind to play even-tempered representative. He couldn't blame them for hedging their bets. Not really. But Christ, couldn't they wait until the fat lady had sung and the war was over? Having the community see them playing both sides didn't look good for their cause.

Slamming the door to his truck, he cranked up and called Norah.

"Hey Leonidas, you snuck out early this morning."

Despite his agitation, Cam felt his heart lighten at the sound of her voice. "Sorry about that. I had a landscaping job to finish prepping for. I figured you needed the sleep, and you looked all cozy in my bed."

"Imagine my surprise when I went to sleep with you and woke up with Hush."

"She's a bed hog."

"She also snores." Norah laughed. "Are you free for lunch or are you working through?"

"Working through. Listen, we've got a problem." He told her about the job fair and his encounter with Vick. "It's not good."

"You had to know that they'd counter with something. They've been too quiet while we put together this Shop Local movement."

"I assumed that was because they were cocky."

"Well, you're not wrong about that. But the

fact is, they wouldn't have to put themselves out there like this if we weren't making a dent in public opinion. It's a waste of their man hours to take applications for a store that isn't built yet when they could've just as easily waited."

"Please tell me you expected this and that you've got some genius plan up your sleeve."

"As it happens, I just might. Finish up your workday, and I'll be ready to tell you all about it when you get home."

Cam said goodbye and disconnected, musing that whatever happened, he could get used to the idea of going home to her.

Norah was drowning in paper and wishing for the swanked out office Mitch had designed her, or at the very least, the series of boards where she could organize and spread out. The open concept of Cam's loft left almost no blank walls for her to co-opt. Cabinetry, shelving, or windows covered almost all of it. So she'd resorted to ludicrous numbers of tabs open in the browser on her laptop and piles on every horizontal surface, except for the sofa, where Hush had been snoring since they came in from an afternoon walk.

A giddy excitement bubbled in Norah's blood, mixed with a low-grade anxiety. This wasn't the killing blow Cam wanted to deliver to GrandGoods and their plans. But like the idea of opening her own firm, this was an option for Wishful she was certain no one had considered before. And it was the only alternative she could think of that would not only maintain the integrity of the town but capitalize on the very things that made it unique.

She just had to convince them it was the right choice.

A truck door slammed below. Hush scrambled up and off the sofa, tail sweeping across the coffee table and upsetting several of Norah's piles in the process. Groaning, Norah sank to the floor to retrieve her research. She'd just managed to gather up the mess when Cam came through the door. Hush gave a delighted bark and began to dance in front of him, wagging her entire butt before starting to bounce back toward Norah.

"For the love of all that is holy, keep her over there until I can get this sorted. That tail might as well be a wrecking ball."

"Wow. Is there actually any paper left in Wachoxee County?"

"Be thankful I restrained myself from taping it all over your walls. It was a near thing."

"You've been busy." He herded the dog toward the treat bucket in the kitchen, peering at some of the stacks on the counter. "You're looking at unemployment rates for the last three decades? Isn't that kind of excessive?"

"Not when you're mapping economic trends and trying to forecast the impact of future actions. It'll be relevant at the debate and something Dr. Brosnan will be bringing up. She's hoping to have her preliminary findings for the second economic impact study by then."

"Here's hoping."

Norah set her stack of papers down and crossed over to him.

"Don't touch me. I'm filthy."

He smelled of earth and man and good, hard work, something her soft-handed ex had never done. Ignoring his edict, Norah rose to her toes to brush her lips over his, careful to keep from pressing up against him, as he really was covered in dirt. "Welcome home."

"Give me five minutes to shower, and I'll show you how much I appreciate you being here to say that." His hazel eyes glinted with promise.

"Five minutes, then come out here ready to listen. I have a lot to tell you. Maybe there'll be time after that for you to show your…appreciation."

With a flash of dimples he disappeared into the bathroom.

By the time he came back in clean jeans and a t-shirt, his hair damp and skin pink from scrubbing, Norah had reconstructed her piles.

He poured himself a glass of tea and came to join her on the sofa, evicting Hush.

"Okay, I'm ready to hear your genius solution, Wonder Woman. Lay it out for me."

Norah almost hated the look of expectant faith on his face. "Wishful is on the verge of bankruptcy. That's nothing you didn't already know. It's symptomatic of a larger economic trend that has been progressing for the last three decades."

The faint trace of humor in his expression faded. "All true, but that's rather overstepping the bounds of the problem we're facing."

"No, it's really not. GrandGoods is only a small part of the full problem. Even if they came, they wouldn't be the answer. They're simply not big enough, and they're going to have further detrimental effect on other businesses in the local economy. Plus, whatever short-term gains they may bring wouldn't be immediate. It would take time to build the store, to stock it and get it open. They alone won't be enough to reverse the larger economic trend."

"All of which we'll bring up at the debate. But how does that fix the problem in the short term?"

"Unfortunately, there is no short-term fix. You can't produce jobs out of thin air, certainly not in this kind of compressed time frame."

Cam set the empty tea glass aside. "So what are you saying? That it's hopeless? That we don't stand a chance of stopping this?"

"I'm saying we have to think bigger than a Band-aid for this situation. If Wishful is going to be saved from economic ruin, you have to realize you're playing a long-haul game."

"If you wanted to depress me, you're doing a damned good job of it."

Norah curled her hands around his and squeezed. "I wouldn't bring this up if I didn't have a plan."

He eased somewhat at that. "I'm listening."

"Do you know why I come here? Why I've always loved coming here?"

"Miranda. Because we're your second family."

She tipped her head to acknowledge the point. "That's part of it. But I love this town for a whole different set of reasons, reasons I'm not sure you can fully appreciate having never lived in the city. Compared to all the other places I've lived since my parents divorced, Mississippi is a whole other world, a whole different way of life. A more…personal way of life.

"I loved Wishful from the first time I came home with Miranda. I love that people smile and nod and speak here. I love that Mama Pearl will dish up a dose of sass to complete strangers, and will remember their order, even when she hasn't seen them in six months. I love that everybody knows everybody, and that you can't get away with shit because somebody will tell your mama. I love that people still have moral values here, that they're generous and open. I love that I haven't been here in three years, but so many people still know who I am and have been keeping up with me through Miranda. I love the town itself because it's adorable and charming, but it's the *people* here who really matter, who make Wishful special."

Cam smiled. "My mom has said much the same."

"The culture and way of life here is, as the reporter said, this wonderful little slice of Southern Americana that simply doesn't exist in urban areas. And *that* is what we need to capitalize on."

"I don't understand. How would we do that?"

"By promoting rural tourism."

He stared at her with abject horror. "You want to turn my town into a tourist attraction?"

"I'm not talking about a theme park, Cam. I'm talking about taking advantage of what makes this town special and bringing in others who would appreciate that personal touch. Rural tourism is a booming trend across the country, and it's a means of revitalizing and diversifying a lot of formerly agrarian and rural communities that have suffered economic downturns, exactly like Wishful has."

"I'm not sure I follow."

"Think about what you show people who come here from out of town. You take them to the fountain, tell them the story, and get them to make a wish. You take them out to Hope Springs. You take them to Dinner Belles or The Spring House. You show them all the things that make you proud of Wishful. And people respond to that."

"I still don't see how that translates into tourism."

"You can't appreciate this because you've always had it. You've always lived here, except for when you were away at college. The fact is, a whopping eighty percent of Americans live in urban areas. They're caught up in the go go go go go, and they want somewhere they can go for a change of pace, for a reminder that there are still places in this country that remember what's important. People *want* to slow down—

whether they realize it or not. Jesus, look at me."

"If you call what you've been doing the last couple of months slowing down, then we need to have a talk."

Norah laughed. "Okay, so maybe I'm a poor example. But think about it. Think about how I couldn't turn off or relax. Even as busy as I've been since we started the coalition, I'm less stressed, less *everything* since I came here. Largely because of you, yes, but also because I finally shifted gears. And it's been amazing to reconnect with that. I want to give that to other people. And I want Wishful to reap benefits."

"You really think people would come?"

"I know they would. This is the answer, Cam. This is how Wishful can take care of itself instead of relying on outside industry. And it's something that can grow and adapt as the town itself does. It's a viable alternative with far more long-term benefits than anything Vick Burgess has up his sleeve."

"Okay." Cam nodded. "Okay, let's do it."

His ready agreement threw her. "Really? You like the idea?"

"I love it. It completely gets at the heart of what I want for Wishful. Sustainable community improvement that strengthens and enhances what's already here rather than changing everything." He lifted her hands to press a kiss to her knuckles. "Someone's been paying attention."

"I wouldn't be good at what I do, if I didn't."

"I'm counting on those rock star capabilities."

Norah grinned, thrilled to be needed, to have his faith in her abilities. "Fantastic. I've got calls in to several people who run the rural tourism campaigns in their towns. I really want to pick their brains about what they've done that was successful. I've got a ton more research to do on it before I can pull together a proper prospectus."

"You've got two days."

She gaped at him. "*Two days?* Are you kidding me?"

"The public debate and the City Council vote is in two days. You've been saying we need an alternative. We've got to let people know about it."

And suddenly that faith felt like the weight of a world rather than motivation. "Cam, I'm good, but I can't possibly have a full work-up to show the public done in two days. I don't know enough about it."

"Then don't do the full work-up. Boil it down to the essentials. I can arrange for you to meet with the Council in private before the debate so you can present to them. They've got to have something else to sway them to vote down this special use permit."

"The permit is specifically about giving them permission for commercial activity on that particular piece of land, right?"

"Yeah. If the permit gets voted down, then GrandGoods has to find another location. It's not a full win. It'd just buy us some time. Unless they decide it's more trouble than it's worth, and they choose to pull out."

"Okay. Okay, so let's approach this not from the perspective of stopping GrandGoods in its entirety. Let's approach this from the angle of stopping them from building on that land. Hope Springs is one of the biggest existing assets Wishful has. It will only stay that way, stay a viable resource, if there's not a big ass store plunked down on its banks. Okay, I can work with that." She reached for a legal pad.

Cam handed over a purple pen. "Get to it, Wonder Woman."

"I require fuel in the form of Chinese," she told him. "It's going to be a really long night."

"Anything you want."

"Bulletin boards."

He laughed. "Seriously?"

"As many as you can beg, borrow, or steal."

"Your wish, milady."

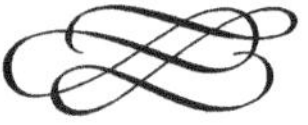

"I NEED A FAVOR."

Cassie shoved up her sleeves and braced herself, all but vibrating with the desire for a mission. "Name it, friend."

Cam leaned across the counter at The Daily Grind and dropped his voice. "We're having an unofficial meeting before the debate tonight. I need you to see that nobody comes upstairs except myself, Norah, and the City Council."

"So you need me to run interference in case a certain pretentious city official happens to show up?"

"Him or anyone else."

Curiosity lit her eyes. "Are we having a covert op planning session?"

Cam laughed. "Nothing so exciting as that. I just wanted a chance to talk to them off book about some stuff before we get to the debate, that's all."

Cassie pouted. "I think we should plot a mission to slash the tires on that new Lexus he's running around in, acting like he owns the town. Prick."

"Vick got a new car?"

"Yep. Top of the line SUV with heated seats and all those bells and whistles, like the automatic stop and back up camera and whatever. He was totally bragging on it to Neil Faber at the latest Rotary Club meeting."

Cam wondered how the hell Vick was affording something like that on the City Planner's salary. Then again, qualifying for the loan and truly being able to afford it were two different things. Vick was absolutely the kind of guy who'd choose appearances over practicality.

"You aren't a member of the Rotary Club. How'd you know about that?"

"Please. I never reveal my sources."

"Fair enough. I appreciate that I can count on your discretion, Cass."

The door opened and Norah came in, laptop bag slung over her shoulder and two of the bulletin boards that had taken over his loft tucked under both arms. Cam hurried over to relieve her of the boards.

"You ready?"

"As I'm going to be." But she didn't have the easy confidence he'd come to associate with her presentations.

Cam knew he'd set an impossible task for her. Part of why she was good was because she was thorough, and less than forty-eight hours was hardly adequate for an in-depth study of the topic. He was relying on her panache and natural persuasion to carry the day.

"You'll be great."

His assurance didn't seem to make much of a dent in the doubts swirling in her eyes.

They'd set up the boards and laid out the folders of informative material at each seat by the time the other Council members arrived. By then, Norah had her game face on, calm and confident.

When she nodded she was ready, Cam launched in. "I realize you're all taking time out of your busy schedules to be here. I thank you for that.

"You wanna tell us why we're having this meeting now instead of as part of tonight's debate?" Connie demanded.

"There are things relevant to the debate that aren't on the agenda tonight, and I wanted an opportunity to present them without interference."

"Meaning you don't want Vick to know about them," Hank said.

"It's no secret there's no love lost between me and Vick, but this isn't about that. Wishful has a problem. A big one. We all know it.

We've all watched it get bigger and bigger over the last few years at every one of our budgetary meetings. Money simply isn't coming into town, into the city coffers at a rate sufficient to support the existing infrastructure, public services, or city salaries. We've all taken pay cuts or cut back hours. The public library is down to a single full-time employee, a couple of part-timers, and a small group of volunteers. The police force is operating on a shoe string, and God help us if we have any kind of fire that the volunteer departments can't handle."

"That's exactly why we want GrandGoods," Connie said. "The sales tax alone from that kind of store would be a Godsend."

"The quarter percent we get above what goes to the state is not going to be enough to support the additional wear and tear on the public infrastructure. And that's all a matter for tonight's debate. The point I'm making here is that GrandGoods is no savior. They'll bring as many problems as they might potentially solve, and they certainly aren't going to fix the long term economic decline we've been trapped in."

"This is all the same song, different verse, Cam," Grace said. "Why are we here now? And why is Norah here? She isn't part of the City Council. No offense, honey."

"I'm here to give you an alternative. Grand-Goods is appealing because it's an option. And up to this point, it's been the only option for y'all to consider. But that's no longer the case."

"Is this more about the Shop Local movement?" Connie asked.

"Despite the fact that the Shop Local campaign is still in relatively early stages, there has already been a twenty-five percent increase in local revenues over the last month. With the recent media exposure, we anticipate that trend will continue—as long as we work to maintain the momentum. What I have in mind is bigger, broader, and will have more impact on the overall economic health of Wishful."

Ed Falk leaned back in his chair and sipped at his coffee. "We're listening."

Cam watched his fellow Council members as she explained the entire concept behind rural tourism. Connie continued to be closed off, face set in annoyed lines during most of the presentation. Grace and Hank both appeared intrigued. And Ed…well who could ever tell what he thought unless he said something?

"You think people would want to come here for fun?" Hank asked.

"I know they will. Wishful and other small towns like it really touch something nostalgic for people who live in the city. Life here is so much more connected in a very real way—person to person, and also person to nature. People would come here to remember how life used to be, how it ought to be. To gain perspective and unplug from the relentless rat race of American society and plug *in* to the important things in life."

"How would we even go about starting something like that?" Grace asked. "Wouldn't it cost a lot of money?"

"Not necessarily. You start with the resources Wishful already has. The cultural identity. The history. The fountain and the lore that goes with it. And, most especially, Hope Springs. Think about all the stuff you show to out-of-towners when they come to visit. The things that you're proud of or that really bring home to outsiders, this is what Wishful is."

She paused and opened the folder in front of her, gesturing the rest of them to do the same. "From there, it's a matter of marketing, like anything else. You start by focusing on day trips. As you can see here, those fall into two categories: long ones, from up to two hundred miles away, and short ones, within about a fifty mile radius. It's the latter that makes the most sense to promote.

"Wishful is exactly halfway between Oxford and Starkville. There are multiple submarkets in both those locations, but just to name a few, you have the potential to tap into the enormous number of people who roll into town for basketball, baseball, and football season at Ole Miss and MSU, who want to attend the game but don't want to be caught up in the crazy by actually staying in town. We're also close enough that both universities could use us as a selling point when recruiting new faculty and students, just like Ole Miss does with Taylor.

"Past day trips, you focus on pass-through visits, both for the day and overnight. Overnights could be weekends or full on vacations. We're less well positioned for that, at the moment, since there's only the B and B and the Mockingbird Motel at the edge of town, with maximum occupancy at both being less than a hundred people, but provided the campaign is successful, and sustainable growth recorded, we could position ourselves as the ideal site for new businesses in the hospitality industry."

Cam jumped in. "There are a lot of options, a lot of directions that could be taken. But the point is that rural tourism is a sustainable option that focuses on what's already here and doesn't run the risk of putting the majority of jobs in the hands of a company that could pull up stakes and leave. That's happened too many times before, and we won't survive it again."

"It's an intriguing concept, to be sure," Ed admitted.

"Sounds like a long-term kind of project," Hank said.

"It absolutely is," Norah agreed. "And it's something that can be adapted to fit whatever budget or staff you have to work with. From a purely pennies perspective, simply setting up a properly designed website, geared to drive interest toward the existing resources you have would be an excellent start."

"Of course, all that depends on those resources remaining available," Cam said. "That means voting down the special use permit for the land by Hope Springs and either sending GrandGoods packing or forcing them to pick a new location."

"In the event we voted down the permit," Grace said, "in order to effectively use Hope Springs as a tourist draw, we'd have to come to some kind of agreement with Abe Costello.

Those aren't public lands out there and the city can't afford to buy the property."

"The specifics of how all that would work can come later. The fundamental issue at stake right now is that this permit is voted down so that it *can* be discussed later. Can I count on you?"

"You know we aren't going to commit one way or the other without hearing the debate," Grace chided.

"Well, I'm happy to take this under advisement," Hank said. "And I'd really like to see additional development of the concept so that we can revisit it in the future."

Ed and Grace conceded the same. Connie said nothing.

Out of additional selling points, Cam adjourned the meeting. "See y'all at the debate tonight."

They filed out, leaving Cam no more confident of their support than when they'd arrived. "I wish I felt better about that."

Norah rubbed a hand down his back. "We

did what we could do in the time we had. It's not the only weapon in our arsenal. Elissa Brosnan is supposed to get here at five with Dillon. Will you be able to join us for dinner to go over strategy before the debate?"

"I'll be there. Do you know if she finished the economic impact study?"

"Not completely. But her preliminary results are enough to call into serious question the methods used by the other firm."

"Well, let's just pray it's enough to make the rest of them waffle."

THE COURTHOUSE WAS PACKED. People were wedged into the wooden benches in the public seating on the main level and up in the gallery. More stood two and three deep around the edges. The coalition was a notable presence, but there were an equal number of faces Norah didn't recognize. Almost all of them were either zoned out or confused.

At the front of the courtroom, Dr. Elissa Brosnan, professor of economics from the University of Mississippi, was engaged in active debate with Arnold Chiles, the representative from the firm who'd produced the original economic impact study. From a purely academic standpoint, Dr. Brosnan was winning. But the entire discussion was taking place at a level of technicality that the vast majority of those present couldn't possibly follow. That wasn't exactly confidence inspiring.

"Are you understanding this?" Miranda whispered.

"Most of it, but I've been up to my eyeballs in this stuff for weeks now."

The Council members were tired. Norah could see it in their postures, read it in their faces. This discussion was closing in on an hour long, and that after almost an hour spent rehashing the issue of infrastructure upgrade that would be required. An upgrade that Grand-Goods vowed to foot the bill for. Damn it.

They were being far too conciliatory. All

smiles, all agreement. Bill Sutto and Vick Burgess were all up in each others' pockets. They even seemed buddy-buddy with Arnold Chiles, which made Norah wonder if there was a connection between them that made Chiles less than an unbiased party. If they could prove it, would it be enough to call into question the results of the study? Or would it just be considered the delay tactic it was intended to be?

"Thank you, Dr. Brosnan, for that…in-depth opinion. You've given us plenty to consider." As the professor took her seat, Sandra continued, "Are there additional concerns anyone wishes to raise?"

Norah knew Cam had been hanging on to the traffic flow issue, but before he could speak, Bill Sutto asked for the floor.

"Thank you, Madam Mayor. I know that there is a great deal of concern about how GrandGoods would impact Wishful. You are a small town with considerable charm, and you don't want to lose that. We absolutely respect and appreciate your position. While it's true that our store would bring in several thousand more vehicles locally per day, there are means of mitigating the impact of that traffic burden so that the character of Wishful remains intact. We took the liberty of having a traffic engineer conduct a study of the existing traffic flow and make recommendations for the best means of minimizing the intrusion into the community." Sutto moved out from behind his table and began to pass out packets to the City Council members.

Shit. By bringing up the issue first, Sutto reinforced the idea that they had the community's best interests at heart.

"We can't trust anything they've paid for," Norah hissed. "They'll have professionals in their pocket to make sure they come across as lily white and innocent."

"Surely the Council won't just swallow it whole," Tyler murmured.

Cam was on it. "Motion to adjourn to allow sufficient time for the Council to review the report."

"Why?" Connie Lockwood demanded. "So you can waste more tax payer dollars trying to find someone to give the opinion you want?"

The audience burst into a flurry of exclamations that had Sandra pounding her gavel for order. Though Norah could see the temper on Cam's face, he held it together, not snapping back at Connie.

"What is her problem?" Miranda muttered.

"She's voting with her wallet," Tyler said.

Dr. Brosnan lifted her hand. "To be clear, I'm here on my own. I'm not being paid."

"There has been a motion to adjourn for the City Council to review the traffic engineer's report," Sandra said.

No one seconded the motion.

"We all know how we're going to vote," Hank said. "Unless there's some other evidence we need to consider—legitimate evidence, not stalling tactics—motion to proceed to vote."

"Second," Connie said, impatient to be done with the proceedings.

Sandra waited, eyes scanning the crowd for

any further objections. A muscle in her jaw jumped, the same way Cam's did when he was frustrated. Norah wracked her brain, trying to think of something else to say, something else to bring up. But the coalition's efforts were exhausted. She met Cam's eyes across the room as his mother reluctantly said, "Motion to vote on the special use permit for the proposed parcel of land is approved."

This was it. The moment they'd been working toward for weeks, pulling out all the stops to sway public opinion and that of the rest of the Council. Norah reached out and grabbed Miranda's and Tyler's hands.

On the front row of the audience, Molly Montgomery stood. "Motion for roll call vote."

"Seconded," Cam said.

"Motion for roll call vote approved."

They would know, without question, who stood where. Norah held her breath as Sandra started.

"Proceeding with roll call vote on the issue of a special use permit allowing commercial construction of a retail space on the proposed parcel of land. Councilman van Buren."

"Aye."

Damn it. She'd thought maybe they'd been able to turn Hank.

"Councilman Falk."

Edgar was the dark horse. Cam said he was never sure which way the older man would vote. His voice rang out clear and confident. "Nay."

One to one.

"Councilwoman Lockwood."

"Aye."

No surprise there.

"Councilman Crawford."

"Nay." Cam's voice came out a couple steps above a growl as all eyes turned to Grace.

"Councilwoman Handeford."

Grace paused as if still deliberating.

Oh please. Oh please. Oh please. Do the right thing. Norah stared hard at the older woman, willing her to give the answer they needed. She cranked down on her friends' hands.

Grace's gaze skimmed the crowd, one final assessment of sentiment before dropping her eyes and giving a quiet, "Aye."

Norah's heart sank.

Sandra's gavel hovered, as if giving the other woman a chance to recant. When she said nothing, Sandra lifted her gavel, reluctance slowing the motion. She rapped once. "The special use permit for the proposed parcel of land is approved by a margin of three to two."

No.

Norah lost whatever was said next because of the roaring in her ears. Or maybe that was the roar of the crowd. Down front, she could see Vick Burgess and Bill Sutto congratulating each other. Both men turned to Arnold Chiles, glad handing him for his role in their victory.

GrandGoods had won.

CHAPTER 18

"HERE, LOOKS LIKE Y'ALL could use this." Tucker handed Cam and Norah glasses of scotch.

Cam tossed his back, wishing the burn of alcohol could mitigate the crushing disappointment of their defeat. Beside him, Norah rolled the tumbler between her hands, the ice cube making a soft *clink* against the glass. She'd said nothing since the City Council meeting adjourned and they'd reconvened at Tucker's downtown apartment. This late, nothing was open, and they'd all felt the need to debrief. Except no one seemed inclined to break the silence.

Breaking the silence meant saying the words. Admitting the truth of their failure out loud would make it real. All that work, all that planning, and Goliath had won after all. Since they left the courthouse, Cam had been second-guessing every decision they'd made, wondering what they'd done or hadn't done that might've tipped the balance. Had it been a mistake to keep the rural tourism aspect quiet? Would it have been better to present it, as undeveloped a plan as it was, in the public forum? Or would the townsfolk have seen it for what it was—grasping at straws?

Would it have been better to not fight at all? To have never had the possibility an alternative in the first place? He was used to disappointment, used to things turning out poorly. He knew how to endure that. But this, the fall from a place of hope, was so much longer, so much harder than accepting that the situation was crappy and was likely to remain so.

Cam looked at Norah, at the shuttered expression in her dark eyes as she stared at nothing, unnaturally quiet and still. The fight had, in a very real way, brought him her. No matter what happened to Wishful, he could never regret the war that had given her reason to stay. So he would bear up under the disappointment and soldier on, grateful to have her by his side.

Miranda sank down on the other end of the sofa and slid an arm around Norah's shoulders. "Honey, are you okay?"

Eyes still unfocused, she shook her head once. Miranda squeezed in support. Cam laid his hand on Norah's thigh, but she didn't take it, only continued to turn the glass in her hands.

"I thought for sure you had Grace," said Mitch, at last.

"Did you see how she looked everywhere in the room except at Vick?" Tyler asked. "Didn't that seem weird to you?"

"Like he got to her in a conspiracy theory sort of way?" Tucker leaned against the wall and crossed his arms. "That sounds like something Cassie would say."

"I'm more surprised by Hank," Cam said. "I felt sure the issue of the wear and tear on infrastructure would sway him to our side. Roads are a big thing with him."

"I just didn't expect it to end like this," Miranda said.

Norah raised her glass and drained it before setting it down on the coffee table with a *crack*. "This isn't over."

"There's nothing left we can do. Legally, there's no other means of stopping construction."

She exploded up from the sofa, stalking to the end of the room before whirling back. Her eyes weren't unfocused now. They flashed with the heat of temper. "There has to be something. Until they break ground—hell, until they open the goddamned doors, there has to be *something*."

The thread of desperation in her voice had Cam crossing to her, running both hands down her arms in an attempt to soothe. "Honey, it's done."

"No. No, it isn't done. *I'm* not done. The land deal hasn't closed yet. There's still time for something to change."

A dangerous and fruitless line of speculation. "Do you honestly think you'll change Abe's mind? You've been trying to do that for weeks."

"So we find someone else to buy the land. Recruit investors."

"Investors from where? No one here has that kind of money or inclination or they'd have done it already."

"Then we go outside of town."

"And what exactly would they be investing in? Part ownership of land we don't want anyone to develop? Who do you think is crazy enough to do that? And who do you think has that kind of money to put into something that won't turn a profit?"

"I don't *know*, damn it. But I'm not going to just accept this. I can't."

"Norah—"

"Burkes don't fail, Cam. *I* don't fail. And I'm sure as hell not going to start now."

"You didn't fail."

"I made you a promise."

"And you kept it. You haven't let me down, Wonder Woman. The rest of the Council did."

"It was my job to convince them."

"It was both our jobs. I didn't pull it off either. But you can't take responsibility for the behavior of other people. We did everything we could do in the time we had available."

"And it wasn't enough." She closed her eyes, her face twisting in pain as she whispered again, "It wasn't enough."

"Hey, look at me." Cam cupped her face, tipped it to his and waited until she opened the eyes swimming with unshed tears. "What happened in Morton—which wasn't your fault, as we already established—isn't happening here. You expressly designed the coalition to support Wishful for the long haul, not just for this one fight. We can still develop your rural tourism campaign. You said yourself it's long-term and adaptable to circumstances and budget. We'll need that now, more than ever, to mitigate the impact GrandGoods will have. And that's going to make the difference in our survival. *You* gave us that option. *You* did that. Maybe it's not everything we'd hoped, but that's not failure."

Norah said nothing for a long moment. Shoulders slumping, she rasped out, "I'm tired. I'm so damned tired." Cam expected her to lean in, rest her head on his shoulder, but she pulled away instead, scooping both hands through her hair.

"You've been running yourself ragged for weeks," Miranda said.

"You know me." Norah flashed a humorless smile. "Full tilt or nothing."

"You'll feel better with a good night's sleep." Cam wanted to bundle her up himself, hold her until she finally relaxed.

"A good week's sleep," Mitch added. "It's time to let yourself crash, sugar."

After another long hesitation, Norah nodded. "Let's go home." It was Miranda she looked at. Miranda she leaned on as she gave a numb and generalized farewell before walking out Tucker's door.

Cam felt a chasm yawning open between them.

Tyler slid an arm around his waist and rubbed his back. "Don't take it personally. She's asleep on her feet and upset. Miranda will take care of her."

Of course she would. That was never a question. But it didn't change the fact that Cam wanted to be the one Norah turned to, who took care of her and eased the hurts.

"It's been a shitty night all around."

"That it has." Mitch crossed over and pulled Cam into a thumping hug. "I'm really sorry how things turned out, cuz."

"If there's anything we can do," Tucker said, "for you or for Norah, just let us know."

Cam sighed. "It's the end of the road for now. And late. Really flipping late. I should get home myself, let Hush out, and get my ass to bed." And hope he actually slept with a hundred pounds of canine draped over his feet instead of warm woman curled against his chest.

Maybe by the time they both surfaced tomorrow, he'd have some idea of the right thing to say.

"You're completely insane." Tucker leaned back in the leather chair behind the wide wooden desk that dominated his law office. "You know that, right?"

"I'm determined," Norah corrected. "And I'm thinking outside the box. Can you do it or not?"

"Yeah, I can do it. The bureaucratic red tape is minimal in a situation like this. The whole thing can be a done deal in ten days, as long as the title is clear. But are you sure?"

"Positive. This is important, Tucker."

"Does Cam know about this plan?"

"No, and I'll tell him when the time is right and not before. I'll remind you of attorney-client privilege and the fact that I will sue your ass if you break it."

Tucker held up both hands in surrender. "I'm not gonna break my ethical code."

"How fast can you have the paperwork drawn up?"

"Should be ready late this afternoon. Tomorrow morning at the latest."

"Put a rush on it. I don't want to take any chances on this going awry." Norah checked her watch. "I need to get going. I've got another appointment."

"I'll call you when it's ready."

As had become her habit when running errands downtown, Norah left her car and walked from Tucker's office. Despite her bravado to Tucker, it was a relief to turn her brain from the true insanity she had just instigated to the meeting that had more than piqued her curiosity.

In the wake of the Council's decision on the special use permit, Norah had posted an update on the coalition website and sent out a news-letter. She hadn't asked for money, hadn't pursued the idea of investors. But she'd made it clear that they were open to further suggestions. Twenty-four hours later, she'd received a phone call from Gerald Peyton, the man who'd inadvertently inspired her rural tourism campaign. He wanted to discuss a business proposition.

Gerald rose from the lip of the fountain as she approached, and there was nothing of the lost about him today. Unlike their first chance encounter, this time Gerald was dressed in a sharply-tailored business suit, a sedate Hermes tie breaking the line of his crisp Oxford shirt, and a Burberry coat draped neatly over one arm.

Once, she'd have been dressed just as smartly, but after two months in Wishful, she'd dialed back to a more comfortable cashmere sweater and jeans. She felt hideously under-dressed. Despite her casual attire, it was easy to slip back into the skin of the consummate professional. She offered her hand. "Mr. Peyton, I hope you haven't been waiting long."

"Not at all. I've been enjoying the chance to slow down and people watch. Would you like to get a cup of coffee?"

Norah angled her head in amusement. "That depends. Do you care if whatever we discuss gets passed around town along with the lunch special? Because both Dinner Belles and The Daily Grind are the town gossip hubs."

"Fair point." His lips curved. "I don't mind, but you might prefer to have some time to think things over before you become additional fodder for dinnertime conversations."

Curiouser and curiouser. "Then perhaps a walk instead?"

Gerald made an *after you* gesture and fell into step beside her.

"I didn't come here looking for you the last time. You were just a reminder that got me looking back at the past. But meeting you, seeing what you'd done here, got me curious.

So I looked you up. Or, as my PA would say, I Google-stalked you."

Just months before, she'd known exactly what there was to find. Her credentials and her reputation had been finely-crafted with great deliberation. But most of that had been through Helios. She hadn't had the courage to see what was left since they fired her.

"The coalition website, that's your work?"

"With the exception of some of the content that came from other members, yes. The design and set up are mine."

"It's been up less than two months, but it's already well-ranked with steady traffic flow."

Norah shrugged. "It's my business to know how to launch things quickly and well." Not that it had mattered in the end.

"But web work isn't your real forte, is it?"

Where was he going with this? "I enjoy it, but no, that's not what I'm known for."

"Skyhawk Industries. New Zinta International. Terraquest. Infinitim Technologies.

All fledgling or failing companies until you took the reins of their marketing campaigns."

"You *did* do your homework." Impressed, she enjoyed the tingle of pleasure at the professional approbation. No one here knew the true specifics of what she'd done for Helios. "While I was the senior marketing executive on those accounts, it isn't fair to take all the credit when I didn't do the work alone. I had a team of talented people."

"You haven't had that here."

She frowned. "I wouldn't say that. What I've been doing here is very different from the sort of work I usually do. The people I've worked with have different skill sets and strengths. That's taken some adaptation."

"The coalition wouldn't have had the results it's had without your leadership."

"My leadership would've meant nothing without the buy-in of the locals. What exactly are you getting at, Mr. Peyton?"

"I wanted to make it clear that I know what you're coming from. I recognize your professional acumen, and I respect the hell out of your capability. And for all those reasons, I want to offer you a job."

Norah stopped walking. "What?"

"Let me back up a bit. I'm the CEO of Peyton Consolidated." He paused, clearly waiting for some reaction. "I can see by the look on your face you aren't familiar with the company. I won't be offended by that. It's part of why I need you."

"What sort of company is it?"

"Historically, we were in the business of business." Gerald gave a wry smile. "My daughter likened it to Richard Gere in *Pretty Woman* before Vivian worked her magic."

"A chop shop. And now?"

"Now we build."

"Build what exactly?"

"A little bit of everything. Hotels. Conference centers. And the last few years, we've branched into urban renewal and revitalization."

"And you want...what exactly? A campaign

for an upcoming project? A new concept for the overarching company?"

"I want you to come run my marketing department."

Norah could only blink at him.

"There's currently a staff of thirty, with the option to expand as the need arises."

Run an entire marketing department for what had to be a multi-million dollar corporation. Was she dreaming?

"I realize this is coming completely out of left field and you'd need some time to consider it. To research my company. But I think we'd be a great fit for your talents."

"Mr. Peyton—"

"Gerald, please."

"Gerald, why me? You're standing here giving me this amazing offer without even conducting a formal interview."

"I find that actions speak louder than words. Yours are commendable. You're driven, intelligent, creative, and you have the kind of moral compass I don't often see in the business world."

"Are you aware that I was…dismissed from my last position for that moral compass?" Might as well put that out there.

"That wasn't how Philip Vargas put it when I called to check up on you."

Oh God, what did he say? Norah was afraid to ask. "And yet, regardless of whatever he said, you're here. Why?"

"The picture he tried to paint wasn't consistent with my own impressions of you, with your actions down here, or with the opinions of any of those other corporations. It's obvious to me that a great deal of the success Helios has enjoyed over the last five years is a direct result of your work, and Vargas is only realizing that in the wake of your absence. He tried to pretend otherwise when attempting to woo me to hire Helios, but I recognize a cretin when I see one. I made it clear I was interested in you, not in Helios."

Norah resisted the urge to do a celebratory

fist pump at that. "I imagine Philip didn't take that well."

"Not so much. It will probably relieve you to know that we do little business in Chicago. Our main offices are based in Denver, with satellites in New York, Atlanta, and London."

"London?"

"I do a fair bit of business in Europe." He began walking again. "Now, I'm not sure what your salary was at your prior position, but I'm certain we could come to an agreement." He named a ballpark starting salary that had her eyebrows winging up. "I realize there are things you would want to tie up here, so start date is flexible, based on your schedule, and we'd cover relocation expenses."

Relocation.

And just like that, the surreality of the conversation faded and the happy little dream bubble that had been building around her popped.

"Thank you. Not only for the job offer but for your obvious faith in me and my capabilities. Not many people would look past what Philip said. I'm beyond flattered." What else could she be when someone offered her dream job on a platter?

His blue eyes sharpened. "But?"

"But, I'm committed to staying here, to building something on the foundation I started." And somewhere, her father was doing the live person's version of spinning in his grave.

"With the town or with the guy?"

"I fell in love with them both." Norah looked around at the bright new face of downtown Wishful. "I have a vision for what this place could be."

Looking intrigued rather than insulted that she'd turned down his generous offer, Gerald angled his head. "Tell me."

She had no idea of his background, but he couldn't run an international company without spending sufficient time in cities that he'd experienced everything she hoped to counter. So she outlined it for him, honing in on all her personal reasons for believing that rural tourism could be a success here. As she spoke, Norah could see that, unlike Cam and the rest of the City Council, Gerald immediately understood her concept.

"There's a real market for that. It's a brilliant way to revitalize this town, if you can pull it off."

"And there's the kicker. The rest of them aren't sold on the idea. Yet. But I'm not done researching and working up a full plan either. Conceptually, the project is still in its infancy."

"It'll be a lot of work."

"I'm not afraid of hard work. And I find that what I've done here is considerably more rewarding than anything I did for Helios."

"So you're going to stay. Really give up the city life?"

She thought of Cam and the family here, so ready to fight for her. "I'm not leaving anything worth keeping."

Gerald's smile was sad. "I hope that works out better for you than it did for me."

Norah wondered if he was talking about the

girl he'd loved and lost but didn't think she had a right to ask.

They'd stopped in front of a sleek, black BMW. "This is me."

"Thank you for coming down and for the offer."

Gerald pulled a business card from his coat pocket and handed it over. "The offer stands, should your circumstances change."

He clearly had more faith in her business capabilities than in the love side of this equation.

Pocketing the card, she bid Gerald farewell. As he drove away, Norah waited for the panic, the second guessing of her impulsive decision. But she felt only a rock-steady certainty that this was where she belonged.

Grinning to herself, she headed for her car. She'd go find Cam and apologize for being distant the last couple of days. Maybe they could go out to Tosca for dinner to celebrate. Because she was going to stay. Really and truly. Better yet, maybe they could get take out from Tosca and celebrate at home.

Her phone rang. She was still smiling when she dug it out and answered.

"Oh thank God. I've been trying to reach you for two weeks."

Her brain took a few moments to shift gears. "Cecily?"

"I was going to email, but I realized I didn't have your personal email, and your company email was already blitzed from the system, and—"

Instinctively wanting to soothe the panic, Norah interrupted her former intern. "Cecily, slow down. Take a breath."

"I've been calling, but you haven't answered. I couldn't even get voicemail!"

Norah realized she'd never unblocked the Chicago area codes. Too late she wondered if Philip had taken any of his frustrations out on her staff. "You've got me now. What's going on?"

"I've been trying to tell you so you could do damage control."

A sick feeling began to brew in the pit of her stomach. "Damage control for what?"

"For Philip. He blackballed you."

THE LOFT WAS empty when Cam got home. Hush raced inside, making a beeline for the back, then coming back looking confused when she didn't find Norah hiding in the bathroom.

"I know, girl. I miss her, too."

Since the Council decision, Norah had withdrawn into a funk. Cam was working hard not to take the distance personally. Miranda assured him she was just licking her wounds. He was willing to bet Norah had spent at least twenty-four hours afterward wracking her brain for something else to do, some last stand. Given the email she'd sent out to the coalition, she hadn't found it. And that had just led to more silence.

The little voice that nudged at him, wondering if she had regrets, if she was going to run, had been silenced by a lot of hard, sweaty labor.

It hurt him that she was so hard on herself. How the hell did anybody make it this far through life without having failed at something? Without being able to accept that sometimes your best wasn't good enough, and it wasn't the end of the world? And it wasn't just a matter of perception on Norah's part. Her track record was irrefutable. She'd more than earned the nickname he'd initially given her in jest.

No amount of logic on his part was going to make her believe she hadn't failed. So Cam figured some redirection was in order. He wanted to focus on the positive to come out of this whole mess—Norah was here. She was staying. And he wanted to take a step forward with their relationship now that every waking second wasn't full of GrandGoods. At least it shouldn't be.

But what step?

For all that he thought they were on the

same page, Cam didn't want to scare her off by pushing too far, too fast. It was hard, so hard, to hang on to his patience since she'd finally admitted she wanted to stay and he began to let himself think of their future. After so many years of waiting for her, he was eager to get started.

She already had a key to his place. That had just been expedience. She'd needed workspace and it was easier to trade off Hush duty. Cam loved having her in his space, loved seeing her dainty girl shoes lined up neatly next to his work boots, loved, too, the myriad of little reminders that she was in his life—like her pens and the favorite wine he kept stocked just for her.

Would asking her to move in scare her off? Would she recognize what he was really saying?

Norah, I love you.

She had to know. It was in every look, every action, every touch. But he hadn't given her the words. Maybe he should just start with that, see where they took him.

As if conjured by his thoughts, she popped up on the caller ID.

"Hey Wonder Woman. I was just thinking about you. Ready to come out of your cave?"

In the beat of hesitation before she answered, Cam felt the tension reach out and grab him by the throat.

"Hey." Her voice was hoarse. As if she'd been talking for hours. Or crying.

"What's wrong?"

"I got a call today from my intern—former intern—at Helios."

No. Oh no. Surely, *surely* they hadn't called to win her back.

"It seems that despite my complete and total absence from Chicago and the entire professional marketing scene, despite the fact that I said nothing about the ethics violations Pierce engaged in to anyone outside your family and mine, Philip decided to hedge his bets and started a smear campaign against me. Two weeks ago. Which I knew nothing about because

I completely unplugged from my professional life and have been hiding out in Mississippi. Two weeks, Cam, for all these vicious rumors to circulate without rebuttal or challenge."

Shit. He didn't know what to say. "How bad?"

"Bad. As in my entire professional reputation hangs in the balance bad. As in, I'm going to sue his ass for libel and slander and whatever else my attorney can come up with bad."

"Jesus." Cam scrubbed a hand over his face. Like she hadn't had enough to cope with. "Look, come over, or I'll come over there and we'll talk through this. Figure out what to do next."

There was another beat of silence.

"I'm already halfway back to Chicago."

Which meant she'd been gone for more than half the day and she'd only just now called him. Cam absorbed that. Her professional life was falling apart, and she hadn't looped him in on this until now. She'd gotten in her car and fucking *left town* without a word to him that she was going.

What else wasn't she saying?

He held on to his temper. "Why didn't you tell me? I'd have gone with you."

"I didn't even think to tell you. I was just so *angry*, I had to act."

They were supposed to be in a relationship and she didn't think to tell him about this huge thing that happened in her life. Didn't come to him for comfort. Didn't come to him for anything.

The silence between them stretched, grew gawky and strange.

"I've been on the phone with my attorney and various other people, trying to find out the extent of the damage."

And this is where he fell in her priority list. Dead last. Or damned close to it.

"When will you be back?" Because they sure as shit needed to talk about this, and he wasn't going to do it from five states away.

"I don't know. I'm not sure how long it will

take to straighten all this out. But I have to see this through. My professional reputation is all I have left."

She had him, but clearly she didn't count that on her list.

"I should know more after I meet with my attorney tomorrow. I'll call you after."

"Yeah, okay. Drive safe."

He hung up and sat in silence, the phone all but crushed in his hand. A neat stack of her legal pads and multi-colored Post-it notes were arranged on the coffee table in front of him. The throw she'd adopted because he kept it frigid during the winter lay abandoned in the armchair, as if she'd just gotten up to pour a cup of coffee. Signs of her were everywhere. And yet after that three-minute conversation, his house felt empty.

Hush, sensing his mood, laid her head on his knee and whined. Cam curled his fingers in her ruff and bent to press his brow to hers.

"Looks like we're on our own for a while, girl."

Hush whined again.

Cam sat up. "You know what? Screw this."

She followed him as he stalked back to his room and began to pack a bag. "We're going for a drive."

CHAPTER 19

"WELCOME TO STARBUCKS. WHAT can I get you?"

Norah looked at the barista who'd served her coffee almost every day of her last two years at Helios and waited a few moments for recognition to click. She tried a smile, "I guess it's been a while, hasn't it, Amos?"

Other than a faint twitch of his pierced eyebrow, his expression didn't change. He didn't remember her. Didn't even make an effort to fake it.

She thought of Cassie and the Daily Grind

and felt a wave of brutal homesickness for Wishful wash over her. That made her think of Cam and wonder how long he was going to stay mad at her for bolting.

Amos cleared his throat.

"Sorry. I'll have a venti Veranda blend." Still rattled from the meeting with her attorney, she added a cheese danish. She took both to a table for two and sat, back to the door. Probably she wouldn't run into anyone from Helios while she was here, except for the one person she was expecting, but she didn't exactly want to advertise her presence.

Her professional life was rapidly descending into the fifth level of hell. Marcus was filing the suit today, but he'd cautioned that she shouldn't get her hopes up. Evidence was going to be hard to come by, as Norah had absolutely had access to all the project materials, and proving she hadn't done what Philip accused her of was going to be very difficult. She needed to work out a plan for damage control, but she wasn't sure how much could actually be done after two whole weeks of no response. Several of her professional contacts outside the firm wouldn't even return her calls. And that left her with very grave concerns about her future employ-ability.

In need of a distraction, and wondering ex-actly what it was she'd turned down flat, she pulled out her laptop and began a search on Peyton Consolidated. Ten minutes into the search, she'd forgotten her pastry. Half an hour more, the last inch of her coffee had gone cold.

Gerald Peyton had built himself a jugger-naut of a company. Its estimated value was over a billion dollars and growing. Company stock was a steady performer, even in the sluggish and unpredictable market. PC was the name behind a very solid and respected segment of the hospitality industry. But it was the past five years she was most interested in. He'd told her they'd made a name for themselves in urban re-newal. She didn't find much directly through the company itself, but she found plenty of press around the country, all of it positive.

Peyton was the real deal, and his company was, by all appearances, a force for good. That had the kernel of an idea starting to tremble in her brain.

"Sorry I'm late."

Norah looked up from her computer screen to see Cecily sliding into the chair on the opposite side of the table. She mustered up a smile. "Hey. Thanks for coming."

Unwinding a chunky heather gray scarf, Cecily shook back her dark hair. "It took me a little longer than expected to slip away. Pierce is overloaded since you left. The guy they brought in to replace you is an idiot, and between the two of them, I'm not sure they can find their own asses without a map and a flashlight. So they've been relying on me a lot."

"They haven't been taking advantage of you, have they? Not making your life more difficult because I'm gone?"

"Apart from more work, no."

Well, that was one tiny relief. "What about

Christoff?" Her irascible PA would likely as not pop off and get himself in trouble on her behalf.

"Pretty sure he's plotting someone's doom. I know for sure there's a voodoo doll in his desk, but he's hanging on. Mouthing off to anybody who has the nerve to bad-mouth you."

Norah grimaced. "Have there been many?"

"Among those who actually worked with you? No. The lower echelons full of the jealous…some. A lot of them don't want to believe you got where you did by sheer hard work and brilliance."

"There was always a segment that assumed I slept my way to the top. A rumor not improved by the fact that I actually dated Pierce. But whatever. I'm not concerned about that. What's the office climate like?"

"Tense. I don't think they realized how much you did until you weren't there to do it. So they've been scrambling to reassign accounts. Several of yours walked when they found out you were no longer there."

That was gratifying. She hoped Helios ultimately lost all the clients she'd helped reel in.

"Well, it isn't going to get any less tense. My attorney is filing a suit for defamation of character today. I'm not sure how quickly Philip will get served, so brace yourself."

"What can I do to help?"

"You've already done plenty just letting me know all this was going on and getting us copies of the emails that went out. I don't want you risking your job on my account."

Cecily scowled. "They're assholes and they're wrong. I know you didn't do what they're claiming."

"I appreciate the faith."

"What on earth have you been *doing* the last few months?"

"I've been in Mississippi. I don't think you ever got to meet Miranda, but you certainly heard me talk about her."

"No I never met her, but I remember her hunky brother."

That wrangled a grin from Norah's lips. "Mitch would be delighted to hear it."

"So you've been visiting all this time?"

"Yes and no. I only planned to be there for a week. But I ended up getting involved in local affairs. Miranda's cousin, Cam, is on the City Council in Wishful, and I helped him start a local coalition against the big box store that wants to build in town. So I've actually been working my ass off with that."

Cecily studied her with a quirk to her lips. "And having something of a local affair while you're at it?"

Norah's cheeks heated. "Am I wearing a sign?"

"You have The Look."

"What look is that?"

"The sort of stupefied, punch drunk, oh my God I met The One and I'm happy look."

"You got all that despite the fact that I'm flipping out over this lawsuit?"

"Yep." Cecily grinned. "Looks good on you. So is it this Cam guy? Miranda's cousin?"

"Yeah." Despite the rocky spot they'd hit, Norah's conviction in that remained unshaken.

"And is Cam as hunky as Mitch?"

"He is."

"Do they have any *other* cousins who are single? Lord knows I haven't been having any luck in this city."

"As a matter of fact, there's one more unattached cousin who's only a couple years older than you. He owns a bookstore and has horn-rimmed reading glasses."

Cecily sighed. "Young, financially solvent. And I do have a soft spot for horn-rims. Maybe I should get myself down to Mississippi."

"I promise you an introduction if you come."

"I'll hold you to it." She nodded to the laptop. "So this anti-big box store campaign. Is that what you're working on?"

"Not exactly. Things on that front haven't turned out all that well." She filled Cecily in on the coalition and the latest blow to the cause. "But all that work ended up having an unexpected consequence."

"What kind of consequence?"

"A job offer." Needing to confide in someone, she settled in and told Cecily about Peyton Consolidated.

"Peyton Consolidated? Seriously? That has to be it."

"That has to be what?"

"Philip's had the new guy and half the firm working on a campaign to woo the CEO. He's made at least three tries that I know of, and the guy keeps saying no. If Philip knows the guy is turning him down in hopes of hiring you, I bet that's why he's going to the mat to ruin you."

"Whether I take the job or not, Gerald isn't going to hire Helios. He told me so outright. But if this is all about loss of business for the firm, then Philip isn't going to just back off. He's not going to stop until my reputation is completely destroyed."

THE BLACK SEDAN cut in front of Cam close enough it should've shaved the front bumper off his truck. Cam slammed on his brakes, laid on the horn, and swore. And, of course, he missed getting through the light. Hush howled her disapproval from the back seat. She'd been a trooper through the all-night drive. Of course, she'd been able to sleep. He'd been fueling himself with truck stop coffee and sugar, and an all too brief three-hour nap at a rest stop somewhere in southern Illinois because the highway was starting to blur and he didn't figure Norah would appreciate him knocking on her door at three in the morning. By now, both he and his dog wanted out of the truck.

He'd expected to show up at Norah's apartment with coffee and breakfast and get to the bottom of things. But she'd already been gone by seven-thirty, and he'd been forced to turn on the friend finder app to track her phone. By the time he made it into the business district almost two hours later, she was on the move again, this time to the north side of the city.

Why in God's name anybody would ever want to live in a place like this, he couldn't fathom. You couldn't get from one side to the other in anything resembling a reasonable span of time, as evidenced by the fact that he'd been chasing Norah all over the damned city and just missing her. There was no rush hour. It was just rush rush rush, all the time, bumper to bumper cars, shoulder to shoulder people. Between the excessive caffeine and sugar, the lack of sleep, and all the freaking people, Cam felt like he was about to crawl out of his skin.

He could've just called Norah and asked her to stay put, but he wanted to see her face when he showed up in her city. Plus, he didn't want to interrupt whatever she had going on in case one or more of these stops were meetings with her attorney. She'd worked so incredibly hard for her reputation. Having it maligned like this…she had to be losing her mind. So yeah, on the drive he'd come to terms with the fact that she hadn't been acting rationally when she left. Mostly.

By now he was exhausted. He just wanted to find her and hold her until everything was okay again. Followed by a nice, solid eighteen hours of sleep. Too late, he wondered if her apartment building allowed dogs.

Miracle of miracles, Norah's dot was still stationary by the time Cam made it back across town to the business district. She hadn't moved by the time he found parking. Not knowing quite where he was headed, he left Hush in the truck and left it running. Anybody considering a carjacking would be deterred by the hundred pounds of wolf-like teeth and claws.

"I'll make this quick as I can, girl. Then I swear, we'll find you a dog park so you can get some exercise."

Hush replied in her sing-song talk, as if wishing him luck. He ruffled her ears and set out at a brisk walk, his shoulders hunched. His flannel-lined Carhartt coat wasn't enough to protect against the ice-edged wind coming off Lake Michigan. He wished desperately for gloves. If this was what Norah was used to, no wonder she'd mocked what they called cold back home.

The dot turned out to be Starbucks. Cam was so chilled by the time he reached it, he was actually glad to see even chain coffee. The place was packed when he stepped inside. A double line snaked back from the counter, past the door where he stood, so he edged aside to get out of the way and began to scan the room for Norah. Voices chattered around him, clipped and rapid, almost like typewriter speech. What the hell was their hurry?

His own urgency seemed to hit slow-mo and melt away as he finally caught sight of Norah just past the station with the cream and sugar. Her back was to him, but he knew that fall of hair, that slope of shoulder. The sight of her neat stack of notepads and a row of colored pens had him smiling despite the bone-deep weariness. She sat with another woman, slightly younger. The intern?

Cam made his way over, hampered by the line of people waiting to doctor their coffee.

Too tired to be pushy, he just waited, edging closer as he could, until he could hear her talking. God, it was good to hear her voice.

"I'm nothing but impressed with what Peyton Consolidated has accomplished. It's an incredible opportunity."

"I'll say. Particularly in light of the lawsuit. People have long memories for scandal. That'd be less likely to touch you out in Denver. So to have the chance at a position like that with a billion dollar corporation… Are you going to take it?"

"It's essentially my dream job on a platter. I'd be a fool not to."

Cam felt her words like a physical blow. Every drop of pleasure at seeing her after his long trip, evaporated. The blood in his ears began to roar, drowning out whatever Norah's companion replied.

It's my dream job on a platter. I'd be a fool not to take it.

Everything they'd been through. Everything she'd told him. Everything she'd promised. And in the end, she was choosing the job over him. Like her mother. Like Melody. Like his father.

She tried to warn you, he thought. *Everybody tried to warn you that this wouldn't work. But you just couldn't leave it alone. Because you're some kind of goddamned masochist.*

Sick and a little dizzy, he turned and walked back into the cold, heading back to his truck and his dog and the life that was, it seemed, too small for everyone who'd ever mattered to him.

There was nothing to say after all.

THE LIGHTS of Denver glittered against a sky fading from fire to night above the line of mountains beyond the city. Norah saw none of it as she stood at her hotel room window and listened as her call to Cam rang through to voicemail. Again.

He'd been dodging her calls for three days. She'd gotten one terse email.

Been working a lot, catching up on all the stuff I

let slide while we were working the GrandGoods campaign. Plus it's warming up, so the season's starting. Everybody's thinking about perking up their yards now that we're mostly past the threat of frost. Keeping busy and holding down the fort.

No endearments. No questions about how the lawsuit was going. Not even a *When are you coming home?* Which was probably just as well, since she had no idea how to answer.

Norah didn't know what to do with the distance that yawned between them, so much more than the physical miles. Hurt and confused, she desperately wanted to talk to him, to have his support through the nightmare of this case. Was he still angry about how she'd left? She couldn't undo that and she'd apologized, so what did he want from her? Because that was a conversation best left for in person, she didn't try to broach the subject. Instead she just said, "It's me. I really miss you. Please call me."

Dropping the phone into her clutch, she did her best to clear her mind and settle her nerves for this dinner with Gerald Peyton. What she'd come out here to do absolutely adhered to her family's mantra of "Go big or go home." It was a risk, a big one. She might be blowing up her last bridge to traditional gainful employment in her field of choice. But Wishful was counting on her, so she had to try.

He was waiting in the lobby when she came down. His shirt, open at the collar, and the sport coat and khakis, hit somewhere between the casual first impression and boardroom dominator who'd offered her the running of his marketing department. He was a man at ease with himself and his surroundings.

"Miss Burke. It's good to see you again."

Norah shook his offered hand. "And you."

Gerald gestured *after you*. "Shall we?"

She followed him out to a late model Land Rover. They chatted about inconsequential things, and Norah tried to pay some attention to the city as they wove through its streets. He pointed out features of interest, shared little bits of local history. She found herself relaxing by the time they made it to the restaurant.

Gerald waited until they'd ordered entrees and received their drinks before leaning forward, both elbows on the table, and steepling his fingers. "I have to confess, I was very surprised to get your call. But very pleased to have you here. Have you changed your mind about my offer?"

A fleeting thought of Cam and whatever lay so very wrong between them passed like a shadow through her mind, but she shook her head. "I'm afraid not. I actually have other business to discuss with you."

He smiled, a kind of secretive chess player's smile, and picked up his wine. "I make it a policy never to discuss business until dessert."

Inclining her head in acquiescence, Norah settled in to play the game of calculated Get To Know You.

"So, if I remember from our last conversation, you have a daughter?"

"Mmm. Tess. She's twenty-four and an absolute ball-buster. You remind me of her a bit."

"I'm sure my parents would be perfectly

horrified to hear me described that way. They worked so hard to make sure I was polite and politically correct. I, on the other hand, take that as a compliment."

Gerald's lips curved as he sipped his Cabernet. "Joe always did worry too much about that crap."

That set Norah back in her chair. "You know my father?" Did she owe this miraculous job opportunity to her dad pulling strings?

"Knew. We were at Ole Miss together. But he was a senior when I was a freshman, so we weren't exactly buddy-buddy. I remember him more from some of the campus organizations we were both in. I doubt he remembers me."

"So you did undergrad at Ole Miss."

"A couple years. I transferred out to University of Washington and finished there."

"That's a big jump."

"I needed a change."

"Because of her? The girl you loved from Wishful?" The words were out before she could think better of it. She held up a hand in apology. "I'm sorry, that's none of my business. Forget I asked."

Gerald shot her an assessing look. "It's a fair question since I mentioned her to you in the first place. Yes, I transferred because of her."

"What happened? If you don't mind my asking."

He swirled the wine in his glass. "I haven't talked about this in years."

Norah noted he said talked, not thought.

"I'm from Memphis originally. Went down to Ole Miss, and sophomore year I met a girl, as you do. Except the girl was already married to her high school sweetheart."

"That must've been hard."

"I chalked it up to bad luck or crap timing that we should be great friends and that's all. But I was happy to have that instead of nothing, so I kept spending time with her. Nothing happened. We were just friends. At least I assumed that's all that was on her side."

"But it wasn't."

"It wasn't. Her husband had joined a fraternity, gotten really into that scene, which wasn't any more compatible with marriage back then than it is now. She was growing up and he was…acting like a typical unmarried freshman pledge. One night, he got hideously drunk at a party and wouldn't give her the keys. So she called me to come get her.

"It was really late, and we didn't think it would look right if I dropped her off back at their apartment. So we just…drove around for hours, talking. We'd always been able to talk to each other, but this was different. More personal. Hopes, dreams, confessions kind of stuff. She admitted she was unhappy in her marriage. And she…said she wished she'd waited for me."

Norah noted the ripple under the calm surface. "That's a lot to put on a friend."

The arrival of their food interrupted the story, and she found herself wishing the waiter away so Gerald would continue.

Once they were alone again, she leaned forward. "So what happened?"

"I don't think she meant to say it. We were

in that kind of dazed, drunk place you get when you've been up all night. But she said it, and she was just looking at me with these big hazel eyes, and I just—well, I'm not a saint. I kissed her. And she kissed me back."

Gerald fell into the thick silence of memory. His Adam's apple bobbed, his hands tightening on his fork. Eventually, he shook himself. "Anyway, long story short, she decided to leave him. Divorce wasn't quite as common back then, but it wasn't unheard of. And she was going to do it. For me. We waited until summer so she'd be able to file the paperwork and get out, have a few months for the dust to settle. I wanted to meet her at the fountain, but she didn't know how long it might take, and since Wishful's a small town, she didn't want anybody to put two and two together. So we were supposed to meet at the Hoka. It was kind of our place."

"What on earth is the Hoka?"

"It was a movie theater in Oxford. Artsy, indie stuff. Used to be an old cotton warehouse. It's gone now, but it was downtown, kind of in

The Gin's parking lot. Neither of us were really into indie movies, so it gave us somewhere to go to talk. Their cafe used to have the best cheesecake." He smiled a little at the memory.

"So you waited."

"I did. I waited for hours, past closing time, but she didn't come. I got worried that her husband had stopped her. He'd never been violent before, but... I drove to Wishful. Went by her house. And I saw them in the front window. She looked nervous, so serious. I thought, for sure, she was telling him then, that she'd just been delayed somehow. And I was ready to run in and get her out, be her getaway driver. But he didn't look angry. He looked...shocked. And then happy. And then he was kissing her, holding her, and they were laughing." Gerald's voice trailed off. His mouth tightened as his attention focused on his steak. "She made her choice, and it wasn't me. I couldn't stay at Ole Miss after that."

Norah's heart hurt for him. To love someone so out of reach and think you had a shot, only to have it taken away. "I don't blame you. Do you know what happened to her?"

He shook his head. "I moved on. Met my wife, built a life."

"Got divorced?"

Gerald glanced at her in surprise.

"No wedding ring."

He flexed his left hand and looked at it for a moment, before turning his attention back to her. "About ten years now."

"She stuck with you, that first love."

"First loves are like that." Shoving away his half-eaten steak, he said, "How about you tell me what else that busy brain of yours has come up with since we last talked?"

Realizing the subject of the personal was closed, she complied. "I have an investment opportunity for you. Something that will, I think, fit with your desire to build something that lasts, leave your mark in ways that are more personal than how you initially grew your company."

"I'm listening."

They talked business for more than an hour, with Norah giving him a far more detailed description of her plan to promote rural tourism in Wishful than the sketch she'd given him in their last conversation, breaking things down into logical phases. He asked good questions, made some suggestions that had her revising some of those phases in accordance with potential areas of investment by Peyton Consolidated. Unlike the hurried presentation she'd given the City Council, this was shaping up to be a legitimate enterprise.

"So you've piggy backed on the concepts we used for the urban renewal we've done and adapted it for a rural market. That's a smart tactic for sliding the concept by me."

"You wouldn't have offered me a job if I wasn't smart."

He flashed a smile that had her, for a moment, seeing the young man he used to be. "True enough. You've snagged my interest, Norah. I love the idea. In fact, I've got some contacts in another little town a couple hours away.

Balenmore. We have a ski lodge near there, and it happens they've done a lot on the rural tourism front. I think they'd be good people to talk to. Can you stay a few more days? Make the trip up?"

"Of course." Rather than the victory boogie she wanted to make, Norah took a big bite of her chocolate mousse.

"I'll make the arrangements."

She finished her dessert while he typed out a message on his phone, presumably to his assistant. When the man decided to move on something, he didn't waste time.

"I should be able to let you know the details by morning in time for you to check out here."

"Perfect. Will you tell me something?"

"What do you want to know?"

"Does this woman you loved have something to do with why you're considering my plan?"

"I'm considering your plan because I think it's a good investment. And because you're damned good at persuasion, which is why I want you to run my marketing department. I haven't given up hope of wooing you." The smile he shot her was calculated to be disarming.

She didn't miss his sidestep. "I'm good, but you didn't get to be CEO of a billion dollar corporation by being easily led. There are other investments, other places you could do this that would bring you more profit."

"Your point?"

"You wanted to make things better for her back then. I think you still want to make things better for her, in case she's still there."

He said nothing for a long moment. "You have a romantic's heart, Miss Burke. I hope life lets you keep it."

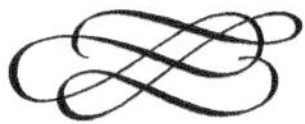

CHAPTER 20

"UH, CAM?"

CAM STABBED his shovel into the pile of mulch and flung it into the newly planted bed before turning to Steve. "Yeah?"

"It's five-thirty."

Cam looked reflexively at the horizon, registering the bleed of colors and the fading light. His crew should've knocked off half an hour ago.

"You want us to start clearing up?"

"Yeah. Sorry about that. I wasn't watching the time. Y'all go ahead and take the gear back to the nursery, check in with Violet. I just wanna finish up mulching this bed."

"You want us to help?" Dewey offered. "You'd finish quicker."

That was exactly what he *didn't* want. "No. I've got this. Y'all have families and dinner to get on home to. I'll see you tomorrow."

His crew exchanged looks but did as they were told. Fifteen minutes later, Cam was alone with the mulch and the lowering sun.

As a rule, Cam oversaw the initial phase of execution for any of his landscape designs before turning over the final wrap up to his more than capable crew. His duties at the nursery made that a general necessity. But since he got back from Chicago, he'd thrown himself into the physical labor, leaving the running of the nursery to Violet so he could work himself to the bone in an effort not to think. Not that it was helping to distract from the epic hole in his life.

He hadn't talked to Norah in four days. He'd spent twenty-eight years of his life without her, and after less than a week away from her, he felt like he was missing a limb. A sensation made all the more unendurable by what he'd overheard.

She was hurt. That much was obvious in her increasingly shorter messages. And he hated it, hated hearing that pained thread in her voice. But even as he knew it made him a coward, Cam couldn't bring himself to take her calls. He couldn't bear to give her a chance to break things off over the phone. If he did, she might not come back at all. Having to come back to Wishful and talk to him in person might change her mind. It had to change her mind. And yet how could he and his small town compete with the career she'd devoted everything to?

While she'd been here, it had been easy to see how it could work. After a bumpy start, she'd taken to small town life like a duck to water. The people loved her, and she'd made connections all over town in her work with the coalition. But was it real or had he just been seeing what he wanted to see? She thrived on the challenge. Now that the challenge was over—and unsuccessful—would Wishful still hold appeal? Would he?

He spread the last of the mulch in near darkness and headed back to the nursery. If he finished the paperwork associated with this job tonight, Violet might not ream him in the morning. Then maybe he'd pick up burgers from Dinner Belles on the drive home as a treat for Hush since she'd been cooped up all day.

Silence lay thick and heavy in the main building of the nursery, interrupted only by the faint buzz of the fluorescent lights. Cam realized he'd been braced for an ambush by Violet or one of his meddling family members. He knew one was coming at some point. It was their modus operandi. They'd poke and prod and harass him until they got to the bottom of his piss poor mood instead of leaving him alone to stew and think. Since he'd rather cut out his tongue than talk about what was happening with Norah, he'd done everything in his power to avoid all of them. As no one had hunted him down, he could only conclude that Norah hadn't been talking to any of them either.

After stowing the last of his equipment and washing at least some of the dirt off in the bathroom sink, Cam holed up in his office to update the inventory and log his hours and those of his crew. Seeing the stack of messages on his desk, he accepted he was going to have to actually come in during business hours tomorrow to deal with the bulk of them. He was calculating how much he could accomplish while Violet took her lunch break, when someone knocked on the outside door.

His gut tightened. It was long past closing time. Anybody out here at this hour was coming expressly to talk to him and it wasn't likely to be about business. For a fleeting moment, he considered just staying where he was, letting whoever it was knock until they got bored and gave up. But given his truck was parked out front, they'd know he was doing just that, so it wasn't like that'd do anything but delay whatever confrontation was brewing.

What if it was Norah?

His heart gave a leap that was somewhere between elation and dread. Her last message hadn't said she was on her way back. But she'd said she missed him. She hadn't told him she was leaving in the first place, so maybe she'd adopted the same policy for the return trip. And for that moment, it didn't matter what was going on, didn't matter about the job or where they stood, because he just needed to hold her.

Cam was halfway across the retail space before he realized it wasn't Norah. His steps slowed as he saw his mother through the window.

Crap. Looked like he was getting ambushed after all.

But when he unlocked the door and pulled it open, he saw she wasn't alone. Edgar Falk was with her.

"Hey baby." Sandra stepped into the store without invitation. Cam automatically bent to accept her kiss on his cheek. "Do you have some time to talk?"

Company was the last thing Cam wanted, but if Ed was here, it probably had something to do with city business. "About?"

"GrandGoods."

That just made him think about Norah and his mood, already black, darkened further. "What is there to talk about? The special use permit already passed."

"Could be we've still got an option." Ed rocked back on his heels and crossed his wiry arms.

Cam found that highly unlikely. "How's that?"

"Well, I'd forgotten about this. It's been forty years since it came up last."

Ed was the closest thing they had to institutional memory in city government. He'd been a representative off and on for the last fifty years. He unfolded his arms and passed over some rolled up papers. "There's a law on the books that'll let us initiate a ballot referendum on any law passed that the public disagrees with.

Makes it a public vote, so you get a true democratic answer to the issue."

Cam unrolled the papers, which turned out to be Xerox copies of city statutes. He read through the pertinent section. "We can overturn the special use permit?"

"If we can get enough signatures on a petition. It has to be a majority of registered voters," Sandra said.

"And it's gotta be turned in within thirty days of the original decision," Ed added.

Which meant they were already seven days down.

"How many signatures are we talking?"

"There are about three thousand people registered to vote here. Unfortunately, unless they submitted the paperwork or unless we get notice from some other jurisdiction, that doesn't eliminate anybody who's moved and doesn't live here anymore," said Sandra. "Updating the records hasn't been a priority since we've had to cut city staff the last five years. We need fifty one percent of that number to initiate a referendum ballot."

"Can people not currently registered to vote register and sign the petition?"

"Yes, though that'll make the overall total of registered voters bigger and raise the number of signatures we'd need as well," Ed said.

Cam needed something, anything to distract him, so he jumped at the chance. "Then I reckon we've got a lot of work to do. Why don't you get up with Molly, get the coalition going on all this?"

"Will you call Norah, see what she suggests on getting the word out?" Sandra asked.

Cam hesitated. If he called her, told her this, she'd probably come back. She'd set aside whatever her personal stuff was for the good of the town, and he might have a chance to win her back, convince her to stay. But there was still the issue of her reputation to fix. She was where she was in part because she'd ignored things up there to deal with stuff down here. If she'd known about the smear campaign from the start, in time to counter, she might not have been so susceptible to the job offer.

He didn't have the right to be selfish and potentially open her to more problems.

"No. She's got her own stuff she needs to take care of in Chicago right now. I don't want to distract her from that. Let's see what we can do with what we've got before I involve her." And maybe when she came back, they'd have some good news to share. News that would make her realize she hadn't failed, that she still had a place in this community and with him.

After hashing out a few more details, Ed headed out, leaving Cam alone with his mother. He made a valiant effort to shoo her along, but she wouldn't be shooed. Sandra Crawford had something to say apparently. Damn it.

"You've been hiding."

"Just working." He shrugged. "There's lots to catch up on that I let slide the last several weeks."

She cupped his cheek and tilted his face down to study it.

Cam endured her scrutiny for a few moments before jerking his head back. "I'm filthy, Mom."

"You miss her."

"Do you expect an award for noticing the obvious?" He got The Eyebrow. "Yeah, I miss her."

"When's she coming home?"

Maybe never? "I don't know. Her ex-boss was supposed to get served a couple days ago." She hadn't left another message saying how that went.

"It's hard when people we care about have to deal with stuff without us. Hard on you in particular."

"Why's that?"

"Because you want to fix things for everybody. Like you dug up the evidence to prove Norah wasn't at fault in Morton."

"Yeah, well, I can't fix this. There wouldn't even be anything to fix if I hadn't talked her into staying in the first place." That was the other thought that had been swimming around beneath his misery.

"You don't know that. Besides, as tough as this is for her, I don't think Norah would trade you to avoid it."

Don't be so sure about that, Cam thought. Some of the doubt must've flickered across his face.

"She wouldn't. I don't know what has or hasn't been said between you, but she loves you. Anybody with eyes can see it when she looks at you."

"For someone like her, love isn't always enough."

His mother frowned. "I don't think that's fair to either of you."

"Maybe not. But it's been a possibility from the beginning. I'm just trying to be a realist."

"How about focusing less on realism and more on having some faith."

It was such a Norah thing to say, Cam felt a stab beneath his breastbone. Because he couldn't take any more of this, he said what he knew she wanted to hear. "I'm sure you're right. I'm just out of sorts."

"You'll feel better once she's home. Meanwhile, why don't you put off that paperwork until tomorrow and head on home. You can call her up on FaceView."

"FaceTime, Mom."

Sandra waved a hand. "Whatever. Call her."

"Yes, ma'am."

Cam walked her out, locking the door behind her and waiting until she'd driven away before pulling out his phone. His thumb hovered over contacts before moving to open the friend finder app. Her name was at the top of the list. He selected it, watching the screen flip to a U.S. map. But instead of zooming in to Chicago, the view shifted west.

To Denver.

"WELCOME BACK." Tucker didn't come around his desk to hug her as she expected.

Norah shrugged it off as a product of him being in lawyer mode. "Thanks."

She'd never been so glad to see Wishful. Between the lawsuit and the trip out to Colorado, then the second round powwow with the attorney handling her case against Helios, she'd been away for nearly two weeks. It felt like a year.

"Have you seen Cam yet?"

Norah shook her head. She'd wanted to go straight to him and assure herself that things were all right between them, but there was business to tend to. "I came here to sign the paperwork first." Something in Tucker's expression set her on edge. "Is he okay? We haven't really talked since I left." *Or at all.* When he hadn't returned any of her calls in the first week, she'd stopped trying. And she'd avoided the rest of the family as well.

"He hasn't exactly dealt well with your absence."

Yeah. Got that.

Looking back, riding her wave of fury

halfway back to Chicago without seeing him first hadn't been the best way to handle things. But he knew what her professional reputation meant to her. She could hardly open her own firm with that in tatters. Now, more than ever, she needed to be able to rely on a job and income.

"Then let's get this done so I can go find him."

"You should also know that there's been a development with the whole GrandGoods thing."

"What kind of development? Is there some kind of problem with this?" Dear God, if this fell through after everything she'd done…

"No, nothing to do with this. Cam will fill you in. But we've got a chance at a Hail Mary."

A Hail Mary in conjunction with what she already had planned? Maybe things were finally turning around. "I like the sound of that." She picked up a pen. "Now, where do I sign?"

The paperwork was minimal, given the nature of the transaction. As she left Tucker's office twenty minutes later, Norah almost felt like clicking her heels together. Now that the deal was finalized, she was excited to find Cam and tell him what she'd done, what she planned. God knew she needed some good to balance out all the bad of Chicago.

This time of day, she figured he'd be at the nursery, so she drove out to the edge of town, mentally rehearsing what she might say.

Listen, I know I handled things badly, but I missed you, and I love you, and oh, by the way, I liquidated every asset I had to buy the land you love to keep the Big Bad Box Store from ruining it.

Surely he'd get over whatever his issue was after that.

Violet looked up from arranging a display of potted daffodils as Norah strode in. "Praise Jesus, you're finally back. Nobody's had any peace. He's been in a Mood since you left. I had to banish him to the propagation house to keep him away from customers."

"That bad, huh?" Norah winced. "Hopefully

I'll be able to improve his mood. Which one is the propagation house?"

Following Violet's directions, Norah made her way around the back side of the nursery to the farthest of three green houses, outside the public space. The thump of bass greeted her even before she tugged open the door and stepped into the damp heat. She stood just inside, feeling her hair frizz and her skin prickle as the driving drumbeat seemed to reach out and resync her heart. Cam was working at the far end of the space, the gentle motions of his hands as he transplanted tiny seedlings into larger pots a strange counterpoint to the angry music. Five Fingered Death Punch. "Bad Company."

It felt like an omen or a wall. So she didn't run to him and slide her arms around him from behind as she wanted.

Hush saw her first, leaping up from where she'd been contentedly chewing on a rawhide to barrel down the aisle. At least one of them was happy to see her. Norah crouched and braced for the impact of Hush's greeting, burying her nose in the big dog's soft fur. By the time she came up from the hug, Cam was looking her way. Looking, but not moving.

Okay, this was a damn sight worse than weird. Norah felt the pleasure at her homecoming leeching away, replaced by wariness.

His expression was shuttered as she approached. Other than using a remote to turn down the music, he didn't move, didn't even put down the pot in his hands, as if he needed a physical barrier to keep her from touching him.

"You're back." Could he sound any less enthused?

"Yeah."

Cue awkward silence. Norah could no more spew her news into that than she could fly. She drank him in, taking in the t-shirt that stretched across his broad chest, the well-worn jeans with stress points faded almost white, and the dirt smudge on his cheek she wanted to reach out and brush away. She was hungry to touch him, to taste him. To tear down whatever this wall was between them. She curled her hands to fists instead.

I'm happy to be home. I missed you. She ached to say it. But not when he stood here like a stranger.

So she defaulted to business. "What's going on with GrandGoods? Tucker said there's been a development?"

He lifted a brow, the biggest shift in his expression since she'd arrived. "You've already seen Tucker?"

"He's taking care of some business for me. I needed to sign some time-sensitive paperwork."

Cam grunted at that.

"So the development?"

He sighed and finally set the pot aside, immediately crossing his arms, as if she hadn't already gotten the message of *hands off.*

"Ed Falk came to see me a week ago. He's old as dirt and is the closest thing we've got to a walking law book for city government in this town. There's a statute on the books that says if we can gather signatures from a majority of registered voters within a month of the passage of a law, the issue becomes a popular vote and can be overturned."

A week. They'd had this development a whole week ago, and he hadn't even emailed her about it. Norah absorbed the sting of that and tried to focus on the news itself. She did the math. "So you've got a little over two weeks left to gather petition signatures?"

He nodded. "Molly's been coordinating teams, getting the coalition out on the streets."

"That's great."

"If we can get enough signatures for a ballot referendum, we're not only seeking to overturn the special use permit but also to implement a store size cap. There is absolutely no reason for any business in a town this size to be bigger than 40,000 square feet. That's less than a third of the size of the store GrandGoods proposes. We think they'd pull out rather than scale down. And a store cap would protect the town from future incursions."

"That's brilliant! What recourse does

GrandGoods have while the petition is going around? Is it something they can try to stop?"

"While the issue is up for vote, no action can be taken. GrandGoods can try to influence voters against the idea of a size cap but they can't move forward even with the purchase of the land until this is settled."

Did GrandGoods even know that the land was off the table entirely? Probably not since she'd literally just finalized the purchase. This was as good an opening as any for her to tell Cam about it, at least.

Norah took a breath. "I have something to tell you."

The tension in the space between them ratcheted palpably higher. "I already know."

"You…what?" Tucker had sworn to keep his mouth shut. Had Abe said something? If Cam knew, why did he seem so pissed?

"I know about Denver and Peyton Consolidated and the job."

It was the last thing she'd expected him to say, and it took her a moment to recover. She hadn't told anyone here about that. Not even Miranda. Unless someone had overheard Gerald's offer. "How did you—"

"I came to Chicago."

He wasn't making any sense. "What? When?"

"Right after you left."

"I don't understand. I never even saw you."

"No, you didn't. I overheard you talking to your friend."

What friend? Who had she seen other than her attorney? Cecily. Of course. And they had talked about the job when they'd met for coffee.

"And you were just…what? Lurking? Why the hell didn't you come to me?"

"Like you came to me before you left?"

She flinched. "Look, I already explained that—"

"Yep, you did. I was under the impression when I left that we still had something to talk about, but you already made up your mind. Without me. Again. So I came home."

Norah's brain scrambled, trying to remember the conversation, what exactly he'd overheard, to understand what it was he thought was going on here.

Cam flashed a bitter smile. "The thing is, I don't blame you. Not really."

That stopped her. "You don't *blame* me?" What was he accusing her of?

"You tried to warn me from the very beginning. It's my fault for pursuing this, for believing you'd be able to change. For thinking I could make you happy."

He thought she'd taken the job. He believed she'd made the decision to walk away from him without even giving him the courtesy of talking about it. That she was capable of being that selfish after everything they'd been through. The insult of that robbed her of words.

But Cam had no trouble jumping into the silence. "So I don't need whatever pretty speech you've prepared to justify all this."

He didn't even want to grant her an opportunity to explain. He was so goddamned certain he knew what was going on. So positive he knew what she would say and do. And none of those views of her were positive.

"Well, if you know everything, then I suppose there's nothing left for me to say." *Except that you're an idiot.*

"Doesn't look like it."

Hush, standing between them, whined and butted her head beneath Norah's palm. Automatically, she threaded her fingers through the dog's fur, using her as an anchor as the world listed hard to one side, the man she loved turning into a stranger before her.

"I won't say anything to the family about this. I don't want to do anything to damage your relationship with them. You can handle that however you want."

Was he patting himself on the back for that? Thinking that meant he was still putting her first, even though he clearly thought she was callous and horrible?

"Listen, I know you'll need to be packing up and going soon, but I hope you can stay long enough to help set up something to get the word out about this referendum. The coalition can use your expertise. It's the last shot we've got, and I know that this, at least, is important to you."

The implication that he wasn't important hung in the air between them.

She could fix this. Could clear it up with a few minutes of explanations. But did she really want to be with a man whose opinion of her could so easily turn? She needed time to think, to get past the insult and the hurt before she decided what to do next.

"Of course, I'll help. I'll get in touch with Molly and see what she needs me to do."

"Thanks."

He picked up another pot, and Norah realized she was dismissed. Bleeding from more wounds than she could count, she turned and walked out, without another word.

THE INITIAL BURST OF temper had already bled away, leaving only a grief so deep Norah thought she'd drown. She didn't dare go find Miranda or Aunt Liz to say she was back. She was too stunned, too raw from Cam's accusations to face anyone from the family. Their well-intentioned concern or advice would break her. She wanted a pint of Ben and Jerry's and a dark room in which to wallow, but that meant stopping at Mc-Sweeney's Market and guaranteed running into *someone* she knew. Not knowing what else to do, she simply drove.

He hadn't fought for her. In the face of his misconceptions, he hadn't questioned, hadn't confronted, hadn't argued. He'd accepted as fact. And he'd let her go. Just like that.

She'd given up her whole world for him.

She found herself at Cam's place before she realized. So ironic that she instinctively came here for solace when he was the one who'd just broken her reality. On autopilot, she climbed the stairs and let herself inside. God, the place smelled like him. Standing in the center of the loft, she waited to feel Cam's rejection echoed through his space, but the apartment was much as she'd left it. He hadn't moved her piles of research. The throw she favored was still draped over the chair. She'd half expected to find her things in a box.

He'd be home in a few hours. A part of her wanted to wait for him, confront him with the truth and set the record straight. But what if this was just an excuse? What if, in her absence, he'd realized he'd been caught up in the rush and he didn't really want her? Certainly, grabbing on to this idea that she was the one at fault would be easier than admitting to his family that he'd changed his mind.

She couldn't do it. She couldn't face another round of rejection from him after everything else she'd been through.

Hands shaking, Norah gathered her stuff. If she was wrong—and oh dear God, she prayed she was wrong—maybe this would be the wake up call he needed. If she wasn't… Then at least she wouldn't have to come back here to face him.

The bag barely fit in the back seat amid the pile of other stuff she'd packed to bring down here. What she'd intended to be the first phase of moving to Wishful for good. Something else she couldn't think about right now.

She needed distraction. Work was the panacea for all ills. Work was her savior. So she called Molly.

"I didn't know you were back!"

"Only just. I wanted to see if you were free to catch me up on what the coalition has done about the petition."

"Certainly, but I thought you'd be with Cam."

So did I. "I've seen him. We agreed that this takes priority."

"Okay then, come on over. I just put a pound cake in the oven."

The two-story ranch was a little worn around the edges. The landscaping needed some upkeep and the siding could use a fresh coat of paint. But everywhere around the house, Norah saw signs of family and permanence. A row of rocking chairs with names painted across the top. Hand-made wind chimes hanging from the eaves. A tree house in the branches of a big sycamore.

Molly opened the door with a broad smile. "Come in, come in. Welcome back."

"Thanks." Norah followed her inside, only dimly aware of the other woman's friendly chatter as she noted the long hallway full of family pictures. Birthdays. Christmases. Sports teams. Dance recitals. Family vacations. The Montgomerys had been here a long time, raised four children, and the place felt full of love and comfort. The kind of home she'd been too afraid to admit dreaming of.

"—told Babette that we really had to work on—" Molly swung around as they entered the living room and stopped. "Norah, honey, what's wrong?"

"Nothing. I'm fine." Why did her voice sound so choked?

"Sweetheart, you're crying."

Mortified, Norah lifted a hand to swipe at her cheeks. "Damn it. I'm sorry. I'm sorry. I didn't mean to—" A hiccupping sob rolled up her throat. Shaking, she clapped a hand over her mouth, struggling to find some semblance of control. But that only made her quake harder. Damn Cam. Damn him for robbing her of this, too.

Molly took her free hand and tugged her down on the sectional. Without batting an eye, she wrapped both arms around Norah. "Go on and let it out, baby. You'll feel better for it."

Too exhausted to keep fighting, she pressed her face to Molly's shoulder and wept. The older woman said nothing, just stroked her back and rocked, while all the stress and strain and heartache poured out, leaving her exhausted and hollow. Even when the tears stopped, Norah stayed put for a few minutes and let herself be soothed.

Then reality intruded again and the embarrassment returned. She'd just completely lost it with this woman who barely knew her outside a professional context. What was the correct response here?

She lifted her head. "I'm sorry."

"You have nothing to apologize for." Molly said it matter-of-factly, as if people fell apart on her all the time. There was no censure, no pity in her eyes, just a kindness and understanding that left Norah feeling out of balance in an entirely different way.

She scrubbed both hands over her face in a

vain effort to erase the damage. "I am…not a crier. My family doesn't encourage that kind of loss of control."

"Sometimes you just need a good purge." Molly handed over a box of tissues. "How long's it been?"

The last time she hadn't been able to choke it down or channel it somewhere else? Well that would be when Cam obliterated her defenses by clearing her name. Before that… "High school, maybe."

"Then I'd say you were long overdue." She patted Norah's hand. "The powder room is just off the hall there. Go wash your face, then come into the kitchen. I'll fix you a cup of tea and we'll have cake. It should be coming out of the oven soon."

Well, if Molly wasn't going to be embarrassed about this, neither would she. Head aching, Norah obediently followed her orders. She deliberately avoided looking in the mirror above the pedestal sink, not wanting to see the damage her crying jag had wrought. On top of all the strain she'd been under the last couple of weeks, she knew it wasn't pretty. The cool water felt wonderful against her puffy cheeks as she rinsed off whatever remained of her makeup. Despite the headache, she felt steadier than when she'd arrived.

Molly didn't turn as Norah came into the kitchen and sat at the island. As she bustled around the room, putting on the kettle and pulling out mugs, Molly said, "You are absolutely not obligated to tell me what that was about. But if you want an ear, you've got mine."

"Thank you." Norah tried to remember the last time her own mother had taken the time to listen and comfort. "Normally, I'd talk to Miranda."

"Hard to do that when she's related to the problem."

Norah started to speak, then closed her mouth.

Molly looked faintly amused. "You've been away for two weeks and you're here instead of there. I'm assuming Cam is at least a contributing factor." She set a cup of tea and a couple of aspirin on the counter.

"You could say that." Norah wrapped her hands around the mug, absorbed the warmth. "It's been a really lousy couple of weeks."

"First rough patch with the two of you?"

Norah scowled. "It's not just that, but yeah. He's being an idiot."

Molly smiled. "Oh, men are good at that. I should know. I raised three. And they're usually convinced they're right." As the buzzer went off, she turned to take her cake out of the oven.

"He's definitely not."

"Did you tell him that?"

Norah sipped the tea, while Molly puttered with the bundt pan and cake rack. "Didn't get a chance." He'd been too busy acting like they'd already had the fight and it was done and this was how things were going to be. And that was so very strange.

After everything he'd gone through to get past her defenses so she'd give their relationship a legitimate try, every gesture, big and small, that proved he cared, why on God's green earth would he come all the way to Chicago and not confront her over what he'd heard?

"There's very little more annoying than being deprived of a good fight."

"Seriously?"

"Sure. I mean, you wouldn't want to fight all the time—that's not healthy—but sometimes it's the same as having a good cry. You need to clear the air, get out whatever's festering."

Had she ever heard her parents fight? Norah didn't think so. They'd always had a completely civil relationship.

"In my family, fighting falls under the same heading as crying: Things Burkes do not do. Arguments are very calm, rational affairs. And, you know what? You're right. They aren't satisfying at all."

"Nobody ever had great make up sex after a civil debate."

Norah's eyes popped wide and she burst out laughing. "That's probably true."

"I've got nearly forty years of marriage to back me up." Molly slid plates of cake in front of each of them and sat. "If somebody's not worth fighting with from time to time, the relationship probably isn't worth fighting for."

"Which is why you have nearly forty years of marriage and my parents crashed and burned after twelve."

"Relationships are all about balance. Wants. Needs. Family. Career. Everybody has a struggle figuring out what their tipping point is. We were lucky that we stumbled on ours early on. Juggling four kids and a full-time job wouldn't have been possible without that."

"Four kids *and* a full-time job?" Norah goggled at her. "My parents couldn't seem to even manage just me and their careers. They could independently save the world, or they could do the family thing. Not both."

"Well, it helped that the career was already established and that we bypassed the baby stage. We adopted all four. But I guess the real clincher is having a true partner. My John was a real trooper. He passed a little over a year ago."

"I'm so sorry." Norah laid a hand over Molly's and squeezed.

"Thank you, honey. I miss him every day. But we found each other early—childhood sweethearts—so I consider myself blessed."

Norah sighed. "I want to be you when I grow up."

Molly's cheeks pinked. "Coming from a bright, capable young woman like yourself, I take that as a huge compliment."

"I can't think of any better role model."

Norah almost toppled off her bar stool as Liam seemed to materialize from thin air and crossed over to the cake.

"He has a sixth sense for baked goods."

As he cut himself a huge slab, Norah wondered if she'd managed to wash away all traces of the tears. Maybe he'd politely ignore the fact that she'd been crying.

No such luck. Turning around with his plate, Liam kicked back against the counter and studied her. "Whatever he did, if he needs an attitude adjustment, I'm happy to give one."

Norah offered a wry smile. "I'm sure Mitch would help."

"Oh, Mitch is a good one in a fight, but for this you want Randa Panda. She fights dirty."

"You know she absolutely loathes that you call her that, right?"

Liam grinned. "Yeah. That's part of the fun."

Norah straightened her shoulders. "If anybody's giving Cam an ass kicking, it'll be me."

He laughed. "I knew I liked you." Walking over, he kissed his mother on the cheek. "Great cake, Mom." Then he and his cake were gone with the same soundless grace with which he'd appeared.

"A man of few words."

"Not always. But when there's cake involved, he's very focused." Molly picked up her own tea. "So, is Cam worth the fight?"

Norah didn't even have to think about it. "More than anybody I've ever known."

Molly gave a satisfied nod. "Good. Do you

want to go kick his ass now or do you still want to go over the coalition stuff?"

"Coalition stuff. He's still at work and what I have to say to him is going to take a while."

She nibbled cake and listened to Molly outline the efforts they'd made so far. Approximately three hundred fifty signatures in the first week wasn't bad, but it was nowhere near the rate they needed to get the referendum.

"We need something to give to people who sign."

"Like a thank you gift?"

"No." She retrieved her bag from the living room and sketched out a quick design. "I'm thinking stickers. YES printed in big block letters and beneath it 'I signed'. That makes signatories walking advertisements. It's vague enough to prompt people to ask 'signed what?' And we should have a second set ready to go for the referendum itself with YES: I voted."

"Oh, that's fabulous. We can have them at every signing station. Every business downtown has a stack of pages for the petition."

"That's a good start but we need more. Bigger. We need a street team. People who are actively out informing people and soliciting signatures. And we'd want them easily identifiable in a way that gets the message across very quickly and visually, so that as word spreads, people can find a petition to sign very easily. I was thinking red baseball caps with YES printed across the front. They're attention getting and very clearly say YES, I support a size cap."

"Richard can have those made up within a few days. I've got a good dozen people I can task with organizing a street team."

Norah scribbled more notes. "Cam said it had to be a majority of registered voters. Can people who aren't registered yet go do that and sign?"

"They can. And for anybody who wants to sign that isn't registered, we've pointed them down to City Hall."

"No you need to eliminate as many barriers as possible. If it's allowed, have stacks of voter registration forms at each petition location so that it saves them from having to go get one. Even better if our business owners can just collect those and drop them off and save people a trip all together."

"I'll check with Sandra to find out the rules on that."

Norah paused in the midst of her notes. "Look, I know you two are close—"

"Don't worry. I won't say anything. Nobody needs to know."

"Thanks. For everything. I really didn't come over here with the intention of falling apart on you."

"Do you feel better?"

"Yeah."

"Then it was exactly what you needed." Molly moved to the sink with her plate. "You're an incredibly strong woman, but I get the sense that you think that means you can't ever lean on anybody else. That needing somebody else to shoulder some of the load somehow makes you weak."

"We Burkes are a self-sufficient lot."

"Self-sufficiency and strength aren't always the same thing. Sometimes the strong thing is admitting you're not and knowing that is absolutely okay."

Norah sighed. "Then I'll have to work on that."

Molly wrapped an arm around her shoulders. "That's the beautiful thing about life, sweetie. We're all constant works in progress."

SHE'D TAKEN ALL her stuff.

By the time Cam got home from one of the crappiest workdays on record, he found that Norah had been by. Hush made a thorough inspection of the apartment and whined when she found no evidence of her favorite person. Everything was gone, down to her last pen—her shoes, her toothbrush, all her office supplies. The key he'd given her lay on the kitchen island without a note. The only things left were the copies of the city financial records she'd gone over for her rural tourism presentation, stacked neatly on the bottom shelf of the coffee table. She'd probably just overlooked them when cleaning herself out of his life.

He'd hoped beyond hope that he'd been wrong, that she'd have some kind of explanation for Chicago and Denver that would make all his imaginings some kind of bad dream. But she hadn't said a word to contradict him. And now this.

They really were finished.

How the hell was he going to get through the next couple of weeks? If she even stayed that long. Who knew when she was due to report to her new job in Denver?

How would he survive after that? Wishful wasn't the haven it had been when he and Melody split up. She'd never really been a part of his life here. But there was nowhere in his town that he didn't associate with Norah now. She'd become a part of the town's fabric. Now he'd only see the jagged tear she left behind.

And wasn't that a bunch of melodramatic bullshit?

Retrieving the remaining half of a six pack from the fridge, Cam sank down on the sofa and pulled out the city financials. Hush scrambled onto her end of the couch and plopped down, staring at him with soulful eyes that seemed to say, *What did you do?* Ignoring his dog and the guilt that look engendered, he opened the binder. The sight of all the color-coded sticky tabs and post-it notes made his throat squeeze tight. This was the only thing she'd touched that she'd left behind.

Christ, he was in bad shape.

The records were arranged in chronological reverse order, beginning with the numbers for the last quarter. He flipped through, fingers tracing the notes she'd made in the margins. Until he reached a point a year before where she'd scribbled *Pattern?* with a number below. He set his beer aside and paid closer attention.

It took him about twenty minutes to figure out what she'd noted, and by then he hauled out his calculator. An hour and a half later, he'd plowed through the rest of the records and had pages of notes of his own. If these numbers meant what he thought they meant…

He called his mother. "Where are you?"

"At Liz and Pete's. What's wrong? Are you all right?"

"I need to talk to you. Stay put. I'm coming over."

Loading up the books and his dog, he drove over to his aunt and uncle's house. The moment he pulled to the curb he had cause to regret not asking his mother to come to him. From the look of things, the entire family was here. A quick, instinctive survey of vehicles showed him Norah's car wasn't among them. Not that it meant anything. She could just as easily have ridden with one of the others.

He wasn't ready to see her again.

But it was too late to change his plan. Grammy was waving from the window. Bracing himself, Cam climbed out of the truck and headed inside. Everyone was gathered in the living room. No Norah. He didn't know whether to be relieved or disappointed.

"What the hell is this? A summit meeting?"

"We were trying to figure out if it needed to be an intervention," Grammy said.

Shit.

"Is Norah with you?" Aunt Liz asked.

The extra beat it took him to find his voice was the kiss of death. "No."

"Then we were right," Reed said. "You are having problems."

"And that's any of your business why?"

"No one knows where she is. She's not answering her phone. And the last person we know saw her was Violet, who said she left the nursery this afternoon looking like you'd punched her in the stomach." Mitch looked like he wanted to return the favor.

That was certainly a switch from what he'd seen. "She was perfectly calm when she left me." No fight, just straight-up rationality, moving on to business as usual. With a short detour to clean herself out of his life with cold, clean efficiency.

"What did you fight about?" Grammy asked.

Cam struggled for patience. He hadn't come here expecting an ambush. His mistake. "We didn't fight." He'd made sure of that, hadn't he? Cutting her off at the first sign of conflict because he couldn't deal with the confrontation and just wanted it over. But maybe she'd been more upset than he thought.

Absolutely nobody looked like they believed him.

"Look, did you try talking to Molly? Norah was going to check in with her on the petition. She's probably holed up somewhere working on a new campaign." Which he could verify with a few swipes of his phone, but God knew that damned app had given him more grief than it was worth. He didn't want to check it again to find her halfway to…anywhere that wasn't here.

Aunt Liz moved off to grab the phone, presumably to follow that lead.

"You can all take potshots at me later. I need to talk to Mom about city business. In private."

They relocated to Uncle Pete's study. Cam shut and locked the door behind them, which caused his mother to arch a brow.

"Not one word about her, Mom."

Sandra Campbell Crawford knew when to choose her battles. Cam fully expected she'd pick this one when he least expected it.

"You said this was something to do with city business." She nodded at the books under his arm. "What are those?"

"The copies I made of the city financial records. Norah was analyzing them for one of her projects. And she noted something unusual."

"What kind of unusual?"

Cam laid out what first Norah and then he had discovered. "It was subtly done, but you see here? The digits are transposed. It starts with small amounts. And if it was just that, maybe we could chalk it up to human error or dyslexia or something. But over the next year and a half, they get bigger and bigger. If I did the math right, we're talking about a difference of near to a hundred thousand dollars of city funds."

"Dear God." Sandra scooped a hand through her hair. "How far back does it go?"

Cam chose his words carefully. "Best I can tell, it started when you were out on medical leave. When Vick took over extra duties because Leigh Billingsly had to go on bed rest. Since she only came back half time after the baby was born, she probably just picked up where the books left off and didn't go back to check the work that was done in her absence."

"Cam, this is a huge accusation."

"I know it. And maybe I'm wrong. But what if I'm not? Vick's been living large when almost everybody's hours and salaries have been cut to the bone. He's just bought an SUV that's almost as much as his annual salary. Where's he getting that money?"

Sandra sat back and sighed. "I just can't believe he'd be embezzling from the city."

"Then how else do you explain these numbers? The system is obscenely antiquated. We've talked about it for years, but we haven't ever done anything about it because there was always some other financial priority. We've got to look into this."

"And we will, but quietly. Both because I'm not willing to make accusations without more definitive evidence and because if it's true, I don't want to spook him into covering his tracks."

Sandra crossed to pick up the cordless phone on the desk. "Robert, it's Sandra. No, no, I'm fine. Listen, are you busy? There's something I need to discuss with you. No, it's probably best if Cam and I come to you. We want to keep this on the down low. I need you to open an investigation into Vick Burgess."

CHAPTER 22

NORAH LEFT MOLLY'S PRIMED to knock Cam down a few pegs and *make* him listen, whether he wanted to or not. So the fact that he wasn't home put a real crimp in her plans. Since she'd rashly left her key after packing her stuff, there was no waiting inside. Damn it.

So she sat in her car. Courtesy of the fact that half her stuff was in the back, she had plenty of clothes to layer for warmth. The temper helped. Her phone kept blowing up with calls and texts from the Campbell clan.

She hadn't listened to the voicemails and hadn't answered the texts. Given that the theme of most had been *Are you okay?* Norah figured that despite Molly's promise of secrecy, someone else had blabbed something. Maybe Liam had spoken to Mitch. She wasn't talking to any of them until she'd talked to Cam himself and had the chance to pry his head out of his ass.

The bravado and the fury wore down considerably over the next two and a half hours. When her watch ticked over to nine and he still wasn't home, she questioned whether he was coming at all. For all she knew, he could be drowning his idiocy in drink up at the Mudcat. When she confronted him, she wanted him sober.

Giving up for the night, she cranked the engine. On the second leg of her K-turn, headlights swept over her car. Cam's truck. Nerves tangled in her belly at the sight of it. Had he been home before now? Seen her initial reaction? She parked her car again and got out, waiting as he did the same.

"Did you forget something?" Flat, expressionless tone. Oh yeah, he'd been home and he was pissed.

He's worth the fight.

"Yes."

Hush ran circles around her, and Norah paused to love on the dog.

"We can work out some kind of visitation for Hush while you're here," Cam said grudgingly.

How civilized of him. She didn't wait for an invitation, just climbed the stairs. After a brief hesitation, Cam followed, unlocking the door. With a sarcastic wave, he gestured her inside. Norah stalked into the loft. Behind her, he shut the door and stood, limned in the lamplight, glowering.

"I came to tell you that this whole non-confrontational, learned helplessness bullshit is not going to work for me."

"Excuse me?"

"I know you've had bad experiences with important people in the past just up and leaving you without you having a say, but you don't come all the way after me in Chicago just to skulk away without a word."

"What do you expect me to do?"

She stepped into his space, close enough to feel the heat of him. "Fight. With me. For me." She laid a hand over his heart and found it pounding. "Because this is worth it. We're worth it."

"So…what? Some grand gesture from me is supposed to outweigh your dream job?" He spun away from her to pace. "How long would that last? How long until you start blaming me for what you gave up?"

She'd planted this idea in his head. When he'd ridden roughshod over her reasons for not being with him. And she'd believed it then. But that wasn't who she was anymore. "That's exactly what I was thinking after I saw you this afternoon. That I gave up my entire world for you."

Back to her, Cam's head drooped, his broad shoulders slumped.

"I've had a really good reminder the last two weeks, of exactly what that world is like. And you know what? My world sucked." He straightened, turning as she continued. "Seventy-hour work weeks. Colleagues who are convinced I got to the top on my knees or on my back rather than through my intellectual capabilities. Professional connections who are more than willing to believe the lies Philip has spread about me. A city where people I saw every single day of the last two years don't even know who I am."

He frowned, confused. Score one for her for throwing him off balance.

"I got headhunted by Peyton Consolidated before I ever left for Chicago. Before I knew Philip had started a personal vendetta against me. Gerald Peyton offered me everything I ever wanted professionally. And I turned him down cold."

"What?"

"I told him what I'd been on my way to tell you. That I'm committed to staying here in

Wishful, to building something on the foundation I started."

He looked like she'd just told him the sky was green. "But the lawsuit—"

"The lawsuit didn't change anything. It's true he left the door open in case I changed my mind. That's what I was talking to Cecily about when you overheard us."

"You said you'd be a fool not to take the job. Under the circumstances, even I agree with you."

With a bracing breath, she took the leap. "Then I'm a fool because I'm not going anywhere." The bloom of terrified hope on his face had her stepping closer, cupping his cheek. "You said you'd always choose me because I was worth the risk. Did you think I wouldn't do the same?"

He reached for her, hands curving around her hips even as he said, "But...you went to Denver."

"How do you even *know* that? You didn't take a single one of my calls." She hung on lest he decide to break the tenuous connection between them.

"I tracked your phone."

"Seriously? You've based your entire freak out on a snippet of eavesdropped conversation and the GPS location of my phone?"

Cam winced. "Yeah?"

Norah shoved back her irritation. "Peyton Consolidated is a big mover and shaker in urban redevelopment circles. I went to Denver to convince the CEO that rural tourism would be an excellent means of diversifying his investments and that he should start in Wishful."

"Wait a minute. You turned this guy's fantastic job offer down and then went to ask him to invest in something else?"

She nodded.

"Did he bite?"

Norah couldn't help but be a little bit smug. "He loved the idea so much, we both went up to Balenmore, Colorado to meet with their tourism coordinator to get an inside look at how they made rural tourism work for them and generate ideas on how we could do the same here."

"So…this whole time you've been gone, you've still been working on a plan to save Wishful?"

"Between meetings with my attorney, yeah."

"Why didn't you *tell* me any of this before?"

"I couldn't tell you before I got back because you weren't talking to me. And when I came to tell you today you didn't want to hear my pretty speech, remember?"

He closed his eyes. "I'm sorry. I was afraid if I talked to you, it'd give you the chance to break things off. Then when you didn't contradict me and I came home and found all your stuff gone, I was sure of it."

"You pissed me off. It really hurt me that you could believe I'd walk away from you so easily."

"It hurt me to think it. I was angry and exhausted when I came after you. And then to hear that…it was like Melody all over again, and I guess it just triggered me."

"Wait, what?" She thought back to what the family had told her. "Aunt Liz said you went up to surprise her and came back in just over twenty-four hours, broken up."

"Yeah. We'd made arrangements to meet on campus. I got there early, in time to hear her talking with a friend, saying she knew she was never going to pry me out of my hick town and she had to find some way to tell me she was never coming back to it. That it was a conversation long overdue but she wasn't a monster who could do that while my mother was on her death bed."

"Okay, leaving aside the fact that you have a serious problem with eavesdropping, Miranda was right. She *was* a bitch."

Cam didn't disagree. "I turned right back around and headed home. Called her from the road to say Mom was having a relapse and that I didn't think it was going to work out between us."

"You let her off the hook."

"Should've done it two years earlier. I knew

when she headed off to George Mason that it wouldn't work. I just couldn't deal with the confrontation then."

"So this afternoon you were trying to let me off the hook and avoid that confrontation?"

"Something like that. If I wasn't what you wanted, I wasn't going to beg and I didn't want to stand in the way of what you did."

It was, in a way, noble and self sacrificing. And completely misguided.

"Why would you do that?"

"Because I love you, and I don't want to be the one to put you in a cage."

"Cam." She cupped his cheek and waited for her throat to unlock. "What we have between us isn't a cage. I'm sorry I went off half-cocked without talking to you. I was panicked and angry, and I didn't think about bringing you into it because you weren't a part of that life. That wasn't meant as a reflection of how I feel about you or us. I could've cleared that up while I was gone, but I didn't want the first time I told you to be in a voicemail. The fact is, I'm stupidly, deliriously, completely in love with you. And I can prove it."

"You already proved it. You're here." He brushed her lips with one of those gossamer, tender kisses that made her feel cherished.

She still had to tell him about the land, but as he pulled her closer, she decided it could wait. "Does this mean we're done fighting?"

"God, I hope so."

"Good, because I'm really ready to make up." Bracing her hands on his shoulders, she leapt, wrapping her legs around his waist and fusing her mouth to his.

Cam took about a nanosecond to get on board with that plan. With a noise somewhere between a sigh and a growl, he hitched her higher. In a dozen strides, he was kicking the bedroom door shut. They fell to the bed, gasping, grasping, rolling, desperate to get to skin.

Norah tugged off his shirt and then her own. Cam helped when it got caught around her shoulders. She took her mouth on a sprinting journey down his torso as she made quick work of his belt and jeans and found only him beneath.

"Behind on laundry," he muttered, dragging her back to return the favor. Both brows winged up as he found her bare as well. "What's your excuse?"

"Optimism. I was banking on fabulous make up sex."

"You make optimism look really good."

They dove at each other, gorging themselves on touch and taste in frantic, greedy bites, as if the speed and heat could eradicate the distance of the past weeks. Fevered, she scissored her legs around his and rolled until she straddled him. Capturing his hands, she curled her fingers through his, pressed them back against the bed and lowered herself, glorying as he filled her in one long stroke. She held at the edge for a long, humming beat, body gripping him, the last of the space between them gone.

At last. She was home.

Cam freed his hands, pulling her down to take her mouth in a kiss that left her branded.

She began to move, driving him with a blistering pace that sent them both careening toward the peak. His tongue danced with hers, echoing the rhythm she set. She took him deeper with every rocking thrust, her muscles coiling, his breath straining as skin slid against slick skin, until she shattered, dragging him into the free fall with her.

Boneless and quivering, Norah lay draped over Cam, her face pressed into his throat. Her heart—or maybe it was his—she couldn't tell—continued to gallop as little aftershocks trembled through them both.

Cam's hand slid limply down her thigh. "That was…"

"Cathartic."

"I was going to say mind blowing."

"That too." She folded her hands across his chest and propped her chin so she could see him. "I missed you. Not just this—although definitely this—but everything else. You're the first person I think about in the morning, the one I dream about at night. You're the one I want by my side, Cam. A partner in the truest sense of the word. I don't ever want you to have reason to doubt that again."

He stroked a knuckle across her cheek, a feather light touch that soothed, even as it aroused. "I'm not perfect. I've got issues, and I'll do stupid things. But I learn from my mistakes. I won't doubt you again."

She kissed him, softly, sweetly and then grinned.

"What're you smiling about?"

"I'm still wearing my socks."

"How is that possible?"

"They weren't all that important in the get naked portion of the program."

He rolled her beneath him. "I take that as a personal challenge." He pressed his hips forward to prove it.

"Then I suppose you're honor bound to rectify the oversight."

Cam shut the door to his truck and, for the first time in his life, stared at his grandmother's house with trepidation. "I can't believe you called a family summit this early in the day."

"It's the most expedient means of putting everybody at ease and catching them up on my situation. You weren't the only one I didn't talk to while I was away." Norah linked her hand through his and dragged him up the walk. "Come on, I'm desperate for more coffee."

So was he, but Cam would've preferred having that coffee at home. Or better yet, skipping the coffee all together and spending the day in bed, sleeping and making love as they'd done most of the night. But Norah had rousted him at 6:30, with little more than a shower and one measly travel mug of coffee to prepare him to face the entire family—all of whom had wanted to string him up the day before.

In accordance with custom, everybody was in the kitchen. And they all promptly stopped talking the moment he and Norah walked in. The weight of their stares hit him like a slap.

Yep, they were still very much on Norah's side, even without knowing the details.

Miranda, clearly at least two cups shy of functional, pinned them both with a furious glare. "You barely talk to me for two weeks, send *one* text to say you're back in town, then you freaking *disappear* for the rest of the day, without answering anybody's call or text. I took a double shift and spent half the night at the ER waiting for you to show up in an ambulance. And now you haul my ass out of bed after only an hour without an IV drip of coffee?"

Without batting an eye, Norah strode up to the lion and hugged her tight. "I'm sorry I worried you. I'm sorry I worried all of you. But I had to talk to Cam first."

Miranda took her by the shoulders and gave her a hard once over. "Are you pregnant?"

Cam choked on the last of the coffee in his travel mug.

Norah's face went slack with shock. "Oh my God. No. *No.*" She spread her hands in the universal sign for *no good.* "Why on earth would you think that?"

"Because you're the most hyper-rational person I know and you've been behaving decidedly *irrationally.* Why else would you call us all together like this?"

"You are kinda glowing," Reed added.

Norah's face went beet red. "I have completely lost control of this situation."

"Well that was your first mistake," Grammy said. "Assuming you were in control to begin with."

"Need I remind you that you're the one who thought facing the Inquisition at this hour was a good idea," Cam pointed out.

"It wouldn't be a bad thing," Aunt Liz offered.

Cam and Norah both stared at her.

"Well it wouldn't! Neither of mine are in any hurry to make me a grandmother."

"Neither are we," Cam said.

Norah poured them both cups of coffee. "I'd rather marry him first, thanks."

"How's Saturday?"

The ripple of surprise swept through the room. Nobody knew which of them to look at. Cam kept his gaze fixed on Norah. She rolled her eyes at him, vexed. "Even if you were serious, you're busy Saturday."

Oh, I am serious. But he let it pass because this wasn't the time or place for asking her. Instead he dimpled at her. "That wasn't a no."

She just arched a brow.

"Okay, I'll play. What am I doing on Saturday?"

She handed him coffee. "Formalizing your design for a park at Hope Springs and meeting with the new owner."

Cam felt the balance of power in the room shift. "I'm sorry, what?"

"Even if the referendum fails, GrandGoods can't touch Hope Springs. It's permanently out of their reach and will be donated to the city."

"How?"

"Because I bought it." And she just sipped

her coffee, calm as could be, as if she hadn't just rocked his world.

"You did what?" Mitch asked.

"I bought the entire parcel of land out from under GrandGoods with cash. Tucker handled the closing. It's why I saw him first when I got back yesterday. I had to sign the paperwork. And before you get angry with him for not telling you, I had him sworn to secrecy because it was supposed to be a surprise. And he's acting as my attorney, so that trumps whatever unspoken bro pact thing you think you have with him."

Cam's brain was still stuck at the beginning. "You bought Hope Springs."

"All 254.5 acres."

"But that had to cost—" Uncle Pete began.

"Yeah, a lot." Norah winced a bit at that. "I liquidated every asset I had. It's why I flipped out when I found out what Philip had done. Given I'm two steps away from being broke, my reputation and employability are kind of an issue."

"Jesus," Cam said. "Why would you do that? Risk that? Have you lost your mind?"

"Nope. Just my heart."

Cam took her coffee away, set it aside with his own. "Norah."

She sighed and linked her fingers with his. "I've never owned anything. Nothing that actually mattered, nothing that meant any kind of roots or permanence. I believe in what we're trying to accomplish here, and I'm not afraid to put my money where my mouth is. I promised I'd save your world, Campbell, and this was my best shot."

He slid his hand up to cup her nape and pressed his brow to hers. "You humble me."

"You should've heard the original speech I had planned." She tipped her mouth up to kiss him briefly, before slipping away to reclaim her coffee and address the rest of the family. "And this concludes the warm and fuzzy good news portion of this morning's meeting. Please collect your caffeine and breakfast pastry of choice and make your way to the kitchen table. Do not pass Go, do not collect $200."

Cam watched the mask slide into place, the smooth, calm exterior over the spine of steel. "It's like watching a Transformer when you do that. Why are you armoring up?"

"Because it's how I survived the last two weeks."

That ominous remark left him with a whole helluva lot of foreboding about whatever was coming next. What had he left her to handle alone?

He sat to her left, Miranda to her right, and the rest of them spread out around the big farmhouse table with considerably less commentary than was usual at a Campbell gathering.

She picked up a croissant. "I want to apologize for how I left, without talking to anybody."

"Emergency protocols apply," Miranda said. "We get that."

"It was still rude. I'm not…good with family. Not your kind of family, where check-ins don't require some kind of performance benchmark. And I'm not good with disasters. Or, to be accurate, I'm fantastic with other people's disasters. I don't have a lot experience with any of my own. So when this one hit, I didn't necessarily handle it the best way possible." This last she addressed to Cam, eyes full of the apology she'd already made.

He rubbed at her shoulders. "I didn't win any awards for how I handled it either. Water under the bridge."

"I'd thought that once I got up there, I'd be in a position to spin some damage control. My old intern got me copies of all the outgoing emails from Philip, so I knew some of what was out there. It's…ugly." Something flickered over her face, before the mask reasserted itself. "Apart from the allegations of professional misconduct, there were a number of more…personal accusations. Between the emails and the affidavits from some of my former coworkers, it was evidence enough for my attorney to file a lawsuit for defamation."

"I'm sensing a gigantic 'but' in everything you're not saying," Mitch said.

She glanced up at him before returning to shredding the croissant in her hands, "But that's about all I can do. I can't stop what Philip started. I can't undo the damage. Even if I win —and that's an enormous *if* according to my attorney, because it's a whole lot of *he said, she said*—there's no putting the genie back in the bottle. My professional reputation is completely trashed. Most of my contacts wouldn't return my calls, and those who did don't want to earn Philip's ire by taking my side. He has a helluva lot more social capital to burn than I do and no compunction about using it to knock me to rock bottom as payback for all the existing clients they lost when he fired me and the new ones who won't go near the firm since I left."

Alone. She'd been dealing with all of this completely alone because he'd been too full of his own imagined hurts to be what she needed. Guilt coated Cam's throat, all but choking him.

If not for him and his cause, his town, she wouldn't even be in this mess. "This is my fault."

Her eyes flashed hot. "Don't be absurd."

"If I hadn't—"

She cut him off. "No. Don't you dare. I stayed of my own free will. I chose you, and I have no regrets."

How could she not have regrets? "But you lost everything you worked for."

"And gained everything that matters. My pride will heal, and I'll figure out some means of earning a living—preferably sooner rather than later because my attorney isn't cheap—but I'm not giving you up. Period. End of story."

"Have you told your parents yet?" Uncle Pete asked.

Norah shifted her attention to him and Aunt Liz. "I just told the only ones who matter. Hell will freeze over before I give my father that kind of weapon."

Knowing what Joseph Burke had said to her regarding what she'd unknowingly been involved with in Morton, Cam could only imagine how he'd twist this to try and bend her. For all the good he focused on doing in the world, how could he not see the damage he did to his own daughter with his expectations?

"What about Peyton?" Cam asked.

"Peyton?" Sandra asked.

Norah ignored that. "What about him?"

"Is the job offer still on the table after all this?"

"We haven't talked about it since I approached him as an investor."

"An investor for what?" Uncle Jimmy asked.

"Ask," Cam said, "and if it is, then take the job."

The burst of temper was immediate. "If you think I'm just going to walk away from—"

"I'll go with you."

It was Norah's turn to stare. "You hate the city."

"I love you more." And God, if he could do nothing else for her, he could do this.

"This is all very romantic and sweet, but

anybody want to clue us in on what the hell you're talking about?" asked Miranda.

Cam jumped in before Norah could minimize it. "She has a job offer from a billion dollar corporation in Denver to come run their marketing department, and she turned it down for me."

"Whoa," Mitch said.

"And I don't intend to reverse that decision. Do you think I don't know what leaving here would mean for you? I'm not dragging you to the other side of the country away from your family."

"Norah, be sensible."

"I am being sensible. You're being impulsive. I appreciate the motivation behind it, but that's not the answer. We've established the economic climate here is crap. The turn around the last couple of months is a start, but only a start. It's no state in which to sell a business. And at that point, you have no control over what a new owner of the nursery would do. There's no guarantee that they'd go to the effort to hire on people like Dewey May to keep him and his family afloat. No guarantee someone wouldn't just come in and turn the nursery into something else entirely. No guarantee that whoever took over for you as City Councilman wouldn't work to overturn everything we've done here. And every bit of that would eat at you, worse than it already does. That powerlessness of not knowing, or worse, knowing and not being able to do a damned thing about it from more than a thousand miles away, would make you miserable. You need to be here. So do I. I'll find another way. It's what I do, remember?"

Frustration simmered at a low boil. Her logic, as always, was undeniable. But there had to be some way he could help fix this. She'd done so much for him, given up so much, and what had he done for her? Chased down some lousy public records?

"How can I make this better for you? I need to do *something.*"

"Help me finish what we started. We're getting this referendum and we're going to bury

GrandGoods. And then we're going to turn this town around. And when all of it is over, and no more disasters are hanging around on the horizon, I'm going to fall apart in an absolutely spectacular fashion and count on you to pick up the pieces." She said it in the same calm, matter-of-fact tone she tended to use when reciting business statistics or weather reports.

He wouldn't have been surprised to see it penciled in on her calendar. *Have breakdown. 8 AM to 5 PM. Schedule massage for tomorrow.*

"In the meantime, I need to work like I need to breathe, so you'll take me back to get my car and let me take over the loft with a quantity of bulletin boards and office supplies that will make it look like Office Depot dropped a tactical nuke on the place."

A hint of a smile tugged at his lips. "Okay."

"What can we do to help?" His mother, as calm and focused as Norah herself.

"That's the other thing I wanted to talk to you about. How long would it take you to set up a town meeting?"

PLEASE LET THIS BE nearly over. Cam sent up the prayer as he pulled open the door to Edison Hardware and stepped inside to continue the petition tally. It was almost time for lunch, and he'd already been by half of the businesses on his list. Aunt Liz and Uncle Pete were doing the others. Avery had been keeping a running tally as they went, and they were close. So close. If the total tipped over their threshold, they'd be spending the next several hours validating that each one was a registered voter. If they didn't get the numbers today, they were out of time.

Tyler stood at the counter, her ponytail pulled through the back of the fire engine red YES cap that matched his. She looked up as he came in and one corner of her mouth curved up. "Hey Councilman, Mr. Cleese here wants to know if signing the petition will decrease his chances of getting called up for jury duty, seeing as it's kind of a civil service."

"Well now, that's something to consider. But I reckon you'd have to take that up with Judge Carpenter." Might as well foist the responsibility for that decision off on somebody else.

Mr. Cleese rubbed the tip of his bulbous nose. "Y'all should check on that. It'd be a real incentive for folks."

"We'll take that under advisement. In the meantime, how about you join the ranks of other fine citizens of Wishful and add your name to the petition?"

After some further hemming and hawing and additional suggestions that were completely out of Cam's power as a city representative, Cleese finally signed the petition.

"Thanks for your support, Mr. Cleese. Here's your sticker." Tyler reached out and plastered the *YES: I signed* badge on the old man's shirt pocket. "You be sure to tell your friends up at Bingo Night."

Cam peeked over to check the petition numbers and texted the total to Avery.

"I thought about adding a suggestion box," Tyler said as the door swung shut.

"Been getting a lot of quid pro quo kinda ideas, have we?"

"A fair number. None actually actionable, I don't think." She leaned back against the counter and crossed her legs. "How are the numbers looking?"

"Overall good. We picked up eleven at No Sweat. Fifteen more at Brides and Belles. Only six at Sanderson's. But it's slowing down to dribs and drabs. Everybody's reporting the same kind of thing. They keep running into people who've already been hit up. I'm not sure how to get beyond that crowd without going door to door."

Tyler pursed her lips. "I heard you spent a fair chunk of time talking to Rosanna Sanderson this morning."

Cam sent her a flat stare. "And who exactly is keeping tabs on how long I'm spending in local businesses?"

"You know perfectly well Cassie can see the door to Sanderson's from The Grind."

"So? She was on my list, same as you and Cassie and more than a dozen other businesses."

"Half an hour just seems like a long time to spend checking on six signatures *in a jewelry store*."

"Any angler knows you've gotta put out better bait if you wanna catch bigger fish."

Tyler grinned at him. "Does that mean there's a bigger fish to catch?"

"If there was, do you think I'd be dumb enough to confirm it? I'm well aware of the state of gossip in this town. Cassie's looking for something to scoop Mama Pearl on, and I am not gonna be it."

"I'm not hearing denials."

"You're not hearing squat." Cam shoved open the door. "I'll keep you posted about the signature total. As soon as Avery notifies us we've got enough, I'll be back by to pick up the pages for signature verification."

"I'll be here. And Cam?"

He paused, looking back at his lifelong friend.

"I'm glad she's back."

"So am I."

Cam made quick stops at Lickety Split and Inglenook before finally working around to Dinner Belles, where Norah had turned a corner booth into an impromptu command center. Against one wall was a markerboard showing the running tally of signatures. Norah herself hunched over a map of the city that showed the individual Council wards, with two others in street team gear. She, too, wore a YES cap, and with the braid in her hair, she looked about eighteen. At least until she started giving out orders like a five-star general.

"Mamie, you hit up the senior center. They're all of a generation where voting actually meant something, so they're probably registered. They just aren't necessarily super mobile and coming into town."

Mamie saluted. "That's a fabulous idea. Autumn, you should come with me." She turned back to Norah. "Autumn's the head librarian. She volunteers at the center once a week. The seniors just love her."

"Do it. We need every asset we've got."

The pair of them headed for the door, flashing cheerful smiles at Cam on their way out.

Cam joined Norah at her booth. "Where's your walkie talkie?"

"Don't tempt me. I'll make you hunt some down for me. You know Cassie would be all over that."

Thinking about what else Cassie was all

over, Cam shot a quick glance at Mama Pearl. Yep. She was giving him a Look.

Jesus.

As if he'd be stupid enough to buy the ring here where anybody and their brother could see and talk about it. Rosanna had just wanted to tell him about her daughter Rory's decision to pursue landscape architecture in college and ask about graduate school suggestions. But that didn't make for good gossip.

"Are those the updated totals?" He nodded to the board behind her.

"Yeah, Avery already copied me on the numbers you sent. We're two hundred signatures in the hole. I'd like to get at least another hundred for padding, just in case we had a fair chunk of non-registered voters signing."

He gave her the same update he'd given Tyler. "Every business in the coalition has about maxed out its customer base. We're running short of places to corner people. Without some kind of captive audience, I'm afraid the only thing we've got left is going door to door."

Norah's eyes narrowed with speculation. "Captive audience…"

"I wasn't actually suggesting we hold people hostage."

"We don't have to. Circumstance already does." With quick, efficient moves, she folded the map and shoved it into her bag, along with the rest of her stuff, before grabbing his hand and tugging him toward the door. "Come on."

"What about your board?"

"Mama Pearl will keep it updated." She pushed out onto the sidewalk and hit the ground at what he thought of as city speed. Woman on a mission.

"Where are we going?"

"Sweet Magnolias."

"Do I get to eat when we get there? Because I think my stomach is trying to devour itself."

"You can scarf while we work. How long do you have before you have to head back to the nursery?"

"Until about three."

"We need more people." She whipped out

her phone and made a series of calls, requesting backup at Sweet Magnolias.

Cam shook his head, holding in a chuckle. *Backup.* God, he loved this woman. Knowing she'd tell him what was up her sleeve when she was good and ready, he just kept walking.

The bakery smelled of vanilla and cinnamon, with a side of sweet cream butter. Or maybe that was icing. Cam started drooling the moment he walked inside.

On the other side of the counter, Carolanne wore her YES cap backward as she piped pink icing on a cake. "Be with you in a jiff," she called, not looking up.

Norah peered into the display cases, the wheels clearly turning. Cam wasn't sure if she was picking out lunch or plotting world domination. These days, it could kinda go either way. There'd been no further updates on the lawsuit, and she'd effectively compartmentalized so that all her focus was on the petition drive.

Carolanne finished the rim of tiny pink

roses around the edge of the cake and finally looked up. "Well, hey y'all. Are you here to check my petition sheets? I'm afraid I don't have too many new signatures."

"I had something else in mind," Norah told her. "We need to make up sample trays of everything you've got on sale today."

"We do? Why?"

"We're turning a negative into a positive. Y'all can't fix the stoplight, so we're taking advantage of our semi-captive audience to hand out pastry samples from Sweet Magnolias, along with information about the petition. So that's advertising for you, getting the word out for us, and linking the whole thing to positive reinforcement with sugar."

"It certainly *sounds* good." Carolanne put the bag of icing aside. "I'll pull together some trays."

"Are you picky about having people in your space or can I come help?"

"Come on back and wash your hands."

There wasn't room behind the counter for a third person, so Cam stood to the side and felt like a useless dolt as the two women spun and cut and made up trays in what seemed like two minutes flat.

"There. Those look amazing." Norah bit into a piece of scone and moaned. "If this takes off, you should consider baking cute little sample size stuff and doing it on a regular basis."

"I wish I'd thought of it before."

Cam snatched a piece of blueberry muffin and popped it into his mouth, pausing for a moment of reverence as the sweet tart flavor melted on his tongue. "So exactly how are we going to do this?"

"Watch and learn, Leonidas." Norah hefted a tray, plastered on a beauty queen smile that would do Barbie proud, and pushed out the door.

Cam followed, clipboard in hand, as she approached a woman in a minivan at the head of the line waiting at the stoplight. After a moment's hesitation, the woman rolled down her window.

"Hi! Can I offer you a sample from Sweet

Magnolias Bakery? We've got blueberry muffins and orange cranberry scones this afternoon."

"Sure, thanks." The woman plucked a piece of scone from the tray.

As she bit into it, Norah went in for the kill. "We're also looking for signatures on our petition. Are you aware that GrandGoods intends to build a store out by Hope Springs?"

Mouth full, the woman nodded.

"We feel that's too important an issue not to be a full popular vote. We're collecting signatures to overturn the City Council decision and make it a public referendum. Are you registered to vote in Wishful?" At the next nod, Norah smiled broadly and offered the clipboard. "Can we count on your support?"

After another brief hesitation, the woman shrugged and took the petition.

Norah took the clipboard back. "Thanks so much! And won't you try the blueberry muffins too? They're delicious."

Norah bid her a good day and moved on to

the next vehicle. Cam watched her repeat the routine twice more before the light changed—Christ, he hadn't truly realized it was this bad—getting signatures from one and stepping back onto the sidewalk as they drove on their merry way.

"Two out of three isn't bad."

"The third one isn't registered to vote in this county." Seeing their reinforcements arriving, she handed him a tray and shoved the petition clipboard into his chest. "You have dimples, sugar. Go use 'em for the cause."

Cam went to work, while Norah trained their backup on the spiel. They fell into a rhythm, going out in pairs, seldom coming in with fewer than two signatures, sometimes more. Between turns, Cam managed to nab a ham and cheese croissant and some coffee. Not exactly the lunch of champions, but it would tide him over. As the lunch hour ended and bled into early afternoon, traffic slowed. Grabbing a freshly refilled tray of margarita cupcakes and strawberry danish, Cam stepped out for his next round.

Only one car had pulled up to the light, an aging Civic with a driver that might as well have sported a T-shirt screaming *Not from around here.* Mid-twenties, with square rim, Hipster glasses, he had city written all over him. Not a registered voter in Wachoxee County. But this wasn't just about the petition, so he stepped up anyway and smiled.

"Afternoon. Can I offer you a sample from Sweet Magnolias Bakery? We've got cupcakes and danish."

"Oooo, gimme. I'm *starving.*" A dark-haired girl leaned over from the passenger seat and reached for a cupcake.

Cam froze as recognition set in. "You're Cecily."

She looked up, surprised. "I am…and I know I would remember if I'd met you."

"No, we've never met. I'm—" *The guy who followed your former boss to Chicago and stood around like some kind of creepy stalker listening to your conversation.* Yeah, no. Not the way to introduce himself.

Now Cecily's eyes were narrowed in speculation. "You're a Campbell. You resemble Mitch." She snapped her fingers. "You're Norah's Campbell!"

That sounded a lot better.

"I am. Cam Crawford."

"And I'm Christoff Bergen," the driver said. "Does somebody want to tell me what's going on?"

"I'm guessing you're here looking for Norah. If you'll pull off and park around the corner there, she's just inside the bakery."

Cecily took a bite of cupcake. "I'd say that's kismet."

Norah turned and nearly dropped the tray full of pastries in her hands, as she watched her former personal assistant walk through the door, trailed by Cecily. "What are you doing here?"

"Now is that any way to greet your loyal minions?" Christoff asked.

"I'm in shock." She hastily set down the tray and opened her arms to pull him in for a hard hug. "It's so good to see you."

"Back atcha, gorgeous." He pulled back and looked her over with a critical eye. "It seems being back below the Mason-Dixon agrees with you. Or maybe it's this tall drink of water over here." His gaze shifted to Cam.

Laughing, Norah made introductions.

"Well, you weren't kidding," Cecily said.

"I'm telling you, they've got good genes in the Campbell family."

Cam shot her a look. "Do I even want to know?"

"Probably not." Norah grinned. Shifting her attention back to her friends, she asked, "Now seriously, what *are* you doing here?"

"We come bearing gifts." Christoff's Slavic blue eyes sparkled.

"Uh oh. I know that look. What did you do?"

"Nothing that didn't need doing. If we can find somewhere a little less public to make our reveal?" he suggested, looking around at handful of patrons, who'd decided to stop for a pastry after being lured in by samples.

"I am suddenly very, very afraid."

"You've got nothing to worry about." Christoff slung an arm around her shoulders.

"Upstairs at The Grind?" Cam offered. "Daniel's on duty. He'll keep anybody out for you."

"Us." Norah grabbed his hand. "You're coming with. I have a feeling I may need moral support for this."

Leaving the other recruits in charge of samples and petition duty, the group of them hiked down the street to The Daily Grind.

"Hail our conquering heroes!" Daniel called as they walked inside.

"Don't count your chickens yet, Danny boy," Cam told him. "We've still got the vote to come."

"I have faith. What'll it be?"

"Y'all go ahead and order. I'll see if it's clear." Cam sprinted up the stairs.

Norah requested their usuals, while Cecily and Christoff hemmed and hawed over what to try. Judging by the look of speculation on Christoff's face, he was thinking he'd take his caramel macchiato with a side of Daniel. When the latter suggested the strawberry hand pie, the calorie conscious Christoff didn't blink before adding one to his order. Armed with pastries and caffeine, they trooped up to the empty second floor.

"Just tell me one thing before we get started. Are you two in trouble? Is my lawsuit against Helios causing you problems?"

"We are *not* in trouble," Cecily assured her.

"But it *is* causing you problems. Damn it. I didn't want any of the blowback to hit y'all."

"Patience, grasshopper." Christoff clapped his hands together. "So, we all agree that Philip and Pierce are douchecanoes, yes? Yes. They've gone to great lengths to smear your name, making claims about your behavior that Cecily and I *know* you didn't actually do. And anybody with a brain at Helios knows you didn't either. Even the people who are claiming to know are just lazy and jealous of your success."

"This is all old ground. It's part of why the lawsuit is stalling out. There's no way to prove one way or the other."

"Yeah, about that," Cecily hedged.

"Oh God..."

"Christoff and I concocted a plan." She pulled out a laptop and turned it on.

"You know Adam in IT?" Christoff asked.

"The one with the dimples and great abs."

"Stupendously fabulous abs. Well, I sweet talked him into setting up the webcams in Pierce's office where we could record remotely, whenever we wanted."

Feeling vaguely queasy, she asked, "You were spying on Pierce?"

"Not exactly," Cecily said. "So Pierce...kind of has a history of making passes at me."

Norah barely trusted herself to speak. "He what?"

"Not, like, serious passes. Not while you were together. Just…vaguely suggestive flirting. He didn't make any *real* passes until after y'all were split."

"The question of Pierce's fidelity is fairly far down the totem pole of sleaze. But if he sexually harassed you, I'll castrate him myself."

Cecily held up a hand. "Not necessary." With a few more keystrokes she opened a file. "You remember how I told you I have a background in theater?"

"Yeah…" Where was she going with this?

"Well, keep that in mind." She turned the computer around and hit play.

The screen was abruptly filled with Pierce, seated at his desk, staring at something on the dual monitors. Paperwork was spread out before him. Projections for some campaign or other. His hair was messy instead of artfully rumpled, and his shirt sleeves were rolled up. The sleek silk tie was loose, his collar unbuttoned. He looked, for the first time Norah could remember, frazzled. That pleased her far more than it should have.

The timestamp in the corner showed it was well after closing when the knock came on his door.

"It's open."

"I have those reports you asked for, Mr. Vargas."

Pierce swiveled away from the monitors to face Cecily, schooling his face into the confident smile that had won more than one account. "Thanks Cecily. You're a lifesaver."

As the door shut, the view shifted to that from the other monitor. Cecily hesitated as she handed over the files, studying him. "You're working too hard."

"Nature of the beast. It's always rough transitioning new members to the team."

"Shouldn't Matthew be transitioned by now?" She perched on the corner of his desk, and his eyes followed the rise of her hemline.

"Well, one would hope. I'm afraid Norah spoiled us."

Cecily laid a hand over his. "It must be doubly hard on you, losing your partner and your girlfriend. You were such a good team."

For just a second, something like remorse flickered over his face. "Yeah, we were."

"You've been so busy picking up the slack, I'm sure you haven't had any chance to even think about yourself and your life outside the company." She edged around the desk, into his space.

Pierce watched her, his eyes sharpening. "Not so much."

"Must be lonely."

"I do find I could do with some company."

She reached out and fingered his tie. "You'd probably work much more efficiently with some stress relief."

And Pierce, damn him, laid a hand on the length of thigh bared by her too short skirt. "Undoubtedly. But I thought you weren't interested."

"I was never not interested. But you weren't available before. And then I thought you needed some time on your own. A girl's gotta be sensible, even with a catch as…impressive as you. Besides, I wasn't even sure I was your type." She jerked a shoulder in lazy shrug that caused the neckline of her blouse to gape.

Pierce's eyes immediately went to the hint of lace beneath and his hand began to knead at her thigh. "Brunette and brilliant? You're absolutely my type."

"I also had to figure out if you were my type."

"And what type is that?"

With a half smile, she grabbed the tie and began to work it lose on every word. "Sexy, handsome, powerful." Tugging him forward until his mouth almost met hers. "A hint of bad boy." She pulled the tie loose and tossed it behind her, nudging him back in his chair.

"Bad boy, huh?"

"Mmm yeah. I've got that fantasy. Lots of girls do." Cecily ran one foot up the inside of his thigh to stroke him through his pants. Pierce jerked, his hands tightening on the arms of his chair.

Smiling and in complete control, Cecily moved forward to straddle him. "The bad ones really turn me on. Especially the really smart bad ones. And I have a feeling that you're one of the exceptionally clever bad boys." She leaned into him and whispered something in his ear that had his hands tightening on her ass, pressing her closer.

"Tell me how bad you really are, Pierce. I can make it really good for you."

"I'm amazing at taking companies with bad press and making the public love them."

Cecily made a moue of disappointment. "I already *know* that. Tell me something I don't know. Tell me a *secret.*"

He started talking, mentioning different accounts and clients he'd worked with, who he'd snowed, how. Cecily proceeded to gradually undress him, touching, stroking, arousing with each secret he revealed.

Norah felt sick.

"I was always jealous Norah got to do those things with you. It's so freaking hot."

"Norah didn't have the stones for it. She was such a Pollyanna, thinking she could be a success in this business being nice. That naive goodness has its place and it totally worked for certain clients, but she never stepped a toe out of line. Not like you. Jesus, Cecily, the things we could do together." He kissed his way down her throat and the camera caught her eye roll.

"But what about all those allegations of professional misconduct your dad made?"

Down to his boxers, Pierce lifted her onto the desk, stepped between her thighs and began to pull off her blouse. "Insurance. Revenge. Whatever you wanna call it. He's pissed that the firm lost a whale of a potential client to her."

"Really? Who?"

"That big real estate development corporation he's had Matthew working on. Peyton Consolidated. Out of Denver."

Oh God, Norah thought. *Cecily was right.*

Pierce kissed a trail down Cecily's collarbone, down toward her lace-covered breasts. "Don't know why the CEO was so hell bent on having Norah. Between that and the other accounts that walked after she left, he had to take drastic measures to protect our remaining client base. What better way to cover our asses than pin it all on her? No way to prove it one way or the other, and we've got the strength of the company behind us. What does she have?"

A door burst open. "The word you're looking for there is loyalty," Christoff said from off camera. "Show's over."

Braced above Cecily, Pierce froze.

"Thanks so much for your cooperation," she said with an innocent smile, and drove her knee into Pierce's groin.

He collapsed to the floor with a series of wheezing curses as she stepped away and began calmly buttoning her shirt. "You bitch. I'll have your job for this. Both of you." Pierce continued to spew threats and invective as he clutched his crotch and tried to get to his feet.

"Oh no." Christoff moved into the line of sight and put an arm around Cecily. "If you or your father lay a hand on either of us, physical or otherwise, the video of that confession is set to go live on every video hosting site, SEO optimized for maximum impact. Pretty sure you don't want any of those clients getting wind of your shenanigans. Now, you're going to issue a retraction countering every single email or phone call your father sent, denying Norah's involvement and clearing her good name, *and* you will convince your father to settle the lawsuit with a generous severance package for the shit you put her through. You have forty-eight hours."

Pierce stared at him, murder in his eye. "Norah would never condone blackmail."

Christoff's grin was just a little feral. "Of course she wouldn't. But thanks to you and your father, she's not here to stop us, now is she? Believe me, honey, nobody has a finer-tuned sense of revenge than a gay man. You'll find our resignations on my desk outside. C'mon Cecily."

The video stopped.

"And sadly, I will not win the Tony Award I so richly deserve for that performance."

"Maggie the Cat ain't got nothing on you," Christoff assured her.

For a few moments, Norah couldn't speak. "Well, I see that your TaeBo classes paid off." She loosed a shuddering breath trying to shake off the skeevy sensation along her skin. "That was… I can't believe…Are you okay? Did he hurt you?" Norah started around the table to check Cecily over, as if it had just happened.

"I'm *fine.* He didn't do a thing to me that four scalding showers didn't cure. He didn't lay a hand on me that you didn't see."

"We saw enough," Norah said.

"The point is, so did he. He did what we asked. Here are copies of the retractions." Christoff handed over a file.

Norah just set it on the table without looking.

"I'm pretty sure what you did was highly illegal," Cam observed.

"Our ass is covered. They won't risk the reputation of the whole firm over this. They'll settle out of court."

Cecily took Norah's hands. "Say something."

"What you did was reckless, dangerous, unethical...and if it had gone another way, you could've faced criminal charges. You shouldn't have risked that for me. Not to mention that you both lost your jobs over it."

"Correction, we both *quit* our jobs over it," Christoff said. "We figure you were our supervisor and will give us amazing recs when we need them. And that aside, we couldn't just stand by and let them keep trying to ruin you. You're worth so much more than that."

Norah felt her eyes prick with tears. "Y'all, I just can't even..."

"You should call your attorney," Cam said.

"I'm afraid to. If any of this comes out, I should probably maintain plausible deniability."

Christoff checked his watch. "Well we're

closing in on forty-two hours now, so you ought to be hearing from your attorney soon anyway."

As if conjured by his words, a phone began to ring. She looked to Christoff. "You're performing voodoo, aren't you? Making deals with sketchy deities. Crossroads demons?"

Christoff only grinned.

But it was Cam's phone. "Avery, what's the update?" He listened for a minute, then nodded. "We're on it."

"Problem?" Norah asked.

"Nope." He broke into a wide grin. "We did it. Forty-eight signatures over our threshold. It's time to validate."

CHAPTER 24

SPEAKEASY SHOULD'VE BEEN CLOSING. After nine on a weeknight, downtown Wishful should've been deserted.

It wasn't.

Cars lined the streets and lights blazed, cheerful beacons in the dark as Norah climbed out of Cam's truck. Exhaustion would set in soon, but for the moment, hunger and anticipation were keeping her going. Cam, Avery, and Sandra joined her and strode toward the pizzeria, where the vast majority of the coalition was waiting for the final ruling on the petition. Judge Carpenter had been kind enough to make it after business hours.

Tucker shoved open the door as soon as they approached. "Well?"

"Let us get in the door," Cam said.

By tacit agreement, the others hung back, letting Norah inside first at the head of their little group. She wasn't about to complain about the spotlight. At their appearance, Tyler let out a two-finger whistle that silenced the crowd and drew every eye to the front. Expression sober, Norah scanned each face, absolutely playing the room, drawing out the tension until she could've heard a pin drop. These were her troops, the people who'd made this happen, so it was pure pleasure to drop the mask and shoot up a fist of triumph. "We got it!"

Cheers nearly blew off the roof.

"The vote is officially set for a week from today!"

A stampede of well-wishers crowded around, shaking hands, slapping backs, giving hugs. Norah's heart swelled at the praise and compliments. In the wake of the nasty from Chicago, she needed that.

As they made their way through the impromptu receiving line, she saw Cam make a face as he got a gander at his own brand of nasty in the form of a smirking Vick Burgess. This was the last place Norah expected to see Cam's nemesis, and she braced herself for some kind of ugliness.

"Coming over to the Good Side or did you just have a hankering for pepperoni pizza tonight?" Cam asked.

"Oh, I'm just enjoying the party. It's the last one y'all will have. This is a delay tactic, like everything else you've pulled. The popular vote will come down exactly the way the City Council decision did. And all this time and effort will have been wasted when GrandGoods moves forward exactly as planned."

Norah joined them, curling her hand

through Cam's. "There's something y'all evidently didn't factor into that assumption, Mr. Burgess."

"And what is that?"

"That the land GrandGoods planned to buy, the parcel tied to the special use permit, is no longer for sale."

"If Mr. Costello is holding out for more money, I'm sure GrandGoods is open to negotiation"

Norah offered her most patronizing smile. "Mr. Costello is no longer the owner. I am. And I can assure you, I'm *not* open to negotiation."

Watching that blow hit home was almost as satisfying as seeing Judge Carpenter sign off on the referendum.

"This is our town, Vick," Cam told him.

No longer smirking, Vick shrugged. "It's no matter. The size cap won't pass. People here want more options and GrandGoods is going to give that to them." Without another word, he shouldered his way through the crowd.

"I'd love to be a fly on the wall when he

breaks that news to Bill Sutto." Their in-house marketing guru couldn't fix this.

"You and me both."

Molly appeared and slipped an arm through Norah's. "Well, it is a delightful thing to see him lose his swagger. Now, tell me what you have planned to kick his ass from here into next century."

Norah opened her mouth to expound on exactly that, but Cam interrupted. "Nope. Not tonight. If you get her started, she'll go past midnight. War council can wait until tomorrow. Tonight is for much deserved celebration. And pizza."

"There should always be pizza." Her stomach growled, underscoring the point. "Go grab a slice. I want to go talk to Christoff and Cecily."

Cam brushed a kiss across her brow and wove toward the buffet.

"I'm glad you worked it out," Molly said.

"So am I. He's totally worth the fight."

"You suit each other down to the ground. You need someone who can appreciate and support your strengths without being intimidated or feeling the need to compete. And he needs someone to push him."

"We balance each other."

"Partners." Molly patted her on the shoulder and disappeared in the crowd.

Norah's friends were perched at a high-top table observing the proceedings with a mixture of amusement and fascination. "Feel like you're on an alien planet yet?"

"I think it's marvelous," Cecily said. "*Everybody* here knows who you are. How cool is that?"

"I'm pretty sure I dropped into an episode of *Hart of Dixie* and Dr. Zoe Hart is going to be sashaying through the door any minute now," said Christoff.

"That's Alabama, sugar."

"Sugar! We all know I'm anything but sweet."

"That is entirely a matter of perspective. What y'all did for me was pretty damned sweet."

"It was pretty damned something, but I don't think sweet is it," Cecily said. "Either way, we felt it was necessary, even if it meant doing a little wrong to right a bigger wrong."

Norah was trying not to think about the potential fallout of their actions, so she changed the subject. "So what's next for the two of you? Are you planning to stay in Chicago?"

"I haven't decided yet. Chicago was fun, but I think I could do with a change of scenery," Christoff said.

"I'm definitely *not* staying in Chicago after graduation in May. But I'm not sure what's next either."

"Don't you still need internship hours?"

"I do." All innocence, Cecily turned to Norah. "I was hoping you could help me out with that. Pretty please?" Hands in prayer position, she batted her clear green eyes.

"You know I'll help however I can. But I'm not coming back to Chicago except to pack up all my stuff and finish moving here."

"I could help you here. Surely there's something with this whole coalition thing I could do."

"I would adore having your help. But we can't afford to pay you. I'm not getting paid on this either."

"So? Not everybody has paid internships to begin with. I had enough overtime with Helios since you left that I can cover my expenses for a while, and it wouldn't be a big deal to sublet my half of the apartment. Cost of living here is bound to be a fraction of what it is in the city. What do you say? I could stay here and finish out the semester working for you."

To have part of her team back was an absolute dream. "We'd have to clear it with your advisor at school, make sure they're okay with the change, but yeah. I'd absolutely love to have you."

"Awesome! Christoff, you should come, too."

"Darling, can you really imagine me *here* for any length of time? I mean, it's charming, but…"

She nudged his shoulder. "It'd give you a chance to get to know the cute barista we saw earlier today."

He angled his head in consideration. "Well, I could at least stick around until this vote is over. Seems like you need all the help you can get."

"That we can," Norah said. "I've got a presentation about my rural tourism campaign for Wishful that would really benefit from y'all's input."

They lost themselves in the familiar and comfortable rhythm of shoptalk as she outlined her main concepts. It felt amazing to have the give and take, other brains that knew how hers worked and sparked new ideas in an instant.

"So are we agreed for now?" Norah asked. "The Dream Team back together again for this one last project?"

"I'm in." Cecily stuck her hand out over the table.

"Oh, what the hell." Christoff added his hand to the mix.

Norah covered them both with her own hand and squeezed. "I'm so glad the two of you are here."

Her phone vibrated. Wondering who was calling so late when everyone she knew was here, she slipped it out. And promptly lost all sense of pleasure when she saw her attorney's name on the display. Instinctively she looked for Cam. He was across the room in deep conversation with Tucker and Tyler. The phone buzzed again. She'd find him after.

"Excuse me, I need to take this." Norah answered, "Hang on just a sec," and hurried outside, away from all the noise. "Sorry about that, Marcus."

"I'm interrupting."

"No, you're not. Really. What's up? It's awfully late for you to be calling." *Please God, don't let them be in trouble.*

"It is, and I'm sorry about that. But there's been a...development."

"A development?"

"One I think you definitely need to hear about."

Oh no. She wrapped her free hand around the back of a bench, clenched it until her knuckles turned white.

"I heard from Helios' attorney. It seems they've had a change of heart from their original position."

"Oh?" She hoped she didn't squeak.

"They're offering a settlement. A severance package of six months' salary, plus all your legal fees."

"That's better than nothing, but six months' salary isn't going to help me if no one will hire me because of the damage to my reputation," she said.

"That's where it gets interesting. I have, in my hands, documented retractions and a glowing letter of recommendation for you, signed by Philip Vargas himself."

"That's…I don't even know what to say. Is it legit?"

The door opened behind her. She knew without turning that it was Cam.

"It's a hell of an offer. You could take it to trial and hold out for more money in damages, but I'm not sure you'd get anywhere, and it might destroy whatever temporary insanity possessed him to make this offer."

Cam moved in behind her, grasping the bench on either side. She leaned into him but didn't release her hold.

"Yeah, no, I agree. Let's take it."

"Okay. I'll make it happen, get the settlement paperwork in the mail ASAP."

"I'll look for it in the next few days. Thanks Marcus." She hung up, shifting to slide the phone into her pocket.

"You're shaking."

"Shock, I think." The long, slow exhale didn't help. "It's over."

When she said nothing else, Cam turned her

to face him. He was braced for the worst, prepared to be her rock.

"And?"

"Helios is going to settle. Six months' salary and attorney's fees, plus documented retractions of all allegations. Marcus said I could hold out for more in damages, but…"

"That's not what this is about for you."

"No. It's so much more than I'd hoped for." Her throat tightened as all the stress and strain of the past weeks came to a head. She pressed a hand to her mouth, shoulders shaking harder as she dropped her head to his chest.

Cam gathered her in, stroking her back in that way he had of soothing. But it wasn't tears that spilled out between her fingers, it was laughter.

She lifted her head and reached to frame his face. "Oh my God. Cam! Their lunatic plan worked! I'm getting my reputation back!"

Fueled by boundless relief and joy, she cut off whatever congratulatory remark he started to make, with an enthusiastic kiss. Dropping back to her feet, she beamed. "I don't know what to do with myself. If I wasn't so damned tired, I'd turn cartwheels."

"Well," Cam said, a trifle breathless, "as it happens we're at a party, so I say we celebrate."

AFTER ATTEMPTING one last head count of the people lining the bleachers in the community center, Cam went in search of the lady of the hour. He found her in a huddle with Cecily and Christoff—her default position the last several days. After the last few months, he'd thought he'd known what Norah was like when she brought her A game. Having her team back showed him exactly how wrong he was. The three of them had a kind of synergy that was a pleasure to watch. They'd turned the Chamber of Commerce press conference about the referendum into an event that drew media—print, TV, and radio—from all over the state, even a few from neighboring Alabama, Louisiana, and

Tennessee. Their David vs. Goliath fight was making regional headlines. In the few days since, the coalition had been contacted by other small Southern towns interested in learning from Wishful's example.

"—not coming tonight, but whenever he makes it down for the initial business meetings with the city, I want to introduce you both," Norah said. "Gerald wants me and my skills, and you're an extension of that in the best possible way. I think Peyton Consolidated could be a good fit for you."

"I certainly won't turn down the connection," Christoff said. "I could learn to ski."

"Has Peyton figured out that if he gives you an inch, you'll take a mile?" Cam asked.

"He hasn't complained yet." Norah moved toward the gymnasium doors with her team at her back. "What's the crowd like?"

"It's standing room only in there. Lotta people came out."

"Good. We'll need them all." Turning to Christoff and Cecily, she put out a hand. "All in." They layered their hands over hers. She looked at Cam, expectant, so he added his to the pile. "Let's lock and load, people." They broke formation, and she stepped into the roar of voices without a backward glance.

The mob inside felt like loosely-controlled chaos to Cam. Too many bodies in one enclosed space, all of them talking. He was pretty sure this might be one of the circles of hell. As he tried to sort out the best means of calling their attention, Norah slid two fingers between her lips and let out a piercing whistle that left his ears ringing. Apparently Tyler had been giving lessons. The crowd silenced, all attention shifting to her.

"That's better."

With a friendly smile, Norah stepped up onto the low stage erected at one side of the room. After a brief glance at the podium, she kept in front of it, at ease and confident in a way Cam envied. He hated public speaking. No matter how often he did it, having to address more than half a dozen people made his skin crawl. She held no notes, no clicker to advance her slides, nothing to keep her hands occupied. Christoff was manning the laptop and projector, a feat he managed with alacrity, since the two could evidently share a mind meld at will.

"Thank y'all for coming out tonight. As you all know, tomorrow is the public referendum wherein the citizens of Wishful have the opportunity to cast their vote for or against a statute that would institute a size cap on businesses operating within its boundaries. I urge you all to uphold your civic duty and hit up the polls." She paused, scanning faces. "But that's not what we're here to talk about tonight."

The PowerPoint presentation popped up on the screen behind Norah, but she didn't give it a glance. "There's been a slow erosion of the tax base, of profit margins, of straight up population in Wishful for the last twenty or thirty years. What we're here to talk about is how it got that way and what we can do to stop it."

Quick and efficient, she spouted relevant statistics, citing the change in population and work force through various stages of the town's economic downturn as the furniture manufacturing industry, and all the peripheral manufacturing that went with it, moved elsewhere. The malaise that seemed to settle over the assembly was palpable. Cam knew her tactics, trusted they'd work, but he wasn't any more immune to the spell she was weaving than anyone else.

"Efforts have been made to recruit other industries that could piggyback on the existing infrastructure and workforce remaining from the manufacturing base. But Wishful is having to compete with larger micropolitans, like Lawley. And even if such an industry set up shop, they could leave. Exactly like Heirloom. And then where would Wishful be? Exactly where it is now. Maybe worse." She paused to take a sip of water and let that sink in.

"More recently there's been the issue of GrandGoods. A big box store that's made a lot of empty promises about the benefits it could bring to this community. Now it's true, if they came, there would likely be some possible short-term benefits. They agreed to contract for local labor to build the store, to use local suppliers for materials where possible. They've even agreed to pay for the necessary infrastructure upgrades to accommodate the exponential increase in traffic and utilities. But that's a slippery slope. Once a place like Grand-Goods gains a foothold, then come other chains. Big businesses that don't know us, don't care about us, and don't add value to the quality of life in this town. With that comes the same kind of sprawl, traffic congestion, environmental degradation, loss of community, and the economic and social segregation that's seen nationwide. And that's touted by many as progress." Her eyes narrowed, her voice dripping with a disdain that had the crowd shifting.

"But I'm here to present to you a different vision of progress. One that plays to Wishful's strengths. The solution lies not in bringing in outsiders to save the town but in leveraging the resources the town already has."

The first glimmer of positive had the

crowd's focus sharpening. Bodies leaned forward, attentive.

Reel them in, sweetheart.

"So we're a little caught in the past. We can play to that. Focus on the glory of bygone days and ramp up the nostalgia. Wishful is a little slice of Southern Americana. A place where people can come and remember what life used to be like. A place that's about community and, most of all, about family." Cam saw her search out Miranda's parents and nod. "It's something that people in this country so desperately long for in a society that's over-connected and simultaneously as isolated as it's ever been. Wishful is a place that can remind people of what's really important in life. It can give the most vital resource and commodity of all: hope. Because Wishful is the town where hope springs eternal. Literally. And we can capitalize on that with a fully developed rural tourism campaign."

Listening to her outline the concept, the assets already in place, and how they might be utilized, Cam recognized the disservice he'd done when he'd pushed her into a quick and dirty presentation for the Council. This was so much more full-bodied and emotionally-charged. All around the room, he could see and sense the tide turning, exactly as she'd said it would.

"Rural tourism has positive benefits for the economy. Most of the revenue generated from outside visitors would stay within the local economy—unlike GrandGoods, whose profits would be returned to the parent company and spent on foreign suppliers. Beyond the gains from direct sales of goods and services to visitors, tourism creates new jobs within the community, which helps prevent population drift and maintains the tax base. Income derived from tourism can help maintain and improve local infrastructure and services, which in turn, improves the quality of life for the community at large. Rural tourism also promotes environmental conservation and protection. Grand-Goods came here planning to buy Abe

Costello's land and build their store right on the shores of Hope Springs, one of Wishful's greatest assets. Well, that's not going to happen. I believe so much in what we're trying to accomplish here that I bought it myself. The property will be donated to the city with express instructions that it be preserved and cultivated into a public park that will benefit locals and tourists alike. Landscape architect Campbell Crawford is here to present the design."

Norah stepped back, arms open to welcome him onto the stage. With a bracing breath, Cam joined her. Feeling the weight of so many eyes, he wished desperately for something to do with his hands. He took up a position behind the podium and gripped the edges to keep from shoving them in his pockets.

"Those of you who know me know I've wanted to put a park out at Hope Springs for years. I've toyed with the design off and on, but I never truly thought I'd get the opportunity to make it a reality."

He shared a long look with Norah that had

his nerves smoothing out. She'd done this as much for him as for the town. She'd given him this dream and inspired bigger ones.

"Tonight, I'd like to give the rest of you a glimpse into that reality."

Behind him, the screen flashed to the first of his slides, and the crowd burst out with audible ooos and ahhs. Through some serious graphic design mojo, Cecily had turned his concept renderings into art that the audience could almost step right into. And that was why someone, someday, was going to pay her the big bucks.

Cam lost himself in the presentation after that, taking his audience on a virtual tour of the park that would both enhance and respect the environmental integrity of his favorite place on earth. By the time he handed the reins back to Norah, he held the assembly in almost as much awe as she did.

"Thanks Cam. That'll be beautiful." She waited for him to step down before she continued. "Now I know this may seem pretty out there to some of you, but the fact is that successful small-town development has mostly shifted away from traditional strategies and is now being driven by smaller, local efforts, with a very inward focus. Those towns that have managed to reinvent themselves aren't focused on luring huge corporations that could pick up and leave exactly as Comfort Coil and Heirloom Home Furnishings did. While funding may be national, regional, or state level, the knowledge base and the action is very much local. Small towns are the heart of the South. While other parts of the country are trying to recover a sense of pedestrian scale and small town life, Wishful is right here with all these qualities intact—just waiting for revitalization. The success of such a revitalization will be as a result of historic preservation, sustainable new development and planning. There has, up to this point, been a significant lack of technical planning skills and resources in city government. That's not meant as a criticism of the system, but a statement of fact. The world has changed and Wishful hasn't had the economic resources or support needed to change with it.

"That changes today. I stand before you as an authorized representative of Peyton Consolidated. Through their non-profit arm, Peyton Consolidated has been at the helm of numerous urban renewal projects around the country." Behind her, the slides flashed by as she listed each, showing the dismal befores and the astonishing afters. "With Wishful, Peyton Consolidated wants to expand its mission to include the revitalization of small town America. The Mayor's Office has been provided with a Memorandum of Understanding from Peyton Consolidated, outlining, in very clear terms, the funding and resources the company is prepared to leverage in support of this venture. In addition, Wishful has been presented with a mentorship agreement with Balenmore, Colorado, a small-town that's made rural tourism a rousing success. They're eager to partner with us in order to help us realize our own rebirth."

Norah spread her hands, the picture of

transparency. "There are no strings here. No hidden agendas. Just the support and resources Wishful needs to bring itself back to life. So think about what you want Wishful to be. Another cookie-cutter, homogenized town, with no cultural identity. Or a beacon of hope in a world where that's an increasingly rare commodity. The future and the decision are in your hands. Please remember that as you head to the polls tomorrow. Thank you."

Thunderous applause followed her off the stage and trailed them out the door into the hall.

"You nailed that."

Norah slipped her hand in his. "*We* nailed that."

"You ever think about going into politics? You'd be great at it. Eloquent. Magnetic. Persuasive."

She shuddered. "No thank you. I'll leave that to you and your mom."

"I'm pretty sure all of them would follow you into war." He tugged her to a stop and pulled her up against him. "I know I'd follow you anywhere."

"Well they don't have to go to battle, just to the polls. Let's hope they turn out in droves and vote the way we want."

"IT'S A REALLY IMPORTANT vote today. We've got volunteer-driven Pollmobiles running in every voting precinct in town until the polls close tonight at nine, so we're expecting unprecedented turnout."

Cam did his best to keep his eyes on the reporter interviewing him rather than letting them stray to the enemy camp set up at the other end of the green, but it was a tough thing. The bright orange tents emblazoned with the GrandGoods logo screamed *look at us!* So did the steady stream of people circulating through them.

"Tell us what the store size cap would mean for Wishful."

He explained the proposed statute as simply and briefly as he could, thinking Norah would've done it with more flare. But the reporter had wanted someone from city government and his mother was MIA at the moment.

When he finished, the reporter turned to her cameraman. "Nearly every business in town is displaying posters in support of the size cap, and as you can see from the sea of red YES caps behind me, the proposed law has a lot of supporters. We'll be back this evening with an update on this important referendum. WTVA News. Deanna Fossett reporting."

Cam didn't get to drop his public face once the camera stopped rolling. They needed the press on their side, so he added a layer of charm to go with the serious. "We appreciate y'all coming out to cover this. Can we offer you some coffee? It's fresh from The Daily Grind."

"Love some," Deanna said.

He directed them into the command center tent the Chamber of Commerce had set up at the fountain end of the green. Inside, Norah was running things with her usual efficiency. Behind her, a markerboard held a running tally of total number of voters going through each polling station. It was being updated on the hour. A few hundred so far, but it was early yet. The real rush would be during the lunch hour and after five.

"How did the interview go?"

"Fine. You'd have been better."

Norah waved that off. "They'll probably do an update for the noon news, the five o'clock slot, and preliminary results for the ten. We'll see if we can't slot your mom in for at least one of those. Maybe Molly for another."

"What are we going to do about GrandGoods?"

"I've sent spies to find out exactly what they're up to."

"Spies? I'm afraid to ask."

"Who do you think volunteered for that task?"

"Cassie. She's not what you call subtle."

"Neither is Mamie, who went with her. But this isn't full scale espionage. It's just two members of the public cruising through some public event they've got going on."

Those same two members came into the command center at a hustle, not a pace Cam generally associated with Mamie. Cassie was practically bouncing, and Mamie's bouffant trembled with her agitation.

While the older woman caught her breath, Cassie saluted. "Agents Callister and Landon reporting."

"I've really got to get you walkie talkies." Norah laughed. "Report in."

"They're giving away free stuff."

"Like koozies, pens, hats?"

"And t-shirts, yeah. But they're also giving away store memberships and discounts that can be used at any existing store."

Norah frowned. "Are they asking for any-thing in return?"

"Just that people hit up the polls, same as us. They're not even asking for proof in advance."

"Did they indicate there's some limit to the number of memberships? Like the first fifty people or whatever?"

"No limit," Mamie said. "They said they want to support the community and are willing to give out free memberships to back that up. The only thing they're having people do is show they have a Wishful address. I got a member-ship myself. Don't have a clue what I'll do with it when they don't come, but I didn't figure it'd hurt anything."

"They're also giving out free pastries," Cassie added. "Store bought, of course."

"Oh, hell no." Carolanne joined the conver-sation from where she'd been helping coordi-nate Pollmobile service. "We can do better than that. Give me a team, and I'll bring my entire inventory out for the cause."

"Do it." Norah called in half a dozen volunteers and dispatched them to Sweet Magnolias.

Once they'd gone, Cam did the math. "At, what, fifty bucks a membership, with a potential for up to maybe a couple thousand people. That's a hundred grand loss right there. Plus whatever they've put into their branded merchandise."

"A hundred thousand dollars is a drop in the bucket for a company like that. They'd make exponentially more than that if they secured a place in the region. Plus, if they *don't* end up coming, they haven't truly lost that much because many of those people won't ever go to one of the other GrandGoods stores before the annual membership expires. It's a smart tactic."

The whole thing had Cam worried.

As usual, Norah read him like a book. She moved in, slipping her arms around his waist. "It will be all right. You just—"

"Have to have a little faith. I know. I've got all the faith in the world in you."

"Then it's time you put your faith in them." She nodded toward the masses.

That feat would've been considerably easier to accomplish had his nemesis not chosen that moment to stroll into the tent. Vick flashed his too white teeth like a shark. "Well good morning to you Councilman, Miss Burke."

"Burgess," Cam said.

"We're having a fine turnout to the polls and an exceptional response to our promotion. Why, everybody's jumping at the chance for a free year's membership to GrandGoods. We've given away six hundred memberships already today."

A number almost equal to the last hour's tally at the polls. It didn't mean anything. Logically, Cam knew that. There'd be people who'd take the deal and vote for the size cap anyway. There would likely even be people who'd take the membership and not vote at all. But some would feel that psychological contract and vote in favor of the store. The question was how many would be wooed.

"It's still early. There are nearly three thousand more people who can vote in this town. And I promise you, the majority won't care about GrandGoods' empty promises."

Vick shook his head in pity. "When are you going to get it through your head, Crawford? GrandGoods is going to be good for this town."

"They've certainly been good to you, haven't they, Vick?" Sandra stepped into the tent, trailed by a handful of other people. Leigh Billingsly, the City Comptroller, looked pissed. Jay Quimby, the resident tech guru, looked smug. Officer Judd Hamilton looked deceptively at ease, but beneath the calm exterior, Cam recognized the same coiled readiness for action he'd displayed on the defensive line of the Wishful Stars football team back in high school. Not until the appearance of Chief Curry, bringing up the rear, did Vick's confident expression falter.

"I beg your pardon?" he asked, innocence with a layer of affront.

"Well, you know how we've been doing

system upgrades at City Hall the last couple of weeks?" Sandra asked. "Jay, here, found some… concerning emails on your computer."

"Email is private."

"In fact, it's not. Everything you do on your work computer is technically the business of the city since your business is to help *run* the city. So imagine our surprise when Jay brought to our attention a string of emails between you and Bill Sutto, making it clear that you've been taking kickbacks from GrandGoods."

"I don't know what you're talking about." Vick began to tug at his collar.

Cam was dimly aware that everyone in the tent had fallen silent, watching the show.

"Turns out, that was plenty of evidence for Judge Carpenter to let us subpoena your bank records," Chief Curry said. "You've been a bad, bad boy, Vick. Our forensic accountant is still going through it to determine the total amount, but at first pass, it looks like, in addition to getting all cozy with GrandGoods, you've embezzled over a hundred thousand dollars from the city."

"This is ludicrous!"

"What's ludicrous is the fact that you are sworn to work in the best interests of this town and its people, and instead you've been abusing your position to line your own pockets." Sandra's voice crackled with temper.

"Victor Burgess, you're under arrest." Chief Curry nodded to Judd, who grabbed Vick's arm, twisting it with a little more force than necessary as he cuffed the older man.

"You have the right to remain silent. Anything you say, can and will be used against you in a court of law. You have the right to an attorney…" Chief Curry finished reading Vick his rights, then he and Judd marched him out of the command center.

That was when Cam realized the camera was rolling and WTVA News had caught the whole thing.

"This is Deanna Fossett, live with a WTVA News exclusive. In a shocking turn of events here in the tiny town of Wishful, where a David versus Goliath battle is being waged over store size caps at the polls today, City Planner Victor Burgess, local champion of GrandGoods and the big box store movement, has just been arrested. Burgess stands accused of taking kickbacks from GrandGoods and embezzling more than a hundred thousand dollars from the city. Mayor Crawford, what do you have to say?"

Deanna tipped her microphone to Sandra, who blinked at the camera. Cam recognized the look on her face as she choked down the more profane remarks that weren't appropriate for addressing the public.

"We are deeply disappointed in the actions of the City Planner. His greed has impacted this city in ways we're only beginning to understand. He has been removed from his position, effective immediately."

"Does this impact the vote today?"

Cam stepped in to take that one. "The vote will continue. The legislation on the ballot today is not specific to GrandGoods, but will impact all future commercial development in the area. We still encourage everyone to make it to the polls today. And we hope that they'll all look at this situation and recognize the cost of doing business with big box stores before they cast their vote for the future of our town."

"There you have it, folks. The vote continues. This reporter will certainly be interested to see how this battle shakes out in the end." She made a slashing motion, and the camera stopped rolling "Well, nobody can say y'all are dull!"

Norah slipped her hand into his. "Nice save. I couldn't have said it better myself."

"I've been paying attention."

"If we could've tailor made a blow to Grand-Goods and their position, I'm not sure we could've done better than this."

"That was all you. We wouldn't have known to look if you hadn't noted those discrepancies in the city financial records."

Sandra laid a hand on her shoulder. "Wishful owes you a debt. For so many things."

Norah smiled. "Just doing what I can to help. Speaking of—" She turned to the still silent crowd gathered in the command center. "Okay people, that was news. I know some of you were snapping pictures and taking video. Pull out your phones and share it! Facebook. Twitter. Text. Somebody get over to Dinner Belles and get Mama Pearl on it. And find Cassie and get things moving over at The Grind. I want every gossip tree in this town singing!"

THE POLLS WERE CLOSED. The command center had been broken down and packed up. Grand-Goods and their tents were gone. In the wake of allegations about offering kickbacks, Bill Sutto hadn't been available for comment to the press, which had swarmed downtown after footage of Vick's arrest had aired. The remaining GrandGoods employees had looked shell shocked, with nothing more to say than

"No comment." Norah and Molly had jumped into the void, talking and talking to get the coalition's message out. And if Norah had used every skill and resource she had to make certain that the news of GrandGoods' less than above board tactics was spread far and wide, she felt not a shred of remorse.

But it was Vick's arrest that remained the hot topic of conversation among the locals. According to the gossip mill, his wife Rebecca was filing for divorce. Judge Carpenter had set bail. Some folks thought it was unnecessarily high, but his wife was one of Rebecca's best friends. Given that Vick's assets were frozen, pending the findings of the forensic accountant, he was still cooling his heels in a cell. Rumor had it there was collusion to make sure he stayed there until all his stuff could be packed up and his ass kicked out of the house. Small town justice at its finest.

Everybody but the die-hards had gone home after the exceptionally long day. Three months of almost non-stop action came down to the results of this night. Those remaining had camped out at the Mudcat Tavern to wait for the referendum results.

Norah hated waiting. Too keyed up to sit, she'd been pacing for the last forty-five minutes. The City Council had gone into an emergency closed session to discuss the ramifications of Vick's actions, so she hadn't seen Cam in hours. It felt wrong that he shouldn't be by her side for the announcement of the results, when they'd been in this together from the beginning.

Miranda stepped into her path, a long neck bottle held out.

"I don't want a drink."

"It's either this or I'm finding a tranquilizer dart. You're wearing a hole in the floor."

Norah took the beer.

"It's going to be fine. Even if the store cap didn't pass, the City Council isn't going to do further business with GrandGoods after what they pulled."

Norah shook her head. "If the store cap

didn't pass, GrandGoods will disavow all knowledge of the kickbacks and put it all on Sutto, claiming he acted on his own. He'll get fired as collateral damage, and they'll send some Honest Abe type with a list of concessions a mile long. We need this legislation."

"Disavow all knowledge?" Miranda snorted. "Are you an expert in corporate espionage now?"

"No, but if I ran their PR division, it's what I'd advise."

"If I were in their shoes, I'd cut my loses and get the hell out." Tipping back her beer, she studied Norah. "Speaking of running PR divisions. What was that whole deal at your presentation last night about being an authorized representative of Peyton Consolidated? I thought you weren't going to work for him."

"I'm not going to run his marketing department. But he needs someone local to liaise with the city, so he hired me on a freelance basis. Between that and the settlement from the lawsuit, I should be in okay shape until I sort out exactly what I'm really going to do for a living."

"Well you know I'm entirely in favor of keeping you as a roommate, if that's what you want. But you might have other plans on that front. It hasn't escaped my notice that you've been spending most nights at Cam's place."

In the wake of Chicago, they'd been reluctant to spend much time apart. "We haven't talked about what comes next."

Mitch swung an arm around Norah's shoulders. "Pretty sure the next steps are marriage and baby carriage. Isn't that how the rhyme goes?"

Norah laughed, figuring it was a sign of how far she'd come that neither idea sent her into a blind panic. "Let's not get ahead of ourselves."

"I was pretty sure he was going to with that crack he made at Grammy's," Miranda said. "'How's Saturday?' my ass. What would he have done if you'd said yes? You're probably the only woman in America who could legitimately plan a wedding in four days."

She'd have done it, too, if she'd thought he was serious. And wasn't that a surprise? But much as he loved his family, an offhand, casual question in front of all of them wasn't his style. If she'd felt just a little pang of regret, she chalked it up to impatience. They were totally fine where they were.

"Who's planning a wedding?" Cecily demanded.

Christoff made a show of picking up and staring at Norah's naked left hand.

Norah freed her hand. "Nobody's planning a wedding."

"Yet," sang Tyler as she strode by.

"You're all completely incorrigible. Regardless of the likelihood of those events—"

"Guaranteed," Miranda and Mitch chorused.

"—in the pretty immediate future, I need to go back to Chicago to finish closing out my apartment and get the rest of my stuff down here. It's a fact that there isn't room for all my stuff at his place. Or yours, for that matter. A lot of it is probably going into storage either way."

"Dibs on that tufted sofa with the scroll legs, if you're getting rid of it," Christoff announced.

"It would be a nightmare with dog hair, so it's all yours."

"Maybe you and Cam need to be thinking about y'all's place. You know I'd design you anything you want. And Lord knows, between the acreage he owns and your land out at Hope Springs, there's no end of pretty places to build a house."

"I hadn't thought about keeping any of it. You know, it's sad, but I've been so damned busy since I got back, I haven't even seen all of it yet."

"Well I reckon you ought to do that before you go donating every last square inch to the city. You could keep a fair chunk for yourself and still give over plenty for the park."

She wanted that, she realized—to walk her land with Cam and Hush and choose a piece to keep. It seemed like a good way to begin putting down those roots she so desperately wanted. Maybe they could manage a picnic over the weekend.

"The news is starting!"

Norah pivoted toward the nearest screen. Hissing admonishments swept the bar until the crowd quieted down. Adele turned up the TVs, all tuned to the same news station. They had to sit through reports of a string of robberies in Columbus, a warehouse fire in Tupelo, and a nasty four car pile-up in Lawley before the view finally shifted to Deanna Fossett outside City Hall.

As she recounted events from earlier in the day, Norah began to bounce on her feet. "C'-mon, c'mon."

"The City Council is still in session and is not available for further comment. Elsewhere in City Hall, results are being tabulated for to-day's referendum ballot about retail store size caps here in Wishful. Poll workers report the biggest voter turnout in city history, with a whopping eighty-five percent of registered voters coming out to weigh in on the issue. We're still waiting to hear preliminary results."

"What is taking so damned long?"

"Paper ballots, sugar," Mitch murmured.

"It is not that hard to count to three thousand in an hour."

"Maybe it's really close and they wanted to double check," Cecily suggested.

Norah hoped to hell it wasn't that close.

"Oh, wait a second. Someone is coming out." Deanna hurried up the steps of City Hall to meet Sandra, and Norah could see the flurry of other reporters doing the same. "Mayor Crawford, what can you tell us about the referendum results?"

Norah reached for Mitch and Miranda's hands and found herself pulled backward against a long, hard body.

"You made it."

"Shh," Cam said.

"—were a lot of ballots to go through. Our team is busy recounting to verify the exact totals, but there is absolutely no question of the results. By an absolute landslide, the statute capping commercial spaces at 40,000 square feet has passed."

The whole place burst into cheers and applause. Several members of the coalition enthusiastically trumpeted with their noisemakers. Behind the bar, Adele and Joe popped the corks on bottles of champagne. And amid all the chaos, Norah held very still, soaking in the sounds of success, her smile spread so wide, she thought her face might crack.

Cam bent to her ear. "You did it, Wonder Woman."

She pivoted in his arms. "*We* did it. With a whole lot of help."

Tucker bounced over, throwing his arms around both their shoulders. In a TV announcer's voice he said, "You two have just saved our town from the Big Bad Box Store! What're you gonna do now?"

Norah and Cam exchanged a look and a smile and answered together. "Sleep!"

CHAPTER 26

"I CAN'T BELIEVE THEY weren't willing to put this off until tomorrow," Norah said. "We've been back in town, what? An hour and a half?"

"I don't set the schedule. I just show up when they tell me," Cam said, as they strode across the town green for a City Council meeting.

"I still don't understand why they wanted me there."

"Don't look at me. I've been in Chicago with you. It's not one of our regularly scheduled meetings. Nobody even sent me an agenda. Maybe they want you to liaise in your official capacity."

Norah scowled. "I could liaise a lot better if I were unpacked and settled. And if I'd *slept* since December."

"Yeah the last three weeks haven't so much maintained our original impression of Wishful being a sleepy little town. On the plus side, nobody looking at you would know you'd been driving for the last seven hours."

Fifteen minutes locked in his bathroom and she'd erased the fatigue from her face and done something with her hair that made her look neat as a pin and ready for the boardroom. It was a fascinating form of female magic.

She brought a self-conscious hand to the twist at the base of her head. "Thank God my suits were in a box at the back of the truck."

"You shouldn't have worn a suit."

"Without knowing exactly what they want me for, a suit is a safer option. It's always better to be over-dressed than under-dressed. Besides, it was this or jeans, and I'm not going before the rest of the City Council in jeans. Especially not at what is evidently a public session."

"Yeah, but I won't be able to pay attention to a thing for imagining getting you out of it."

She slid him a look that was part exasperation, part heat. "Behave."

"Where's the fun in that?" He tugged open the door to the courthouse.

The halls were empty other than the security guard, George Buckley, one of Violet's brothers. An easy smile split his dark face. "Welcome back."

"Thanks, George. How's it looking in there?" Cam asked.

He and Norah walked through the metal detector, collecting their stuff on the other side.

"Pretty good crowd for a mid-afternoon session."

"Hopefully it'll be a quick one. It's been a long day." Cam escorted Norah to the main door of the courtroom. "This is where I leave you. I've gotta go in the other door."

"Where should I sit?"

"Somewhere down front." Cam kissed her quickly, resisting the urge to linger. "I'll see you on the other side."

Norah stepped through the door. Cam smiled to himself.

"She suspect anything?" George asked.

"Not a thing." She wasn't gonna know what hit her.

Cam hurried down the hall to join the rest of the City Council and his mother at the front of the courtroom. It wasn't as full as it had been for the vote on the special use permit, but still the floor level benches were pretty packed. Norah had found a spot on the second row beside Miranda and Piper. As Cam slid into his seat beside Ed, his mother rapped her gavel and brought the session to order.

"Thank y'all for joining us this afternoon. We'll jump straight on in. The forensic accountant has finished her investigation. The former City Planner did, indeed, embezzle $124,000 from city accounts over a period of several years. He has failed this city and is currently awaiting trial."

That spawned considerable murmured comment from the peanut gallery, but they quieted as Sandra continued. "The City Council has conducted its own investigation into how this egregious crime remained undiscovered for so long. Without getting into the long details, it boils down to antiquated record keeping and a perfect confluence of circumstances, such that those responsible for oversight were lax in their duties. I take responsibility myself for not being more diligent upon my return to office after my cancer treatment. That being said, a number of changes are being made moving forward to prevent something like this from ever happening again, not the least of which is a brand new electronic accounting system designed by Jay Quimby."

Sandra went on a bit longer about the rest of the changes and reiterated a policy of transparency to prevent mismanagement of city funds. "Further details are available for those who are interested. However, none of this is why we called this special session of the City Council."

As his mother surveyed her audience, Cam thought she'd been taking lessons from Norah on how to play the crowd.

"Four months ago, our town was struggling financially. Yes, at the civic level, some of that was because of the criminal actions of the City Planner. But even without that added burden, Wishful has been in a long-term economic decline for the last two decades. It seemed that the only way out of that was the recruitment of and dependency on some larger industry, like the ones the town was built around. When no opportunities of that nature became available, we were susceptible to the lure of promises made by GrandGoods, a big box store that would've changed our way of life."

She paused and shot a look in his direction. "Councilman Crawford was the lone voice of dissent. He made the unpopular choice, the hard choice, to do whatever he could to protect that which we hold dear. And in doing so, he brought in the assistance of a young woman with more grit, determination, and hope than any single person I've ever met."

Cam watched, fascinated and amused, as Norah actually sank lower in her seat, as if to shrink from all the eyes turned in her direction.

"She almost single-handedly revived the Chamber of Commerce. She was the primary force behind the founding of the citizen's coalition. At her request, we had a literal army of volunteers help makeover Main Street. As a result of her tireless efforts, we've seen a display of community spirit unrivaled in the last twenty-five years. Her Shop Local campaign has brought a forty percent increase in local revenues since its inception, and that number only seems to be going up. She is the brain behind the YES Cap campaign and one of the reasons this referendum saw record numbers at the polls. And, as if all that weren't enough for an entire team of people, when all seemed lost and everyone else gave up, she kept the faith and gave us the answer for how Wishful can save itself, complete with linkage to the resources to enable us to do exactly that. Norah Burke, can you please join us down front?"

Cheeks faintly flushed, Norah rose from her seat and edged into the aisle, looking a trifle embarrassed as she made her way through the gate from the visitors' gallery to stand in front of the Council.

"Norah, you have given of your expertise, your time, and your personal resources, all in the name of supporting this town you've decided to make your own. We owe you a debt that can never be properly paid because you cannot put a price on the gift of hope. But we came together today to honor you and your endless contributions to Wishful."

Sandra stepped down from the bench and brought her the engraved plaque, while the room erupted with applause. Cam's heart fairly burst with pride as Norah accepted it and then his mother's embrace. Sandra gestured to give Norah the floor.

With a helpless look at the audience, Norah lifted a hand to her cheek. "For probably the first time since any of you have known me, I don't know what to say."

A faint ripple of laughter swept through the assembly.

"Thank you. I'm so honored. But really this doesn't belong to just me. I might've had the ideas, but I couldn't have executed any of them without help from all of you. The success isn't mine, it's Wishful's."

"Well, we're glad to hear you say that," Hank said.

Norah turned back to face the Council.

"See, there's the matter of the vacancy in the City Planner's office," Grace said.

"And we can't think of anyone better suited to the job than you," Ed said.

Norah blinked. "You're…offering me a job?"

"Normally we'd do a formal interview, get references, the whole shebang," Sandra said. "But in this case, your actions over the last four months more than answer all our questions.

You're smart, dedicated. You're above reproach. And you consistently put Wishful first. That's exactly what we want in a City Planner. We realize we've put you on the spot, so you don't have to give an answer right now. Take some time to think about it."

She turned her gaze on him, and Cam knew her answer even before she spoke it. "I don't have to think about it. Yes. There's nothing else I'd rather do."

"You totally knew they were going to do that." Norah poked an accusatory finger in Cam's arm.

He grinned, unrepentant, and draped an arm around her shoulders. "I totally did."

"Well, I'm glad I wore the suit since I was up there in front of *all those people*."

"You could've gone up there in shorts and a t-shirt and it wouldn't have diminished your accomplishments or how much we all appreciate them."

"Yeah, but the suit looks better in pictures."

"Can't argue with that."

"It was your idea to make me the new City Planner, wasn't it?"

"I might've put the bug in their ear when we were discussing qualifications for the position. But I couldn't have gotten you hired all on my own. The decision was unanimous. No contest. No discussion. You were made for this job."

"I think maybe I was."

"C'mon, I want to show you something." Cam steered her across the green, toward the fountain. "I've been instructed to inform you that the honors don't end with just a plaque."

"They don't?"

"Nope. You're getting a burger named after you at Dinner Belles. And Cassie is creating a drink in your honor for permanent inclusion on the menu at The Grind. The General Burke."

Norah gave a happy sigh. "You know, I have

no idea what cockles are, but that just warms my heart all the way down to them."

"Pretty sure that makes you an official local. There's no getting rid of us now. We've got our hooks in you too deep."

"You had your hooks in me from day one. You and your silly dog."

"It was a masterful plan, if I do say so myself."

He pulled her to a stop beside the fountain, keeping her tucked close against his side. "What do you see?"

She looked but couldn't tell what it was he wanted her to home in on. "Did they clean it?" As far as she could tell, it still had the same patina of age it always had.

"Look closer."

Her gaze skimmed the edges, the base, the pool of water with its glinting treasure beneath. "I still don't know what you want me to see."

"Okay I'll chalk it up to the fact that you're wiped out. Here's a different question. What do you *hear?*"

Norah listened closely. A faint breeze rustled the leaves of the massive oaks shading the green. Voices from people walking down Spring Street and Main carried back on the wind. And underneath it all, the soft burble of…water.

"It's running!" She could see it now, the faint trickle of water. Not a lot, but something where there'd been nothing for years.

"It is. I noticed it before we left for Chicago last week."

"Did they finally figure out what was wrong with it?"

Cam tugged the plaque from her hand and set it aside, pulling her to sit beside him on the fountain ledge. "Nobody's touched it."

"But it's running again. Why would it just spontaneously start up?"

"I have a theory." He said it in a tone that clearly expected skepticism.

"Lay it on me."

"Well, actually it was sort of your theory. Do you remember the day we made our wishes?"

"Sure. Hard to forget when I got my wish."

That distracted him. "What was it?"

"For my time here to show me what my path was, what I was meant to do. I'd say I pretty much got my answer today."

"I got the wish I made that day, too."

"Yeah? What was yours?"

"I wished for a miracle to save Wishful. We got you."

Norah's heart squeezed. "Cam. You are the sweetest thing." She leaned in, brushed her lips over his.

"Don't know that it's sweet if it's just plain truth."

"Flatterer." She settled back. "So what was your theory? Or my theory. Whatever."

"You said that the fountain dried up as hope in Wishful did. Over the last four months, you gave that back to us. You saved us in more ways than one. Me most especially." He leaned over and trailed his hand through the water, scooping a coin up from the bottom.

"What are you doing? You can't do that.

That's somebody's wish."

"Sure I can. It's mine." He turned his hand over to show her. But it wasn't a coin in his palm. It was a ring. Diamond, flanked by sapphires and filigree. Gorgeous and sparkling in the late April sun.

Norah's throat closed up.

"I could've asked you that day at my grandmother's, but it was always meant to be here. Source of hope. Font of wishes." He took her limp hand in his and smiled. "I love you. I want to spend the next fifty or sixty years showing you how much while we build a life and a family together and keep right on saving this town, side by side. Say you'll grant me my wish and be my wife."

She swallowed hard. He was so steady, so perfect. So hers. It was worth every hour of work, every moment of frustration and doubt, every turn in her life, because all of it had brought her here, to him.

When she couldn't make a sound, she just nodded. Cam's fingers were warm and sure as he slipped the ring on her finger, then raised it to his lips.

Norah still didn't make a peep. She was positive if she opened her mouth, she was going to burst into happy tears.

"Wow, speechless twice in one day? That's got to be a new record."

That surprised a laugh out of her. "Don't get used to it."

He cupped her face and drew her close. "I wouldn't dream of it."

"I love you so much, Campbell."

When he kissed her, she tasted his smile, and it was sweet, as life was sweet.

"Let's go home before anybody sees us." He pulled her to her feet.

"What?" She laughed.

"Once this hits the wind, it'll take us five hours to cut loose, and I've got a mind to celebrate."

"I can't argue with that."

As they headed for his truck, Norah looked around at the town she'd adopted as her own and reflected that life would never be dull in the place where wishes came true.

CHOOSE YOUR NEXT ROMANCE!

Who do you want to see next in Wishful?

IF YOU'RE in the mood for some hotness in a toolbelt, you will want to jump to Book 2, *Know Me Well.* Lovers of best friend's older brother romances will *adore* Riley and Liam's story.

Do you want to know all about the guy who broke Tyler's heart? Then you'll want to nab Book 3, *Be Careful, It's My Heart.* This second chance romance capitalizes on my absolute love of the movie *White Christmas,* as some of our favorite Wishful citizens band together to save the old Madrigal theater by putting on a community theater production of the story. Piper pulls some shenanigans in the name of matchmaking that you won't want to miss!

A complete and up-to-date list of all my books can be found at https://kaitnolan.com.

THE MISFIT INN SERIES
SMALL TOWN FAMILY ROMANCE

- *When You Got A Good Thing* (Kennedy and Xander)
- *Til There Was You* (Misty and Denver)

- *Those Sweet Words* (Pru and Flynn)
- *Stay A Little Longer* (Athena and Logan)
- *Bring It On Home* (Maggie and Porter)

RESCUE MY HEART SERIES
SMALL TOWN MILITARY ROMANCE

- *Baby It's Cold Outside* (Ivy and Harrison)
- *What I Like About You* (Laurel and Sebastian)
- *Bad Case of Loving You* (Paisley and Ty prequel)
- *Made For Loving You* (Paisley and Ty)

MEN OF THE MISFIT INN
SMALL TOWN SOUTHERN ROMANCE

- *Let It Be Me* (Emerson and Caleb)
- *Our Kind of Love* (Abbey and Kyle)

WISHFUL SERIES

SMALL TOWN SOUTHERN ROMANCE

- *Once Upon A Coffee* (Avery and Dillon)
- *To Get Me To You* (Cam and Norah)
- *Know Me Well* (Liam and Riley)
- *Be Careful, It's My Heart* (Brody and Tyler)
- *Just For This Moment* (Myles and Piper)
- *Wish I Might* (Reed and Cecily)
- *Turn My World Around* (Tucker and Corinne)
- *Dance Me A Dream* (Jace and Tara)
- *See You Again* (Trey and Sandy)
- *The Christmas Fountain* (Chad and Mary Alice)
- *You Were Meant For Me* (Mitch and Tess)
- *A Lot Like Christmas* (Ryan and Hannah)
- *Dancing Away With My Heart* (Zach and Lexi)

WISHING FOR A HERO SERIES (A WISHFUL SPINOFF SERIES)
SMALL TOWN ROMANTIC SUSPENSE

- *Make You Feel My Love* (Judd and Autumn)
- *Watch Over Me* (Nash and Rowan)
- *Can't Take My Eyes Off You* (Ethan and Miranda)
- *Burn For You* (Sean and Delaney)

MEET CUTE ROMANCE
SMALL TOWN SHORT ROMANCE

- *Once Upon A Snow Day*
- *Once Upon A New Year's Eve*
- *Once Upon An Heirloom*
- *Once Upon A Coffee*
- *Once Upon A Campfire*
- *Once Upon A Rescue*

SUMMER CAMP
CONTEMPORARY ROMANCE

- *Once Upon A Campfire*
- *Second Chance Summer*

ACKNOWLEDGMENTS

I am always humbled by the number of people who help me get a book from that twinkle in my eye to fruition, and this one, in particular, has been no exception. I have so many people to thank!

My brilliant cover artist, Robin Ludwig, as always, you far exceeded my expectations!

My dear friends Melissa, Erica, and Alyson for a regular supply of small town hilarity that makes me bray with laughter and provides a constant source of inspiration,

My beta readers, Julie, Lauralynn, Melissa, and Erica,

My critique partners Susan Bischoff, Claire LeGrand, Jessica Fritsche, and Liana Brooks, this book is so much better because of your input and the many, many people who talked me off the edge of crazy during my pre-release spaz, especially Lisa Kroger, who knows when to give me a Gibbs slap to get over myself.

Love and thanks to you all!

Kait is a Mississippi native, who often swears like a sailor, calls everyone sugar, honey, or darlin', and can wield a bless your heart like a saber or a Snuggie, depending on requirements.

You can find more information on this

RITA ® Award-winning author and her books on her website http://kaitnolan.com. While you're there, sign up for her newsletter so you don't miss out on news about new releases!